"You'll be ok," I lied to Josephine, whispering in soft German in her ear. "I love you."

Perhaps the driver of the oncoming train didn't see the blood on the stairs, the mothers holding their children close as they cowered behind grey pillars and fluorescent vending machines. Perhaps he did see it, but like a hedgehog before a cement lorry was so bewildered by the events, he couldn't manage an independent original thought and so, training overriding initiative, he slowed down.

Faced with sirens above and a train below, the man with the gun looked around the station once more, did not see what he wanted, turned and ran.

The train doors opened, and he climbed on board.

Josephine Cebula was dead.

I followed her killer on to the train.

Praise for the novels of Claire North

Praise for

TOUCH:

"*Touch* is a brilliantly balanced knife's edge of a book—fast-paced and thrilling, it's somehow also languorous, thoughtful, intelligently intimate. Kepler is a thoroughly absorbing and sympathetic anti-hero, trying to minimize harm while striving for survival. I am left staggered into an awed slow-clap at everything North has accomplished here. *Touch* is touching, horrifying, magnificent; step into it, and it will step into you."

—*NPR Books*

"The high stakes and breakneck pace of the plot will draw readers in, and the meditations on what it means to be human and to be loved will linger long after the last shot is fired."

—*Kirkus*

"As masterful as her debut...[a] fast-paced, imaginative novel... There is plenty of conspiracy and intrigue in this deftly paced novel, but North also poses subtle questions about identity and love."   —*Washington Post*

"Claire North has set her marker down as a here-to-stay talent. This is another excellent read with so much imagination packed into its pages the quality dazzles."   —Peter F. Hamilton

"Touch is little short of a masterpiece...both a thought-provoking literary treatise on what makes us human, and a genre-thriller that rattles on at a breakneck pace. Excellent."

—*Independent*

Praise for

THE FIRST FIFTEEN LIVES
OF HARRY AUGUST:

By Claire North

The First Fifteen Lives of Harry August
Touch

TOUCH

CLAIRE NORTH

www.redhookbooks.com

Copyright © 2015 by Claire North
Excerpt from *The First Fifteen Lives of Harry August* copyright © 2014 by Claire North

Redhook Books/Orbit
Hachette Book Group
1290 Avenue of the Americas
New York, NY 10104
www.HachetteBookGroup.com

Printed in the United States of America

RRD-C

Published in hardcover by Redhook: February 2015
Originally published in Great Britain in 2015 by Orbit, an imprint of Little, Brown
First U.S. paperback edition: August 2015

10 9 8 7 6 5 4 3 2 1

Redhook is an imprint of Orbit, a division of Hachette Book Group.
The Redhook name and logo are trademarks of Hachette Book Group, Inc.

The Hachette Speakers Bureau provides a wide range of authors for speaking events. To find out more, go to www.hachettespeakersbureau.com or call (866) 376-6591.

Library of Congress Control Number: 2014953910

ISBN: 978-0-316-33592-8 (hardcover)
ISBN: 978-0-316-33591-1 (paperback)

TOUCH

Chapter 1

Josephine Cebula was dying, and it should have been me.

She had two bullets in the chest, one in the leg, and that should have been the end of it, should have been enough, but the gunman had stepped over her expiring form and was looking for me.

For *me*.

I cowered in the body of a woman with swollen ankles and soft flabby wrists, and watched Josephine die. Her lips were blue, her skin was white, the blood came out of the lower gunshot to her stomach with the inevitability of an oil spill. As she exhaled, pink foam bubbled across her teeth, blood filling her lungs. He – her killer – was already moving on, head turning, gun raised, looking for the switch, the jump, the connection, the skin, but the station was a shoal of sardines breaking before a shark. I scattered with the crowd, stumbling in my impractical shoes, and tripped, and fell. My hand connected with the leg of a bearded man, brown-trousered and grey-haired, who perhaps, in another place, bounced spoilt grandchildren happily upon his knee. His face was distended with panic, and now he ran, knocking strangers aside with his elbows and fists, though he was doubtless a good man.

In such times you work with what you have, and he would do. My fingers closed round his ankle, and I

jumped

slipping into his skin without a sound.

A moment of uncertainty. I had been woman; now I was man, old and frightened. But my legs were strong, and my lungs were deep, and if I had doubted either I wouldn't have made the move. Behind me, the woman with swollen ankles cried out. The gunman turned, weapon raised.

What does he see?

A woman fallen on the stairs, a kindly old man helping her up. I wear the white cap of the hajj, I think I must love my family, and there is a kindness in the corner of my eye that terror cannot erase. I pulled the woman to her feet, dragged her towards the exit, and the killer saw only my body, not me, and turned away.

The woman, who a second ago I had been, shook away enough of her confusion to look up into my stranger's face. Who was I? How did I come to be helping her? She had no answer, and finding only fear, gave a howl of she-wolf terror and pulled away, scratching at my chin. Breaking free, she ran.

Above, in the square portal of light at the top of the stairs: police, daylight, salvation.

Behind: a man with a gun, dark brown hair and synthetic black jacket, who wasn't running, wasn't firing, but was looking, looking for the skin.

On the stairs, Josephine's spreading blood.

The blood in her throat sounded like popping candy when she breathed, barely audible over the racket of the station.

My body wanted to run, thin walls of an ageing heart pumping fast against a bony chest. Josephine's eyes met mine, but she didn't see me there.

I turned. Went back to her. Knelt at her side, pressed her hand over the wound nearest her heart, and whispered, "You'll be OK. You'll be all right."

A train was approaching through the tunnel; I marvelled that no one had stopped the line. Then again the first shot had been fired not thirty seconds ago, and it would take almost as long to explain it as to live it.

"You'll be OK," I lied to Josephine, whispering soft German in her ear. "I love you."

Perhaps the driver of the oncoming train didn't see the blood on the stairs, the mothers holding their children close as they cowered behind grey pillars and fluorescent vending machines. Perhaps he did see it, but like a hedgehog before a cement lorry was so bewildered by the events, he couldn't manage an independent original thought and so, training overriding initiative, he slowed down.

Faced with sirens above and a train below, the man with the gun looked around the station once more, did not see what he wanted, turned and ran.

The train doors opened, and he climbed on board.

Josephine Cebula was dead.

I followed her killer on to the train.

Chapter 2

Three and a half months before she died, a stranger's hand pressing on hers, Josephine Cebula said, "It's fifty euros for the hour."

I was sitting on the end of the hotel bed, remembering why I didn't like Frankfurt. A few beautiful streets had been restored after the war by a mayor with a sense of undefeated civic pride, but time had moved too fast, the needs of the city too great, and so a bare quarter-mile of Germanic kitsch had been rebuilt, celebrating a lost culture, a fairy-tale history. The rest was pure 1950s tedium, built in straight lines by men too busy to think of anything better.

Now grey concrete executives sat within grey concrete walls, quite possibly discussing concrete, there not being much else in Frankfurt to get enthused about. They drank some of the least good beer Germany had to offer, in some of the dullest bars in Western Europe, rode buses that came on time, paid three times the going rate for a cab out to the airport, were weary when they came, and glad when they departed.

And within all this was Josephine Cebula, who said, "Fifty euros. Not negotiable."

I said, "How old are you?"

"Nineteen."

"How old are you really, Josephine?"

"How old do you want me to be?"

I added up her dress, which was in its own way expensive, in that so little fabric worn on purpose could only be the consequence of high fashion. A zip ran down one side, tight against her ribs and the curve of her belly. Her boots were tight around her calves, forcing them to bulge uncomfortably just below the knee. The heel was too high for good balance, which showed in her uneasy posture. I mentally stripped her of these poor choices, pulled her chin up high, washed the cheap dye from her hair and concluded that she was beautiful.

"What's your cut?" I asked.

"Why?"

"Your accent isn't German. Polish?"

"Why so many questions?"

"Answer them and three hundred euros are yours, right now."

"Show me."

I laid out the money, a note at a time, in clean fifty bills on the floor between us.

"I get forty per cent."

"You're on a bad deal."

"Are you a cop?"

"No."

"A priest?"

"Far from."

She wanted to look at the money, wondered how much more I held, but managed to keep her eyes on me. "Then what?"

I considered. "A traveller," I said at last. "Looking for a change of scenery. Your arms – needle marks?"

"No. I gave blood."

A lie, one I didn't need to call her on, it was so weak in both conception and delivery. "May I see?"

Her eyes flickered to the money on the floor. She held out her arms. I examined the bruise in the nook of her elbow, felt the skin, so thin I was amazed my touch didn't dent it, saw no sign of more

5

extensive needle use. "I'm clean," she murmured, her eyes now fixed on mine. "I'm clean."

I let her hands go; she hugged her arms around her chest. "I don't do any stupid stuff."

"What kind of stupid stuff?"

"I don't sit around and talk. You're here for business; I'm here for business. So, let's do business."

"All right. I want your body."

A shrug; this was nothing new. "For three hundred I can stay the night but I need to tell my guys."

"No. Not for the night."

"Then what? I don't do long term."

"Three months."

A snort of a laugh; she'd forgotten what humour sounded like. "You're crazy."

"Three months," I repeated. "Ten thousand euros upon completion of contract, a new passport, new identity, and a fresh start in any city you name."

"And what would you want for this?"

"I said: I want your body."

She turned her face away so that I might not spot the fear that ran down her throat. For a moment she considered, money at her feet, stranger sitting on the end of her bed. Then, "More. Tell me more, and I'll think about it."

I held out my hand, palm up. "Take my hand," I said. "I'll show you."

Chapter 3

That had been three months ago.

Now Josephine was dead.

Taksim station has very little to recommend it.

In the morning dull-eyed commuters bounce off each other as they ride down the Bosphorus, shirts damp from the packed people carriers that serve Yenikoy and Levent. Students bound through the Metro in punk-rock T-shirts, little skirts and bright headscarves towards the hill of Galata, the coffee shops of Beyoglu, the iPhone store and the greasy *pide* of Siraselviler Caddesi, where the doors never close and the lights never die behind the plate-glass windows of the clothes stores. In the evening mothers rush to collect the children two to a pram, husbands stride with brief-cases bouncing, and the tourists, who never understood that this is a working city and are only really interested in the funicular, cram together and grow dizzy on the smell of shared armpit.

Such is the rhythm of a thriving city, and it being so, the presence of a murderer on the train, gun tucked away inside a black baseball jacket, head bowed and hands steady, causes not a flicker as the Metro pulls clear of Taksim station.

*

I am a kindly old man in a white cap; my beard is trimmed, my trousers are only slightly stained with blood where I knelt by the side of a woman who was dead. There is no sign that sixty seconds ago I ran through Taksim in fear of my life, save perhaps a protrusion in the veins on my neck and a sticky glow to my face.

Some few metres from me – very few, yet very many by the count of bodies that kept us apart – stood the man with the gun beneath his jacket, with nothing in his look to show that he had just shot a woman in cold blood. His baseball cap, pulled down over his eyes, declared devotion to Gungorenspor, a football team whose deeds were forever greater in the expectation than the act. His skin was fair, recently tanned by some southern sun and more recently learning to forget the same. Some thirty people filled the space between us, bouncing from side to side like wavelets in a cup. In a few minutes police would shut down the line to Sanayii. In a few minutes someone would see the blood on my clothes, observe the fading red footprint I left with every step.

It wasn't too late to run.

I watched the man in the baseball cap.

He too was running, though in a very different manner. His purpose was to blend with the crowd, and indeed, hat pulled down and shoulders curled forward, he might have been any other stranger on the train, not a murderer at all.

I moved through the carriage, placing each toe carefully in the spaces between other people's feet, a swaying game of twister played in the busy silence of strangers trying not to meet each other's eyes.

At Osmanbey the train, rather than growing emptier, pressed in tighter with a flood of people, before pulling away. The killer stared out the window at the blackness of the tunnel, one hand grasping the bar above, one resting in his jacket, finger perhaps still pressed to the trigger of his gun. His nose had been broken, then restored, a long time ago. He was tall without being a giant, hanging his neck and slouching his shoulders to minimise the effect. He was slim without being skinny, solid without being massy, tense as a tiger, languid as a cat. A boy with a tennis racket under one arm knocked against him, and the killer's head snapped up, fingers curling tight inside his jacket. The boy looked away.

I eased my way around a doctor on her way home, hospital badge bouncing on her chest, photo staring with grim-eyed pessimism from its plastic heart, ready to lower your expectations. The man in the baseball cap was a bare three feet away, the back of his neck flat, his hair trimmed to a dead stop above his topmost vertebrae.

The train began to decelerate, and as it did, he lifted his head again, eyes flicking around the carriage. So doing, his gaze fell on me.

A moment. First stony nothing, the stare of strangers on a train, devoid of character or soul. Then the polite smile, for I was a nice old man, my story written in my skin, and in smiling he hoped I would go away, a contact made, an instant passed. Finally his eyes traced their way to my hands, which were already rising towards his face, and his smile fell as he saw the blood of Josephine Cebula drying in great brown stripes across my fingertips, and as he opened his mouth and began to draw the gun from his shoulder holster I reached out and wrapped my fingers around the side of his neck and

switched.

A second of confusion as the bearded man with blood on his hands, standing before me, lost his balance, staggered, bounced off the boy with the tennis racket, caught his grip on the wall of the train, looked up, saw me, and as the train pulled into Sisli Mecidiyekoy, and with remarkable courage considering the circumstances, straightened up, pointed a finger into my face and called out, "Murderer! Murderer!"

I smiled politely, slipped the gun already in my hand back into its holster, and as the doors opened behind me, spun out into the throng of the station.

Chapter 4

Sisli Mecidiyekoy was a place sanctified to the gods of global un-originality. From the white shopping arcades selling cheap whisky and DVDs on the life of the Prophet Muhammad to the towering skyscrapers for families with just enough wealth to be great but not quite enough to be exclusive, Sisli was a district of lights, concrete and uniformity. Uniform wealth, uniform ambition, uniform commerce, uniform ties and uniform parking tariffs.

If asked to find a place to hide a murderer's body, it would not have been high on my list.

But then again –

"Murderer, murderer!" from the train, voice ringing at my back.

In front confused shoppers wondering what the commotion might be and if it'll get in their way.

My body wore sensible shoes.

I ran.

Cevahir Shopping Centre, luscious as limestone, romantic as herpes, could have been anywhere in the world. White tiles and glass ceiling, geometric protrusions on a theme of balconies and floors, not-quite-golden pillars rising up through foyers where the shops were Adidas and Selfridges, Mothercare and Debenhams, Starbucks and McDonald's, its only concessions to local culture the kofte burger and apple cinnamon sundae served in a plastic cup. CCTV cameras lined the halls, spun slowly to track suspicious kids with saggy trousers, the well-heeled mum with shopping bags loaded into an empty pram, infant long since abandoned to the nanny and the face-paints stall. About as Islamic as pig trotters in cream, yet even the black-veiled matrons of Fenir came, children grasped in gloved hands, to sample halal pizza from Pizza Hut and see whether they needed a new kind of shower head.

And yet, at my back, the sirens sang, so I pulled my hat down, my shoulders up and ploughed into the crowds.

Chapter 5

My body.

The usual owner, whoever he was, perhaps assumed that it was normal for shoulder blades to tense so tight against the skin. He would have had nothing else to compare his experience of having shoulders with. His peers, when asked how their shoulders felt, no doubt came up with that universal reply: normal.

I feel normal.

I feel like myself.

If I ever spoke to the murderer whose body I wore, I would be happy to inform him of the error of his perceptions.

I headed for the toilets, and out of habit walked into the ladies'.

The first few minutes are always the most awkward.

I sat behind a locked door in the men's toilets and went through the pockets of a murderer.

I was carrying four objects. A mobile phone, switched off, a gun in a shoulder holster, five hundred lira and a rental car key. Not a toffee wrapper more.

Lack of evidence was hardly evidence itself, but there is only so much that may be said of a man who carries a gun and no wallet. The chief conclusion that may be reached is this: he is an assassin.

I am an assassin.

Sent, without a doubt, to kill me.

And yet it was Josephine who had died.

I sat and considered ways to kill my body. Poison would be easier than knives. A simple overdose of something suitably toxic, and even before the first of the pain hit I could be gone, away, a stranger watching this killer, waiting for him to die.

I thumbed the mobile phone on.

There were no numbers saved in the directory, no evidence that it was anything other than a quick purchase from a cheap stall. I made to turn it off, and it received a message.

The message read: *Circe*.

I considered this for a moment, then thumbed the phone off, pulled out the battery and dropped them into my pocket.

Five hundred lira and the key to a rental car. I squeezed this last in the palm of my hand, felt it bite into skin, enjoyed the notion that it might bleed. I pulled off my baseball cap and jacket and, finding the shoulder holster and gun now exposed, folded them into my bundle of rejected clothes and threw them into the nearest bin. Now in a white T-shirt and jeans, I walked out of the toilets and into the nearest clothes store, smiling at the security guard on the door. I bought a jacket, brown with two zips on the front, of which the second seemed to serve no comprehensible purpose. I also bought a grey scarf and matching woolly hat, burying my face behind them.

Three policemen stood by the great glass doors leading from the shopping mall to the Metro station.

I am an assassin.

I am a tourist.

I am no one of significance.

I ignored them as I walked by.

The Metro was shut; angry crowds gathered round the harried official, it's an outrage, it's a crime, do you know what you're doing to us? A woman may be dead, but why should that be allowed to ruin our day?

I got a taxi. Cevahir is one of the few places in Istanbul where finding a cab is easy, an attitude of "I have spent extravagantly now, where's the harm?" lending itself generously to the cabbie's profit.

My driver, glancing at me in the mirror as we pulled into the traffic, registered satisfaction at having snared a double whammy – not merely a shopper, but a foreign shopper. He asked where to, and his heart soared when I replied Pera, hill of great hotels and generous tips from naïve travellers bewitched by the shores of the Bosphorus.

"Tourist, yes?" he asked in broken English.

"Traveller, no," I replied in clear Turkish.

Surprise at the sound of his native language. "American?"

"Does it make a difference?"

My apathy didn't discourage him. "I love Americans," he explained as we crawled through red-light rush hour. "Most people hate them – so loud, so fat, so stupid – but I love them. It's only because their masters are sinful that they commit such evils. I think it's really good that they still want to be nice people."

"Is that so."

"Oh yes. I've met many Americans, and they're always generous, really generous, and so eager to be friends."

The driver talked on, an extra lira for every four hundred merry words. I let him talk, watching the tendons rise and fall in my fingers, feeling the hair on the surface of my arm, the long slope of my neck, the sharp angle where it struck jaw. My Adam's apple rose and fell as I swallowed, the unfamiliar process fascinating after my – after Josephine's – throat.

"I know a great restaurant near here," my driver exclaimed as we rounded the narrow stone streets of Pera. "Good fish. You tell them I sent you, tell them I said you were a nice guy, they'll give you a discount, no question. Yes, the owner's my cousin, but I'm telling you – best food this side of the Horn."

I tipped when he let me out round the corner from the hotel.

I didn't want to stand out from the crowd.

*

There are only two popular municipal names in Istanbul – the Suleyman restaurant/hotel/hall and the Ataturk airport/station/mall. A photo of the said Ataturk graces the wall behind every cash counter and credit card machine in the city, and the Sultan Suleyman Hotel, though it flew the EU flag next to the Turkish, was no exception. A great French-colonial monster of a building, where the cocktails were expensive, the sheets were crisp and every bath was a swimming pool. I had stayed before, as one person or another.

Now, locked in the safe of room 418, a passport declared that here had resided Josephina Kozel, citizen of Turkey, owner of five dresses, three skirts, eight shirts, four pairs of pyjamas, three pairs of shoes, one hairbrush, one toothbrush and, stacked carefully in vacuum-wrapped piles, ten thousand euros hard cash. It would be a happy janitor who eventually broke open that safe and reaped the reward that would now for never be the prize of Josephine Cebula, resting in peace in an unmarked police-dug grave.

I did not kill Josephine.

This body killed Josephine.

It would be easy to mutilate this flesh.

There were no police yet at the hotel. There had been no iden-tification on Josephine's body, but eventually they'd match the single key on its wooden bauble to the door to her room, descend with white plastic suits and clear plastic bags, and find the pretty things I'd bought to bring out the natural curves in my

in her

body, a fashionable leaving gift for when we said goodbye.

The intermediate time was mine.

I toyed with going back to the room, recovering the money stashed there – my five hundred lira was shrinking fast – but sense was against the decision. Where would I leave my present body while I borrowed the housekeeper?

Instead, I went down a concrete ramp to a car park even more universally dull in its design than the Cevahir Starbucks. I pulled the car key from my pocket and, as I wound down through the foundations of the hotel, checked windscreens and number plates for a hire number, pressed "unlock" in the vicinity of any likely-looking cars and waited for the flash of indicator lights with little hope of success.

But my murderer had been lazy.

He'd tracked me down to this hotel, and used the parking provided.

On the third floor down, a pair of yellow lights blinked at me from the front of a silver-grey Nissan, welcoming me home.

Chapter 6

This is the car hired by the man who tried to kill me.

I opened the boot with the key from his

my

pocket, and looked inside.

Two black sports bags, one larger than the other.

The smaller contained a white shirt, a pair of black trousers, a plastic raincoat, a clean pair of underpants, two pairs of grey socks and a sponge bag. Beneath its removable plastic bottom were two thousand euros, one thousand Turkish lira, one thousand US dollars and four passports. The nationalities on the passports were German, British, Canadian and Turkish. The faces, alongside their endlessly changing names, were mine.

The second, far larger, bag contained a murder kit. A carefully packed box of little knives and vicious combat blades, rope, masking tape and stiff white cotton bandages, two pairs of handcuffs, a nine-millimetre Beretta plus three spare clips and green medical bag containing a range of chemicals from the toxic through to the sedative. What to make of the full-body Lycra suit, thick rubber gloves and hazmat helmet, I really didn't know.

I nearly missed the fat Manila folder tucked into an inner

pocket, save that a corner of it had caught in the zip and showed brown against the black interior. I opened the folder and almost immediately shut it again.

The contents would require more attention than I felt able to give for the moment.

I closed the boot, got into the car, felt the comfortable fit of the seat, checked the alignment of the mirrors, ran my hand around the glove compartment to find nothing more exciting than a road map of northern Turkey and started the engine.

I am, contrary to what may be expected of one as old as I, not in the least bit old-fashioned.

I inhabit bodies which are young, healthy, interesting, vibrant.

I play with their iWhatevers, dance with their friends, listen to their records, wear their clothes, eat from their fridges.

My life is their life, and if the fresh-faced girl I inhabit uses high-powered chemical cocktails to treat her acne, why then so do I, for she's had longer to get used to my skin, and knows what to wear and what not, and so, in all things, I move with the times.

None of which prepares you for driving in Turkey.

The Turks aren't bad drivers.

Indeed, an argument could be made for their being absolutely superb drivers as only split-second instinct, razor-sharp skills and relentless determination to be a winner could keep you both alive and moving on the Otoyol-3 to Edirne. It's not that your fellow drivers are ignorant of the concept of lanes, merely that, as the city falls away behind and the low hills that hug the coast begin to push and shrug against you, the scent of open air seems to provoke some animal instinct, and the accelerator goes down, the window opens to let in the roar of passing wind and the mission becomes go, go, go!

I drive rather more sedately.

Not because I am old-fashioned.

Simply because, even at the loneliest of times on the darkest roads, I always have a passenger on board.

Chapter 7

The single most terrifying drive of my life.

It was 1958, she had introduced herself as Peacock, and when she whispered in my ear, "You want to go somewhere quiet?" I'd said sure. That'd be nice.

Five and a half minutes later she was sitting behind the wheel of a Lincoln Baby convertible, the roof down and the wind screaming, swooping through the hills of Sacramento like an eagle in a tornado, and as I clung to the dashboard and watched sheer drops twist away beneath our wheels she screamed, "I fucking love this town!"

Had I been experiencing any sentiment other than blind terror, I might have said something witty.

"I fucking love the fucking people!" she whooped as a Chevy, heading the other way, slammed on both its brakes and its horn as we barrelled towards the lights of a tunnel.

"They're all so fucking sweet!" she howled, pins unravelling from her curled blonde hair. "They're all so fucking, 'Sweetie, you're so sweet!' and I'm all, 'That's so sweet of you' and they're all, 'But we can't give you the role because you're so sweet, sweetie' and I'm like, 'FUCK YOU ALL!'"

She shrieked with delight at this conclusion and, as the yellow glow of the rock-carved tunnel enveloped us in its heat, pressed harder on the accelerator.

"Fuck you all!" she screamed, engine roaring like a baited bear. "Where's your fucking bitter, where's your fucking bile, where's your fucking balls, you fuckers?!"

A pair of headlights ahead and it occurred to me that she was now driving on the wrong side of the road. "Fuck you!" she roared. "Fuck you!"

The lights swerved, and she swerved with them, lining up like a jousting knight, and the headlights swerved again, wheels screeching to get out of the way, but she just turned the wheel again, face forward, eyes down, no going back, and though I rather liked the body I was in at the time (male, twenty-two, great teeth), I had absolutely no intention of dying in it, so as we lined up for the kill, I reached over, grabbed her by the bare crook of her arm and switched.

The brakes gave off a primal scream of metal tearing metal, of tortured air and shattered springs. The car spun as the back wheels locked, until finally, as gentle and inevitable as the crash of the *Titanic*, the side of the car slammed into the wall of the tunnel and with a great belch of yellow-white sparks we scraped our way to a standstill.

The motion knocked me forward, my head bouncing down on to the hard steering wheel. Someone had tied little knots between all the neurons in my brain, making thick bundles of uncommunicative squelch where my thoughts should have been. I lifted my head and saw that I left blood on the wheel; I pressed a peacock-blue glove against my skull and tasted salt in my mouth. By my side the very pleasant young body I had been inhabiting stirred, opened his eyes, shook like a kitten and began to perceive for himself.

Confusion became anxiety, anxiety panic, and panic, having only a choice between rage or terror, went for the latter option as he screamed, "Oh God oh God oh God who are you who the fuck are you where am I where am I oh God oh God . . . "

Or words to that effect.

The other car, whose intended role had been the agent of our sticky demise, had pulled itself to a stop some twenty yards from us, and now the doors were open and a man was barrelling out, red-faced and cavern-skinned. As I blinked blood from my eyes I looked up to see that this gentleman, white-collared and black-trousered as he was, carried a small silver-barrelled revolver in one hand and a police badge in the other. He was also shouting, the great roaring words of a voice which has forgotten how to speak, words of my family, my car, police commissioner, going to burn, going to fucking burn . . .

When I had nothing to contribute on this subject, he waved the gun at me and roared at the boy to throw him my handbag. It too, like all things to do with me, was peacock-blue, adorned with green and black sequins, and glistened like the fresh skin of a shedding snake as it tumbled through the air. The man with the gun caught it awkwardly, opened it up, looked inside, and dropped it at once with an involuntary gasp.

Now no one was shouting, only the *tick-tick-tick* of the car engine filling the hot gloom of the tunnel. I leaned over to see what contents could possibly have induced this blissful respite from head-pounding noise.

My fallen handbag had spilt its contents in the road. A driver's licence which informed me that my name was, in fact, Peacock, a curse clearly bestowed upon me by parents with a limited sense of ornithological aptitude. A tube of lipstick, a sanitary towel, a set of door keys, a wallet. A small plastic bag of unknown yellowish powder. A human finger, still warm and bloody, wrapped in a white cotton handkerchief, the edges ragged where it had been sawn away from the hand.

I looked up from this to see the man with the gun staring at me with open horror on his face. "Damn," I rasped, pulling my gloves free from my hands one long blood-blackened length of silk at a time, and holding out my bare wrists for the cuffs. "I guess you'd better arrest me."

Problem with moving into a new body, you never quite know where it's been.

Chapter 8

I judged myself to be halfway to Edirne by the time the sun began to set, a hot burst lighting the tarmac rosy-pink before me. Close the window of the car for even a few minutes, and the rental smell crept back in, air freshener and chemical cleanliness. The radio broadcast a documentary on the economic consequences of the Arab Spring, followed by music about loves lost, loves won, hearts broken, hearts restored once again. Cars coming from the west had their headlights on, and before the sun could reach the horizon, black clouds swallowed it whole.

I pulled into a service station as the last of the day began to fade, between two great pools of white halogen light. The station promised fast food, petrol, games and entertainment. I bought coffee, *pide* and a chocolate bar containing a grand total of three raisins, sat in the window and watched. I didn't like the face that watched back from the reflection. It looked like the face of someone without scruple.

Otoyol-3 was a busy highway at the best of times, and though the signs promised Edirne as you headed west, they could equally have offered directions to Belgrade, Budapest, Vienna. It was a road for bored truckers to whom the mighty bridge from Asia to

Europe across a plunging gorge was no more and no less than a tedious bottleneck, and the sight of Aya Sofia on the banks of the Golden Horn nothing more than a mental tick box proclaiming, *Only ten more hours to home ...*

Families, six to a five-seater car, tore through the station like prisoners freed from their cells. The parents and one regrettable grandmother who'd insisted on coming too bickered, while the children whooped, their eyes opened to the irresistible truth that what they'd needed their whole lives was a plastic water gun and a pair of x2 magnification binoculars.

I needed to ditch my car, sooner rather than later.

When had the face in the window made this decision? I wondered.

Probably around the same time it chose not to swallow a slow-acting but incurable poison.

Possibly the same instant it received a text message on an unused phone: *Circe.*

The moment it realised it wasn't alone.

A man asked me if I had the time.

I did not.

Was I going to Edirne?

I was not.

Was I OK? I looked ... different.

I was fine. Dealing with some personal stuff.

Everyone always respects a guy who's dealing with personal stuff.

He left me alone.

In the half-gloom of the parking lot a pair of lovers screamed at each other, their blooming romance destroyed by the trauma of trying to map-read in the dark. I got back into the car, turned the radio up high, wound the windows down to let in the cold and headed north, towards Edirne.

Chapter 9

I've always liked Edirne. Sometime the haunt of princes and kings, in recent decades it had fallen into grubby disrepair, worn like an old man who knew that the holes in his cardigan were a badge, not of shame, but thrifty pride. In winter slush turned grey in the gutters of the straight dual carriageways, while in summer boys and men gathered to compete in the annual wrestling tournament, buttocks shining, oiled torsos gleaming, clawed hands locked across the arched backs of their beefy opponents as they rolled in the sand. I have never been tempted to participate, even in the skin of champions. For sure, the city lacked any of the great "come-hithers" of Istanbul, save for a silver-capped mosque built by yet another Sultan Selim with a penchant for marble, and a pleasant-looking hospital founded by a Beyazid who loved to both conquer and repent – but for all that it had a proud integrity of purpose and design which invited the visitor to remember that Edirne didn't need to be flashy to be great.

I parked the car by a fountain decked with giant metal sunflowers.

I took the bags from the boot, put a hundred lira and one of the passports in my pocket, snapped one bracelet of a pair of handcuffs on to my right wrist, popped the key in my inside jacket pocket, pulled the sleeve down to hide the steel, slung the bags across my back and walked away through the quiet Edirne night.

Sodium lamps stood out from the walls where once torches had burned, the pinkish bulbs captured in old iron hooks. Magnolia apartment blocks squatted between ornate 1800s mansions, now transformed into flats for busy families, the grey-blue light of the TV flickering behind the balconies. A cat hissed from behind a laundry line. A speeding bus parped its hooter at a neglectful motorbike. A restaurant owner waved goodbye to his favourite customers as they staggered home through the night.

I headed towards the white-lit walls of the Selimiye mosque, for where there are great monuments to regal expenditure, there are hotels.

The receptionist was dozing off in front of a TV drama, the story of identical twin brothers played by a single actor. In the final scene they stood together and shook hands upon a hill. On the left side the weather was overcast, oppressive. On the right it was cool and fair. Where their hands met, a line sliced through the sky and the earth, tearing it in two. The credits rolled, the receptionist stirred. I laid my Canadian passport down on the table, and said, "Room?"

The receptionist read the name in the passport carefully, trying not to lose any syllables.

"Nathan Coyle?"

"That's me."

Everyone loves a Canadian.

The hotel was three floors in total, in a once-wooden building now fused into a mixture of brick and timber. There were no more than twelve guest rooms, nine empty, and silence in the corridors.

A girl with baggy eyes, straight black hair down to the small of her back and a jutting chin showed me to my room. A double bed dominated a small floor beneath a sloping ceiling. A window opened on to two inches of balcony. A radiator sat beneath a wooden bracket supporting a small TV. A bathroom, whose four walls I could touch by standing in the middle, smelt faintly of lemon and toilet products. The girl stood in the door and said, in heavily accented English, "It OK for you?"

"Perfect," I replied. "Can you show me how to use this?"

I waved the TV remote at her. She barely managed to suppress the rolling of her eyes.

I smiled a toothy smile of North American doubt and confusion. Her hand came out to take the remote, and as it did, I reached behind me, snapping the free bracelet of the handcuffs shut around the radiator pipe on the wall. The sound caused the girl's eyes to rise, and as they did, I pressed my left hand against hers, wrapping the fingers round the remote, and switched.

My fingers jerked.

The TV popped on.

A newsreader laughed at an unheard punchline, lost to the airwaves. A weather map appeared behind him, and as if to confirm that nothing could be quite as wonderful as the weather, he laughed again, at grey skies and falling rain.

The man before me, 25 per cent of whose passports declared him to be Nathan Coyle, Canadian national and no bother to anyone, staggered, one knee buckling. He tried to climb back up, the handcuffs clattering on the radiator, turning blearily to blink at the metal bracelet holding him down.

I watched. His breathing, the sharp in-out of a body suddenly shocked and confused, slowed. His nostrils flared, and I counted the two, three long breaths he took, and by the time they were done, so was he, body tense, head high, respiration back under control.

I said, "Hello."

He pressed his lips together and stared up at me, and it seemed to me that he saw

not me, not I that-is-she-who-lives-at-the-hotel, but me

I, myself

and I felt my breath catch in my throat.

He looked without speaking from his crouch on the floor, right arm half-pulled back behind him as he strained against the handcuffs. I hovered outside his arms' reach and said, "You're going to eat poison."

Silence from the floor.

"Two questions are keeping you alive. First: who do you work with, and will they keep coming? I'm assuming that they will. People like you always do. Second: why did you kill Josephine Cebula?"

He stared up at me like a wounded cat and said nothing.

My body had been on its feet too long, the taste of cigarette smoke in its mouth, the weight of a day pulling my spine out and down. My bra was uncomfortable, done up too tightly at the back, and the piercing in my left ear was fresh, throbbing from a gently escalating infection.

"You're going to eat poison," I repeated to no one in particular. "All I want are answers."

Silence from the floor.

"This relationship is going to be difficult for us both," I said, then, "Left pocket."

A flicker of his eyebrows. His free hand turned instinctively towards his left pocket, then hesitated, and before he could consider further, I reached down and grabbed his fingers.

Switched.

The girl with the optimistically tight bra staggered. I reached into my jacket pocket, pulled out the keys stashed therein, unlocked the cuffs and, as she reeled forward, I rose, caught her under the arms said, "You OK, miss? You came over dizzy."

Incredible, the willingness of the human mind to believe in that which doesn't scare it.

"Perhaps you need to sit down."

Chapter 10

My first switch.

I was thirty-three years old.

He was probably only in his twenties, but his body felt a lot older. His skin flaked in little white clouds as he scratched, a great rasping of dry flesh beneath cracked yellow nails. His hair was turning smudged grey, his beard grew in erratic patches from a once-scarred chin, and when he beat me to death, he only did it for the money to fill his belly, and his belly was so empty

my belly was so empty

as I discovered, when I switched.

I didn't want to touch him, since he had just killed me. But I didn't want to die alone so, as my vision flooded like wine in a cup, I reached out and grabbed his shoulder as he pulled my purse from round my waist, and in that moment I became him, just in time to see myself die.

Chapter 11

Awake at 3 a.m. in a hotel room.

The light still on.

Nothing on TV.

This body needs sleep.

I need sleep.

Sleep does not come.

A mind that will not stop, thoughts that will not cease.

At 9.40 a.m. a woman called Josephine Cebula left a hotel room in Istanbul, heading to the waterfront. Three days ago she'd met two new friends, who'd said please join us, we'll teach you how to fish off the Galata bridge.

I'm too beautiful to fish, the mind that wore the body of Josephine Cebula had thought. Are you sure you don't want me to change into someone more appropriate?

Fishing would be delightful, my fresh red lips proclaimed. I've always meant to learn how to fish.

By midday I'd seen someone in the corner of my eye, and by 12.20 p.m. I was running, grateful that my shoes had flat soles, for the crowds of Taksim, for the easy way out, my bare fingers flicking from skin to skin as I searched for a suitable exit route, and then, as I stumbled against the body of a woman with swollen ankles and the taste of coconut in her mouth, the gunman at my back had fired, and I had felt the shot tear through my leg, felt flesh burst outwards and arteries snap, seen my own blood sprinkled on the concrete in front of me, and as I closed my eyes against the pain and opened my mouth to scream, my fingers had tangled against those of a stranger, and I had run and left Josephine Cebula to die.

And then

inexplicably

he'd killed Josephine.

She was fallen and I was gone, but he put two bullets in her chest and she died, even though he was coming for me.

Why would anyone do that?

In a hotel room, 3 a.m., and my left leg ached, though there was no sign of scarring or apparent cause for pain.

A Manila folder from Nathan Coyle's lethal travelling bag.

I'd glimpsed it when I stole his car, and now, as the night crawled towards dawn, I spread its contents across the bed and looked again, and saw the faces of my life stretched out before me. A single name was written across the front of the file: Kepler.

It seemed as good a name as any.

Chapter 12

I checked out of the Edirne hotel at 7 a.m. Breakfast was from a bakery around the corner, which served hot croissants, cherry jam and the best coffee I'd had in this body so far. With my bags on my back and hat pulled down low, I went looking for the first bus to Kapikule, and out of this country. In a murderer's body I couldn't think of any good reason to linger.

How unusual it felt for me to be the innocent in any crime but my flesh to be the hunted.

The thought made me smile all the way to the ticket booth.

There were eleven people on the short bus ride to Kapikule, which seemed apt, as the bus was no more than a converted minivan with a paper sign in the front which read, KAPIKULE. LEV OR LIRA ACCEPTED, NO CHANGE GIVEN.

An ageing man and his aged mother were sitting in the twin seats behind me, bickering.

She said, "I don't want to."

He said, "Mother . . ."

She said, "I don't want to and that's that."

He said, "Well, you've got to, Mother, you've got to, and we've

31

had this conversation and this is your future as well as mine so we're going and you've got to and that's it."

She said, her voice rising almost to the point of tears, "But I don't want to!"

Their conversation continued in this vein all the way to the station, and doubtless beyond.

Kapikule was a non-place on the edge of not-anywhere-really. Not so long ago I would have avoided it and picked up the train I wanted directly from Edirne's central station. But these were difficult times, lines suspended for lack of pay, terminals withering as the flow of people dried up with the work.

The station was a two-storey building of no discernible merit whatsoever, lit in fluorescent white. In another country it might have been a grim commercial development filled with little shops doomed to fail, or a well-intentioned residential undertaking whose purpose had been corrupted by dubious landowners looking to sell on to MegaMart International. As it was, it was neither of these things.

The ticket clerk sat with his chin resting on the palm of his hand as I approached. His cap was pulled down over his eyes, but when he looked up at the arrival of money on the steel counter before him I was excited to see that here was the last man left in the world who thought that a Hitler-Chaplin moustache was the pinnacle of stylish facial hair.

I pushed cash and my Turkish passport towards him. He regarded both as a doctor observes a severed leg, waiting to see if there may yet be a body attached.

"What?" he asked.

"Belgrade," I said.

His sigh as he took my money – and ignored my passport – was the profound heave of a man aware that, strictly speaking, you have him. You have him and really he has to oblige, but, damn it, a kinder man would have walked away, let him rest, rather than trouble him with this ticket-selling business.

"Train is this evening," he grumbled, pushing the meagre papers towards me. "You'll have to hang around."

"Is there anything to see in Kapikule?"

His look could have cowed a cobra. I smiled my most charming smile, slipped the tickets into my passport and said, "I'll find somewhere to nap."

"Don't nap here," he barked. "Station property."

"Of course it is. How silly of me."

I was reluctant to wait anywhere too public.

By now the police may have found my body's fingerprints, a hair fallen from my fleeing head or some other symptom of a cock-up which I knew not of, and begun to trace its movements. Perhaps they – the great unknown "they" – have followed CCTV footage from the moment Josephine Cebula fell down the stairs of Taksim station, all the way back to a hire car pulling into a car park beneath a hotel, and, if they are especially skilled at their job, an alert could have been issued for my hire car, now sitting in the shade of a cypress tree opposite a fountain where metal sunflowers grow.

Or perhaps not.

Perhaps the police were baffled.

Who was I to say?

I took shelter in a tiny pink-stone chapel by the banks of the river. I was in Turkey, but the neatly ordered dusty fields beyond the water, their crops uprooted for the harvest, the soil already turned for next year's seeding, were in Greece. A spit and I could be there, and for a moment I considered it – quick knife to the wrists and then away I'd go in the body of a Greek farmer, breath smelling of garlic, shoes scrubbed with sand.

A priest with a great black beard approached me as I sat in the furthest pew, legs crossed upon a stone bench. He addressed me first in Greek, a language where I have never been strong, and hearing my accent raised his eyebrows in surprise, and switched to Turkish.

"This church was founded by Constantius I. He was travelling through the empire and came to this place, where he drank the waters of the river. That night, as he lay sleeping, the Virgin Mary came to him and bathed his feet and hands, and daubed his lips with the water from this stream. When he woke, he was so taken with the vision that he ordered a monastery built here. It was a thriving place: pilgrims came to wash their feet and dream of the Madonna. Then the Ottomans knocked down all but this little chapel you see now, but Sultan Selim the Grim came to this place while hunting, and lay down to rest by its banks and dreamed the same dream that his predecessor, Constantius, had dreamed. When he woke, he washed his hands and feet in the waters and proclaimed the river blessed, and said it was a crime to do any further harm against the walls of this place. He left this." His hand swept the wall, brushing over the faded remains of a great golden scrawl of near-vanished paint, running across three feet of the wall nearest the altar. "The sultan's *tigra*, stamp of his authority, so that should any man ever threaten these walls again, we could take him inside and show him the word of his master. He saved this chapel, though the pilgrims did not come again."

I nodded the slow nod of the theologically well-meaning, eyes running from the signature of the sultan to the sad smile of the Virgin Mary above it, and asked, may I go down to the river and see if it washes my sins away?

The priest's eyes widened in horror.

Of course you can't, he exclaimed. The river is blessed!

Chapter 13

The body of Nathan Coyle.

Upon reflection, he's not really my type. The muscles under my arms and across my back are a little too gym-built, maintained by the lifting and dropping of weights for no apparent purpose. Years of running have strengthened my cardiovascular system, but my left knee aches after too long motionless, and the pain grows steadily until relieved by stretching. I am a little long-sighted – undoubtedly excellent vision at a distance, but close to I find myself inclined to squint. I can find no sign of contact lenses or glasses in my bag. Perhaps he'd been meaning to go to the optician. More likely he simply hadn't realised that squinting was not the norm, having no experience save his own.

A file labelled "Kepler" sat on my lap.

The bench on the Kapikule platform was cold, hard, metal. The wind was from the east, the smell of rain on the air, the Belgrade train running twenty minutes late.

I have no interest in going to Belgrade per se. My aim is to get out of Turkey, away from the police hunting my face. But Coyle's passports are North American, north European, and there is a text on my phone which reads *Circe*, and a murder kit in my bag, and though it would be simple to kill this body and move on, I remember the feel of the bullet as it went through my leg, and though I ran and Josephine died

yet it was me he aimed to kill.

The file on my lap was laid out chronologically, photos and documents. An introduction lamented that no further information on entity Kepler was available than these thin pages of lives stolen, time lost. Not a footnote, appendix or watermark suggested who the author was.

I turned through sheaves of notes, stiff glossy photos, faces and names I barely remembered, until I reached the most recent photo – my photo. Josephine Cebula.

A copy of her Polish passport, found in the hands of her Frankfurt pimp. Her face, devoid of make-up and joy, was plain and grim, but no less than the face which had greeted me in the morning mirror.

A photo, snapped on a street corner, her face half-turned away as the photographer swept by, a moment captured, frozen, discarded.

The police record for the first time she was arrested, released nine hours later. She wore a short leather jacket that exposed her belly button, a skirt that barely covered her behind, and a bruise beneath her right eye as she glared at the camera.

The boarding pass I'd used when I caught the plane from Frankfurt to Kiev, ready for a languorous trip down the Crimea. I'd travelled business class, dressed in new, bright clothes, and as the stewardess poured me whisky I'd felt an itching and realised that Josephine was a smoker whose needs I had failed to indulge. Landing in Kiev and cursing all the way, I'd bought a box of nicotine patches and sworn that, by the time I gave her body back, she'd be clean, physiologically, if not mentally.

A picture of me, leaving the hotel in Pera, the sun on my face and phone in my hand, for I was young and rich and beautiful, and if these qualities lend themselves to one thing, it is the making of quick and easy friends. I remembered that day, that sunshine, that dress. It had been three days before I was gunned down on the steps of Taksim station, shot by a stranger. For three days they'd watched me leading my life, until they were ready to make the kill.

My nails dug into the palm of my hand, and I let them dig. A little blood, right now, wouldn't go entirely amiss.

I flipped through to the report on Josephine. A violent mother who swore she loved her daughter and wept on Josephine's shoulder every time she was released from jail. A boyfriend who'd told her that it was OK if she slept with his friends; in fact, he needed the money to pay for all the pretty things he'd bought her. A flight to Frankfurt, a flight from everything, thirty-two euros in her pocket and the author had no doubt she'd intended a better life, a good life for herself, but it seemed that Josephine's situation was untenable until the entity known as Kepler arrived and offered her money for murder.

I stopped.

A list of the dead. Dr Tortsen Ulk, drowned in his own toilet. Magda Müller, stabbed to death in her kitchen by a stranger, her daughters asleep upstairs. James Richter and Elsbet Horn, found in each other's arms, their eyes ripped out and insides spread across the floor of the cabin of the little boat they were sailing up the Rhine. Though the police had never linked the killings, lamented the author, we have done so, for these victims were part of us, and it was by Josephine's hand, and at Kepler's command, that they all died.

I read the words once and, not sure I had understood, read again.

They were no different on the second look, and no less lies.

The Belgrade train shrieked like a metal mother-in-law, white sparks bursting from its wheels as it crawled to a halt in Kapikule. A few lights were still on behind the blinds of the couchettes. Doors opened here or there, thick orange panels swinging out, metal stairs dropping down. The train had once been orange and blue, Bulgarian Railways' finest. That colour was long since lost, obscured beneath layers of spray paint, the pride of the line overwritten by the pride of the kids who haunted the terminals at either end of the line. I smelt urine from the toilet that guarded the door, heard the illicit pressure pump of a passenger committing that ultimate offence – flushing while in the station – and turned to find my cubicle.

A cabin for six, four of the beds already taken. A husband, wife, teenage son occupied three; in the other was an old man who chewed something herbal with the circular grinding of a camel's jaw and lay on his back to read articles about ancient cars and journeys through the east. The family had a makeshift feast, which they passed up and down the three-bunk tier they inhabited. Hard-boiled eggs, slices of ham, pieces of goats' cheese, crumbling bread that shook golden shards across the floor. With every crunch of the knife through the loaf, the old man with the car magazine flinched, as if the blade were cutting bone.

I climbed into the top bunk as the train jerked into motion, put my bag of clothes beneath my head, my bag of weapons beneath my feet, and lay back to think. Metal bunk below, plastic ceiling above, the space between barely wide enough for a tomb.

No one came to check the passports.

Chapter 14

There are many ways to catch a ghost sitting in the body of a loved one. Basic questions – name, age, father's name, mother's name, university – can be answered by any well-informed inhabitant, but it takes a matter of minutes to probe a little deeper.

First place you lived when you left the family home?

Name of your primary school headmistress.

First girl you ever kissed.

Or – my personal favourite – can you play the violin?

The delight with that particular enquiry is of course when the ghost, relieved to be asked something it can successfully answer, stands up and rattles off five favourite tunes in the key of G, only to be informed upon the final semibreve that the body's natural owner has never held a violin in all her life.

First skin I ever jumped to, the first question I was ever asked, I failed.

I was an empty-bellied killer, and the constable who pinned me to the watchtower floor wanted to know my name.

So I told him.

"Not *that* name," he growled. "Not the poor soul you killed. I want to know *your* name."

I had beaten a stranger to death, and that stranger, me.

I was a killer caught with blood on my hands.

"What's *your* name?!"

I was a flake-skinned youth, the weight of a club across my neck, the pressure of a knee against my back, two ribs cracked, one eye swollen, never to see right again. And like the men who beat me, I too was curious to find the answer to that most thorny of questions.

What's your name, bastard? Murderer, butcher, liar, thief. What's your name?

When they threw me into Newgate, in the hot pits where the masses went, fifty to a room – forty-seven and three bags of flesh by morning – I laughed the hysterical laughter of a mind too shattered to remember that it should weep. When the judge sentenced me to hang by the neck until dead, my knees buckled, but my face was empty and my soul was calm. When Fat Jerome, king of the underbelly of the prison, tried to get there first, his great wet paws around my throat, I didn't fight him. I threw up no defence, made no noise, but consigned my soul to Satan, to whom, it seemed, it had no choice but to go.

Yet it transpired I did not want to die, so with Fat Jerome murdering the murderer who had murdered me

rather inevitably, upon reflection,

I looked back into my murderer's face from Fat Jerome's eyes, and forgot to squeeze.

My killer fell to his knees, gagging for air, his face red, eyes popping. A small crowd had gathered, pinioning us together, body to body, sweat to sweat, and one voice said, "Why didn't you finish him, Jerome? Why'd you let him live?"

I couldn't speak.

"I'll do it, Jerome!" piped up another, a crooked-lipped thief with a brand on his hand who desperately wanted to impress the king of the cellar, the lord of the throng.

My silence was taken for consent, and with a little whoop the spry-limbed convict leaped forward and drove the end of a spoon into the socket of my killer's eye.

Chapter 15

Sleeper train is a misnomer.

Starting-awake-in-the-night train is more apt.

As drivers change and carriages are shunted in and out of platforms in the dark, the journey towards Sofia is a stop-start of teeth-grinding screeches and head-bobbing rattles. You do not sleep on a sleeper train, but rather doze in and out of a fitful sense of unconsciousness, aware that this is not awareness, that the thoughts with which you think this are not thoughts at all, and so infused with so profound an understanding of your condition, you sleep to wake again ignorant that you slept at all.

We reached Sofia at 4.23 a.m. I would not have known, but the lone passenger had set his alarm to buzz at 4.15 a.m. precisely. It made the sound of a nuclear siren, a klaxon that knocked the entire compartment awake with a clenching heart. He rolled out of his bunk dressed in yesterday's clothes, picked up his bag and left without a word. I tweaked the blind back as we passed into the station. The sun was still down over the city. A lone luggage handler waited on the deserted platform. I pushed my wafer-pillow higher against the back of the bed and rolled over to sleep.

The blind stayed down as we pulled away from Sofia. A city, its history and people, its stories and its tragedies, holds no interest to me at 4.23 a.m.

The Serbians did check passports.

At Kalotina-Zapad a team of fresh hard-jawed officials boarded the train, while the grimy-eyed crew of the previous night disembarked, wheeling their little cases to the opposite platform and the journey home. The new officials wore smart peaked hats and scuffed blue coats. As we pulled away from the station, they knocked on every compartment door, calling out, "Tickets, passports!"

Tickets and passports were taken away for inspection. I handed over my Turkish identity, the name newly learned, and lay back in the bunk, wishing we could open more of the window as the Bulgarian countryside flashed by. I had no great fear of detection this side of the border. No matter how good the Turkish police, international arrest warrants take time.

As my details were inspected and my tickets stamped, I flicked through the file marked Kepler.

Nearly a hundred photos and names, faces, glimpses of old CCTV pictures, arrest warrants, family photos. Records of interviews and documents logged, emails sent and phones hacked. Some of the faces in the file I barely remembered; others had been part of me for years at a time. There the beggar I had met in Chicago whose face, when shaved, turned out to be barely a boy's, and whose body I enrolled, as my very last act in it, on a catering course in St Louis, reasoning there were worse places to begin again. Here the woman from St Petersburg whose companions had loved her and left her, and who I'd found wandering the streets without the money to get home, and who hissed, "Vengeance against all false friends ..." There the district attorney in New Orleans who, sitting beside me in the bar, had said, "If he testifies, I can blow this case wide open, but he's too goddamn scared to come to court." And I'd replied, "What if I could get him there?"

Here, over ten years of my life, laid out in neat chronological order, every jump, every switch, every skin, tracked and documented and filed for future reference, right up to the very last page, and Josephine.

Someone had spent years tracing me, monitoring my every move through records of amnesia, the testimonies of men and women who had lost an hour here, a day there, a few months at a time. It was a masterpiece of investigation, a triumph of forensic detection, right up to the point where, without explanation, it took it upon itself to lie shamelessly and brand both me and my host murderers.

I pulled a few pictures from the file.

A woman, sitting in the window of a café in Vienna, her cake untouched, her coffee growing cold.

A man in a hospital gown, a tawny beard spreading across his round sagging belly, staring out of the window at nothing much in particular.

A teenage boy, his hair stuck up in ozone-destroying spikes, giving two fingers to the camera as he waggled his pink pierced tongue. Definitely not my type but perhaps, given the circumstances, his presence in my file was fortuitous after all.

Chapter 16

As the train slowed into Belgrade, I checked my belongings.

Passports, money, weapons, mobile phone.

I put the battery back in the phone and thumbed it on.

It took a while to work out its location and then grudgingly conceded that yes, it was in Serbia, and sent me a text message to inform me of the same and ask me to enjoy my stay. I waited. Two new messages. The first was a missed call, no message, number unknown. The second was a text message. It read: *SOS Circe.*

Nothing more.

I thought about it a moment, then turned the phone back off, removed the battery and put them away at the bottom of the bag.

What may be said of Belgrade?

It is a bad city in which to be old or cantankerous.

It is a fantastic place to party.

The station is a monument to triumphant 1800s ambition, a palace of fine lines and handsome stones that put Kapikule to shame. Step outside and taxis honk, cars scrunch head to tail, trams and trolley carts compete for space beneath the spider's web of overhead power lines feeding the transport system, and a couple of tower blocks stand still, grey and empty where once – not so long ago – NATO cruise missiles fell. A proper heart-of-city station, the smell of the rivers pushes back against exhaust and cigarette smoke as the Sava and the Danube collide, determined to prove that whatever meagre definition of 'river' you've been working on up to now, you ain't seen nothing yet. It is easy to believe, when you stand on the shores of the Danube, that the world is an island after all.

By night the barges that hug the waterfront turn up the music and the disco lights, and the young come out to party. By day the pedestrianised streets of central Belgrade are swamped with the fashionable come to buy fashionable things, to sustain their sense of fashionability, while on the edge of the city the old folk sit, men with drooping cigarettes and time-sunken eyes, who stare at the swaggering world and are not impressed.

Cross the waters of the Sava, and long shadows are thrown by the tower blocks and industrial slabs of communist dreams with such catchy names as Blok 34, Blok 8, Blok whatever. It is a place perhaps more real than the dream of exclusive boutiques that line Prince Mihailo, where life is not glamorous, and fashion serves no purpose apart from provoking envy and contempt.

I checked in at a hotel that was one of a thousand hotels run by ten companies the world over. I used the German passport and the woman exclaimed in poorly accented *Deutsch*, "Ah! Welcome you here very much!"

My room, unlike in Edirne, had the space, uniformity and whitewashed luxury expected by any bug-eyed European traveller who is now too tired to want to think about where the kettle is or watch anything other than CNN sports reports or repeats of *CSI*. I locked my case away, put a few hundred euros in my pocket, tucked the Kepler folder under my arm and went in search of an internet café.

On page 14 of the Kepler file there was a photo of a man.

His hair was dyed black, his nose, chin, ears, jaw burst with pieces of metal, he wore a T-shirt with a white skull on it and, if it hadn't been for the prescription-strength glasses on his nose and the textbook on *Prüfungs Gemacht Physik* in the background, I would happily have dismissed him then and there as your average happy punk.

The note in the file read: "Berlin, 2007. Johannes Schwarb. Short-term inhabitation, long-term association?"

Looking at the leering expression on the studded face, I shuddered to think that I had ever even considered habitation of that flesh, brief though it had been.

Chapter 17

He was sixteen, I was twenty-seven, and he was hitting on me in a Berlin nightclub.

"No," I said.

"Come on ..."

"No."

"Come on, babe ..."

"Absolutely not."

"Come on ..."

The bar was loud, the music was good, I was Christina and had a taste for mojitos, he was Johannes Schwarb and he was high.

He waggled his tongue at me like a flailing fish, revealing the stud protruding from its flapping pink surface. "Young man," I said, "you are all of thirty seconds away from self-harm."

My statement, true as it was, didn't seem to be comprehended by Johannes, who kept on writhing whichever parts of his body he still had some sort of control over up and down against the stool by my side. He hadn't mustered the courage to writhe against anything living, so the furniture would have to do. For a brief moment I contemplated doing the unthinkable, grabbing his face and putting my tongue down his throat, just to see what happened.

Odds were, he'd be so shocked he'd bite, and it seemed unfair to leave Christina with a swollen tongue and the taste of vodka.

Then his friend ran up, and she was fifteen, and she was crying, and she pulled at his arm and said, "They're here!"

"Babe!" he wailed. "Can't you see I'm ...?" A gesture attempted to take in the curves of my body, the shape of my dress, the look of murder in my eyes.

"They're here," she hissed. "They want the money."

Her eyes darted across the dance floor, and his followed, red capillaries wiggling through the whites, body half-falling as he twisted to see the source of the disruption.

Three men with the faces of those for whom a party was a source of profit, no more, were heading across the floor with the determination of a Roman road. Johannes whooped, stuck both his arms in the air, revealing a well-pierced midriff, and shrilled, "Hey! Motherfuckers! Come get it!"

If they heard this statement, the three gentlemen were unimpressed.

"You have to go. Please, run!" whimpered his companion, tugging at his arm.

"Fuckers!" he roared, face open with delight, eyes staring at some fantastical outcome only he could see. "Come on then, come on!"

I tapped the girl, tears still flowing down her face, politely on the shoulder. "Drugs?" I asked.

She didn't answer, and didn't need to. Johannes whooped. A blade flicked open in the fist of one of the approaching men.

"Right then," I muttered, and put my hand on Johannes' arm.

Jumping into an inebriated body is an entirely unpleasant experience. It is my belief that the process of getting drunk is a cushion to the actual reality of being drunk. Bit by bit the mind grows accustomed to swaying room, burning skin, churning stomach, so though every aspect of your physiology screams, poison, poison, it is the gentle and pleasant acquisition of the state that prevents the experience from becoming a thoroughly vile event.

Jumping straight from a reasonably sober body into one riding high on more noxious substances than I cared to guess at was like taking a standing jump from a trotting pony to a speeding train.

My body jerked, fingers tightening on the bar as every part of me tried to rearrange itself in some other place. I tasted bile, felt mosquitoes feeding inside my head. "Jesus Christ," I hissed, and as Christina swayed and opened her eyes beside me, I pressed my hands against my skull and turned, and did my very best to run.

The skin of strangers as it touched mine was an electric shock that rippled through my arms, ran down to my stomach and made the sack full of puke I carried beneath my lungs swish like the ocean against a cliff. I heard the girl shriek and the boys run, staggered against a man with coffee skin and avocado eyes, beautiful in every way, and wanted to fall into him then and there, damn Johannes.

The fire exit was shut, but not locked, the alarm long since disabled to let the smokers, sniffers and shaggers out into the alley at the back. I stumbled, forgetting that I wasn't in a dress, wasn't in Christina's fancy shoes. I crawled up the stairs to street level, reached for the nearest dumpster, pressed my head against the cold stinking metal and was profoundly, and gratefully, sick.

The fire door slammed shut behind me.

A voice said, "You're dead, Schwarb."

I lifted my head to see the fist, which collided with the hard bone beneath my eye. I fell, hands scraping along the tarmac, vision spinning, heard tinnitus break out loud in my right ear, coughed thin white bile.

The three boys had an average age of nineteen, twenty at most. They wore knock-offs of sporty brands: baggy trousers and tight T-shirts which emphasised in clinging polyester just how few muscles they had to celebrate.

They were going to kick the crap out of me, and with my head auditioning for soprano, I couldn't precisely put my finger on why.

I tried to get up, and one of them swung his fist again, slamming it into the side of my face. My head hit the ground and that was fine, that was completely fine, because at least with most of me on the floor, there was less of me to fall. The same thought seemed to occur to one of the boys, who grabbed me by the scruff of my shirt and began to haul me upright. I caught his wrists instinctively and, as his nostrils flared and his eyes widened, I dug my fingers into his skin and switched.

Johannes in my hands, my heart in triple figures, Christ, my fingers wanted to strike, my muscles wanted to strike, every part of my body was buzzing with adrenaline and I thought – why the hell not?

I dropped Johannes and turned, putting my entire body into the blow, knees and hips, shoulders and arms, twisting and rising to deliver a punch under the chin of my nearest companion. His jaw cracked, a tooth snapping as mandible hit cranium, and as he fell back I leaped on top of him, my knees into his chest, my face against his face, and pushed him down, screaming with a voice only freshly broken. I hit him, and hit him again, and felt blood on my knuckles though I wasn't sure where it had come from until the third boy grabbed me by the throat, yelling a name which I guessed had to be mine. As he pulled me off the bleeding mess beneath my knees, I grabbed his arm where it lay across my neck

I had an arm across the boy's neck, but I made it better, putting my left forearm across my right to pull tighter as the boy, bewildered and confused, writhed and wheezed and wiggled in my grasp. I kicked his left knee, and as he dropped, I held on tighter, suspending him by skull alone until his eyes began to roll and his fighting grew less, at which point and at last

I let him go.

And turned, breathless, to Johannes.

He sat, blood running from a wide cut across his face, palms dirty and scratched, staring at me with mouth open, eyes wide. I looked at the two boys on the ground, and saw that they weren't going anywhere any time soon. I looked back at Johannes. His lips were twitching from side to side, unsure of which torrent of thought they should express. When he finally found something, it was not the sentiment I had expected. "Oh my God!" he whispered. "That was *incredible!*"

Chapter 18

That was then.

Belgrade, the body of a man who might or might not have been Nathan Coyle.

I bought an hour of internet time in a café behind the dark-domed cathedral of St Sava, opened a packet of biscuits and a sweet fruity drink, and went online.

I needed a hacker.

Though when Johannes Schwarb went online, he did so in an altogether different guise.

Christina 636 – Hi, JS.

Spunkmaster13 – OMG! How are you?

Christina 636 – I need a favour.

Chapter 19

More photos in the Kepler file.

Faces and memories. Places seen, people travelled.

I pulled one from the folder.

Horst Gubler, US citizen. First contact with entity Kepler, 14 November 2009.

Current residence – Dominico Hospice, Slovakia.

Good on the Slovakians.

No one else would have taken him in.

It takes twelve hours to travel by train from Belgrade to Bratislava.

By plane the journey is barely worth the taxi down the runway.

Get stuck on a plane, however, and your options are far fewer than they are on a train of several hundred diverse weary travellers. As for getting a gun through an airport – a train seemed the easier option.

I caught the 6.48 from Belgrade to Bratislava.

Notes on the train from Belgrade:

It is a mish-mash of carriages and compartments, some Serbian, some Slovakian, some Hungarian, most Czech. A surprisingly high number of seats are designed for disabled passengers, though none are to be seen. An entire carriage is assigned for passengers who have children under the age of ten on the wise assumption that twelve hours with a mewling infant in close proximity is enough to drive anyone to a criminal act. The restaurant car sells variations on a theme of sandwich, soup, tea, coffee, biscuit, cauliflower and cabbage, all carefully reheated in the microwave to your exacting desires. The train crosses three international borders, though passports are checked only once, and were it not for a slight variation in the spelling of "toilet" as you pull in and out of long platforms, you might not notice the transition at all.

I turned my

this body's

mobile phone on as we crossed from Serbia to Hungary. There was one new message. It read: *Aeolus*.

Still no number.

I turned the phone off again, pulled out the battery, pushed it back to the bottom of the bag.

"Seven hundred euros," said the traveller at the bar. "Seven hundred euros, that was my bill last time I went travelling. I thought the EU was supposed to sort that shit out. I thought they were changing things – you make a call in Europe, it's like you make a call to home, you know? How do they let the phone companies do that? How do they let them rob you like that and pretend it's OK? You know the worst part?"

No, what was the worst part?

"All the calls I made, I made for work. On my personal mobile because my work phone was broken. And the fuckers wouldn't pay the bill. 'Your fault,' they said. 'Your fault for not paying attention to the fine print; you can't ask us to foot the bill for your mistake.' Like fuck. *Fuck*, I say fuck. What do you call the recession? What do you call government? All we ever do is pay for other people's greed and vanity, that's all we're good for, men like you and me."

So what did you do?

"I quit my fucking job, didn't I?!"

And how's that going?

"Shit. Like shit. I'm going home to live with my mother. She's eighty-seven and still thinks she's married, stupid hag. But what's a man to do?"

I bought another bottle of water and a packet of crisps from the restaurant-bar, wobbled my way back to my seat, and slumbered through the long Hungarian countryside as we tracked north, chasing the Danube to Slovakia.

Chapter 20

I was going to visit Horst Gubler.

Not because I liked the man, but because at some point whoever wrote the file on Kepler had also visited. If I was lucky, I
might even be wearing the right face for the trip.

This is how I met Horst Gubler:

She said, "I want him to pay."

Her hands were clamped around the whisky glass, her face tight,
shoulders stiff. She sat on the terrace of her white-wood house as
the sun set over the weeping willows and said in a thick Alabama
drawl, "I want him to suffer."

I ran my finger round the rim of my glass and said not a word.
The evening was settling in pink stripes across the horizon, layers
of cloud and sun, cloud and sun, stretching away towards the river.
The next house along flew an American flag; two doors down
from that, a couple stood with a baby in a pram, talking to their
neighbour about neighbourly things. Obama was president and the
economy was burning, but in this tiny corner of the USA it
seemed that no one wanted to care.

Except her.

"He raped her," she said. "He raped her and he's done it to others, and I don't give a fuck what the law says, because he did it and he's got away with it before and he'll get away with it again. I want Gubler to pay."

"Dead?" I asked.

She shook her head, thick black curls catching on her shirt. "Death is a sin, Bible clearly says so. But Bible don't say nothing about draining his accounts, shutting down his house, turning away his friends and marching him to the ends of the fucking earth in nothing but ashes and sackcloth. They tell me you can do that. They tell me you were an estate agent once."

I took a sip of whisky. It was bad American stuff, distilled on estates bigger than the average English county, advertised as wholesome goodness for men who believed that the wearing of a flat cap equated to an understanding of universal truths. Sitting opposite me, in a white shirt and vanilla skirt, was Maria Anna Celeste Jones, whose ancestors had been stolen from Sierra Leone, and whose home was Mississippi, and whose vengeance was absolute.

"How did you come to hear of me?" I asked.

"I was worn." Her voice was flat, to the point. "As a skin. That's what you call it, right? I was seventeen and in the gutter. This guy comes up to me. 'You've got beautiful eyes,' he says, and he touches me, and I go to sleep, and when I wake it's six months later and a girl sits by me on the bed and says, 'Thanks for the ride.' There's fifteen thousand US dollars under the bed and a letter from NYU, saying hey, well done – you got in."

"Did you go?"

"I burned the letter. Then two weeks later I wrote to them to say that the letter had got lost in the post, would they send me another, and they did, and I went and learned the law. And I learned other things too. Like how folk who move from body to body sometimes keep the same email address. The one who wore me – he went by the name of Kuanyin, and left his internet account details on the hotel computer when he cleared out of my skin."

"I know Kuanyin," I murmured. "She – she's a she, last I

checked – is sloppy. Many are. Did she ... " I toyed with my words, trying to find the right combination "... leave you as she found you?"

Maria Anna Celeste Jones looked me in the eye, and her stare was iron, her will unbreakable. "He – she – fucked people with my body. Ate, drank, stole six months of my life, got a manicure, cut my hair, dumped me in some city I'd never seen. Kuanyin gave me more money than I'd had in my life and got me enrolled at a college, and I never looked back since. So no. She didn't leave me as she found me. Dumb question, don't you think?"

I sipped whisky, let the moment settle, linger, cleared my throat. "But you didn't want revenge."

"No. Not on her. Not any more." Her fingers tightened round the glass. "Gubler. Kuanyin recommended you. Said you were good at this. Said you were an estate agent."

The edge of the glass hummed as I ran my finger round it. I couldn't meet Maria Anna's eyes. "Did she explain what that meant?"

"Told me enough. Gubler, he's rich, successful, and he's gonna run for Congress and he's gonna get in, because what he can't buy with cash he'll sell with lying. He's lining up the fund-raisers, and he rapes poor black girls because he knows he can get away with it, and because we *let* him get away with it. Us. The law. Because we gotta protect everyone equally, but some people – some we protect more equally than others. And if I'm doing one thing with my life, now that it's mine, I want it to be this. Take Gubler down. Do it for money, do it for reward, do it because you'll find it fun and need a new fucking body – I don't care why you do it. Just get it done."

Her voice didn't rise, her gaze didn't flinch. Her words were recorded messages played at the morgue, a testimony from beyond the grave, the gentleness buried beneath thick wet earth a long time ago.

I drained the last of the whisky down, laid my glass on the table between us, and said, "OK."

*

Four days later she wore a blue ball gown cut to highlight the tightness of her waist, the roundness of her buttocks, the softness of her legs, and I wore a man with no chin and a new suit, who sold bad cars to gullible people and had tried the same with me. We stood on the steps of a museum dedicated to a great battle of the Civil War, where men who believed and men who were merely there because circumstances had collaborated against them had clashed on a field and fought no less hard for the reasons that brought them. From within came the sound of harmless music played by an inoffensive quartet, the bubble of well-heeled voices in high-heeled shoes, the chink of glass upon glass, the busy bustle of money flowing out of people's mouths, into people's ears, as deals were struck and pledges made for plans not yet written down.

Maria Anna held a silver-edged invitation. I held out my hand, a partner inviting her to the dance and said, "May I?"

Her face was locked as she held out her hand to me, but the fingers, when they brushed mine, trembled.

I squeezed her palm reassuringly, and saw her flinch.

I jumped.

The car salesman staggered, groaning in confusion, but I was already sweeping up the steps in a wave of taffeta and rose-hip perfume, my hair pinned too tight to my head, my heart racing so fast in my chest I felt briefly dizzy and knew it was not *my* presence which made it beat, merely the thought that I might be present, which a moment ago had been all that filled Maria Anna's mind.

And yet she had taken my hand.

I handed over my invitation with barely a glance at the boy who took it, and the boy who took it waved me through with more than a glance at the body I wore. Maria Anna, tall and graceful, her long neck accentuated by the single pearl she wore in the hollow of her throat, hands sticky – physiological reaction to stress a little over-contained. As I swept into the main gallery of the museum, the guests in tuxedos and gowns swirled and swept around black-iron cannon, monuments to the dead, glass cases containing the pistol of a general, the uniform of a colonel fallen in a charge, the banner of a regiment wiped out upon some gunpowder-blasted hill. Through all this, the crowd chatted and bantered, the past set out to be picked over like last night's TV.

I caught a glass of champagne from a waiter as he passed, and drifted towards a display of regimental photos, grainy and beige, sipping my drink and waiting for the rushing in my blood to slow down, pass. The hypertension eased a little at a time, muscles so tight it seemed the nerves themselves couldn't process their presence. I let my gaze sweep the crowd, seeking out Horst Gubler from among his adoring fans.

He didn't take much seeking. The noise around him was a swell in the turning sea and, unlike his more meagre guests, he didn't have to move to find the party, but rather the party twisted to come and find him. I eased my way through, smiling a dazzling smile at all I passed, until I stood close and a little to one side, listening as he regaled the gathered masses with the story of a time when he had caught a fish, and met a minister, and watched the sun set on a Saudi oil field. When the audience laughed, I did not, and my silence caused his gaze to turn and light on me.

His eyes swept me from bottom to top, top to bottom, sticking to my skin, before his face opened into a smile of recognition and delight.

And at his smile something twisted beneath my stomach and he said, "Why hello. I remember you *very* well," and, though I was perfectly functional and my body liked to exercise two or three times a week and eat sensible food, I tasted bile. Quickly, I reached out towards his smiling, wobbling face, palm up and replied, "Yes you do."

He shook me by the hand.

Later, when asked to recall Horst Gubler's speech at the museum, kinder listeners would report that he seemed rather strange in the minutes leading up to it, hardly himself at all. Harsher listeners — and the press — would report that he was clearly drunk, there being no other explanation for his actions.

59

Everyone, regardless of personal bias or inclination, would remember the first thing he said upon taking the stand, immortalised in journals across the state.

"Hiya, all!" the body of Gubler cried, silencing the audience with the jingling of a silver spoon upon a crystal glass. "So glad you could all be here, so glad! There's just one thing I'd like to say before we kick off with the evening's festivities. President Obama – what a faggot."

Three days later I was on a plane to Slovakia, Horst Gubler's passport in my hand, credit cards in my pocket. Of his assets – which turned out to be a mere 1.8 million dollars and a great deal of bluff – twenty thousand dollars went into a Swiss bank account for an unnamed roaming traveller, eighty thousand went to an ex-wife, and the remainder was bequeathed, along with any outstanding assets, to a charity dedicated to the victims of rape, violent crime and domestic abuse. They were so grateful, they sent me a plaque, framed in brass, which I forwarded on to Maria Anna Celeste, with my compliments.

Chapter 21

Slovakian?

Not a word.

I speak French, German, Russian, Mandarin, Japanese, English, Swahili, Malay, Spanish, Arabic, Turkish, Farsi and Italian. Based on these I can roughly comprehend a wide range of locally similar languages, though comprehension is never the same as being able to reply.

Hungarian? Czech?

Not a clue.

Only a few borrowed words – toilet, TV, credit card, internet, email – that sprung up too fast and too late for the linguists of their nations to have any better idea.

I got off the train a few stops short of Bratislava.

When first I visited Slovakia it was a beautiful land of mighty rivers, great fields across fertile plains, pine tree hills rising on the horizon and the distant jingling of cattle bells from the blue-grey walls of the evening valleys. There may even have been some traditional dress – though at the time tradition was a concept yet to be romanticised into its knee-kicking glory.

Communism, as always, had not been kind to this idyll. With

as much tenderness as a tank in a trench, villages of rustic stone and tiny cared-for chapels now boasted squat apartment blocks and concrete industrial zones, fallen into disrepair almost as soon as they had risen. Rivers, once running clear, now flowed sluggishly through the flatlands, their surfaces decked with thick green scum that grew back as quickly as it was cleared. The land still held much beauty, but it was spotted through with the remnants of an industrial ambition stretched too far.

I stopped in a bed and breakfast in a town with an unpronounceable name. A bus ran every three hours to Bratislava, twice a day on Sundays. One church, one school, one restaurant, and on the edge of town one supermarket, which sold, as well as cured meats and fish, garden furniture, bathroom parts and small electric cars.

The owners of the bed and breakfast were a husband and wife, and only one other room was occupied by a pair of Austrian cyclists come to pedal the gentle low roads of Europe. I waited for the building to go to bed, then let myself out into the night.

The one-church town was also a one-bar town.

The one bar was playing 1980s pop songs from one CD. On the dance floor teenagers desperate to get out, get away, writhed against each other, too horny to go home, too frightened of their companions to actually have sex.

I looked for the one person who might be interested, and found her, sitting back from the dance floor, watching in the dark. I sat down opposite her and said, you speak English?

A little, she said.

But for what she did, a little was more than enough.

I bought her a drink, which she barely touched.

Her English was better than she claimed, and her French, we eventually discovered, was superb. She said, where are you staying?

The boarding house.

That won't do at all, she replied. If you're interested, I know somewhere quiet.

Quiet was perfect.

Quiet was exactly what I needed.

*

She lived on the very edge of town. The front door locked heavy behind us, the walls were hung with photos of ancient grand-mothers, their hands resting proudly on the shoulders of their sons.

Her room consisted of a bed, a desk, a couple of hand-me-down works of art put up by a tenant generations ago who hadn't liked them enough to take them away and left hanging by a lazy landlord. Under the bed were books on economics, chemistry, mathematics. On the small crooked desk, old plates gathering mould, and pieces of foil, stained with powder. She kicked the books aside, took off her jacket and said, you ready?

The track marks in her arm were faint but visible. The thin white scars across her wrists were in neat little rows, running up to her elbow, fading and old but made worse by scratching. I said, how old are you?

She shook her head.

Are you ready?

I smiled and replied, something a little kinky?

I gave her the key before I pulled out the handcuffs. It never serves to give the wrong impression. She looked briefly shocked, but her professionalism managed to restore her smile quickly enough and, gesturing at the bed she said, come on in.

I lay down on the bed, let her cuff my right hand to the bed-stead, and as she lent back to admire her handiwork, I caught her left wrist with my free hand and
    jumped.

"Hey there," I said, as the body beneath me blinked bleary, unfocused eyes. "I think we should talk."

Chapter 22

The scars on my arms itched.

Hidden beneath my tights were fresher scars on the inside of my thighs, still burning, crying out for the scalpel and the antiseptic wipe.

Nathan Coyle – or at least the man whose Canadian passport so proclaimed him to be – lay handcuffed to the bed beneath me. I sat down beside him, crossed my legs, put my chin in the palm of my hand and said, "You've got some text messages."

His eyes focused on me, and with clarity of vision came clarity of thought.

Clarity of thought, it seemed, was not impressed with its conclusions.

His jaw tightened, his fingers tensed.

"I'm guessing," I said, "that they're security checks. The first was *Circe*, the second *Aeolus*. Having no idea who to reply to or what to say, I didn't respond. Your colleagues must know by now that you're in trouble. Good news for you, unless they shoot you like you shot Josephine."

He lay motionless. Flat. The angle of his arm cuffed to the bedhead couldn't have been comfortable, but he was a tough guy. Tough guys don't fidget.

"I read the Kepler file," I added, fighting the urge to scratch my arms. "It's mostly correct – I'm impressed – but you don't appear in my file, and based on what I can remember I'm reasonably confident I never touched your body, right up to the point you shot me with it. So it can't be personal. Met any ghosts before now, Mr Coyle?"

Silence.

Of course.

Tough guys, they wake up handcuffed in strange places, gun down women in stations, get possessed and marched halfway across Europe by an invading consciousness, but it's nothing they can't handle.

"I considered mutilating you," I breathed, barely aware of the words as I spoke them, and had the satisfaction of seeing something twitch in Coyle's face. "Obviously not while I was inhabiting, I have never had a taste for such things. But I still hope that your colleagues, whoever they may be, may hesitate to kill you, as you killed my Josephine, and that hesitation could yet save my life."

Silence.

"In Edirne I asked two questions. Having spent some time in your body I now have a couple more, though the direction of the enquiry hasn't changed. Who are you working for, and why did they lie about Josephine?"

He levered himself, just a tiny bit, further up, and for the first time his eyes met mine, and stayed.

"It's lies," I breathed. "Most of the file is fine, but then it gets to Josephine and it's lies. Your employers wanted her to die as well as me. Why is that, do you think? Who are these people she's meant to have killed? People have always tried to kill my kind, down the centuries. It is inevitable, given what we are. But you shot Josephine in the leg, and even though I fled, even though you *knew* I'd fled, you still put two bullets in her chest. And I don't understand why. I want this to end well. You're a murderer, but you didn't act alone. You're alive because you're the only lead I have."

I waited.

So did he.

"You'll be wanting to think," I concluded. "I understand." My fingers crawled against the soft inside of my arms, tracing scars, wanting to scratch. I pulled my hand away, stood up, hoping that motion and speed would distract from the physiological urge. He watched me. I smiled. "This body –" I gestured head to foot at my skin "– she's maybe seventeen? Self-harm, drug use, prostitution and schoolbooks under the bed. Not my problem, of course. This is just a rest stop, no business of mine. Tell me: do you like what you see?"

Did tough guys have opinions?

He didn't seem to.

Perhaps the discipline in suppressing terror also suppressed thought.

"You think," I said. "I'll potter."

And I did precisely that.

I swept the grubby pieces of foil into a plastic bag, scraped the crumbs off her desk, opened the window to let in cold night air. I straightened her books, folded her clothes where they'd fallen from the lopsided wardrobe, threw out two pairs of tights with irredeemable holes. I realigned the not-quite-art on the wall, and as I went through the drawers I pulled out a small packet of pot, another of cocaine, and added them both to the rubbish. The bottom drawer was locked. I forced it with a kitchen knife, and from within produced a collection of well kept medical scissors, bandages and a single silver scalpel. I hesitated, then threw the sharps away, left the bandages intact.

Coyle watched me from the bed, sharp as a cat, silent as a paw in the night.

His stare was a distraction. I have stood up before the US House of Representatives, and been witty and vibrant and in control, but then I wore a three-thousand-dollar suit, ate a two-hundred-dollar lunch, and I was fabulous because it was what I was meant to be.

This girl – whoever she was – was not fabulous. With her fraying tights and her welted arms, the temptation to hide behind her frailty, to curl up into my skinny bones, shoulder blades sticking out like chicken wings, chin down, neck tight, was as natural as night. Yet still Coyle watched me, and it wasn't me he watched, but *me*, myself, and no shadowed eye or buried face could alter the object of his interest.

Unsettling. Unwelcome and unfamiliar. Exciting.

I concentrated hard, my every step measured, and went about imposing what should be upon the what was of the bedroom. Cleaning a room is an extension of cleaning a body; changing its furniture as well as its clothes. Everyone needs a hobby, and every-one was mine.

Then Coyle said, "You're an arrogant son of a bitch."

"My God!" I exclaimed. "He speaks."

"You fuck with her life—"

"Do you mind if I interrupt you before this becomes emotive? I am here to talk to you. And as you cannot think when I am in residence, I need a host to let you mull the fruity depth of our conversation. I don't deny that I bore easily, and naturally I regard the skins I wear as something of a project, as anyone would, as everyone does. Some people knit; others take up yoga. If this were a long-term habitation, I would absolutely consider the latter – I feel my knees would benefit from the regime. But it isn't, so I do what little I can in passing, and you, before you hold forth on the theme of my monstrosity, should be relieved that rather than tidy and bin some junk, I didn't pull your fucking eyes out with my fingernails."

His lips sealed once more.

I hopped back on to the end of the bed, tucking my knees up to my chin, wrapping my scarred arms across the thin bony shins, staring into his grey, dark eyes.

"You tear people to pieces," he said at last.

"Yes. Yes, I do. I don't deny it. I walk through people's lives and I steal what I find. Their bodies, their time, their money, their friends, their lovers, their wives – I'll take it all, if I want to. And sometimes I put them back together, in some other shape. This skin," I flicked a stray piece of hair behind my ear, "is going to wake up in a few minutes, frightened and confused because several hours of her life have vanished in a flash. She's going to think I raped her, maybe drugged her, did something to her body, her belongings, which are the only symbol she has of achievement in her life – in most people's lives. She's going to be frightened not because of any pain to her flesh, but because someone walked in and violated the home where she lives. And perhaps she does what she does when she feels alone. Perhaps she cuts, perhaps she sniffs, perhaps she drinks and then finds a guy to pay for all of the above. I really don't know. But you and I needed to talk."

A slight intake of breath. "Did we?"

"It would have been as easy for me to walk you through Chinese customs with five kilos of heroin strapped to your belly as it is to have a conversation. If you talk to me, you might have a chance."

"You steal life, you steal choices – her choices."

"Not right now. In a few hours her body is her own again and we'll be gone. A few minutes, a few seconds, everything changes. Or nothing at all. What you do when that moment comes is all that matters."

"A thief is a thief."

"And a killer a killer. That is the extension of your argument, is it not?"

He shifted, barely, against the bed. "What do you want?"

"You killed Josephine," I answered, a mere breath in the chilly gloom. "You know how I feel about these things. Why did you try to kill me, Mr Coyle?"

"You tell me."

"Sometimes it's easier to fight than to have a conversation."

"You'd talk to the smallpox virus?"

"If it had stories to tell me of plagues it had seen, of great men it had visited, of children who lived and mothers who died, of hot hospitals and cold freezers in guarded trucks, I'd buy it a three-course meal and a weekend in Monaco. Don't compare me with a DNA strand in a protein shell, Mr Coyle; the argument is beneath us both. Your passports, your money, your weapons; you're clearly organised, part of a wider operation. You keep yourself in excellent shape – I haven't been following the diet or doing the press-ups, I'm afraid. And now you kill people like me." I sighed. "For no better reason, I'd guess, than because we exist. Did you think you were the first? Sooner or later someone always tries. Yet here we are, as persistent as death itself. In two separate continents through two different paths, two entirely different yet functionally identical species of vulture evolved, nature filling a void. No matter how many of us you kill, we keep on recurring, nature's hiccup. Here it is, then," I murmured. "You killed my host, who I loved. You may find the concept hard to believe, but I *loved* Josephine Cebula, and you killed her. You killed her because there was a note in her file which said she wasn't just a host, she was a murderer. This was a lie. Your masters lied to you. That, and only that, is something new."

"The file didn't lie," he replied. "Josephine Cebula had to die."

"Why?"

"You know why."

"I really don't. The names in the file – the corpses she was meant to have left behind – Tortsen Ulk, Magda Müller, James Richter, Elsbet Horn. I hadn't heard of them until I read them, and the manner of their death – brutal, sadistic perhaps. Josephine was not that woman. She lacked motive, opportunity and means, and if you'd done your own research you'd know that. She was my skin, nothing more, nothing less." He wasn't meeting my eyes. I caught his chin, pulled his head up and round, forcing his gaze to meet mine. "Tell me why."

"Galileo," he said. I froze, fingers tight across his jaw. He seemed surprised to have heard himself speak. "For Galileo."

"What is Galileo?"

"The *Santa Rosa*," he replied. "That was Galileo."

I hesitated, looking for something in his face, something more, and as I did, he struck, his left hand slamming up in a fist, into my face. I cried out and fell to one side, rolling off the edge of the bed.

He scrambled up on to his knees, pulling at the handcuffs, ripping with both his hands at the metal chain, even as the bedpost cracked and begin to splinter. I staggered to my feet and he swung one leg into my belly, but I caught his foot, and as he ripped his hand free from the bedpost I flailed against his trouser leg, felt ankle beneath my fingertips

and that was the end of that.

Chapter 23

We have always been hunted.

My first encounter with this truth was in 1838. I was in Rome, and how they found me I will never fully know.

They came in the night, men in thick leather gloves and black masks with long sweet-smelling beaks, plague doctors hunting a most unusual disease. They had tied rope around their sleeves, ankles and waists so that I might not burrow my fingers against their skin. Two of them sat on my chest while a third locked a collar on a three-foot pole around my neck then swung me up by my throat. I wheezed and scrambled and kicked and tried to catch at a hand, a hair, a foot, a finger – any stranger's skin – but they were careful, so careful, and as they marched me on the end of my collar through the midnight streets, like a naughty dog on his master's leash, they reminded each other, beware, beware, don't get too close to the demon-devil, don't let his fingers so much as brush yours in passing. In the dead dark of the night Roman emperors with broken faces, dead gods with shattered limbs, the weeping eyes of the Holy Mary and the hooded glares of the scuttling thieves as they slipped into the stone alleys between the leaning, stinking homes looked down and showed no comfort.

In a stone cell beneath a stone tower built by a long-dead Roman and renovated by a long-dead Greek, they clamped me down with iron shackles to a wooden chair, so no part of my body could move. Then came the priests and the doctors, the soldiers and the violent men, who beat me with long cudgels, and swung incense in my face and said, begone, evil spirit. In the name of the father, the son, the holy ghost, I banish you, begone.

On the third day of my captivity three masked men entered the room with a woman whose eyes were red from weeping and who tried, at the sight of me, to throw herself at my feet, to kiss my gloved and bound hands, and who was immediately restrained from crossing the line of salt that had been sprinkled around my chair.

And she wept, and cried out, my son, my son, what demon has done this to you?

If they hadn't broken my ribs, poisoned me with their remedies and fed me no more than a little water and soggy bread with a very long spoon, I might have said, these men, good mother. These men that you see before you, they have done this to me. Come a little closer until your ear touches my lips, and I will tell you how.

As it was, they had, so I didn't, but sat limp and broken before her while she wept and wailed and called out for her boy and against all demons, until she was calmed and given a cup of wine with a little something extra to drink, and sat upon a low stool.

Then the leader of my tormentors, a man in a great red cowl and huge crimson gloves that swelled outwards from his wrists, only to be clipped back in and tied to his forearm, knelt down before my mother and said, "Your son is dead, and in heaven. What you see here is a mockery of his flesh, a ghoul in the rotten body of your boy. We could have executed it without telling you, but you are his mother, and to not know the fate of your son is worse than knowing what horrors this creature has performed."

At this, she wept a little more, and I almost admired the compassion with which my would-be killer bestowed mercy on a mother.

Then he went on: "This demon has fornicated with your son's flesh. It has lain with both women and men. It has worn your boy's face as it commits sin upon sin, revelled in its power, delighted in its wickedness. With every act it commits it brings dishonour upon the memory of your boy and it must die. Do you understand this, good mother? Do you forgive us the deed that we must now perform?"

The woman looked up from this angel of death, to me, and I breathed, "Mother . . ."

At once my killer clamped his hands tight around the woman's own and hissed, "It is not your son. It is the demon. It will say anything to live."

And so my mother looked away from me, and with tears running down her face she breathed, "God have mercy," though upon whom she did not say.

I twisted and screamed, called out for my mother, mother, please, as they led her away, but she didn't look back, and I didn't entirely blame her for in truth I didn't know her name.

The next day, in the half-dawn light, they took me out to a courtyard framed with grey stone and locked shutters. They had a mansion which had once belonged to great men, but in this age of steel and smoke had fallen hard by, a cracked monument of imperial ambition.

A pyre had been built in the middle, and the red-robed masters of my demise stood round it, heads bowed, gloved hands folded across their chests, a single brazier smouldering at the foot of the stake. Ritual makes murder easier; it is something else to concentrate on. Seeing the pyre, I kicked and screamed some more, and they dragged me to the foot of the stake and pushed me to my knees. A priest stood before me, long black robes draping around his black-clad feet. He raised his hands to bless, if not exactly me, then the body he was about to commit to the flame, and it occurred to me that his robe, while extensive, could possibly obscure an excess of hairy leg. The question of what lay beneath a priest's cassock was not one I had considered too deeply before,

73

but now it seemed of absolute import and so I let myself collapse, falling against my own collar, dragging it down, even as it pulled into my trachea, cutting off breath. The guard who supported me was pulled forward by my weight and as I hit the ground, the priest started back, surprised at his own power to induce such an extreme reaction in the penitent. For the briefest moment I felt the pressure on my throat weaken and so I opened my eyes, pushed up off my belly and with teeth bared shoved my face up and under the priest's robes and bit as hard as I could against what lay buried there.

I felt hair on my skin, cloth in my eyes, tasted blood on my mouth and even as the priest cried out in shock and distress, I

jumped, and staggered back, yelping, my black robes billowing around my legs. At my feet the shackled body was pulled back, a bludgeon to the head. I hopped away, hands shaking, and exclaimed in perfect Italian, "In the name of God, go in peace!" then scrambled away, gasping for breath.

Blood drifted down the inside of my calf from the fresh bite mark in my flesh, but no one noticed. Meanwhile, the bewildered body opened his eyes, and as they chained him to the stake he cried out, what is this, who are you, help me, help me, what's happening?

I looked around at my silent companions. Thick gloves, long robes, no easy way in. A guard took a flame from the brazier, and as he laid it to the kindling the body on the stake saw me and screamed, "Father, help me, please!"

A gloved hand fell on my shoulder and a voice said quietly in French, "He did not touch you, did he, Father?"

I looked into a pair of eyes above a tight red mask and shook my head. "No," I replied. "My robe protected me."

The eyes narrowed, and it occurred to me that I had no reason to think the body I inhabited could speak French at all.

The Bible fell from my hands, and even as the robed man turned to his companions, I knocked the hat from his head and tugged the mask from his face, pulling one arm across his throat and pressing my other hand over his eyes and as he began to fight I switched, spinning to drive my elbows straight into the belly of the black-robed priest. My body was tall, old but lean, and I had a dagger and a pistol on a black cord which now I pulled and fired at the first man who turned to fire at me. The flames were catching on the kindling beneath the pyre, black smoke rolling up as the body began to scream, but the red-robed men were moving, reaching for weapons, calling out in alarm, and I bent my head forward, put my elbows together and charged head first at the nearest man, slamming into his chest and knocking him to the ground. A gunshot rang out and something exploded inside me, tearing through lung and bone. I fell back, the echo of the shot ringing in my ears, not so much pain as shock opening inside my chest. The man who'd fired stood not fifteen feet away, reloading his pistol. I crawled on to my feet, felt blood swirl around me, and ran at him, pulling my glove free from my right hand, as he reloaded, raised his pistol again and fired.

The force of it spun me through a three-hundred-and-sixty-degree pirouette, and as I fell I reached for the nearest object I could find, which happened to be him, and my fingers tore the robes from his chest. I felt the warm touch of a collarbone and

blessed relief, blessed merciful relief I jumped

a body with its bones still intact

a bloodied corpse that clung to my collarbone clung no more, fell at my feet, lungs broken, chest shattered, face covered in its own blood.

Now men were shouting, pistols drawn and daggers raised, but in the confusion no one quite knew who to shoot at, so I turned and looked for the exit, for the way I had come, and as the flames rose behind me, I hurled my gun to the ground and ran.

Behind me, on the pyre, a man whose flesh was popping and hair was catching flame screamed as his legs began to sizzle in the heat.

I ran.

Chapter 24

I, whose enemies call me Kepler and whose body, as it boarded the 7.03 bus towards Bratislava, answered to the name of Coyle, have in recent years tried my best.

Which is not to say that the standard of my best is especially high.

In a small room in a small flat in a small town a girl with scars in her arms sat awake, and afraid, in a room she herself could not remember tidying, ready to live a life no one else but she could possibly live.

A blink of the eye, and all things change.

Consequences are only for the ones who stay behind.

The bus rattled through tiny villages, picking up an old woman here, a pair of teenage lovers there, no more than six or seven passengers at any time, heading through Slovakia.

My stop was unmarked, but the driver knew the place, pulling up by a shrine to St Christopher and a mud path framed by a tunnel of beech trees. The ground was soggy with the mulch of fallen yellow leaves as I walked to a grey tomb of a building surrounded by gardens of sloping grass and still lily-spotted ponds. A small fountain was dried up and clogged with moss by the front door. Metal grilles had been nailed on the outside of the windows. A wooden board proclaimed, DOMINICO HOSPICE, PLEASE SIGN IN AT RECEPTION.

Under communism mental health was easy. Depression, schizophrenia, bipolar disorder or, worst of all, the manifestation of any views contrary to those held by the state were simply the expression of a diseased mind best kept isolated from the body politic. To be ill was to be at fault. You, said the state, you who weep when you look upon the harsh truths of this world, see so clearly the lies that people tell – you have done this to yourselves. And so must be thankful for whatever little mercy the country throws your way.

We call it a disease, a doctor once whispered to me in the backstreets of Vienna, but a disease is not nearly as easy to blame as people.

Communism had fallen, but ideas fall more slowly than men.

This I'd known when, all those years ago, having drained his accounts and disowned his family, I marched the body of Horst Gubler to the gate and proclaimed, help me, I think I am possessed.

The receptionist asked for my name.

Nathan Coyle, I said, in my best Canadian accent. It sounded almost identical to my American accent, except for my pronunciation of the letter 'z', a refinement entirely wasted on the Slovakian matron behind the desk.

I'm a nephew of Mr Gubler, I said. I've come to see my uncle.

She looked astonished.

Goodness, she said, you didn't say you were his *nephew* the last time you were here, Mr Coyle!

Didn't I?

Perhaps I wasn't thinking straight.

Remind me when it was that I last dropped by?

There is a picture in the Kepler file of Horst Gubler.

It shows a man in his early sixties, sitting with his back to the window. He has two chins: the first sharp, pointed, the second

77

longer, lower, sagging towards the base of his neck. His hair is salt-white, straight, cut short, his eyes grey; his nose is hooked and, on lesser men, might seem oversized but fits his features well. He looks away from the camera, half-turned towards some unseen stranger, wears hospital blue and seems surprised to have been caught there, framed by the setting sun. In another life he might have been a genial uncle, a teddy-bear Santa, or perhaps, had circumstances permitted, a trusted Congressman and abuser of women. Yet here, now, he was all that he was – a man of no wealth, friends or even citizenship, for he accused himself of many crimes, burned his US passport when he entered Slovakia, gave away his assets, dismissed his friends, and acted, indeed as he proclaimed when entering the mental home, as a man possessed.

I was led through halls smelling of disinfectant and boiled onions. Behind heavy metal doors that buzzed when opened the abandoned of the nation sat in silence, watching daytime TV. A recent donation from an unknown benefactor had bought an art studio, a small room with wide windows looking north, whose door stood locked – for the funding, while generous, could not support a teacher and the paints as well.

"We like the patients to be expressive," explained the matron as she led me through the halls. "It helps them find themselves."

I smiled and said nothing.

"I don't approve," said an old man, sitting in a chair alone, a knitted cardigan too small about his tiny shoulders, his lower lip thrusting forward until it nearly stuck out beyond the tip of his nose. "They don't know. When they find out – that's the day. Then they'll come back just like I said."

Of course they won't, Matron smiled. You're talking nonsense again.

A corridor up some stairs, a locked security gate. More doors of thin wood, most standing open. Outside each a rack for paperwork – records of appointments, blood pressure, medication, and a few scant photos for those who wanted to remember, of families who'd long since walked away, children who never came to visit, a home that the patient would never see again.

Horst Gubler's door had no photos.

It stood ajar, and when Matron knocked, she didn't wait for an answer before opening it.

A single bed, chair, desk, sink. A PVC mirror, carefully laminated and glued to the wall. A window with a grille over it, which looked west towards red-leaved trees growing bare with the coming cold.

"Horst," said Matron, and then, in heavy English, "Look who's back."

Horst Gubler rose from his single chair, put down his book – a much-thumbed swashbuckler of minimal merit, and looked at me. He held out a clammy hand and stammered, "P-p-pleased to meet you."

"You remember Mr Coyle," chided matron. "He came to see you not five weeks ago."

"Yes. Yes. He did." He must have, for Matron said he did and so it must be. "I h-hoped," his tongue tangled on the word, but he scrunched his eyes up tight and then forced himself on, "you were from the embassy."

"Horst –" a sad shake of the matron's head was enough to bow Gubler's eyes to the ground "– we've talked about this."

"Yes, Matron."

"Mr Gubler doesn't remember things clearly, does he?"

"No, Matron."

She turned to me, her voice ringing out for every ear. "It's common among patients suffering psychotic episodes to seem lucid during the event but amnesiac following it. Mr Gubler's psychosis – a belief in possession – is a fairly typical mechanism, thankfully less common among Western societies than it has been." She beamed, a little chuckle swelling up from within her bosom as she added, for the ease of all concerned, "Things keep getting better, that's what we say!"

I laughed because she laughed, and my eyes flickered to Gubler, who stood mute and still, head bowed, hands folded in front of him, and said not a word.

*

79

He sat on the edge of his bed, fingers clinging to it as if he might drop.

I closed the door as the matron walked out, then sat in the chair opposite him, studying his face.

I barely knew it. For weeks I had regarded it in the mirror, let it grow a shabby beard that blurred rather than enhanced its features. Yet even when searching for means to punish that face, striving with all my might to rip Horst Gubler to shreds, there had been a pride in the eyes, a crinkle in the lips which I could not erase. So long had I stared at that reflection that I had come to loathe it, for no matter how sad I waxed my features, how deeply I scrunched my eyes or wrinkled my nose, the glowing defiance of the man who got away with it always burst through.

No more.

I had done everything I could do to destroy this face, but only at the very end, when I stood before a stranger in a strange land and told a single truth – "I am possessed" – had I achieved my aims.

The face was broken now, my work concluded.

I said, "Hello, Mr Gubler."

"H-hello," he stumbled, not raising his head to look at me.

"Do you remember me?"

"Yes, Mr Coyle. My memory is better now. You came here with your p-partner."

"Ah yes, my partner. Forgive me, I have several partners – can you remind me which partner I came with?"

His eyes flashed up, for this was a test, surely, a test of his mind, and he would not fail. "Alice. Her name was Alice."

I smiled and shuffled a little closer to him on the edge of my chair. He flinched, head twisting away to one side.

"Do you remember what we talked about, Mr Gubler? The last time I came to see you?"

A dull, single nod.

"Can you tell me what it was?"

"You wanted to know about my h-history. It was a psychotic break," he added, voice rising in case he had made a mistake. "I was not possessed; I had an episode arising from marital and work-related stress."

"Absolutely," I replied. "I remember you telling me about it. How did you say it began? A woman touched you. She had dark skin, a blue dress; she shook your hand and the next thing you knew . . . "

"Here." His voice was a bare whisper. "I was . . . here."

"Yes, you were." I leaned forward, threading my fingers together between my knees. "And what else did you tell us? About being possessed?"

"Not possessed, not possessed."

"There was something else, wasn't there," I murmured. "When you woke up here, your hand was in a doctor's hand and you looked up at him, and what did he do next?"

"Not possessed," he repeated sharply, knuckles white where they gripped the edge of the bed, spine curved, jaw slack. "Not possessed."

"Did you tell me and Alice about the doctor? Did you tell them how he smiled at you?"

"Smiled, glad to see me, he smiled, taking care of me."

"Did you tell us the doctor's name?"

I was a few inches from Gubler now, my knees bumping his, fingers almost close enough to brush his, and as my hands swayed, he jerked back, springing off the edge of the bed and pushing himself against the wall. "Don't touch me!" he screamed. "Bastard shit! Don't fucking touch me!"

I recoiled, raising my hands, placating, palms out. "It's OK," I breathed. "I'm not going to touch you. No one's going to touch you."

Tears balanced on the rim of his reddened eyes, waiting to fall, his breath fast, body twisted into the wall away from me. "Doctor forgot," he whispered, and his speech was fast, clear, and completely sane. "He forgot that he touched me. How'd they explain that? How'd they make sense of it?" His eyes rolled back to me, and there it was, just for a moment, the hardness that had haunted me in the mirror, cutting through the drugs. "You understood, sat there, she held the camera and you said you understood. You believed me. Did you lie to me? Did you fucking lie?"

"No," I replied.

"Did you fucking lie?!"

"No. I don't believe I did."

"Are you ... laughing at me?"

"No."

"I've been waiting years. Friends, embassy ... they're cunts. They're all fucking cunts. They say there's a hold-up, the courts have a backlog. You said you'd make it better. What do you want?"

"Everything," I breathed. "Everything you remember about me and Alice. I want you to tell me what I said, what she said, what I wore, what she wore. What language did I speak, was it Slovakian? Was she tired, did she look happy, sad, young, old? Everything."

"Why?"

I looked down at my feet, then untangled my fingertips and stood up. I tucked my chair under the desk, ran my hand through my hair and sat down beside him, close enough to, very carefully, lay my hand on the leg of his trouser, feel the warmth of his calf underneath. I took a slow, careful breath, then looked him straight in the eye.

Our gazes met and, for the first time since I had walked into that room, he saw *me*.

My fingers tightened around his leg, pressing warm into his skin.

"Why do you think?" I said.

Chapter 25

Evening in Bratislava.

A computer in a café, bad coffee in my mouth, Coyle's bags stuffed beneath my chair.

An email to an account I'd set up a lifetime ago and never closed down, from an individual who identified themselves as Spunk-master13.

Times changed, but not Johannes Schwarb.

A report on the passports carried by Nathan Coyle – clean, save for the Turkish identity, which the Istanbul police were seeking. A man suspected of shooting a woman dead on Taksim station had hired a car under that name, then driven his escape vehicle all the way to Edirne in the night.

I made a mental note to burn the Turkish passport, and began to reply.

Spunkmaster13 was already waiting in the chat rooms, and he appeared before I could type more than a few words on to the screen.

Banal pleasantries were exchanged along with the panoply of smiley faces and vanishing ninja emoticons that seemed to form the greatest part of Johannes' vocabulary, until:

Christina 636 – I need you to do another check-up for me.

Spunkmaster13 – Sure, what?

Christina 636 – Registration number. It's for a car driven by two people – a man called Nathan Coyle and a woman called Alice White. They visited an asylum in Slovakia, signed in at reception, logged the registration details of the vehicle they visited in. An inmate describes the woman as aged approximately 29–35, short blonde hair, 5'5–5'8, slim build, fair skin, blue eyes. Can you check?

Spunkmaster13 – In my sleep.

Christina 636 – One more thing – the name Galileo mean anything to you?

Spunkmaster13 – Dead white guy?

Christina 636 – I was given names – Galileo and Santa Rosa.

Spunkmaster13 – I got nothing.

Christina 636 – Never mind. And thank you.

Chapter 26

Bratislava, as night fell.

The sky was turning the colour of a two-day bruise, a stripe of golden sunlight skimming the western horizon, trying to peep through beneath the promise of rain.

I hadn't been to Bratislava for decades. Ten beautiful streets in the middle, a castle on a hill, trolley buses and a great deal of anonymous architecture beyond. It was a city that most tourists covered in two days. An hour from Vienna by boat, the same by train through flood plains, it was hard to shake the feeling towards this would-be national capital that there was somewhere a little more interesting nearby.

The internet café where I connected with Johannes served sweet pastries turning hard around the edges. The lights in the square outside were cold white over pale stones, and as it began to rain the gutters sparkled and shimmered with the rush of water to the riverside below.

I stepped out of the café into the downpour and regretted that I hadn't stocked up on all-weather gear during those few breathless minutes in Istanbul when I had first met the body of Nathan Coyle. After all, I had no idea how long I was going to be in residence.

I scampered through the rain as it tap-danced on the sloping roofs and thundered down from the straining metal gullies. The solemn statues on the churches dripped from the ends of their chins and noses, angel wings shed waterfalls across the wooden doors of medieval monuments. The cables on the trolley buses snapped great white stars as they swung through the running streets, while the four-towered castle upon its hill vanished into a yellow rectangle of light hanging over the distorted darkness of the city.

I ran, my trousers soaking, my stomach empty, a bag of someone else's secrets bumping on my back, past the half-shadowed faces of men with coats pulled across their heads, fighting for a cab; women with umbrellas turned inside-out, hair clinging to their pale, cold faces; teenage girls whose shoes were now too impractical for walking in, holding them by their heels as they waded through the riverine streets. And for a moment my fingers itched and my face was heavy with cold and I glanced at

a woman with beautiful black hair down to the nape of her spine, her shoulders bare, icy in the cold, the jacket that should have adorned it slung over one arm as she struggled unexpectedly into thicker clothes, a man at her back, the taste of chocolate on her lips, and she looked beautiful, and her life looked serene. Tonight, perhaps, she dines with the man she loves, and he loves her, and when the rain stops they will stand together on a balcony

– for certain she has a balcony –

and look down on the river in the cold night air and have no need for words.

She turned away, and I scuttled on, for everyone's life is greener on the other side.

My hotel was a hotel for tourists, right on the river. A bar protruded out over the water's edge, purple LEDs framing the balustrade, and the sound of glass chinked against its neighbour. The lobby was lined with pictures of old Bratislava, dead princes and noble kings; the receptionist spoke five languages, all fluently, all with a smile, and when I slid the key card into the lock to my room, the door slid open without a sound, into warmth that was a little too hot and an interior that smelt of fabric softener.

I had a bath.

As I sank deep into the tub I ran my fingers over the markings of a life lived. Round white scar on the left upper arm where, a long time ago, I'd had the BCG jab. I remembered a time when bodies carried smallpox scars; now they were marked by vaccinations. Another faded scar ran straight through the webbing between thumb and forefinger on my right hand, and there, below my ribcage, the prize-winner – a great pinkish slice, the zigzag of brisk stitching done by a busy hand still apparent around the grinning flesh. I traced the mark, felt the thickness beneath the skin, and guessed a knife, rammed in from the side and then slid across the stomach. The wound had long since healed, and I had to applaud Nathan Coyle for the density of functional muscle he'd built up in the intermediate time, but the scar remained, like a slag heap above an exhausted mine.

Horst Gubler had recognised Coyle, and that was good. My borrowed face had some utility after all.

More importantly, he'd given me a name, a partner, someone else to look for. I was in no great hurry to backtrack through the faces of my life, but if in doing so I could also trace the men who had ordered my death

ordered Josephine's death

then I would do so.

And if this body, hot water running off its arm and seeping into the places between its toes, died in the attempt?

That didn't bother me at all.

Chapter 27

Memories of ghosts.

Anna Maria Celeste Jones, sitting with her back straight and her eyes front.

I was worn, she said. As a skin.

Beauty is a hard attribute to measure. I have been a long-necked model with golden hair, my lips fresh, my eyes wide, my skin silk. And in this guise I found it hard to walk in my tight red heels, and bewailed how quickly my skin lost its sheen when not pampered with a regime more time-consuming than sense. The volume of my hair was lost after a single wash, the fullness of my lips cracked within a day. No more than a week was I this model of fine proportions before irritation at the maintenance drove me on to simpler pastures.

It is not beauty, in an eye, a hand, a curl of hair. I have seen old men, their backs bent and shirts white, whose eyes look up at the passers-by and in whose little knowing smiles there is more beauty, more radiance of soul, than any pampered flesh. I have seen a beggar, back straight and beard down to his chest, in whose green eyes and greying hair was such handsomeness that I yearned to have some fraction of him to call my own, to dress in rags and sweep imperious through city streets. The tiny woman, four foot eight of purple and pearl; the chubby mother, her bum heaving against denim jeans, her voice a whip-snap between supermarket aisles. I have been them all, and all of them, as I regarded myself in their mirrors, were beautiful.

In 1798, sitting upon the shores of the Red Sea, I first discovered this simple truth: that as one of us who move from flesh to flesh, life to life, I was not, in fact, alone.

Chapter 28

My name was Abdul al-Mu'allim al-Ninowy, and I had chosen the wrong side; or perhaps, fairer to say, the wrong side had chosen me.

I came to Cairo in 1792, as the Ottoman administration collapsed and Egypt fell to whichever Mameluke strongman could muster the sharpest sword. Abdul al-Mu'allim al-Ninowy was such a man, who lived away from the stink of the city in a white mansion with a courtyard of trickling fountains and kept three wives, one of whom I loved. Her name was Ayesha bint Kamal, and she had a fondness for song, wine, poetry, dogs and astronomy, and had been married off cheap and young by her father, who understood wine and dogs and disapproved of the rest.

I met her in the bathhouse, where I was a respected widow young enough to be physically comfortable, old enough to escape excessive pursuit for my wealth. In the steamy confines of the women's room, away from the ears of men, she and I had laughed and talked. When I asked what her position was, a frown had played across her plucked eyebrows and she replied, "I am the junior wife of Abdul al-Mu'allim al-Ninowy, who sells wheat to the Turks and cotton to the Greeks and slaves to everybody. He is a great and a powerful man. I would be nothing, if I were not his."

Her words were level as the stones on which we sat, and the next day I was the fourteen-year-old serving boy who bought al-Mu'allim his bread who no one noticed or cared for. Five days after that, having gathered sufficient information to fulfil the role, I was al-Mu'allim himself, slightly paunchy in my early forties, with a magnificent beard that needed constant attention, lips that tingled just before rain and overly long nails that I trimmed on my first day.

Naturally, upon habitation I set about reordering the household. Some slaves I sold; some servants I traded away. Friends who came to the door whose faces I did not know were politely rejected and informed that I had a fever, and sure enough fear of plague kept even my most loyal associates from knocking on my door, save for one cousin who hoped – who prayed, no doubt – that this was the fever that took his uncle from the world, and his cash from the vault.

Of my two senior wives, one was an absolute harpy. On learning that she had a sister in Medina, I recommended – for her health, both physical and spiritual – a pilgrimage, for which, naturally, I would pay. The middle wife was far more pleasant company, but it took her a few scant days to suspect that I was not myself, and so, to avoid the whispering of my household, I again suggested a pilgrimage – far, far away, preferably by camel with a lame foot.

They both loathed the idea, nearly as much as they loathed each other, but I was the grand man of the household and it was their duty to obey. The night before they were to depart my senior wife came into my room and screamed at me. She tore at my clothes, and when I was unmoved, she tore at her own, dragged her nails down her face, pulled clumps of her hair in thick fistfuls from her head, and screamed, "Monster! Monster! You swore you loved me, you made me think you loved me but you have always been a monster!"

My dear one, I replied, if this is so, would you not be happier away?

At this she pulled her robes wide, revealing a body well kept for its age, nourished but not to excess, loose as a pillow, pale as summer cloud.

"Am I not beautiful?" she cried. "Am I not what you desire?"

She did not look at me in the morning as I bade her farewell.

The majority of my affairs so settled, I moved what remained of my household to a mansion by the waterfront, and invited Ayesha to dine with me. Alas, for the first few weeks I could find nothing of the gentle woman I had met at the bathhouse, and wondered if I had not made a terrible mistake in leaving my wealthy widow. Ayesha would not meet my eye, nor answer in anything other than short affirmations, demonstrating such coldness in her manner that it dampened her veiled beauty too. I wooed gently, as a fresh lover might, and thought I saw no change until one evening, as we picked over fresh dates and cold leaves, she said, "You are very much changed, my husband."

"Do you like the change?"

She was silent a while, and then replied, "I loved the man I married, and honour him, and pray daily for his soul. But I confess, I love the man who I see before me more, and am glad of his company, for as long as it may last."

"Why did you marry me, if not for who I was?"

"For money," she replied simply. "I had a good dowry, but that is not an income. You have income. You have prestige. You have a name. Even if you had not the first part, two together beget the third. My family lacks for any of these. By my union with you, I secure their advancement."

"I see," I murmured, unsure of what al-Mu'allim would have said to all this, and choosing, therefore, to say as little as possible.

At my reticence, Ayesha, rather than draw back, smiled. For the first time she raised her eyes to my face, and at that my heart ran fast. Then – a gesture almost unheard of at the dinner table – she reached over to touch my hand. "You do not recall," she breathed, and there was no accusation in it, merely a statement of understanding, of discovery, "very well."

For a moment, panic. But she simply sat, her fingers resting in my palm, and when the sun was down we stood together by the water's edge and I said, "There is something I must tell you. Something you may not understand."

"Don't tell me," she replied, sharp enough to make me flinch. Sensing my withdrawal, she repeated, softer, "Don't tell me."

"Why don't you want to know?"

"I am sworn to you. I am tasked to honour and obey. While I do this in duty, and sincerity, my soul is clean. Only in these last months, however, have I found joy in my duty. Only with ... only these last few months. Do not speak the words that might tarnish the joy we have. Do not wipe away this moment."

So I said nothing. She was my wife, and I was her husband, and that was all that we needed to know.

It lasted six years, in which my wife lived with me in wealth – wheat, cotton and boys being profitable markets at nearly any time, and there the matter may have rested, until the French came to Cairo. When the rage of the Egyptians against their remarkably moderate oppressors grew too great, conspirators came to my door, asking for arms, influence, money – all of which I politely refused.

"Your city is held by the infidel!" they exclaimed. "How long until a Frenchman violates your wife?"

"I really couldn't say," I replied. "How long did it take until they violated yours?"

They left, muttering against my impiety, but their comings and their goings were already being watched, and when the revolt began and the cannon fired and the heavens cracked and Napoleon himself gave the order to blast down the walls of the Great Mosque and massacre every man, woman and child who had taken refuge inside, my name was called in the round-up of the living dead amid the thunder-blasted carnage of the Cairo streets.

The teenage boy, now grown to a man, whose body I had first inhabited when I came to inspect the household of al-Mu'allim came running to me. "Master," he exclaimed, "the French are coming for you!"

My wife stood by, silent and straight. I turned to her, said, "What should I do?" and meant the question, for to become some French officer — the obvious recourse — would in that single breath, that second of transition, end the life I had, all that I had lived to obtain. "What should I do?"

"Al-Mu'allim must not be found in this city," she replied, and it was the first time in six years that she had looked at me, but spoken my body's name. "If you remain, the French will take you and kill you. There are boats on the river; you have money. Leave."

"I could return . . . "

"Al-Mu'allim must not be found," she repeated, a flash of anger pushing at her voice. "My husband is too proud and lazy to run."

It was the closest she had come to admitting my nature, for though her fingers were in mine, her breath mixed with my breath, she spoke of my body as if it were some other place.

"What about you?"

"Bonaparte wants, even now, to prove that he is just. He puts up signs across the city, which proclaim 'Do not put your hopes in Ibrahim or Muhammad, but put your trust in he who masters empires and creates men.'"

"That doesn't inspire me to believe in anything," I replied.

"He will not murder a widow. Our servants, wealth and friends will protect me."

"Or make you a target."

"I am only in danger while al-Mu'allim remains!" she retorted, the tendons pressing against her neck as she swallowed down a shout. "If you love me — as I think you do — then go."

"Come with me."

"Your presence here brings me danger. Your . . . who you are brings me danger. If you love me, you would not bring me harm."

"I can protect you."

"Can you?" she replied sharply. "And who are you to protect me? Because my husband could not do so much, even if he loved me enough to try. When all this has ended, perhaps you may come back to me, in some other shape."

"I am your husband . . . "

"And I your wife," she replied. "Though never before has either of us had need to say it."

Ayesha bint Kamal.

She stood upon the banks of the river, one hand across her belly, a blue scarf across her head, her back straight and the serving boy crying silently at her side.

I left her as Cairo thundered to the roar of infidels.

Leaving is one of the few things I am good at.

Chapter 29

In 1798 by the banks of the Nile I wore the body of a man whose life no longer interested me. The waters of the river spilt out into the long grass until you believed that the water was without end, drowning the earth.

I took al-Mu'allim south, far from the French as they battled Mameluke cavalry before the slopes of the Pyramids. My body grew thin, my nails began to yellow and I would have abandoned it then and there, for it disgusted me, a withering corpse. Then I remembered my wife, and my oath to keep her husband safe, and I clenched my fists and lowered my eyes, and kept going.

Though the French were far from the higher reaches of the Nile, yet even here their deeds were condemned by the cataract-eyed imams, who cried, infidel, infidel, they violate us, they violate Egypt! The further from Cairo I went, the more violent the rumours became. The city was burned; the city was lost. Every woman was raped, every child butchered on the steps of the mosque. After a while I gave up contradicting the tales, as my veracity only served to mark me out as a traitor to the jihad rising in the sands.

I headed towards the coastal mountains of Sudan, until I came at last to the Red Sea where it looked out towards Jeddah. There, as news of a great naval defeat came whispering down the waters, I sat to watch the ocean and resolved at last to make a change.

There were few ports along the western coast of the Red Sea, but the battles in the desert and the chaos at the mouth of the Nile, where Nelson had shattered the French fleet, created a buzz among the tiny fishing craft and semi-piratical lateen-sailed skiffs. Excellent profits were made as they shipped, stole and scuppered war goods heading north towards the Mediterranean. One ship in particular caught my eye, an ancient schooner long past its retirement day. Its captain was a grinning Dinka chief, with a great sword on his belt and two pistols slung with piratical glee across his chest. His crew were as multicultural a melange as I had ever seen, from his Genoan lookout to the Malaysian pilot, who communicated through a mixture of poor Arabic, reasonable Dutch and obscene gesticulation. Of most interest to me, however, was the one passenger they were carrying for their crossing to India, who stood silently at the prow of the ship in a cloak of black, studying the waters and saying not a word.

He was a man barely into his twenties, tall and lean with perfect ebony skin, well-muscled arms and coiled black hair, who held himself aloft with the glory of a prince and was, upon interrogation of the crew, revealed to be precisely that: a prince of the Nuba travelling to India on a diplomatic mission.

"Does anyone know him?" I asked. "Does he have family or servants in attendance?"

No, no one knew him, except by reputation, and he had come to the ship without servants but with a vast quantity of cash. His personality was a closed book; his history, doubly so. It was with this in mind that I, still in the body of al-Mu'allim, followed him, the night before sailing, into the tiny port town. I trailed him between the crooked mud houses of the cliff-clinging streets, reached out to touch him on his arm, and as I went to jump, heard in my head the screaming of vampire bats, felt tiny vessels bursting behind my eyes, tasted iron on my tongue, and as I fell back, gasping from the attempt, the beautiful prince turned, his face also drained of blood, and exclaimed, in flawless Arabic:

"What the *hell* are you doing?!"

Chapter 30

Restless sleep, restless memories in an anonymous hotel room in . . .

where, precisely?

Bratislava.

What in God's name am I doing in Bratislava?

Sleeping on top of a file that dissects the life of the entity known as Kepler. Rolling in sheets pulled too tight across the bed that wrap themselves around the body of the murderer called Coyle. I'd burned the Turkish passport, scattered the ashes down the toilet. I'd always known that I'd have to ditch an identity eventually; I was simply waiting to find out which one.

A thought, in the night. It hits so hard, so fast that I bolt upright, wide awake.

The Turkish authorities have no reason to track my British, Canadian or German passports, but that was because they didn't know what to look for.

Whereas Coyle's colleagues, whoever they might be, knew all of Coyle's names.

*

A racing mind at 4 a.m. The street light is a yellow rectangle on my ceiling, the shape of the window. The rest of the room is deepest blue, the not-dark of the city.

I had been careful – so careful. Careful to avoid security, careful to slip over the borders quiet and fast, lest someone check my passports too particularly. Johannes had told me my Turkish passport was blown, and so it was destroyed. But buoyed up by that overconfidence I had let the hotel receptionist at the desk scan my German documents.

Was that enough?

I had trusted in border posts to be sluggish in their checks, for hotels to keep records rather than immediately search databases or contact the police. Were I merely evading a national agency, my precautions would be enough.

But I wasn't just hiding from a police force. Whoever had given me the name of Kepler cared nothing for the sanctity of borders, the discretion of a hotel. And even if I were safe for tonight, having paid in cash, if someone looked hard enough

and for certain they would

as matters stood, the body of Nathan Coyle could be tracked.

A face in the mirror at 4.30 a.m., grey by fluorescent bathroom light. I've worn better faces, I've worn worse. I could get comfortable with these features, given time, but no amount of scrutiny can offer me the answers I need. The eyes are heavy, the mouth is slack, the scars tell me no more and no less than that the original occupant of this flesh wasn't always great at making friends. Are the frown lines his or mine?

I gather up my belongings, put the handcuffs in my outer jacket pocket, key in my inner, and head out into the city, no rest for the wicked.

Chapter 31

She calls herself Janus.

On the shores of the Red Sea she wore the body of a Nuba princeling, and when I tried to move in on this most desirable of properties, we both came away with a stinking hangover.

Over a hundred and fifty years later she came to me in the body of a seventeen-year-old girl, and said, "I'm looking to relocate."

We met in a bar on East 26th Street. Her body had been out in the sun, which was impressive, as in Chicago in the rain-soaked autumn of 1961 the only flushing I saw was from vodka and wind-burn.

The place had been a speakeasy once upon a time. The man with the greying chin and fading hair who stood behind the bar polishing a glass had once stood behind the very same long wooden counter cleaning coffee mugs with an old towel, ready for the cops to bust in and the clients to bust out. He still ran a quiet joint, one of the few left as the 1960s came roaring across the world, and still kept the good stuff in a locked cabinet, hidden away beneath the bar.

Janus wore blue, I wore Patterson Wayne, a businessman from

Georgia I'd acquired the day after he liquidated his assets into a suitcase of cash, and the day before his company flopped, taking with it forty-seven employees and sixty-three private pensions. He was healthy, and of that age which the young respect and the old envy.

She said, "I'm absolutely divine, make no mistake. Have you felt my skin? It's brushed silk, and my complexion! Do you know I don't wear any make-up? I don't need to! It's just sensational."

Her skin was indeed very smooth, and though she had to be the only woman in downtown Chicago who wasn't adorning her features with the garish colours of the decade, yet the absence of paint only served to draw the eye, novelty in a crowd.

"There's just one problem," she murmured, head tilted away from the lone proprietor and his eager ears. "When I picked this skin up, I thought she looked just radiant. It was at the bus stop, and she was heading north anyway, and I thought ... why not? It's obvious no one's interested in the girl, except for the usual, so a few months, a few years, it could be delightful. Only the problem ... " A conspiratorial palm pressed gently into her own belly. "I know," she whispered, her voice quivering with delight at its conspiratorial outlay, "why I had to leave in the first place, and I reckon it's only five months more until I pop."

I pushed my bourbon to one side, rested my elbow on the bar, pulled a slim black notebook from my inside jacket pocket and a stub of pencil. "What precisely are you looking for?"

Janus sucked in her lips judiciously. "Male, unmarried, twenty-five, I think – although I can go with younger so long as he looks like he can hold his own, I won't be having boys – thirty-two at the maximum, any older just isn't worth the effort. Unmarried, naturally. I'm not interested in excessive body hair. I don't mind the regular shave, but the all-over carpeted look is very 1880s. I'd *love* it if he has a place to live already, no further west than Princeton; if there's a mortgage that's fine, but I don't want to handle the paperwork on an initial purchase."

I licked the end of my pencil-scrubbed fingertip, turned the page of my notebook. "Any academic qualifications, career prospects?"

"Absolutely. I'm looking at a long-term investment. I want to start a company, I want to have a family, I want ... what do you want, Mr Patterjones Wynne?"

The question came so suddenly, at first I wasn't sure I'd heard it. "Me?"

"You. What do you *want*?"

I hesitated, pencil balanced on the edge of the page. "Is that relevant?"

"First time we met you wanted ... whatever her name was."

"Ayesha," I murmured, and was surprised how quickly the name was on my lips. "Ayesha bint Kamal. She was ... but I had to go."

"A woman," she concluded with a twitch of a shoulder. "A wife. A normal life. What do you want now?"

I considered, then laid my notebook down, looked her in the eye and said, "I want what everyone wants – something better."

"Better than what?"

"Better than whatever life it is I happen to be living right now."

A moment which could have gone any way at all.

Then Janus grinned, slapped me on the shoulder and exclaimed, "You're gonna be really busy with that. Good luck!"

I sighed and picked up my notebook. "What else were you looking for? Acceptable health issues, inoculations ...?"

She shrugged, shoulders swelling, elbows tucked in. "OK," she said. "You want to talk shop, that's fine. No fallen arches." She jammed her finger into my thigh with each vital word. "You may call it petty, but I have no time for them. I don't mind spectacles – lend a certain dignity – but tinnitus, eczema – any sort of sense or skin disorder – absolutely out, and I don't want any surprises in the sexual area again, thank you very much."

"Height?"

"Over five foot six, but I don't want to be a freak. At six two you're respectable, at six five people start to wonder."

I made a note. "I take it we're looking at years, not months?"

"Yeah. You could say that."

"Any goals I should be made aware of?"

She considered. "Well," she said at last, "I wanna build a life, marry a girl, find a house and have a baby. If you can get me someone who's been to Harvard, that'd be just peachy."

Chapter 32

Fifty years later I walked through the pre-dawn streets of Bratislava, bag over my shoulder, handcuffs in my pocket, and I was angry.

It was that blue-grey hour of deepest cold when any heat from yesterday has finally dissolved in the night, nothing to replace it but the hope of sunrise yet to come. In the doorway of a supermarket, shutter down over the windows, slept a beggar man, dead to the world, blue bag pulled up around his head. From the slumbering square of Mileticova a garbage truck roared and grumbled as it scooped up and crushed the tatty remnants of market day, its yellow lights spinning off the grey-white walls. On the Danube a cargo ship of orange paint and rusting sides, riding high in the water, chugged and churned its way towards Vienna. I headed towards the swooping arch of Apollo Bridge and saw beneath it a single street sweeper sitting on a bench, his trolley resting while he had a fag, his eyes gummy and bags full of fallen leaves.

He glanced up as I approached, but saw no threat in me. I reached into my pocket, pulled out the handcuffs, snapped them round my wrists, pinning them in front. At the sound, he looked up again in time for me to put my hands across his shoulder, press my fingers into the soft skin where collarbone met neck and switch.

Nathan Coyle swayed as I rose to my feet, and before he could move I punched him, not particularly hard, but hard enough, in the shoulder. He stumbled and tripped over his own retreating feet, tried to brace his fall, found his hands cuffed and landed badly. I knelt on top of him, my right knee cracking, my body sticky and warm beneath its protective jacket, and before he could speak I laid my arm across his throat, pressed one hand against his cheek and hissed: "Who are you working for?"

I wanted to shout, but the river caught all sound, spun it outwards, bright and clear for all to hear, so I pressed harder against his neck and snarled, "Why did you kill Josephine? Who are you working for?!"

I'd caught one of his arms beneath my knee; now he tried to break free of my weight, rolling to the side, but I drove my fist across his face, pressed the full weight of my body on to his chest and screamed without screaming, roared without the lion's lungs, "What do you *want*?!"

"Kepler ..." The word barely made it out through my weight on his throat, rattling like sand down a mountain. "Galileo."

"Who's Galileo? *What's* Galileo?"

"*Santa Rosa.*"

"I don't know what that is."

"*Santa Rosa.* Milli Vra. Alexandra."

"What are these? What does it mean?"

He tried to move again, and at the curl of my lip he desisted before that mistake could go any further. "He kills because he likes it," he whispered. "He kills because he can."

"Who? Galileo?"

He didn't answer, and he didn't deny. I pressed my elbow against his trachea until his eyes boggled. "I am *not* a killer," I hissed. "All I want is to live."

He tried to speak, tongue waggling, and for a moment I

thought about it. This face that had looked back at me from the mirror, now animated with someone else's fear. This face had killed Josephine Cebula.

His cheeks were flushing swollen red, now heading for purple blue.

I pulled back with a snarl, letting him gasp for air, head bouncing in an effort to inhale. "Who are you working for?" I breathed, pressing my fingers into fists inside their heavy, smelly gloves. "Who's coming for me?"

He lay and wheezed, and said nothing.

"They'll kill you too. If they're at all like you, they'll come for me and shoot you in the process."

"I know," he replied. "I *know*."

He knows but he does not care.

I can't remember the last time I was willing to die.

"Why did you kill Josephine?"

"Orders."

"Because she was a murderer?"

"Yes."

"Because she killed people in Germany? Dr Ulk, Magda Müller – them?"

"Yes."

I grabbed a fistful of shirt, pulled his face up towards mine. "It was a lie," I hissed. "I did my research; I went over every inch of her life before making an offer. Your people *lied*. She killed no one, she was innocent! These are the fucking people you'd protect? What do they want?"

I could feel his breath on my face. It smelt of cheap toothpaste; when his mouth was mine, I hadn't noticed. I let go; he dropped back on to the cobbles, lay breathless beneath me.

"What do you want, Mr Coyle?" I asked, squeezing my shaking hands tight. "Forget the ones who sent you, the ones who lied. What do *you* want?"

He didn't reply.

"What would you do if I let you go?" I didn't look at him as I asked the question.

"I'd put a bullet in your brain before you could touch another soul."

"That's what I thought." Then, "I know about Alice." An almost infinitesimal thing, a little pulling of muscles around the eyes, the chin, but it was as good a reaction as I was getting from him. "I went to see Gubler. He recognised me – you. Said you were nice, understanding, almost. Said you went to visit with Alice. You know, covert operatives shouldn't leave their car registration number on the reception desk."

His breath picked up a little speed. "You won't find her."

"Sure I will," I replied. "And even if I don't, she'll find you. Wearing your face is the biggest come-hither I can conceive. Maybe she'll tell me why Josephine died."

I eased my weight off his chest, slipped down to the stones at his side. Coyle lay still on his back, hands cuffed in front of him, staring up into the rain. "I . . . followed orders."

"I know," I sighed. "You're just the foot soldier."

He opened his mouth to speak.

I grabbed his hand.

I couldn't imagine he'd have anything interesting to say.

Chapter 33

A boat to Vienna.

The Danube's flat silver waters are wide enough in places to mistake it for an inland sea. Travellers cross the border from Slovakia to Austria without noticing, passports merely glanced at by the conductor on the boat. Drowned wooden sheds for long-departed fishermen greet you along the waterside, in the waterside, the windows washed away by the flood. It is not fit for luxury yachts, but an industrial river, a practical river of great flatlands washed with silt. Factories feed off it; behind the fields squat little towns with long names where no one asks too closely the secrets of their next-door neighbours. The Austrians value their privacy, and so in silence the villages sit on the edge of the river, waiting for a change that never comes.

I shouldn't have hit Coyle.

My face feels tender, red. In a few hours I'll have a whopping bruise.

I have crossed into the Schengen zone, and can temporarily discard my passports as irrelevant. My spoken German is good enough, and if I was ever to disappear, this is the time. A new body, a new life, a new name. One dense crowd, perhaps leaving the cathedral or in a busy market, and I can switch bodies ten, fifteen times – untraceable, no matter how good your resources. Swallow poison and, before the drug can take effect, jump away, leave Coyle to his well-deserved fate. Move on to the next life, bigger, better than before. The next life is always better.

Josephine Cebula, dead in Taksim station.

I will not run.

Not today.

The boat moored just beyond Schwedenbrucke. On the west bank old Vienna, tourist Vienna, the city of spires, palaces, *Sachertorte* and Mozart concerts, ten a cent. On the east bank the antique rectangular windows of the city dissolved into the white concrete and iron-elevator apartment blocks of post-war Europe. I headed west, into the old city, past prim-buttocked matrons in their tight skirts walking pampered dogs on tight leashes through the immaculate streets. Past stiff-necked gentlemen with their briefcases polished black; hawking migrants selling DVDs from open rucksacks, chased away by the blue-capped police who know that drink and drugs are only a problem when the burgo-masters of the city perceive them. I walked beneath the faces of stone cherubs, sad to see their streets defiled by the presence of uncouth strangers; past statues raised in stone to emperors and their steeds, empresses and their noble deeds, and dead generals famed for fighting Turks and civic dissent. I passed an art gallery showing an exhibition entitled Primary Colours: the Post-Modern Revival, whose posters explained that within you could find canvases painted entirely in red, blue, green, and, for those who were feeling radical, yellow, with a single pinpoint of white daubed in the bottom corner to draw the eye mystically in. Some had artistic titles – *Aneurism Lover* was a canvas of solid purple with a tiny tracery of blue just visible if you squinted. Others, such as two canvases of solid black, shown side by side, were simply *Untitled*.

I walked on by. I like to believe that I move with the times, but sometimes even I miss the 1890s.

An antique shop was tucked into the base of a great white

mansion with a brass-plated door facing a square decked with a fountain of gurgling dolphins and raging ocean gods. When I pushed open the door, a small brass bell rang, and the air within smelt of old paper, feathers, copper and clay. A pair of Chinese tourists – never going to buy – stood examining a little marble statue bearing the face of a stern-eyed bishop with a sagging chin, but at my approach they giggled and put it down, like children caught fiddling with the keyhole in a vending machine. A man, his hair inclining towards grey, forest-green trousers faded to thin patches around the knees, stumbled out from behind a counter bedecked with skulls, pots, papers and the obligatory models of St Stephen's spire, looked at me and stopped where he stood. "I told you already," he blurted. "Go away!"

For a moment I forgot my body, and blushed, hot and suddenly ashamed. "Klemens," I blurted. "I'm Romy."

His hands, which had been flapping in the air, as if by wafting alone I could be propelled through the door, froze. His face tightened, lips peeling back. "You shit," he spat, the thickness of his accent tying up around the word and making it greater. "I have nothing to say, and you come here like—"

"I'm Romy," I repeated, stepping forward. "We went to the opera together, rode the Ferris wheel. You like green beans but hate broccoli. I'm Romy. I'm Di'u. I'm me."

Chapter 34

Klemens and Romy Ebner.

They appear approximately one third of the way through the Kepler file.

They met in 1982 at a dinner in Vienna and were married five months later. She was Catholic, he was lapsed, but the service was before the eyes of God, and their dedication was absolute.

Their first child was born in 1984, and sent to boarding school at fourteen, to return to the family home no more than twice a year. Klemens loved walking in the forested hills that bounded Vienna; Romy did not, and so the walking boots stayed at home and he looked at the horizon from the windows of the Brunerstrasse tram on his way to work.

When he joined a choir, she said he sang like a chipmunk. When she started attending meetings at the local church hall, he enrolled in a cooking course, but his food, she said, was foreign muck and she had no time for it. When she retired, to dedicate herself to herself, he stayed working, longer and later to support their needs, and found that, alone in the evening gloom of the shop, he did not mind his own company.

When I met them, I was Trinh Di'u Ma, trafficked from her

home aged just thirteen years old, whose parents, some five years later, had paid an estate agent to find her and bring her back. They had no money to give, so they bartered away the only currency they could think of – six months of their daughter's body, in exchange for her safe return home. I had taken the deal and regretted it, for on acquiring Trinh from the brothel in Linz, I spent the best part of a month engaged in nothing but medical tests and detox. When the pain grew too great, I jumped from Di'u into the body of the nurse who watched her, and sat with my head in my hands as she screamed for heroin, please God, please, just give me what I need, I'll do anything.

Even when the last opiate had been flushed from her system, and I walked wobbling from the hospital door, I felt the emptiness in her mind, longing in her blood, and wondered whether I, riding the mere echo of dependence, could make it to Vietnam without breaking.

Sitting in the departure lounge of Vienna airport, my arms around my knees, a fake passport in my pocket and caffeine buzzing around my head, I felt the avoidance of the well-dressed travellers more than the stares of the security guards. When the customs officers, having no better reason than my age, race and fading scars, took me to one side and strip-searched me, their hands running over every part of my body, their machines beeping at my bare goosebumped flesh, I stood with arms open and legs apart and said nothing, felt nothing but an overwhelming desire to get out.

I nearly left her then, abandoning Di'u with her ticket for Hanoi and no recollection of how she got there, until a man, seeing me hunched beneath the seats, came up to me and said in badly broken English:

"Are you OK?"

Klemens Ebner, in a yellow jumper and appalling beige trousers, knelt by the side of a shaking Vietnamese girl and said, "Miss? Ma'am? Are you OK?"

Behind him, Romy Ebner, stiff-backed in black and blue, exclaimed, "Get away from her, Klem!"

I looked up through Trinh Di'u Ma's hazy eyes into the eyes of the only man in the world who seemed to care, and he was beautiful, and I was in love.

Two weeks later I knocked on a heavy black apartment door in Vienna, wearing the smart sandals and well-worked feet of the local postman, and said, "Delivery, please?"

Romy Ebner answered it, and as she signed the packet and returned my pen, I caught her by the wrist and jumped.

Chapter 35

Back in the body of Nathan Coyle, I sat in the darkest corner of the tightest café in Vienna and ate lemon cake with a cherry on top while Klemens gripped his tiny cup of coffee and failed in his mission not to stare.

"How did you end up as him?" he asked, voice low against the customers coming in for lunch. "As this man?"

His crinkled eyes were enough to suggest dislike, his voice confirmed active hate. I shrugged, scooping yellow cake on to the end of my fork, and tried not to take it personally. "He came looking for me," I replied. "I take it you've met him before?"

"He came to the shop, asking about you," he grumbled, sipping espresso a droplet at a time. "Not in terms of a name, or a description of your ... your qualities. He knew my wife had had blackouts, a few days here, a few days there, and wanted to know if I had experienced the same."

"What did you tell him?"

"I said no."

"What did you tell him about your wife?"

Klemens smiled, and immediately frowned, joy and guilt taking turns to wash across his features. "I told him that my wife seemed absolutely fine, and then said she couldn't remember what she'd done yesterday. I told him that we'd been to the doctor a few times, but he couldn't find anything wrong with her, and that I wasn't very worried about it."

"And was he ... I mean, was *I*," I grunted, "happy with this reply?"

"You were ... neutral. Your partner seemed unconvinced."

"Ah, my partner. Alice?"

"That was the name she gave."

"What's she like?"

He blew thin steam off the top of his coffee and considered. "She spoke German with a Berlin accent, liked to be in charge, walked around like a man, very tough, very proud. She was on her phone a lot, made notes, took a few photographs – I asked her not to – she had short blonde hair. She wanted to be tougher than anyone else in the room. I thought it weakened her, trying to be all that."

"Are the two mutually incompatible? Femininity and toughness?" I asked, and to my surprise and secret pleasure, Klemens blushed. He had a good blush, which swelled up beneath his neck and circled round the rim of his ears.

"No," he mumbled. "Not at all ... Just I thought she was maybe trying too hard to be ... something she didn't have to be."

I grinned and had to resist the urge to put my hand on his. His eyes met mine, then looked away, down into the blackness of his coffee cup. "She left me a card. An email address, contact number. Would it help you?"

"Yes. Christ, *yes*, it's exactly what I need."

"Then it's yours," he said. "Just ... use it well."

A single rectangle of card with just three lines of text – email address, phone number, name: Alice Mair. He pulled it from the mess of his wallet, from cards he'd never used and memberships he'd forgotten he owned, and as he pushed it towards me, our fingers touched, I lingered, and he shied away.

"This is ... unexpected," he admitted.

"I'm sorry. I didn't mean to visit like this."

"It's ... fine. I know that it's you. There must be reasons. This man you're ... this man you've become. Did he hurt you?"

"Yes."

"I thought as much," he murmured. "You don't strike me as someone to do something for no good reason."

"He killed ... someone close to me."

"I'm sorry."

"He was aiming for me."

"Why?"

"It's something that happens," I replied. "Every few decades someone new learns of our existence, realises all that we could do and gets scared. This time ... "

"This time?"

"This time there were orders to kill my host, as well as me. That's never happened before. My host was an innocent. I made her an offer and she said yes. Now she's dead and the people who are coming for me invented lies to justify it."

He was leaning away, a motion he probably didn't notice himself perform. My face belonged to a murderer, and though it wasn't to a killer that he spoke, yet some reactions are ingrained deep in decent men. "What will you do?"

"Find Josephine's killer. This body pulled the trigger, and for that ... but it was also following orders. Someone gave orders that she had to die. I want to know why – the real why."

"And then?"

Silence between us. I smiled, and it didn't reassure. "More coffee?"

"No. Thank you."

His eyes were locked on to his coffee cup, reading the future in its depths.

"How's your wife?"

A flicker to my face, then away. "Good. Well. Busy. She's always very busy."

"And ... you're happy?"

A brief flicker of his gaze, a shift on his face, gone as quickly as it had arrived. "Yes," he said softly. "We're happy."

"Good. I'm glad."

"You?" he asked. "Are you . . . happy?"

I thought about it, then laughed. "All things considered . . . no. Not at all."

"I'm . . . sorry to hear that. What should I call you?"

"I'm called Nathan."

"I . . . will try to call you that. Is it your name, or is it . . . " A flicker of fingers at my borrowed skin.

"It's his," I replied. "I lost my name a long, long time ago."

Klemens Ebner.

He is, if you look through the weariness, the slouched shoulders and the abandoned dreams, a very easy man to love. It is perhaps the simplicity of his affection, the patience of his understanding and loyalty that makes him too easy to love, for his love is taken for granted by many, who give back nothing in return.

I came to him first in the body of his wife. I did my research, for if nothing else I was a good estate agent, and knew how to pick up a life that was not my own, move it about like so much money on a Monopoly board. The first night that I wore Romy Ebner I said, let's go out for dinner. Let's have something Thai.

Klemens Ebner loved Thai food, so we had a platter of spicy treats: duck stewed with cashew nuts, coconut rice, prawn crackers, rice noodles, tofu steamed on a bed of garlic and mushrooms. When we were done I said, come on, there's a concert round the corner, and it was Brahms and I held his hand as the violins played.

At home, in the dark, we lay together in a creaking bed, and made love like teenagers just discovering their own flesh, and in the morning he held his arms around me and said, "You are not my wife."

Of course I'm your wife, I exclaimed as my heart started in my chest; don't be foolish.

No, he replied. My wife hates the things I love, because she hates that I can love anything besides herself, and when we make love, it is to appease me, because sex is dirty and flesh is vile and it is only because men are weak that such things must be so. You – this woman in my arms – you are not my wife. Who are you?

And to my surprise, I told him.

I am not Romy Ebner. I am not Nathan Coyle, I am not Trinh Di'u Ma, sobbing in her father's arms even as I slip away from her body, relieved to be gone. I am not Josephine Cebula, dead in a Turkish morgue, al-Mu'allim lost by the Nile, or the empty-eyed girl sitting in a village in southern Slovakia, scars on her arms and drugs in her veins, do you want to try something kinky tonight?

Once every few years I return to Klemens Ebner and his wife, who he will never leave, and for a few nights, preferably over a weekend with no social obligations, he commits delightful adultery with the woman he married, and we sail the river and ride the Ferris wheel and live as tourists do, hand in hand, until I leave, and he loves the body I leave behind.

My file calls me Kepler.

It will have to do.

Chapter 36

Klemens asked me if I wanted to stay.

He didn't want me to, but asked anyway, out of good manners.

Thank you, but no.

In all the times I've worn his wife I've managed to avoid ever having to meet her for more than the briefest instant of physical contact, and frankly I'm not sure I want to start now.

He says:

If you're in trouble . . . you could be me. For a little while. If you need to.

His offer of a bed was false, his offer of a body is real.

I have to remember not to kiss him when I say no, thank you.

He says:

The man you are now? This . . . Nathan? Are you going to kill him?

The words come tangled, courageous and scared.

Maybe, I reply. Maybe.

He nods, digesting my words, then says:

Don't. Life is a beautiful thing. Don't kill him.

Goodbye, Klemens Ebner.

Goodbye, Nathan.

We shake hands formally, and then, as I move away, his fingers touch my arm, the inside, where the skin is soft. He's frightened, but his fingers stay, barely resting on my skin, and if there was a moment, it would have been then.

I do not look back as I walk away.

Travellers' hotels.

Seen one, seen 'em all.

This one had a couple of cranky computers in the hall, accessible for half-hour stretches for residents' internet access. Of the many email accounts I ran, only one had content more interesting than an invitation to buy three new coffee cups at 72 per cent of their original price or anti-cellulite cream for the modern woman.

The email was from Johannes "Spunkmaster13" Schwarb, and came with a business disclaimer at the bottom pointing out that any information contained within was confidential, and that the value of your investments might go down as well as up. He'd forgotten to remove it before pressing 'send'.

The email was short and to the point.

It had the registration number of a car driven to a hospice in rural Slovakia.

The name of the woman who'd hired it from Eurocar in Bratislava.

The credit card she'd used to secure the transaction.

The last eleven places that credit card had been used.

Five of the eleven were in Istanbul, on the days leading up to the death of Josephine Cebula.

All the rest were in Berlin.

A name and address were at the bottom.

Alice Mair.

Nice to meet you at last.

Chapter 37

An estate agent has two primary roles.

The first is the acquisition of long-term investment property. Male or female, young or old, there's no point moving long term into a skin unless you know its social situation, criminal record and medical history. I have known seven of my kind hospitalised for asthma, angina, diabetes – all of which could easily have been avoided if they'd done their homework – and two have died of the same, their physical conditions striking so hard and so fast that they couldn't even get a good grip on the paramedic to jump away. Had one known enough about her target to check the inside jacket pocket, she would have found the epinephrine right there, ready to go. She would have lived but for ignorance of her own wardrobe.

The second role of a good estate agent is exhaustive research for short-term loans.

To take an example.

"I wanna be Marilyn Monroe."

1959 Hollywood may have had the glitz, the glamour and the flashing lights, but the Scarlet and Star Diner on North Arlen

Boulevard served the worst scrambled eggs this side of the Greenwich Meridian. I prodded them gingerly with my fork while on the other side of the booth the body of Anne Munfield, forty-two years old, said, "I wanna be her, just for a few days. There's a party on Friday, the whole town's talking, and I thought, maybe Tony Curtis, maybe Grace Kelly, maybe I'll go as a politician or even just a waiter, whatever – but then I thought. Marilyn. Just for a few days, a couple of nights, even. I wanna be Marilyn Monroe."

My eggs, when prodded, oozed a thin liquid that might have been water, might have been undercooked grease – whatever it was, it could have formed the perfect medium for the evolution of some primeval monster.

"So . . . ?" asked my companion, leaning across the rubber table-top. "Whatcha think?"

I laid my fork to one side. The inhabitant of Anne Munfield went by the name Aurangzeb, for reasons which largely evaded me as, by her own confession, she'd been ghosting for less than thirty years and had been raised in her previous life on a farmstead in Illinois. Even had she not admitted to her youth, her behaviour would have been self-explanatory.

"All right," I murmured. "Let's go with this for a moment. Why Marilyn?"

"Jesus, why not Marilyn?" she exclaimed. "She's got this sleek little body, and it's perfect, but it's also real, you know, I mean, she's got a real arse and real tits and a real belly and you might call it chubby, but it's not that – it's just real."

"The word is she's also prone to alcohol and pills."

Aurangzeb threw her hands up in frustration. "Who isn't in this town? You seen some of the faces round here – it's like they've been eaten by crabs. I heard you were the guy for this. I heard you were good. This body I've got, it's got more money than sense – I can wire you whatever you need, whatever currency, I've got the signature down perfect. Just gimme this? OK?"

Anne Munfield might once have been a dignified middle-aged woman, serene and calm, quite possibly vegetarian. Now her face twisted with wheedling desire, her eyes looking up like a meek puppy afraid of a master's slipper. Such juvenile imploring did not suit features better made for motherhood.

My eggs oozed oily water and my body craved cabbage. I had never liked cabbage, but now my stomach ached for it like a baby for mother's milk, and Aurangzeb whined, straining every muscle, every fibre and vein beneath her skin with the need to be someone new.

"If I do this," I grunted, "I want to be absolutely clear – one night, two at the most, and you're out. Marilyn Monroe wakes up on Monday morning with a stinking hangover and a feeling that she's missed something insignificant and that's it. The end. No more, no less. Are we agreed?"

Aurangzeb whooped, punching the air in her glee, and I felt a momentary pang of shame that a body as beautiful as hers should be so ugly to my eyes.

It didn't take much to research Marilyn.

She was one of the first movie stars not only to court the press, but seduce it, invite it round with an intimate suggestion, bathe with the press, share two straws to one milkshake with the press and, when the press looked up from its mug with a creamy moustache, it was Marilyn's metaphorical – and not so metaphorical – handkerchief that dabbed the offending mark away.

A little more research was required to get the important – and perhaps more interesting – information on the people around her.

I spent half a day as a chipper black woman by the name of Maggie who brought coffee to all the execs in Fox; another three hours as a harried producer with thinning hair and what felt suspiciously like undiagnosed sciatica. I hopped around for three minutes as a security guard, two as a gaffer, seven as a costume girl and finally, angling for the exit, forty-five seconds as a minor movie star whose name I forget and whose mouth reeked of aniseed.

Out in the clearer air, my body – my preferred body – was waiting for me by the car.

"How'd it go?" he asked.

"I hate this town," I replied. "Every mouth aches from smiling too much."

He shrugged. "Works out well enough. Hey, you in tonight?"

"I was thinking about it, why?"

"The Dodgers are playing. I thought, you wanna go?"

I thought about it. "Why not? I'll change into someone less sensible."

So saying, I took his unresisting hand, and jumped.

The Dodgers don't interest me.

Baseball doesn't interest me.

Sports trivia.

If you suspect that the body you're sitting opposite is a ghost, I recommend sports trivia as a method of detection. A body wearing a Dodgers shirt should, if it paid for the threads, know the score – but what self-respecting ghost wastes time on detail like that?

That's the kind of thing you pay estate agents to do.

Straight white streets through the straight grey grid of LA.

My body is young, stronger now for a decent meal, with a mole under my left armpit that I find perpetually fascinating and have to force myself not to fiddle with in public. He is also that most vital of employees for a jobbing estate agent – a clean, cooperative gofer.

I had met my body beneath freeway 101.

It was the place where dreams went to die. The failed actors, the porn stars who'd been too late to get the treatment. The handyman turned out when the studio went under, the scriptwriter who'd never quite hit the money. The drug dealer who'd lost his haul in the last bust, the kid whose father was in lock-up and whose mum couldn't cope. It was the dead night-time stain of the city, the hollow-eyed place that peeked out between the brightness of the street lights. It was a dangerous place to walk alone at night. It was the perfect place to find unwanted flesh.

He wore stinking grey fabrics falling off him like the wrappings from a rotten mummy. His beard was down to his collarbone. His hair appeared grey, but when I squatted down opposite him and put a twenty-dollar note into his foul black hat, he told me his name was Will and he was twenty-two years old.

"Are you on drugs?" I asked.

"Jesus," he groaned as the cars rumbled by overhead. "What kinda question is that?"

"A question that could change your life," I replied. "There's more than just money on the line."

His head turned one way, then the other, twisting down like a swan examining its feathers. "No. You think I got the cash to pay for that shit?"

"What brings you here?"

"I fell for a guy."

"So?"

"They don't take kindly to sodomy in Texas. If it'd had been a white guy, maybe my folks would've been OK. Maybe they wouldn't. With all the shit that went down, didn't really stop to ask."

"You got family, friends here?"

"I got folk who look out for me," he replied, bristling.

"That's . . . not what I meant."

His eyes narrowed. "Spill. Don't dance – talk."

I sat back on my haunches, hands spilling over the tops of my knees. "In five seconds' time you'll be standing up, but you won't know how you got there."

"What the—"

I grabbed his wrist and switched.

Five seconds later he was standing up and didn't know how he'd got there.

"What the fuck did you do to me?" he breathed.

I swayed, my body a little dizzy from the two rapid jumps, in and out. "I want you to listen to me carefully. There sometimes comes a moment – so fast, a flash in the pan – which can change your life. It's the two seconds in which the driver of the truck failed to hit the brakes. It's the single breath where you said something stupid, and you should have said something kind. It's the moment the cops bust in through the door. Everyone feels it, that moment where their lives hang on a knife's edge. This is one of those moments."

"Who are you?" he stammered. "What the fuck are you?"

"I am a ghost. I live through other people's skins, wear the flesh of strangers. Quickly, painlessly, and without memory of the event. I'm not going to ask for a decision now. I'll keep my distance and let you think it over. I'm in town for a few weeks running some errands. What I want – what I need – is a semi-permanent body I can touch base with when the day is done, which won't get up and walk away when I'm not in residence. Do you understand?"

"Fuck no!" he said, but he wasn't shouting, wasn't screaming, wasn't running, which was in itself good news.

"The deal is simple. I'll clean you up: new clothes, haircut, money, identification, whatever. I'll put down six months' rent on an apartment, somewhere nice, stock up the fridge, and put five thousand dollars into an account in whatever name you choose. If you have culinary preferences or sexual concerns, we can negotiate. In exchange, I get your body for three weeks."

He shook his head, but it wasn't anger or rejection. "You're fucking insane," he breathed.

"I am asking politely," I replied. "It will be far more convenient if we enter into this arrangement willingly. If you doubt my word then it is my intention to leave this body tomorrow lunchtime. This host, unlike you, I acquired for the purpose of the bus ride to LA. He will not remember how he got here, he will not remember how he came to be wearing these clothes or where the insole that he sorely needed for his left shoe came from; the last three days will be a blank to him, and absolutely he will not remember how one thousand dollars in used notes came to be in the bottom of his suitcase. He may panic, he may run, he may do all sorts of things that alas I cannot influence or control, or he may take this for the gift it is. When he wakes, he too will be on that knife-edge that can change a life, and whether he dances or whether he slides will be his call. You just want to talk; that's fine. You want to dance? Be at the junction of Lexington and Cahuenga tomorrow. It's a good deal – consider it."

So saying, I walked away.

Chapter 38

I hate LA.

Endless straight lines from nowhere particular to nothing much especially.

Even the places that should be green – parks and "recreation areas" – are no more than a slab of fenced-off concrete where the kids sit and drink while waiting for something more interesting to pass them by.

But say what you will for Los Angeles, you can always find someone willing to do something if it'll cut them a break.

At 12.03 p.m. I left my host for the body of a passing stranger, walked far enough along Lexington for my former host not to suspect, then crossed over the street to where Will was waiting, squinting against the noonday sun.

"Hi," I said, and to his credit he didn't jump. "Make your mind up?"

Two weeks later we sat on the concrete stands of the stadium, he eating popcorn, me in the over-tanned, dry-skinned body of a handy stranger, when Will put his hand on my arm and said, "I can see you now."

"See what?"

"You," he replied. "Doesn't matter who you're wearing, where you've come from; I wait by the car and when you come to find me, I know it's you."

"How?"

He shrugged. "I dunno. Something in the way you walk. Something in the way you look. Something old. I can recognise you, whoever you are. I know who you are now."

I tried to answer and found I had nothing. My eyes were hot, and I turned my face away and hoped he didn't see me cry.

Chapter 39

The Kepler file made no mention of estate agents.

Its list of my bodies was far from comprehensive. Details were pieced together based on the testimony of witnesses, medical reports, but by definition the bodies I had worn had only gaps in their memories to offer, not hard information.

Nowhere did it tell of my previous employment.

If it had, perhaps Nathan Coyle would have tried that much harder when he came to pull the trigger.

A good estate agent will spend months researching a target.

For long-term habitation, a clean skin is advisable: those with no social connections or economic expectations, whose sudden alteration will not be noticed. The ideal candidate is, naturally enough, the comatose patient whose family have given up hope. With no one else at home, it's as clean as it comes to pick the body up for whatever purposes you so desire. The downside of acquiring a body whose original inhabitant is in a vegetative state is you cannot always guarantee the extent of the biological trauma the body itself has suffered. Some muscle atrophy is inevitable; I find that bladder control and various secretions such as tears, saliva and snot can also take a hit, though these can be nursed back to stability with patience, a quality many of my kind lack.

In rare cases ghosts have been known to jump into a vegetative patient only to discover that as well as higher brain activity, muscle control and coordination are entirely out of the window, and so they remain, trapped, awake, paralysed, screaming without a voice, shrieking with no sound, until someone, God almighty be praised, some nurse or passing janitor, accidentally brushes their naked skin, and they can move out again. I once spent two days in such a state, until my body was given a sponge bath, and when I escaped into the nurse I fell on to the floor, weeping with relief to have a body back.

Whatever the risks, a long-term habitation of a clean skin is almost invariably preferable to one with an established history. An estate agent can help: they can teach you the names of brothers, fathers, mothers, daughters, colleagues, friends; they can show you where your skin keeps the car keys, help you learn the signature, fake the accent, tell the tales, to ensure that the leap from skin to skin happens with minimum fuss to the moving ghost. Hopping into any well-established skin is hard; ghosting into Marilyn Monroe was utterly insane.

"She's taking drugs," I said as Aurangzeb sat in my flat and drank my wine. The great glass window of the living room looked out and down from the LA hills on to a city like a circuit board, red and yellow twinkling in the smog beneath us.

"So?" she asked. "Who isn't in this town?"

"She's mixing drugs and drink."

"Come on." Aurangzeb rolled her eyes. "Having me in residence will be a lucky break for the girl! Couple of clean days, you know?"

"Have you had much experience of the physiological effect of dependency?"

"A day – two at most – I think the body will make it a coupla days without going to shit, you know? Gimme the stuff I can use. Who's she sleeping with, what's her agent's name, who's the guy she owes money to, that sorta stuff. Is she ..." She shuffled forward eagerly. "Is she sleeping with Kennedy?"

"Even if she is," I replied, "Monroe's response is coyness, and I suggest you try that yourself. The golden phrase is 'I don't really want to talk about that now.'"

"Whatever – I can do that."

"She's no dope," I added quickly. "Whatever you do, don't play her as a dope. She becomes vapid as a defence mechanism, is blunt when she's sure of her power. You can't be sure of anything with this level of research, so for God's sake play it empty. But not dumb."

"I don't know what you're so worried about," said Aurangzeb, stretching her stockinged legs across my tabletop. "I thought you'd be up for this."

"Honestly," I replied, shuffling my papers out of the way of her heeled shoes, "I don't see the point."

"You don't see the point of being Marilyn fucking Monroe?" she squeaked.

"No. Is it wealth you want? There's richer people out there. The body? There are prettier bodies. You want fame? You want to feel adored, adulated for a night? They're not adoring you, it's not *you* they'll praise. You want to experience that high, find the body of a dresser or a stage manager, and as the actor goes on for their final bow, grab them by the wrist and walk out to the roaring of the crowd. Or learn to do it for yourself. Find a pretty body – an anonymous pretty body – and I'll jump into producers and casting directors in any studio in LA and tick that box by your name right up to the moment when you turn to the camera and smile your cosmetic moonlit smile."

Aurangzeb had rolled her eyes when my words began, and now she rolled them again as I finished. "You want me to *work*? I could be Clark Gable like that." She snapped her long manicured fingers. "I could walk Laurence Olivier naked round London; I could be fucking Marlon Brando – I could be Marlon Brando fucking – and you wanna tell me to sit back and take, what, five years out of my life, maybe ten, to get what I could get in a day? What the hell is wrong with you?" She leaned forward, legs swinging down, eyes bright. "I heard things about you. I thought you were the kinda guy who *lived*."

"What kind of things did you hear?" I asked softly.

"That you were a guy who tried things out. That you'd been the fat soprano, the airline pilot; you'd shaken hands right into the Oval Office. I heard you did stuff too, like, back in the war. I heard that there were more forgetful soldiers staggering around central Europe in 1943 than there were fucking V1s dropped on London."

"I had no idea Janus gossiped so much. And what did you do in the war?"

"Moved about. America. Canada. I thought it'd be cool to hitch a ride with a GI on a ship to Europe, once the U-boats were going down, but in the end I tagged along with a co-pilot and faked food poisoning over the Atlantic. Way easier. I saw the liberation of Paris."

"And what was that like?"

"It was shit," she replied. "Guys marching up and down and people waving and bands playing, and I thought, where were you last week, where were you yesterday, when you didn't know if you were gonna wave the fucking tricolour or the swastika? Then I found out that the guy I was wearing was a collaborator and that dampened my mood." She slammed her hands down into her thighs and exclaimed, "The war was so fucking lame!" and it occurred to me that, for all her curving clothes and pampered hair, in every way, in every flail of her arms and the way she sat with knees apart, Aurangzeb was through-and-through an American male.

I pinched the bridge of my nose. "OK," I breathed. "We need to get you walking in some higher heels."

Chapter 40

A direct train runs from Vienna to Berlin. It is a white monster decked out with the square red letters DB – Deutsche Bahn. With its origami white cabins and stainless-steel sinks, the slick Berlin sleeper was a triumphant two fingers raised against the Balkans Express.

I had a two-bed berth to myself. With the mattresses folded into the wall, it was a bright white triumph of spatial engineering. Unfolded, you had to squeeze between bunk and wall like an eel through a cracked sluice.

Outside, the full romantic cliché of the German night became apparent, criss-crossed only by the light of the yellow-skimmed autobahn as we raced it north. Low moonlit mist clung to the fields; towns flared, puddles of whiteness; great rivers wound between black hills, little villas of white concrete and clean glass peeking out between the trees, where the stressed families of München and Augsburg went to relax. When the train began to curve east, it did so in a great sweep, luxurious as the painter's brush drawing the final curve of a woman's breast.

I watched the landscape go by, my bed made but untouched. Every body grows used to its own smell, but even I could tell that

I stank. The water from my sink ran either too hot, or too cold, with no middle ground.

At 1 a.m. I heard the shuffle of the stewardess as she made her rounds down the slumbering train. I snapped a bracelet of my handcuffs on to my left wrist, leaned out of my door and whispered, "Madam?" Even at that hour, her smile had been engineered to dazzling perfection. "Madam," I murmured above the heartbeat of the track beneath us, "could you help me?"

Of course, sir. It'd be a pleasure.

I gestured her into the cabin. She followed, eyes curious, smile open. With one person the cabin might have been called cosy; with two it became suffocating.

"May I . . . " she asked,

and I reached out, caught her wrist, jumped.

Nathan Coyle. He was getting better at recognising his own symptoms: as he swayed, dizzy at the release, he tried to lash out, flailing wildly, his hand striking the compartment wall with a *thump* that made him wince. I caught his hand and snapped the handcuffs to the rail on the higher bunk, waited for the dizziness to pass.

Pass it did. He felt the restraint on his left wrist, saw the hand-cuff, groaned and slouched back against the wall. "Right," he grunted. "Where now?"

"Train to Berlin."

He raised one drooping eyebrow to examine me. "What are you supposed to be? I thought you only went in for whores and garbage men."

I smoothed down my uniform. "I think I look rather smart. You missed the joy that was Kapikule, or the Balkans Express, or Slovakian buses, so you probably lack the appreciation for a smiling face as it stamps your ticket that I have. Thankfully, you and I will both benefit from Deutsche Bahn's breakfast tray with marmalade."

"I hate marmalade."

"I like it," I retorted. "I could eat pots of the stuff."

He straightened a little, turned to fully examine me. "Are you . . . threatening me with breakfast condiments?"

I tucked a loose strand of hair behind a delicate ear, and said, "I have an address for Alice Mair."

His fists tightened. "She'll be ready for you," he breathed.

"I know. By now your friends will be scouring Europe for you – or rather me, or let's say us. That they haven't found us is something we can perhaps both be grateful for. I've been through the Kepler file and I can't work out what deed I directly performed that could induce such personal hatred in you. Professional dislike and business animosity I can comprehend. In the last ten years I have worn prostitutes, beggars, criminals, liars, killers, thieves. I haven't always been . . . I was not always what I am now, but surely you can see, I have tried my best." I shivered, suddenly cold in my uniform shirt. "Your file is a lie. Perhaps you assume I've killed, that I've . . . worn a body for a night, ridden high on the sex and heroin, and left it to die of the overdose, alone on the hospital floor. I have lived longer than you know, and I have carved . . . turmoil through my past. You talked to my hosts. Were they unhappy? Were they left naked and alone? As samples of my species go, you must be able to see, you must know . . . I am a bad choice of target."

He didn't speak, didn't move. I hissed in frustration, my thin arms wrapped tight across my bony chest. "You presume the high ground. Most murderers do. But it was me you should have killed, not Josephine."

Was that hesitation in his face? A quiver of a thought more than hate? It was hard to tell. I had spent too much time in his features, not looking at them.

"Who is Galileo?" I asked and saw his weight shift, one foot to the other, then back again.

"How long has it been?" he said. "It was only a few minutes ago that I shot you in Taksim; a second ago you were a bin man in . . . some place. Somewhere else. How long has it been, really?"

I dredged my thoughts back. "Five days? And it wasn't me you shot."

"Yes, it was," he replied, sharp as a tack through the toe. "It was you I shot; and a tragedy that it wasn't you who died."

"But your orders were to kill Josephine too."

"Yes."

"Why?"

"She was compromised."

"By what?"

"You know."

"I really don't."

"She killed our people."

"She really didn't, but I can see this argument getting circular."

He tugged loosely against the cuff around his wrist, irritated rather than testing its strength. At last: "You must be very intimate with my body."

"Yes."

"What do you think?" he asked, twisting so I could admire it fully. "You have an unusual perspective. Do I fulfil your requirements? Is my face stern enough, are my legs of a suitable length, do you enjoy the colour of my hair?"

"A stern face is not the consequence of the body that bore it."

"I cannot imagine my face in any shape other than the look I give it."

"I can," I retorted. "You've looked after yourself, that much is clear. Hard to say whether you've fallen foul of that fine line between fitness and vanity. I was curious about the scar across your stomach. Also you need to think about spectacles." His mouth twisted in surprise. "Take it from an expert; you'll be wanting reading glasses sooner rather than later."

"My eyes are twenty twenty!"

Amazing, the indignant pride people invest in natural processes.

Astonishing, how deeply vanity is ingrained.

I tried to put my hands on my hips, but in the confined space of the cabin I could only manage one hand on one side. "Are you saying that to impress me?" I asked. "Because I imagine, having been in residence for a while, that you're the kind of man to take pride in his physical prowess, but there's no point being foolish when it comes to your eyesight. I've had cataracts, infections, long-sightedness, short-sightedness, partial blindness . . . "

"Not you!" he snapped. "Not you. Someone else's eyes, someone else's blindness."

"Me," I replied. "I, myself. These are the things I have experienced. I have walked bodies into courtrooms because they were too afraid to speak. I've held a skin down while they gave me the general anaesthetic because the tumour-ridden schmuck was too scared of hospitals to go through the treatment. Think whatever you want about who I am, but don't waste your breath denying my experience."

He tried bristling for a moment longer, shoulders high and eyebrows low, but the effect was too conscious now, and he abandoned it. I slunk down on to the bottom bunk. My nails were shellacked to a fascinating firmness. My back ached, my uniform belt was tight, and as I pressed my hands against my spine, a thought struck me. "Am I . . ." I blurted. Coyle stared at me, one eyebrow raised. I ran my hands carefully across my midriff, pressing deep into my soft skin, feeling for something beneath the warmth. "I think I'm pregnant."

The train rattled, and no one spoke. Then the tiniest shiver passed down Coyle's spine, his shoulders jerked and he gave a single, high hoot of merriment.

"Bloody hell," I groaned.

Coyle's laughter subsided as quickly as it had come. Outside, fields of freshly turned earth stretched away to the flat horizon. A full moon sat in a cloudless sky, promising icy winds and frozen soil come morning. I pressed my hands against my belly and felt something turn which wasn't my stomach. "This is . . . peculiar," I said.

"You're not enamoured of the joy of childbirth?" asked Coyle. "I thought you would have given it a go, just for the experience."

I scowled. "During times of stress I have been known to make . . . unexpected jumps. And while I'm sure giving birth is a wonderfully life-enhancing experience, if it comes with the associated baggage of planning, expectation and the optimism of another eighteen years of happy nurturing by the family fireside, when there's a fifty/fifty chance that you might mid-convulsion find yourself a mewling infant still attached by an umbilical cord to a shrieking and confused woman, I'm sure you can see why the exercise might lose some of its appeal."

An idea dawned on Coyle's face. "You could . . . *ghost* into a foetus?"

"What a truly ghastly idea."

"You've never tried."

"Absolutely not."

"Never been tempted?"

"Not in the least. I have no delusions about the joy of physicality. Having inhabited almost every size, shape and form of body you can possibly imagine, the only conclusions are these: exercise when you're still young enough to appreciate it, look after your spine, and if you have the option, use an electric toothbrush."

"Decades of stealing bodies and that's your big conclusion?"

"Yep."

"How long have you been a ghost?"

I glanced up and saw his eyes bright upon me. "Wouldn't you love to know. How'd you get that scar across your stomach, Mr Coyle?"

"You know it's not my name."

"Curiously enough, that doesn't bother me. A few hundred years." His eyes flickered, and I leaned forward, one hand pressed instinctively over my belly. "A few hundred years," I repeated, soft against the bouncing of the train. "I was murdered on the streets of London. My brains were bashed in. As I lay there, I caught the ankle of my killer. I hated him, feared him, dreaded him for killing me, and was so frightened of dying alone, I needed him, longed for him to stay with me. Next thing I knew, I was staring at my own corpse. I was arrested for it, an irony which has never entertained. Not a glamorous beginning, truth be told, but it seems the urge to live outweighs all other instincts."

"Who were you when you died?"

"I was . . ." the words drifted somewhere at the back of my throat " . . . no one of significance. What about you, Mr Coyle? How'd you get that scar?"

Silence.

"Galileo," he said and stopped.

I waited.

"Galileo," he tried again. "Stuck a knife in me."

"A ghost?"

"Yes."

"Why'd he stab you?"

"I was the last one left standing."

"Where?"

"*Santa Rosa.*"

"You said these things before."

A small shake of his head, a smile. He can't believe what he's saying. Now would not be the time to question the notion.

"There's . . . a rumour," he murmured. "A myth. Over time the story has outgrown the seeds that sowed it. Yet for all that, there is some truth in it. A ferry ride, a few hours, across the Straits of Malacca, perhaps through the Baltic Sea. The engine stops, and as the passengers and crew wait for rescue, a body is found. The body is . . . someone, doesn't matter. Throat cut, blood on the deck and everyone panics until someone points out that the killer cannot have escaped being seen, must have been caught on camera, drenched in blood. They look. They find the murderer, who sits huddled in a toilet, shaking with fear, blood on his, her – whoever's – face, on their hands, their clothes. We have the killer, they say. As soon as the engines are fixed we shall take this murderer to the police on shore.

"Then another body is found, intestines pulled out, eyes popping up at nothing, tongue lolling in a vacant mouth, and everyone goes, it is not the killer we have caught, or perhaps who we've caught is working with someone else, and the panic spreads, and this ferry has too few staff to too many passengers, no hope of order, so the captain orders all passengers to a muster point. Everyone stay in one place, he says, no one move, and we shall be safe. Safety in numbers. It is a comforting thought until the first mate sees that at the muster point on the first-class deck the passengers are all dead. Some have blood on their hands, some on their faces; some tried to bite the ears off their neighbours; some ran; some fled, but one remains, standing, grinning at the camera, before he too waves goodbye and is, within a few minutes, himself found dead.

"In the three hours it takes the coastguard to board the ferry and fix the engines, seventeen people are dead, five are in a critical condition. And when the forensic police examine the corpses, they find that each body carries the stamp of someone else's DNA, as though for every victim there was a different murderer, a different set of fingerprints on the blade. Do you know this story?" he asked, gaze returning from a distant place.

"Yes," I said. "I know it."

"Do you know the names? Of the ships, of the dead?"

"Some," I replied. "There was a frigate in 1899 off the coast of Hong Kong. A cruiser in 1924. A ferry in 1957, though that was never confirmed – someone opened the cargo bay doors and the living went down with the dead. Something similar happened in 1971: twenty-three dead, the authorities claimed pirate attack. A yacht in 1983 off the coast of Scotland. Two people died on board, a small body count by his standards, but still him. We all know the rumours."

He nodded at nothing at all. "*Santa Rosa*," he breathed. "October 1999."

"You were there?" I asked.

"Yes. I killed a man. I don't remember doing it, but I opened my eyes and there was blood on my hands, and a man with a hollow of blood filling the indent beneath his throat. He was alive, but when he breathed, bubbles popped, and then he wasn't alive, and I was holding the knife and a woman stood in front of me and watched me watch him die. She took the blade from my fingers – it was a kitchen knife from the canteen – and put one hand on my shoulder like a mother and stuck the blade in me, rocked it around, smiled and didn't say a word. They classed me with the dead until the pathologist called out that I had a pulse. Then they called me murderer. Which, in a way, I was."

"Galileo?"

He nodded, though barely at me or the word I spoke.

"You should have said," I breathed. "I could have helped."

"Helped?" The word choked out, almost a laugh. "You're a fucking ghost. What good are you to anyone?"

"Might've been some. I've met your Galileo."

Now his head turned, eyes striking like an axe on ice. "Where?"

"St Petersburg, Madrid, Edinburgh, Miami. Not since Miami."

"You're sure?"

"Yes."

"How?"

"Contrary to popular opinion, not every ghost you meet is inclined to once-every-twenty-years outbreaks of psychopathic extermination," I replied. "Those that are, you tend to remember."

"Tell me!"

"Why?" I breathed, and saw him almost flinch. "You are hell-bent on killing me. You killed Josephine, and for all that this is a perfectly friendly little encounter, give or take my hormonal condition and the handcuffs, I find it hard to simply forget the turbulent nature of our relationship. You'd kill me, Mr Coyle, because a ghost nearly killed you. I am not that ghost. You'd kill me for what I am. Why should I help you find Galileo?"

His lips thinned; he turned away, then as quickly turned back. "Because if you didn't help me, knowing anything at all, it would prove that you are the monster I think you are."

"You think that anyway. Give me something more. Why did you kill Josephine?"

"Orders."

"Why?"

"Because I respect the men that give them. Because the file said . . . " His tongue tangled on the words. "Because the file said she murdered four of our researchers. She did. Not you – her."

"Why?"

"She attempted to infiltrate one of our projects. A medical trial. You should know this."

"I know some. She needed money, a medical trial in Frankfurt, something for the common cold. They rejected her when they realised she was a hooker. I did my research too, before making a deal with Josephine Cebula."

He shook his head. "It wasn't for the common cold."

"You astonish me. What was it?"

"Vaccinations."

"Against?" He didn't answer. A thought. I leaned back, feeling the idea settle like dusty cobwebs on clean skin. "Oh. Against us. You were trying to find a vaccine against us. Did it work?"

"Not with four of our researchers murdered."

"Wasn't me."

"But it was Josephine. I saw footage, CCTV. I saw her with blood on her hands. Then you came to Frankfurt, made her an offer. What were we to think?"

I inhaled the words. I wasn't sure if I trusted myself not to have a violent physical reaction. My fingers pressed over my belly. "You believe . . . that I became Josephine because of some medical trial? You think she and I launched some kind of *attack* against your people? Conspired to murder Doctor whoever-it-was and all his happy brood?"

He thought about it. "Yes. That is what I believe."

Smell of detergent on my fingertips, a memory of fruit tea at the back of my throat. I counted backwards from ten slowly, and said, "You're wrong."

Coyle did not reply.

The train was slowing, carriages clunking against each other as we decelerated towards a siding. I wondered how this body would cope with pregnancy. It seemed a stick-skinny thing, frail ankles and tight waist. I wondered if fruit tea was any use against morning sickness.

"Who do you work for?" I asked.

He shook his head.

"You know I'll find out."

"Tell me about Galileo."

"I'm going to keep on wearing your body, Mr Coyle, until someone shoots me in it. You want a happy outcome, I'm going to need more information."

"You need information?" His voice was a half-laugh, having nothing better to do with itself. "Ten minutes ago it was midday in Istanbul. A man touched me on the train and I was somewhere else, wearing new clothes, talking to someone new. You've stripped me naked, talked with my tongue, eaten with my mouth, sweated and pissed and swallowed my spit, and you need information? Fuck you, Kepler. Fuck you."

Silence.

The train bounced across an uneven set of points, slowing now, the engine winding down. Perhaps there was a station nearby, a midnight traveller looking for a ride. Perhaps a siding where we might sit for a few hours while the driver had a cup of coffee, smoked a cigarette on the side of the track. The engine chunked to itself, unwilling to sleep.

I felt my hands on my belly and wondered what my child would grow up to be.

Perhaps he'd work on the railways like mum?

Perhaps she would dream of being something more.

A politician, perhaps, who in thirty years' time would stand before the nation and proclaim, "My mother rode the tracks between Berlin and Vienna to support me in my youth, so that the future I could make would be better than the life she lived."

Or maybe none of the above.

Maybe my child would grow up quiet and alone, a mother perpetually travelling, postcards from abroad, a sense that her life was not her own.

"Galileo," I said, staring at nothing in particular. "You want to know about Galileo?"

An intake of breath, his eyes on my face.

I told him.

Chapter 41

St Petersburg in 1912, and you could almost believe the Romanovs had got away with it. I had heard the rifles crack in 1905, seen barricades in the street and believed, as had many others, that the dynasty's days were numbered. The social reforms could not keep up with the demands of economics; the political reforms could not keep up with the changes in society, and so, kicking its way into the twentieth century, it had seemed inevitable that some part of Russia would get caught on the wire.

Yet in 1912, dancing beneath the chandeliers of the Winter Palace, silk gloves rolled to my elbows and hair held high with silver and crystal, I could believe that this world would last for ever.

I was Antonina Baryskina, seventh daughter of a grand old duke, and I was there to demonstrate an eligibility that my host singularly lacked. Antonina, sixteen years old, was already branded a flirt, a harlot in the making, and worst of all the kind of woman who would sleep with a proletarian largely because her daddy forbade her from doing so. No coercion, wheedling or downright threat had yet coaxed Antonina into reforming her ways. As rumours threatened to burst into flame, a Moscow estate agent by the name of Kuanyin approached me with an unusual commission from the father.

"Six months," she said. "Beautiful woman, beautiful life. There is, I think, no existence on this earth more refined than the Baryskina girl."

"And in return for this . . . refined existence?"

"It is asked that you manifest a maturity worthy of the rewards that are bestowed."

"To what purpose?"

"To prove to the world that Antonina Baryskina is open for business."

I loved being Antonina Baryskina. She had a beautiful bay mare who I rode every morning regardless of the cold; owned a cello which she had almost never played but whose strings, when pressed, sang like the weeping of an widowed god, and as I danced, and laughed, and discussed the current political climate and the state of the weather, the rumours of Antonina-that-was fell away, and across St Petersburg eligible men queued to catch a glimpse of this reformed heiress.

The bores I ignored; the handsome and the witty I permitted to visit me in my mansion on the banks of the canal, feeding them coffee and Turkish delight. Several brought prepared verse and song to entertain me, and I clapped my hands and felt really quite giddy at the rapt adulation of so many noblemen. I have waved my banners with the suffragettes, marched for civil rights and the equality of man, and still feel a flush of excitement at the recollection of handsome men reciting verses to my honour.

In time, my father came to me and said, "You are receiving a great many eligible visitors to this house, and I think the time has come to discuss marriage prospects."

He had never known how to speak to his daughter. He knew even less how to speak to the mind that now wore his daughter's flesh. I said, "The commission was to keep me away from treasure-hunting lieutenants and unwise sexual behaviour long enough to undo the potential smirch on my name. Nowhere did our arrangement extend to finding marriageable material."

It takes the full force of a magnificent Russian beard to truly bristle, and bristle it did. "I do not suggest that *you* marry the gentlemen!" he retorted. "Simply that we must start laying the groundwork for my daughter."

After some haggling I agreed to dine with the top ten most eligible and wealthy bachelors my father could find. I dismissed four on the first encounter for behaviours ranging from the boorish to the barbaric, while retaining the other six at the end of a very long social leash. In time my father came to respect my judgment and, for a few brief moments, would almost forget that it was I, not his daughter, who he addressed.

"You are aware," I said one day, "that when my tenancy expires, the individual these gentlemen have come to admire will be replaced by, if you don't mind me saying, your daughter."

"My daughter desires only one thing in this world – to be adored," replied my father as we sat in the gloom of his swaddled coach, bouncing its way over the Moscow cobbles at the gorging hour of night. "As it was, that need made her a thoroughly unadorable creature. It is my hope that, once she realises that she is already adored, thanks to your groundwork, she will settle down and become rather more manageable. Even if she does not, it is satisfactory for now that her reputation has been salvaged, and perhaps in a few years, when we have beaten the demon out of her, she can return and reclaim the reputation you have made."

"You are not concerned by the ... unorthodox nature of our relationship?"

"To which relationship do you refer?"

"To mine and your daughter's, perhaps," I murmured. "And pursuant to that, my relationship to you and yours to your child."

He was silent a while as we rattled through the chittering night-time streets. At last: "On accepting this commission, it was necessary that you acquainted yourself with my family's history. Did you do so?"

"Of course."

"Then you have done more than my daughter," he grunted.

"Whatever your motives may have been. You will be aware that my family has a long history of military service. My father, in particular, fought in the Crimea and was applauded for gallantry."

"I have read the same."

"Lies," he replied flatly. "My father did not fight in the Crimea. His body was in attendance and by all accounts warred gallantly, yet of the battles engaged, the foes struck down, I assure you my father had not one memory. He could not bear the sight of blood but is famed to this day as a mighty warrior. Can you conceive of how this situation came to pass?"

"Yes," I breathed. "I rather think I can."

He straightened, half-nodding at a purpose unseen. "You wonder why I would permit – forgive me, that is not the word – why I would invite you to assume the role of my daughter. You consider it unfit for a father? I would answer to you this: that if you were to have a gangrenous leg cut off, or to stand before a lover and declare that your love is dead; that if the necessity of your position commanded you to kill a friend, to stick a knife into the throat of a man who has ever been loyal – what would you give *not* to do it? And what would you give for it to be done?"

"What makes you think another would do what you cannot?"

"Because it is not *your* lover you destroy, yet they, in looking on you, are destroyed as truly. My daughter derides her birth and damns her family, and yes. This is better."

The halt of the carriage came with a two-three of rocking bodies and the stamp of horses' hooves by the kerb. For a moment my father did not move. Then, "There is a question I would ask."

"Please."

"When we met, you wore my servant's body, and said, call me Josef, the name of the man you wore. Now you wear my daughter, and say, call me Antonina and you ... speak alone with men, and wash yourself before the mirror and ... engage in those personal acts of womanhood that I would rather not consider too deeply. Here is my question: who are you? When you are neither Antonina nor Josef, who are you when you lay my daughter's head down to sleep?"

I considered this problem. "I am a well-bred daughter of Russia. I am a cellist with a love for a bay mare that I spoil greatly. I am polite at the dinner table, charming with those who merit my attention and dismissive to those young gentlemen whose intentions are inclined only towards my modesty or my wealth. All this is true. What else matters?"

He shifted, readying himself to speak, so I reached out with my gloved fingers, resting them on his liver-spotted hand. "Did your father ask who it was who slew his way across the Crimea?" I breathed. "Did he want to know?"

"No. I don't believe he did. There were rumours of . . . some vile things permitted in my father's body, and yet I suppose in war vile things are accepted."

"Then ask yourself this – do you want to know who it is you have permitted into your daughter's flesh?"

I saw his Adam's apple rise and sink in the half-gloom of the carriage, Then, with a brighter bark he exclaimed, "Well, what is it we are seeing tonight, Antonina?"

What we were seeing was a show of minimal merit, and that night as the curtain fell I applauded the actors and smiled at the audience, and a reasonable percentage of the audience applauded me, for I was beautiful and wealthy, the perfect picture of who Antonina should be.

And then in the crowd that swirled beneath the chandelier of the lobby – for no one of society came to the theatre just for the play – a chubby finger prodded my elbow and a small voice said, "I know who you are."

I looked down and beheld a little girl, her hair done up in doll-like curls. Her tiny dress of pink silk clung to an undeveloped chest, yet she wore rouge on her cheeks and as her fingers brushed my arm, I felt a buzzing in my teeth like a wasps' nest doused in smoke.

"Do you?" I murmured, studying the face that studied mine.

"Yes. I love your dress."

"Thank you, Miss . . . ?"

"Senyavin. I'm . . . oh!" A tiny hand went to her mouth, holding back a giggle. "Am I Tulia or Tasha? We look so alike, I can't always tell, and mummy calls us both 'angel'."

I drew further into the candle-washed gloom of the theatre, pulling my cape tight across my thin shoulders. "And how long has your mummy called you that?"

"All my life, I suppose," replied the child, "But it's only been two weeks." Her head tipped to one side, staring at me crookedly. "I burned Tulia's dolls' house. Or maybe Tasha's. The rooms were painted in pink, and I wanted them blue, and they said no. So I burned it. What do you do?"

"I salvage the reputations of young women too naïve to realise what a good reputation is worth," I replied. "But in two weeks' time, I imagine I'll be someone else."

"Only two weeks?" asked Senyavin. "I'm moving out tonight. Look." She pointed across the room, a chubby finger lancing a man in a bright red sash and curled dark moustache, standing iron-straight in the centre of the foyer, slim glass between three fingers. "Do you like what you see? He's beautiful, yes?"

"Very pleasant."

The girl turned back to me, face full of concern. "I wanted to let you know," she explained. "When I realised who you were, I wanted you to understand that he's mine. I love him already. I love his sweat. I love his smell. His eyes smile even when his lips are still, his hair is soft and falls that way across his brow by nature, not hard work. He works to keep his hands still, but they still twitch at his side, bursting with energy, and when I kiss a woman with his lips she'll cry out, no, I can't, no, and then kiss me harder because she knows what I know. She knows that I am beautiful. If I could keep him for ever, I would, just like this, perfect. But people get old, flesh withers, so now – now I need to be him while he's still perfect, before his face changes. He's so beautiful, I thought, what if you try to move in? That couldn't happen. Too much noise, not enough room. So I thought I'd say hello and tell you. He's mine. I love him. Touch him and I'll rip your eyes out and feed them to my pussy cat."

So saying, little Senyavin smiled a delightful smile, grabbed two fingers of my hand with her fist and shook it goodbye. I stood in silence and watched her as she skipped brightly away.

That was what I believe to be my first meeting with the entity known as Galileo.

It was not my last.

Chapter 42

On the train to Berlin Coyle stood in silence, eyes half-closed as he digested my words. "You're older than you seem."

I shrugged. "I move with the times. My skin, my clothes, my body. I own an MP3 player, I have a piercing in my tongue. I choose to have piercings, tattoos, cosmetic surgery; I choose to be who I am, and a lot of the time I choose to be young. Youthful flesh induces a youthful character, since the physical pains and social responsibilities that temper a nature don't usually affect a twenty-two-year-old with a penchant for punk. I like it that way; it suits my inclination."

"What were you, originally?" he asked. "In . . . your body, your first body, I mean. Man, woman – what were you?"

"Does it matter?"

"I'm curious."

"What do you think?"

"I thought man. It seemed . . . I don't know what it seemed, perhaps it was something assumed, what we always assume."

"And now?"

"Women were beaten to death in dark alleys as well as men," he replied. "What's your name?"

"Kepler will do just fine, as Coyle works for you."

"You have no preference – for either sex, I mean?"

"I have a preference for good teeth and strong bones," I replied. "I have a preference for clear skin and, I must admit it, I have something of a weakness for red hair, when I find it, and it's real. Say what you will for the nineteenth century, at least you weren't being continually wrong-footed by convincing dye jobs."

"You're a snob."

"I've been enough people to recognise when they're trying too hard to be something they're not. I can help you," I added. "If Galileo wore you, used you – if he's your target – I can help you."

"How would you do that?"

"You have something else?" He didn't answer. "Who are you working for?"

Silence.

"Do you believe what they told you about Frankfurt? Do you believe they were trying to make a vaccine?"

Silence.

"Josephine was a host of convenience. We made a deal because she needed the cash and I wanted a change. My involvement need not equate to your employer's destruction, but I need – I would like – you to give me some reason, some tiny shadow of a doubt as to why, when I find them, and find them I shall, I do not destroy them all."

Our gazes locked. I had looked into Coyle's eyes in the bathroom mirror for days, and all I had seen in them had been contempt. "They try their best," he said. "The best that can be done."

A scowl pulled at my lips – too pretty, too happy with the prospect of motherhood, assuming my body had noticed its fate, to be so distorted. "Not good enough," I said, grabbed him by the hand and switched.

Chapter 43

I lie awake on the sleeper train, and remember ...

Marilyn Monroe.

What a bloody stupid idea that had been.

On a hot autumn evening in suburban LA I slipped into Louis Quinn, aspiring actor, model, full-time waiter, and, balancing a tray of champagne on my fingertips, went to visit the stars.

The house was a mansion, and the mansion – as with every building in LA – had a swimming pool. She was reclined beside it, champagne in one hand, hair unkempt and laughter shrill. They say that the camera adds five pounds to anyone it films. It is no more than we do to ourselves already, judging every fold of flesh as if it were a newborn monster. I have worn slim, beautiful creatures, stood naked before a mirror and suddenly seen that I am fat, or wrinkly, or somehow less than what I seemed to be when I beheld myself through the eyes of a stranger.

Marilyn Monroe was, to my mind, more beautiful off the screen than on it, for even with her chubby belly and bulbous chin, she dressed herself to the pleasure of her own eye, and that gave more satisfaction than any costumier could have achieved.

Except perhaps tonight. It seemed to me, looking at her spotted pants and loosely tied bikini, that someone had dressed for the character of Marilyn, rather than the woman she should have been, and it made her ugly.

I laid my tray down and slipped from my waiter into the producer queuing for her attention, and as the waiter staggered bewildered behind me I leaned down to whisper into Marilyn's ear:

"Aurangzeb."

Her features crinkled as if she'd bitten a sour plum. She rolled her head round slowly, fixed me with a glower and hissed, "What the hell are you doing here?"

"Might we have a word in private?"

"I'm with my friends!"

"Yes, you are. We should talk."

"Fine." She scowled, grabbing a towel and slinging it around her midriff. "It was getting dull here anyway."

She led the way to the end of the garden, where green hedges had been trimmed into the shape of a squashed-nose cat, a dog with his paws raised, an umbrella in a cocktail glass and other such offences against topiary. When secluded behind the nearest of these, she rounded on me and snapped, "What?"

"It's been five days," I said. "In and out, we agreed – two days at most."

"Jesus!" she exclaimed, throwing her hands up in a parody of frustration. "What the fuck is wrong with you? These people *love me*. They think I'm great – better than the real Marilyn. People have been asking what I've been taking, whether I'm seeing someone, I'm so much calmer than I was, so much more ... you know ... more!" She flapped, unable to find the words. "I just had John Huston *beg* me to do another film, said I'd be perfect."

"And that's delightful. But what do you plan on doing when they put you in front of a camera and you can't act?"

"This is Hollywood! People will see the picture because I'm in it, not because of what I'm doing."

"It's not that I'm averse to you destroying a career, if it comes to it, but sooner or later people *will* talk, people *are* talking, and I will not be responsible for creating the single noisiest scandal that has ever affected our kind. If Marilyn Monroe loses a week of her memory, that's OK. That's practically par for the course in this town. If she loses six months, or a year, or five years, and wakes up at the end of that in some B-movie with her knickers on her head because that's all you were capable of pulling, then we have a problem and I will not go down as the estate agent who brokered that. So I'm telling you now – get out. Find a different body."

"No."

"No?"

"No." Aurangzeb had worked hard on that pout. "I'm here now. I'm doing it. I can make this work."

I stood back a pace. "That your final answer?"

"Yes."

"All right."

Her lips parted in surprise, then opened in a shriek of laughter. "That it? That all you gotta say to me?"

"That's it," I replied. "I'm going to find the waiter I walked in here in – he had nice hands – and get out. Might go somewhere chilly. Canada, perhaps. Alaska. See the Northern Lights."

"Jesus, you *are* the lamest thing *ever!*"

"Sure. I'm lame. I've had the loud life and now I like the quiet. I've also spiked your champagne."

The laughter forming on her breath froze, diminished, shrank. Her face twisted through a kaleidoscope of emotion, none pleasant. "You're lying," she blurted. "You wouldn't dare."

"Sure I would. I came in here as a waiter. If there's one thing we're good at – one thing we ought to *excel* at, you and I – it is blending with the crowd. Enjoy the stomach pump."

I turned. I walked away.

"Hey!" she called after me. Then, "Hey . . . you!"

A void where my name should have been. If she'd paid more attention to the file I'd compiled for her, she could have found my picture right there, neatly annotated for her attention, but

156

Aurangzeb was lazy, hadn't bothered to do her homework. "Hey!" she shrieked, loud enough for people to turn. I smiled serenely, walked over to where my bewildered waiter was trying to gather his thoughts and, laying my hand on his arm, I murmured, "You all right, son?" and jumped.

Playing the violin, speaking French, an intimate knowledge of the Dodgers.

If all these fail, and you really, really want to know if your target is a ghost in hiding, gastro-enteritis is another great way to go.

Chapter 44

Sleeper trains never pull into their final destination at a reasonable hour.

6.27 a.m. is not a good time to start the day.

No shops are open, no coffee is to be found except cheap brown sludge for the earliest of the early-morning commuters who are too harried or hung over to care. You can't check in at a hotel, but must sit on what luggage you have in whatever café will take you and wonder why you didn't fly.

The weather was notably colder. Over the last five days the skies had darkened with the soil, and as I shuffled blearily on to the glass-and-steel concourse of Berlin Hauptbahnhof, my breath condensed in the air.

I like Berlin.

I liked it before it was levelled, and I like the way it was rebuilt. The architects of the new Berlin didn't fall into the trap of believing that all that went before must be perfectly resurrected, nor that the past as a whole should be buried. Rather they fused the best that had been with the best innovation had to offer, rejecting the concrete-tower-block solution adopted by so many 1950s town planners and instead embracing apartment living, broad streets and the planting of as many trees as their budget could buy. In West Berlin this created a wealth of greenery, grown up over the years into balmy groves lining genteel streets, and great parks where children could hide between the gnarled roots, sounds of the city lost through the undergrowth. In East Berlin the development had been less idyllic, and only now were the trees planted beginning to grow into their full leaf beneath the functional towers and sensible estates of the industrial planners in a hurry to get grinding.

I like the vegetables you can buy in Berlin, fatter and sweeter than the usual supermarket stuff; I appreciate how easy it is to be a cyclist in the city, with ways through the parks, pedestrianised roads and traffic that yields at every green light to the mob of two-wheeled commuters that has saturated the street before it. I like the schnitzel, the creamy potatoes, the beer, the noise where it should be noisy, the calm where it should be quiet. I have no time for boiled sausages, or boiled vegetables of any nature really, and cannot for the life of me comprehend why anyone would still insist on serving dishes whose whole cooking process consisted of exposure to water, to freely invited guests.

The fact that Alice Mair, partner of Nathan Coyle and a woman who would probably, if the company she kept was anything to go by, be quite content to kill me on sight, lived in this same well-ordered city only mildly dampened my spirits.

First task – a place to stash Coyle.

I bought the least bad coffee I could find and went in search of an internet café.

Estate agents have always existed for my kind, in one way or another. They are a useful tool when you are in a difficult situation: an expert in whoever you need them to be, they can salvage a body gone wrong, help you find your path to a body that will go right.

The estate agent in Berlin went by the name Hecuba.

I tried phoning her office, and the number was disconnected.

I tried emailing her from a dummy account, and the message pinged back immediately: not recognised, no one home.

I deleted the email account with which I had attempted contact and moved cafés before continuing my search.

I sent out a few emails to a few contacts – Fyffe, Hera, Kuanyin, Janus. Only Hera replied and no, she hadn't heard from Hecuba for years.

I even tried Johannes Schwarb, who replied immediately that no, that site had been taken down, and hey, you in Berlin, you wanna hang out?

Thanks, Spunkmaster13, I replied. I'll let you know.

Hecuba was nowhere to be found.

Irritated, I tried a few more mundane sources. The process was slower, and the euros ebbed away as I trawled through vague memories of half-heard names and faces, until I stumbled on one which was familiar. She'd got herself a haircut, a brand new suit and some fifteen years of experience, but Ute Sauer was still my skin.

I called her up from a payphone.

I don't do that any more, she replied.

Wouldn't ask if it wasn't important. Willing to beg, I said.

She was silent a long while on the end of the line. Then, "Zehlendorf," she said. "I'll pick you up. Who do you look like today?"

Zehlendorf is twee.

From its still-standing buildings of old Germany through to its semi-detached houses framed with grass and running water, Zehlendorf is the place to buy hemp handbags, straw sunhats and a sense of organic, universal belonging. In summer it is the Berlin countryside without the inconvenience of leaving the city. In winter the sounds of happy children's choirs are inflicted on innocent shoppers as they shuffle through snow-crusted streets. Ute picked me up from the U-Bahn. She drove a silver hybrid, and as she pushed the passenger door open with one hand, with the other she swept a pile of CDs on to the back seat, Mozart quintets and *Little Songs For Happy Children*. I ducked in beside her, and as we pulled away her car wheedled at me, demanding seatbelts be worn.

"I hate it when it does that," grumbled Ute. "I can't put my shopping in the front seat any more. It's like we're all fucking children, being told by machines what we can and can't do. Ridiculous, just ridiculous."

Ute Sauer.

When I first met her, she was seventeen, lived in East Berlin, and her father had been arrested by the Stasi.

Get me to the West, she'd said, and my body is yours.

That it is, I replied, but not perhaps in the way you think.

A few years later the Wall fell, but Ute remained on the books of the local estate agent as what she was – a clean willing skin, perfect for short-term engagements or quick reconnoitring trips. She charged an hourly rate for her body and was prepared to let you borrow her car if you promised to obey the speed limit and not double-park. The ideal body to wear on the way to being someone else, Ute prided herself on her dignity, clean health and modest dress. When I left Berlin, she'd stayed on Hecuba's books, running errands for ghosts about town, waiting on the sidelines as Will had waited for me in LA; save that Ute had made a profession of the occupation.

Now we drove through Zehlendorf as the sun rose over the shedding trees, and she said, "I have to pick the kids up at 2.30 from school. Will this take long?"

"Possibly. I tried calling Hecuba, but there wasn't an answer."

Short auburn hair, square face, Ute must have been a stubborn child, evolved now into a mother who knew how to get her way. "Hecuba is dead," she said. "The office was raided, wiped out."

"Who did it?"

"I don't know. I didn't look. I have children now."

"You're safe?"

"No one has come after me, if that's what you're asking."

"That's exactly what I'm asking."

"Then I am safe."

"Do you recognise my body?" I asked.

She glanced at it from the corner of her eye. "No. I've never seen you before. Should I have?"

"No," I breathed, sinking back into the seat. "You shouldn't. I need a place to stash this body for a while."

"Why?" Her voice harder than the tarmac beneath our wheels.

"I don't believe this body to be a threat to you – he's primarily interested in me. But he has attempted to kill me, and if that's a problem, please, say so, and I'll go and there'll be no hard feelings."

Her lips curled in, as she tasted, chewed and digested the idea. Then, a single brisk shake of her head. "My husband sells real estate. There's a house we can keep him. Can we sedate you?"

"Yes."

"Good. We stash, we sedate, you run your business, and I'm at the school gate by 2.30 p.m. Do we understand each other?"

"Yes. Thank you."

"There will be no charge. You ... and I have an understanding. For services previously rendered."

"That's very kind."

"Half past two," she said. "The clock is ticking."

The house was a square mansion of timber and glass with architecturally immense windows built on to balconies of terracotta. Empty rooms were waiting for happy people, white walls too bright to be besmirched, a kitchen too clean to cook in, and a bathroom of polished black stone. I rummaged through my bag for the handcuffs and Coyle's medical kit of needles and blades. I pulled my sleeve up, disinfected the hollow of my elbow, rubbing to bring up the vein, and injected the sedative straight in. The fluid was cold as it entered my body, then warm as it spread. I handcuffed myself to the nearest radiator, both hands behind my back, while Ute disposed of the needle. She knelt down beside me and said, "Is it working?"

I giggled and didn't know why. A flicker that might have been a smile – and I hadn't yet seen her smile – passed across her lips. "I'll take that as a yes," she said, slipping her hand into mine. "Shall we?"

" ... dance?"

Her voice, my words.

I looked down on Nathan Coyle as he opened his eyes. I pulled a sock and a roll of gaffer tape from his bag, stuffed the first in his mouth and wrapped the other across as an indignant blare of sound tried to push up from between his lips. Ute's body was older than the last time I'd worn it, her knees creaked, cartilage wearing thin. Coyle kicked against the floor, strained against the radiator. His eyes moved without focusing, and he tried to snarl again, the sound deteriorating before it had a chance to grow.

"Bye," I said to the rolling whites of his eyes.

I drove back into town in Ute's car. It seemed to me unimaginable that Ute had a single point on her driving licence, and to sully this record induced a childish fear in me. Getting your body a parking ticket and walking away without paying the fine is the height of rudeness.

There was something numb in my chest, a weight I couldn't explain. It was not pain, nor discomfort, nor chills nor an irritant to be scratched. I was halfway up Schönhauser Allee before I realised it was the emptiness left by a surgical scar, a place where flesh had been cut away. Had I focused any awareness on it, it could have dominated my senses, but the need to drive safely and not disturb any of Berlin's highly pedantic policemen pulled my senses away from full understanding.

Ute had not spoken of her scars, and I would not ask.

I parked the car round the corner from Pankow, left the key in the ignition and waited for a dark-skinned businessman to walk by. His hair was short, his shirt was long, his shoes were smart, and as he passed I said, "Excuse me, do you have the time?"

His stride faltered in merely considering whether or not to answer, and as he looked to his watch, my hand curled around his wrist, and I jumped.

Ute swayed a little, supporting herself against the side of the car. I caught her by the shoulders, dropping my briefcase to the ground, and waited for her gaze to come back into focus.

"It's . . . been a while," she said.

"You all right?"

"Fine. I'm ... fine. How am I doing for time?"

"Plenty. And thank you."

She glanced at her watch, scrunching and unscrunching her face as the hands shifted back into focus. "I can wait one more hour," she said. "If you need me."

"I'll be fine. The important thing was stashing Coyle."

"Is that his name?"

"No," I replied. "But it'll have to do."

She looked me up and down, assessing my body, then said, "Is that your style now?"

"No," I grumbled, picking my briefcase up in a sulky sweep. "And I've got athlete's foot."

Neat streets of neat houses. A neat bakery, selling neat loaves on neat trays. Cars, neatly parked, and bicycles politely dinging. Berlin is a city which knows how to keep up appearances.

I walked the few blocks to a neat yellow apartment block on a perfect right-angle corner. Up a cobbled path lined with bins for paper, tin, plastics and organic recycling, to a thick blue door. I looked down the list of names by the buzzer. Alice Mair hadn't bothered to disguise hers.

Wheels rattled on cobbles. I turned to find an elderly lady behind me, a shopping trolley in her hands, hat low on her head. The curvature of her spine pushed her head out almost horizontally from her shoulders, and as I stood aside, she went into her pocket for her door keys. With a slight shudder of apprehension, I reached out and touched her hand.

I hate being old.

Switching from legs which swing along merrily to hips of crumbling calcium and not much hope of repair is a quick path to injury. I took a step and nearly fell over, misjudging the stability of my own bones. I took another far more conservative step and felt tremors rush up my knees and shake my spine. My left hand was curled around the keys in my pocket, and as I pulled them out I saw twitching fingers, skin like a withered date. Half-bending to get a better look at my keys, aches down my back, it occurred to me that to drop them now would be a minor catastrophe all of its own.

Behind me a confused man with a battered briefcase thought about asking me where he was, how he came to be there, but who asks doddery old ladies anything these days?

Alice Mair lived on the third floor.

I took the lift and left my trolley on the landing.

I buzzed a brass bell once, twice. No reply. I considered knocking, but my knuckles felt hollow and my arm no stronger than a roll of paper soaked in rain.

I buzzed again.

A voice called out in German, "Coming."

The door opened an inch, on the chain. I fixed my face to a foolish, denture-filled smile and said, "Have you seen my keys?"

A single eye, sky blue, peeked through the gap in the door. "Your . . . keys?"

"I had them," I explained. "But I lost them."

The eye considered.

Everyone knows that ghosts are vain; why would we be anything else? I am told that the old do not notice that age has come upon them until they are in the full throes of pain, in much the same way as an asthmatic assumes that the breath they struggle to draw is the same struggle fought by all men. No ghost ever chooses to be old.

"A moment," said the voice.

I heard the rattling of the chain, and the door swung wide. A woman, five foot five, with blonde hair cut short and a hint of freckle across her flushed cheek, stood in jogger's T-shirt and Lycra pants, and as she opened her mouth to offer some charitable advice to the ageing neighbour who stood on her doorstep, I smiled my most sublime of smiles and caught her by the hand.

I don't think she even had time to be afraid.

"Ma'am," I said as the old woman blinked before me, "do you need help getting your shopping into your flat?"

Chapter 45

Impressions of the body of the woman called Alice Mair.

Good teeth, chemically whitened; nice hair; unplucked softly curving eyebrows. A twinge in my shins that might be the result of too much running in cold weather. Eyes seem good and she's wearing sensible shoes. Itchy nose. A relief to be young again.

I lock the door behind me and inspect my apartment.

Walls painted a shade of not-quite-white which designers probably dubbed "pearl". Flat-pack furniture, cream curtains hanging down before the windows. A flat-screen TV, a couple of magazines about women's boxing and the plight of the polar bear. On the wall a collection of semi-Impressionist paintings bought three for two at a clearance sale of inoffensive art. Alice's bed was freshly made, with matching duvet and pillow covers, but her laptop in the kitchen by a gently cooling cup of coffee was passcode protected. I patted my hips and felt no pockets, then spotted the phone on top of the microwave. It too was passcode locked.

I opened drawers, rummaged through books and pieces of old paper, checked the trash, the recycling bag beneath the sink. No pictures of friends, address books, handy lists of Christmas presents bought for helpfully notated colleagues. No files, no folders, no holiday snaps – nothing in this apartment to indicate even the slightest kind of external existence, save, of course, for the nine-millimetre pistol in her bedside cabinet. Alice was not about to win any awards for hospitality.

I sat on a soft padded sofa in a cream padded room, drinking the remains of Alice's coffee, and tried to think.

Of all the paths available to me – and they weren't a highway of choices – only one seemed to have any particular merit in it. Even so, that merit was questionable.

Walk away?

No reason for Alice Mair to have more than a glimmer of a doubt about my occupancy of her body. I could knock on the old lady's door right now, pick up the conversation where we left off, get out, get away. Someone would find Coyle eventually. I could be a long way away before anyone even bothered to look.

And somewhere in Istanbul Josephine Cebula would be buried in an unmarked grave, and the man who seemed to have nothing to say but Galileo, Galileo, Galileo would walk away unscathed.

(A little girl in St Petersburg – touch him and I'll rip your eyes out and feed them to my pussy cat.)

I picked up Alice's phone, pulled out the battery, grabbed her laptop and, on further reflection, a warm jumper, wallet, U-Bahn pass and gun, and headed out into the cold light of day.

Ghosts are vain.

We are also largely ignorant.

Want to be a rocket scientist? Hijack one for a few days, and if anyone asks you anything at all, say it "needs further investigation".

Want to be President of the USA? He shakes a lot of hands on his way out of convention centres; if you are a particularly cute little girl in a pink flowery dress, your odds of receiving the blessed touch increase hugely. The same can be said of popes, though the language skills required for a popish possession exceed those for the White House.

Want to go to university? Freshers' week – my God, but freshers' week! What a glorious opportunity to acquire clean skins – a great mass of strangers far from home, grab yourself a handy history student and be spared the indignity of actually having to take A levels to get there.

Which is not to say that we don't occasionally try. I have several bachelor's degrees from reputable institutions and nearly half a medical degree. Any guilt I experience at having deprived my hosts of their university experience is offset by the thought that the first-class degrees I acquired in their name were a perfectly good academic outcome, better than the STDs and 2.2s they may have obtained without my intervention.

Though self-improvement is a ludicrous notion to those of us who switch bodies like a new pair of shoes, who leave behind every purchase and every obtainment on the instant we jump, yet I am not wholly ignorant.

Although I know my limits.

I am not, for example, a computer hacker.

Christina 636 – OK. I need your help again.

Spunkmaster13 – Waaay! Lets paaarrtyyy!

Chapter 46

Johannes Schwarb.

Encountering him face to face brought back the uncomfortable recollection of those few minutes I spent in his skin – of alcohol, drugs and fists in a dark corner of the night.

We met in the McDonald's on Adenauerplatz, where the almost-Mediterreanean cafés, Teutonic bars and ubiquitous clothing outlets of Kurfürstendamm met the sharp offices of well-to-do solicitors and the grand apartments of big-time bankers, and where the taxis were never for hire.

The burgers were bad, the McCroissant unmentionable.

When Schwarb – Spunkmaster to his friends – walked in, I barely recognised him. Dressed in a black suit with grey pinstripes, his thin hair gelled back against his skull, his chin was neatly shaved and even the tiny diamond stud in his right earlobe seemed like a sad attempt at being radical by a man who had long since sold his revolution for guaranteed investment bonds. The fact that he ordered a double burger with extra fries, extra mayonnaise, extra *everything, yeah!* seemed a little more in character, and when I slipped into the booth beside him, he exclaimed, "Oh my God, you're *hot* again! You're ... you're so ... you're ... " He gestured furiously up and down, and failing to find anything else, concluded, "You're sexy!"

"How have you been?"

"Me? I'm immense. I'm ruling the world, you know?"

"I thought you were a financial adviser."

"An independent financial adviser," he corrected. "An *immense* independent financial adviser."

"I had the impression that was a position of respectability, responsibility, of nine to five ... "

He flattened his burger with the palm of his hand, creating a rich goo of processed vegetables squished against processed meat. "I get three hundred and fifty euros an hour to tell people stuff they could have got off the internet. I'm like – of course I'm good, I know what I'm talking about – but these guys, these money shits, they just want everything, you know? They want big returns on investment for no risk and I say you gotta spread your bets."

There must have been something incredulous in my stare, for he added, "Hey – you looking for financial advice?"

"I'm really not."

"Nah. You're looking for computing shit, aren't you? The digital age, twenty-first century, pow!" Before I could answer, he scooped up his burger and took a bite worthy of a shark.

I waited for the worst to pass, then: "I need three things. I need access to a laptop; I need access to a phone; and I'm going to need to access some password-protected machines, I think."

"You think?"

"I'm pretty sure."

"OK. Can't we just do it remotely, hello the global age?"

"I don't yet know where these computers are."

"Right ... "

"I'm sure I'll spot them when I find them."

"OK ... "

"Can you just knock me up a USB stick or something?"

He stared at me in expert horror. "You've just got no clue, have you?"

Without consciously doing it, I realised I was batting my eyes. "That is why I came to an expert."

Chapter 47

The sun was setting by the time I left Schwarb, Alice Mair's fingers turning daisy-white in the cold. I had drunk tea as he tampered with laptop, telephone; played with software; tutted and cursed and performed the technological equivalent of summoning sagely demons and learned ghosts to help him in his enterprise.

After he had unlocked the laptop, he set about unlocking the mobile phone.

I sat with Alice's computer on my knees and flicked through email, news sites and a small but respectable collection of strategy games.

Her email was personal, not professional.

A sister in Salzburg, forwarding a picture of her latest scan. An arrow drawn across the grainy image pointed to a bundle of white that might, in time, come to have a head, a pair of legs and a thumb it sucked in its mother's womb.

A college reunion; ten years since we graduated, can you believe it? No? Have a drink with us and maybe you won't have to.

A series of requests, notifications – this person on that network is looking to make a friend. This stranger wants to share a file. This person likes your online dating profile. You've used a false name and called yourself an account manager, but the picture you posted of yourself, Alice Mair, is beautiful. You wear a blue dress and seem surprised at your own femininity, delighted at how silly and free you feel, a moment captured by the lens.

The history of Alice's life is on this computer, ready to be read.

The story of her job, however, is not.

Only one file, still lingering in the "Recent Downloads" folder. She hasn't yet wiped it, watched it from a temporary file and then forgot it was there.

A video.

A CCTV camera catching a moment, a woman in a hood and miniskirt. She's taken off her high-heeled shoes and carries them by their straps between the spread fingers of her left hand. She's on a path by a river, maybe a canal; the water is still and the bank is low, I can't tell from this angle. She walks quickly, then slowly, seems to feel the gaze of the CCTV camera on her, looks up, looks round, smiles at what she sees, smiles into the camera. Her hands are smudged with something dark. She kneels down before the screen and runs her hand across the tarmacked path. Sometimes she stops, running her fingers across her palms, around her wrists. She's writing. Ink is darker than that, paint is thicker, but the liquid staining her skin, darkening her tights, smeared across her face, is suitable for the challenge. It isn't her blood, which is why she stops occasionally to scrape a little bit more on to her fingertips from the streaks across her flesh.

When she stands, the words she has written are just about visible.

Do you like what you see?

Josephine Cebula's eyes linger on the camera, asking the question that is written at her feet.

She walks away.

I check the date/time stamp on the video.

Schwarb checks it as well, looking for a forgery beneath the image.

I look for associated files, find a list of names.

Tortsen Ulk, Magda Müller, James Richter and Elsbet Horn.

Murdered in Frankfurt. Their deaths were not clean; it was not assassination or burglary gone astray which killed them. They suffered before they died, and their killer enjoyed the experience.

Coyle blamed Josephine, but I had studied her life and knew she had not done it.

A face frozen on the screen, staring up at the camera.

Do you like what you see?

I closed the laptop, told Schwarb to keep it hidden.

"What do you want to do?" he asked.

I left his office as the sun went down. In my pocket was a USB stick, its rubber sheath cut into the shape of a cheerfully waving penguin.

I went to a department store at the eastern end of Kurfürstendamm. When the Wall fell, East Berliners had flocked to these hallowed walls of commerce, their priorities clear: smelly soap and soft socks. I bought a pair of trousers, pulling them over the Lycra jogging pants. It was all very well looking like you could run the marathon, but how useful pockets were.

I bought two cheap mobile phones with a few euros' credit in each and headed east, towards Potsdamer Platz. At the old Checkpoint Charlie a museum had been built to the great Mauer which had eaten its victims whole, but at Potsdamer Platz it was hard to believe that the concrete monster had ever stood at all. Reflective glass was lit up by brilliant splashes of light; LED screens ran constant shimmering shapes round the curves of the overhanging buildings; the sound of voices fought against the clatter of feet beneath the shop windows and the calls of waiters as they pushed their restaurant doors wide to offer sushi, pad thai, prawn crackers, mulled wine, venison stew, hot dumplings and vodka. Beneath the origami-steel roof of the Sony Centre your only purpose was to buy, spend and make merry, as brightly and as lavishly as you possibly could.

With the winter coming on, the authorities had built not only an ice rink but a small ski slope and "Winter Wonderland", where children screamed and nervous couples worried about the safety of their ankles. I bought myself a ticket to the ice rink, and was caught short when asked what size boots I wanted.

"Do you ... want to check?" asked the woman behind the counter when my silence grew too long.

"Thanks," I mumbled. "I can never remember."

A pair of ice skates later, I sat on a hard wooden bench at the side of the rink while music played and lights spun in magenta blobs across the ice. Hundreds were already skating, thick gloves pulled up high. None were professionals; professionals would not have been seen dead at Potsdamer Platz. Teenagers clung to each other for support and whooped when one fell, only for the collapse of one to topple a neighbour, who toppled the next, until with a *swosh* of metal on ice the whole pack went tumbling, feet up, bums down, faces wet with laughter. Around the edge of the rink those who had always known they didn't want to skate, had never wanted to skate, didn't want to skate now, clung to the wall, shuffling one foot over another while their sleeker, more prepared companions *whooshed* up and down.

I did up the last knot on my boots, patted my pockets to check that all I needed was there and turned on Alice's phone.

Notifications began to appear – calls missed, messages received – a dozen in total. I put the phone in my pocket and pushed my way on to the ice. I joined the circling mass of the crowd, laughed when they laughed, turned when they turned, and felt the sense of companionship that can only be found from doing a ridiculous thing with those who are as ridiculous as yourself. In that moment I loved Berlin, I loved the cold, the ice beneath my feet, the laugh that came from my throat, beautiful and vibrant, and I loved Alice Mair.

The best things cannot last for ever. Reality interferes like a bullet in the back.

After a few laps, the heat rising beneath my jumper even as my face grew numb, I felt the phone ring. I swung to the edge of the rink and answered.

"Hello?"

"Where the hell are you?" barked a voice – male, irritated, a strong French accent lacing his German.

"Potsdamer Platz. Skating."

"What are you doing skating?"

"I like skating, I find it invigorating. I also went shopping, had a bite to eat, a pleasant walk . . . "

"What are you—"

"I should explain," I cut in. "Alice isn't in right now."

Silence.

"Who are you?" he breathed at last.

"Your file calls me Kepler," I replied. "Your file is full of lies. In fifteen minutes' time, if you are not on this ice rink with a copy of *Frankfurter Allgemeine* under your left arm, Alice Mair is going to slit her wrists."

"I'm half an hour away."

"See you in fifteen," I replied and hung up.

I skated for a few more minutes and realised I was smiling.

Chapter 48

Ten minutes after the body of Alice Mair answered the phone, I stumbled forward, my fingers brushed the back of the neck of the woman in front of me, and I switched.

Within fifteen seconds I was four bodies away and skating towards the exit.

Alice Mair stood where I'd left her, in the middle of the crowd, phone in her pocket, a stranger asking if she was OK. She did not move. She was locked, a piece snapped into place that could only be unbent by breaking, a woman frozen colder than the ice beneath her feet. Her eyes stared at nothing, and as the stranger asked again, are you OK, are you all right, her head turned to the woman who held her elbow, and she did not speak.

I sat down on a bench to peel off my boots, discovering that I had thick socks with reindeer faces on them and the beginning of blisters, and when I looked up again Alice's shoulders were shaking, tears threatening to puncture her features.

Watch her: a thought strikes, and her hands move to her face, then hesitate, unsure whether to touch.

Watch her.

No one seems disgusted by her; she's in no pain, perhaps her body has not been sullied and here it comes, the one question she wants to ask.

Exactly how much have I violated her flesh?

There's another.

Exactly who has violated her flesh?

She dare not ask while the world turns around her, alone in the middle of the ice.

Alice Mair.

She will not cry.

And here – the next thought, see how it strikes into the blackness of her eye – I must be nearby.

Who held her arm when she opened her eyes?

Who is looking?

Who went away?

She turns now, ankles wobbling in her boots, and she's looking for me. And I am sitting here, undoing my laces, knocking my blades together in a shower of shaven snow. I am happy for her to look, and in a moment she'll reach into her pocket for her mobile phone, and then stop and think and . . .

there we go. She thinks and does not touch her phone. Clever, for the nasty creature that has been wearing her flesh like so many old clothes may have done things, she knows not what.

Now she is recovering her wits, she checks one last thing – the time – for how many hours has it been, how many days, since her body was acquired, and how many minutes have passed since she was freed? Will she have a sense of me? Will there be some residual instinct which tells her where I am and . . .

No.

There will not.

There is no one more humiliated, wretched or alone than the woman who waddles to the edge of the rink, knees knocking in her borrowed boots. She lowers herself gingerly on to the edge of a bench, then puts her head in her hands to hide the growing tears.

I feel . . .

. . . almost nothing at all.

I have seen this all before.

I jump from my reindeer-socked girl to a man in a checked shirt; from him to a woman composing amorous text messages, to the green-sweatshirted man scrubbing the sodden floor around the edge of the ice rink. He'll do. Part of the furniture.

I scrub, and when I look up, a man is standing behind Alice, a copy of *Frankfurter Allgemeine* under his left arm. He studies her. His trousers are tucked into his socks, his socks secured with yellow bicycle clips. His shirt is tucked into his trousers; he wears his belt tight. Somewhere beneath the outer layers I suspect skin-tight Lycra covers his flesh. He wears several layers of glove, tucked inside the sleeves of his jacket. The only part of his skin that is exposed is his face, and even that is rimmed with hat and scarf.

I think he must be very hot under all those protective layers.

I think it unlikely that he came alone.

I finish scrubbing my patch of floor, twist the mop into the bucket, then turn and begin to wheel my work towards the door. I catch sight of one of Alice's colleagues by the exit without even trying; there are only so many people who come dressed in full-body suits to an ice rink. He has a colleague nearby. They work in teams, one to monitor the other, a sensible precaution. I shuffle past the front desk, smiling at the receptionist, who grunts in reply.

In the heaving halls beyond I spot two more of Alice's comrades. I walk past them without a glance to the rubbish bin smelling of vinegar into which I had tucked a plastic bag containing Alice's wallet, her gun and my spare phone. Someone has thrown coleslaw on top of it. I scowl, wipe the bag clean and, as a security guard walks by, say, "Excuse me?" and grab his wrist.

I catch the plastic bag before it can drop, smile nicely at the befuddled boy, his hand still on my wrist, and walk away.

I had bought two mobile phones.

The other one was in Alice's pocket.

I thumbed on the phone from the bag and called a number.

Somewhere in the spinning mass of the ice rink a phone rang.

Perhaps it was still in Alice's pocket.

It rang a very long time, until . . .

A man's voice, the same voice which had answered before: "Yes?"

"Hi there," I said, sticking to German. "You've found her then?"

"I thought you wanted to talk."

"I did. I do. We shall. You seem to have brought some friends."

"What do you want, Kepler?"

I sucked air in between my teeth. "As of seven days ago, nothing. Nothing at all. Peace and quiet, to live my life, whatever life that happened to be. You refocused my interests. I have Coyle."

"Prove it."

"Scar on his stomach, claims twenty-twenty vision, is clearly mistaken, doesn't like marmalade, four passports and a murder kit in the boot of his car, shot my host on the stairs of Taksim station and didn't look back. Would you like his collar size too?"

A silence, a pause, a breath, the sound of the ice rink, cheap pop and easy screams, in the background. "Tell me what you want."

"I want to know why Josephine Cebula died."

"You know that already; you were there."

"I read your file. I was hoping, however, that you were senior enough to know why it lied."

"It doesn't."

"I will kill Coyle," I said, "if that's what it takes to get your attention. Who is Galileo?"

A slight intake of breath, a little drawing back. "Why Galileo?"

"As with everything to do with my kind, it's personal."

Someone tapped me on the shoulder. A woman's voice, excuse me, do you know where I can find a toilet?

"Very well," said the voice on the end of the phone. "You have made your interests clear."

A tap again on my shoulder, the toilet, please, do you know where the toilet is?

I have already forgotten that I am a security guard, but then who asks security the way to the bathroom?

Something hot bit into my skin above my right shoulder blade. For a moment I considered ignoring it, an irritation, nothing more. Then my left knee buckled, and as I staggered forward, I felt something sharp sticking out between flesh and bone.

Damn.

I looked for skin and all I found was darkness.

Chapter 49

Drugs wearing off from my system.

The security guard I am wearing is a big man, a tough man; he can take being knocked out. The fact that he is strapped to a chair inside a glass box at a location unknown he'd be less happy about, if he were aware of the situation. Thankfully, he is not.

I underestimated Coyle's friends.

Did they spot the switch or did they follow the amnesia?

Should have been more careful; should have jumped into someone old, or a child, or a stranger with frail knees. No one ever looks for a ghost in a body with arthritis.

I consider my cage, and my options. My cage is made of clear glass panels that run floor to ceiling. A clear glass door is set in a panel directly ahead of me. Around the glass walls, another room, larger, concrete, encases my transparent cage. A red metal door leads from this place, to location unknown. There is a fluorescent light above my head – too high to be any use. The man with the pistol by the door wears a hazmat suit. Rubber gloves, rubber suit, rubber boots, plastic visor: he's dressed for disaster. Not an inch of bare skin anywhere, and the joins sealed up with tape. It would almost be funny in another life.

My consciousness must have been reported, for the one metal door, a grille secured over its window, opens from the outside and lets in two more hazmat-suited captors. I can give both the false names they like to lie by: Eugene, Alice.

"Can I have a glass of water?" I asked.

No one seemed in a hurry to provide. No one entered through the clear door of my clear cage, but Eugene turned left to circle, and Alice turned right.

"Kepler, isn't it?"

Eugene's voice. I strained my neck in time to see him leave my field of vision, circling in the passage defined by concrete walls on the left, glass walls on the right. A cheap trick. It implied a mind not entirely confident of its ability to intimidate without the added antics. That seemed unfortunate; insecurity is often the mother of aggression.

"It's a name as good as any other."

"Where's Coyle?"

"No."

"No?"

"You want Coyle; I want out. Our situation hasn't really changed."

"You underestimate your importance to us, Kepler," and there he was, back in view, a wasp circling its prey. "The welfare of Nathan is of great concern – naturally – great concern, and we will do whatever it takes to protect him. But you – you are of even greater concern still, as I'm sure he would have explained, had you bothered to talk to him."

"We talked," I replied, shrugging against my bonds. "We talked about life, love, guns and Galileo." The chair I sat on wasn't secured to the floor – it creaked as I pushed against it.

"What is your interest in Galileo?"

"If I tell you, do I get a drink of water?"

He hesitated. Every good negotiator needs to understand that no matter how many cards they hold, still they must play to stay in the game. "We have no desire to see your host suffer need-lessly."

"I'm imagining that your definition of 'needlessly' is not like mine?"

A little sigh. Poor Eugene, the hard-pressed senior manager. I wondered what his blood pressure was like, if his shoulders ached. "Where is Nathan?"

"Handcuffed to a radiator with a gag in his mouth," I replied. "Why did Josephine die?"

"Where is Nathan?"

"The gag is made of sock and packing tape. Josephine."

"You seem to care a great deal for a former host."

"She and I had a deal."

"Yet you would permit harm to come to the body you currently wear?"

"I permit nothing," I replied. "You make your decisions and act on them; I cannot influence that. To live I must have a host; I die when my host dies. Let's not put the moral burden on biology."

"Where is Nathan?"

"We could help each other, you and I."

Eugene stopped in his circling, turned to face me. He held up the penguin-shaped USB stick I'd slipped into Alice's pocket. "What's this?"

"An autobiography."

"A virus, perhaps? Something more . . . complicated? You program it yourself, or did you ask a friend?"

"I'm a ghost. Everyone knows we're pig ignorant."

"So you do have friends."

"Or friends of friends; these things grow grey."

"You seem to like society."

"I do. People are easier to collect than things. Did you get yourself checked out with a rape kit?" I asked Alice, who was hovering on the edge of the cage. Her lips thinned; her face did not change. "Of course you did. My restraint wasn't a reflection on your body. Simply that sex, in this context, would have been a monumental waste of time."

"Kepler." Eugene's voice snapped my attention back to him. He held the USB stick up for me to see, then laid it on the floor and, with the heel of his boot, ground it into silicon and rubber. "You *will* tell me where Nathan is. That is your only purpose."

I put my head on one side as he lifted his foot from the crushed electronics that had almost – but not quite – been Spunkmaster's finest piece of work. "I could tell you about the time I met Kennedy," I suggested. Eugene resumed his march round my cage. "Or the thirty seconds I spent as Churchill? Let me regale you with stories of the rich, the glamorous and the dead; or maybe you want to know how it felt, how it really *felt* being black, young and free beneath the podium of Martin Luther King. I heard him speak and I knew, I absolutely knew, that the suffering of my people was not a stigma, but a badge of noblest pride, and that those who had fallen were not crushed, but were Newton's giants, bearing us steadily up. Or maybe not," I concluded sadly. "Maybe you're not that interested in other people's point of view. So go on. Do whatever it is you're going to do to . . . Who am I?" I tried to get a better look at my own body. A few too many beers had settled on my belly, showing as a bulge of muscle and fat competing for which was going to get the final metabolic say. "Was I carrying ID?"

"You claim to care for your hosts but you would let harm befall the body you currently inhabit?"

"Desperate times," I replied. "You'll hurt me regardless of who I am; perhaps the most equitable solution to this question would be if I jumped into one of you? Then you could beat, torment, torture – whatever – one of your own employees. That's fairer, don't you think? This . . . whoever I am . . . is just a bystander, whereas your team signed up for this job in full awareness—" I caught myself, smiled. "No, maybe not in full awareness. Maybe not that. But with some awareness at least that the precise circumstances we now find ourselves in might arise. So go on. Be the man. I'll be right here."

Eugene was smiling behind his visor. It was an automatic smile, hiding truth. "Everyone else can leave."

He was the boss.

They left.

Eugene sank down on to his haunches before me, one hand pressed up against the transparency of my cage.

I waited, testing the restraints on my wrists and feet, and wondered how much force the chair would take before it smashed.

Then Eugene began to undress.

He undid the tape that sealed his gloves to his sleeves, his boots to his trousers, his helmet to his neck. He pulled his head free with a shake of peppery hair, peeled back the zip on his suit, revealing a white vest beneath. He tugged his boots off, untangled his legs one limb at a time to reveal grey underpants and black socks. His legs showed more sign of age than his face, hollows settling around the inside of his calves, digging into the fat behind his thighs. Then he pulled his vest off, and his chest was bone and white scar tissue. I could not call it skin, as I had never seen skin which had been so scoured, burned and rearranged and yet claimed the title. He spread his arms so that I might see the dunes welt and weal, the electric burns across his back, down his spine, whose effect was to seem to shrink his vertebrae into a swollen chain of pinkish-grey disfigurement. Thin lumps stood out on his shoulders, golf balls of improperly healed muscle and bone.

He turned, and turned again so I might fully appreciate the spectacle, then this old man in his underpants faced me at last, pressing his palm against my cage, and said:

"Do you like what you see, Kepler?"

(Do you like what you see?)

"You may have met the one who wore me when this was done. He called himself Kuanyin, the god of mercy. It was an operation that went wrong. There was a tear in my suit, he managed to get his little finger into the gap. I don't recall the events that followed. I take three different kinds of medication, painkillers. I piss acid, I breathe fire. My body was violated in every manner there is, and still Kuanyin would not leave, would not speak, would not do anything but scream and weep and shit blood for three weeks, until at last his spirit broke along with my body, and he begged to die.

"A former colleague of mine volunteered to save me. He was

seventy-two years old, his wife was dead, he had no children, and thirty years of smoking had left his lungs in a poor state. He came to where they held me and took my hand, and I remember opening my eyes to see him smiling down at me, this friend, this man who had trained me, and then his smile faded, and he looked up, and he was not my friend at all, he was Kuanyin, who had the arrogance to call himself merciful. They put two bullets through his head right there and buried him in my friend's grave with all the honours of a life well lived. It was a good ending. I hope you'll agree to a similar arrangement when the moment comes. Because it will come. So, Kepler," arms spread wide, hazmat suit at his feet, "do you like what you see?"

(I love it, Janus replied. I love it I love it I love it!)

"I knew Kuanyin," I answered, taking my words slowly, familiar sounds on an unfamiliar tongue. "She was kind."

"The only kindness I saw Kuanyin perform was in the manner in which he died. I want you to understand this. I want you to understand what we are. Do you understand?"

"Yes."

"Are you afraid?"

"Yes."

"Then be merciful to yourself, if no one else. Where is Coyle?"

I licked my lips. "One question . . ."

"Where is Coyle?"

"Just one, and I'll tell you. I'll tell you, and when this is done you can find a nice body with a terminal disease, and I'll go."

He waited, broken flesh and breathing silence.

I closed my eyes, trying to shape the words. "I've been thinking about Frankfurt. Your organisation was running a trial, a vaccination programme – vaccinating against me, my kind. Four researchers were killed, and you blamed Josephine – blamed me. I studied Josephine's life. She was no killer, but when I became Alice, I had a look on her computer, and there it was. CCTV footage from Frankfurt, the night of Müller's death, and Josephine smiled at the camera. She smiled and it wasn't her, we both know it. Not Josephine, not *my* Josephine. I made her a deal and she had no idea what I was, she didn't know what it meant to be worn. But your CCTV footage predates the time when I met her, so if she had been worn, she cannot have been aware of it. Grabbed in the night perhaps by the man she'd slept with. A few hours vanish, a few minutes. She closes her eyes in a stranger's hotel room, and when she blinks, she is there still, though her hands feel cleaner than they were, and two maybe three hours have passed her by. Is that the time, she asks, and a stranger says, yes, yes it is, doesn't time fly when you're having fun? And she walks away, not knowing that in the bathroom by the door the tap is still washing away someone else's blood, scrubbed from her fingertips."

Eugene ran a finger along a line of scarring across his belly – habit, fascinated by his own flesh, eyes focused on nothing, body moving on automatic. "You haven't asked a question yet."

"I want you to understand it, before I ask. You told Coyle that Josephine killed those people under my orders but that it was her choice. You blamed me for another's crimes without evidence. You sent Coyle – a man with a history – to kill me, and through all of this I think about Galileo. Where Galileo fits into all of this. Because Josephine killed no one. I studied her life, it wasn't her. But a few hours here, a few hours there, perhaps – just perhaps – her body killed someone. And the manner in which it was done is all Galileo. Every step of the way. So, either you're a fool, giving orders that do not conform to your stated intentions, or you're nothing more than a pawn. My question, therefore, is this: have you been losing time?"

Silence.

He paces.

He turns.

He stops.

He paces again.

Is he considering the question or simply his answer?

He paces again.

Stops.

Says, "No."

That is all.

"All right then," I replied. "You're just another foot soldier."

His eyes flickered up to mine, then away again. "Where is Coyle?"

Fingers running over scars.

"Rathaus Steglitz," I said.

"An address."

I gave him one.

Chapter 50

Waiting in a prison.

Boring, waiting for the excitement to begin.

I remember:

(Do you like what you see?)

(I love it! Love it love it love it!)

Kuanyin.

I remember her as decent, if aloof.

I remember her as a her, beautiful in a Congolese woman, her hair pinned back, the scar marks just visible on her wrists from where the blades had slashed, as she proclaimed, "She said she would try again."

And what did you do?

"Why, I took her away from there."

And what will you do when she wakes? Kuanyin, goddess of mercy, what will you do when the woman you are wearing opens her eyes and the grief that you walked away from is still fresh in her heart?

"I will open her eyes in a safe place, with no knives nearby," she replied. "She chooses death because it seems simpler than life. I will make that decision hard."

I heard Kuanyin speak, and I was impressed.

"Do you like what you see?"

"You're very beautiful," I replied. "Very kind."

Only later did it occur to me that I never asked *when* she intended to give the body back.

And then, as far from the austere coldness of Kuanyin, there was Janus, who stood in front of a mirror in an apartment in Brooklyn and said, "I love it!"

It was 1974, and though the Cold War raged and Nixon still clung on by his ragged fingernails, there was a sense in the air that these were the times that would change all times.

Her brief had been nothing remarkable. Her ambitions bordered on the banal – a house, a family, a life to call her own. A clean body with no past, no baggage. I just needed to get her started.

I had found the skin at freshers' week.

"I love it! Love it love it love it!"

Michael Peter Morgan, twenty-three years old, about to start an economics doctorate. His first degree was from Harvard, his parents, both dead, had left him a sizeable inheritance. An awkward youth with almost impossibly black hair, thick eyebrows and shoulders that curved forward before the gaze of other men, at first I had dismissed him as a candidate. However, look again and somewhere beneath the hooded eyes and clenched fists, a handsome man was struggling to break free.

The second Janus slipped into his body like a hot dressing gown after a cold shower, my suspicions were confirmed. His shoulders rolled back, his head rose, his knees unlocked, and as Janus stripped before the mirror, he, who was an instant before a she, puffed his chest out and exclaimed, "Wow, do I go to the gym?"

"You did tae kwon do at Harvard."

"Oh I can *see*!" he shrilled, turning his naked body this way and that. He raised his arms and squeezed the muscles tight, squeaking with satisfaction. "How long do I take to grow a beard? Do you think I need a beard?"

"Morgan shaves every three or four days, not very well."

"I think I'd suit grizzled. Adds masculinity. How much do I have in the bank?"

"Fifty thousand dollars."

"And what do I do?"

"You're about to begin a doctorate."

"So I'm qualified?"

"Highly."

"Is my doctorate in something exciting?"

"No," I admitted. "I suspect . . . for these purposes, no."

"It's fine, I can do without the doctorate. Now – I can't quite see – my arse, would you call it tight?"

I considered his arse.

"It seems very nice."

He slapped it with a loud crack of palm on buttock, feeling around the flesh on his bum, his thighs, his belly. "Jesus," he said. "Tae kwon do is the shit, isn't it?"

"You haven't practised for a while. I thought you would be pleased by how well you retain the benefits."

"Hell yes! Though I always find it's easier to stay at a level when I'm a guy." His gaze, wandering round Morgan's room, settled on the wardrobe. Throwing the doors wide, Janus' face dropped. "So yeah," he grunted. "Shopping trip tomorrow."

I tried not to drum my fingers on my knees. "Do you think you're going to take it?"

An overdramatic sucking in of air followed this enquiry, before Janus' face split into a delighted grin. "Just one question – do you think I can get away with wearing yellow?"

Janus was Michael Peter Morgan for thirty years.

He married.

Had children.

Lived well and, from what I can tell, never once jumped away. Such a life is a luxury that only an estate agent can provide. It is the luxury of wooing a wife over many a rocky year, the empowerment of worrying about a mortgage, the privilege of going to the doctor for an ingrown toenail. It is the joy of friends who love you for the words you speak and the thoughts you think, the honour of being honoured for the deeds you yourself have achieved. It is a name, an identity, which becomes through years of labour entirely yours. A thing that is almost real.

I do not know what the original Morgan would have done with his life, had he lived it.

Questions of "what if" are not an estate agent's occupation.

Do you like what you see?

Chapter 51

I don't know how long it took them to get to Rathaus Steglitz.

To find that Nathan Coyle was not, in fact, there.

Eugene, restored to full hazmat glory, entered the room, then the room within the room, my transparent cage, without a word. He marched forward, drew his right hand up to his left shoulder, and on the backstroke hit me as hard as he could across the face.

It was a slap more than a punch, but the shock of it reverberated down to my very toes.

"Where's Nathan?" he said.

I shook my head.

He hit me again.

"Where's Nathan?"

And again.

"Where's Nathan?"

On the fourth stroke his hand became a fist, and his fist sent my chair over sideways, and my head bounced against the floor, and a tooth rattled in my mouth, and I thought, that'll cost someone some day, losing a tooth like that, and the chair that I was secured to creaked under the strain.

Bored with hitting me, he tried kicking, and the third time he kicked my kidneys, something inside went *pop*. A feeling like a blister bursting, the warm glow of fluids seeping into places within my body where such fluids should not seep.

Had he stopped hitting me, I could probably have found some reason to answer his question. As it was, he didn't, so I couldn't, and when he stamped down on my little finger hard enough to crack it, it occurred to me that Eugene's personal problems were getting in the way of his professional integrity. Then he stamped again, and I largely stopped thinking.

"Where's Nathan?"

I gasped, "Steglitz. He's in Steglitz."

Eugene kicked again.

"Steglitz!"

He grabbed a fistful of hair, his gloved hand digging into my scalp, pulled my face close. "You're going to die in this place, Kepler."

Ghosts have one defensive move.

We move.

A tale was told of one of my kin who, pursued for her life, hid in the body of a mother. She was eight months pregnant, and as the captain of the killers demanded her name – which the ghost did not know – she hid in the only place left to hide, in the body of the near-born child within its mother's womb.

Of the consequences of this – life, death – the story is more vague, but the lesson survives: when cornered, a ghost will always run rather than fight.

Now seemed as good a time as any to buck the trend.

I slammed my head, as hard as I could, into Eugene's visor. Hair tore from my scalp, Eugene staggered back, a thin plastic crack in the sheet across his face. I rolled on to my knees, then dropped back as hard as I could on to the chair.

Plastic snapped beneath me. I tried to move my hands and found that one was free, the leg that had held it broken wood. My other hand was still cuffed to the seat of the chair, which was either a terrible dragging weight or a weapon. I looked up into Eugene's startled features and swung the chair into his face. The crack spread through his visor like a spider's web, and he fell to the side as the weight of my makeshift club slammed into the side of his head. Others were moving, one reaching for a Taser, Alice for a gun. I tried to charge them, but my feet were still cuffed and I fell forward. I saw the man with the Taser bring it up to fire, and raised the chair in front of me. The electrodes hissed and spat as they struck, a buzz through my palms and the *pop-pop* of the gun. An arm went around my neck from behind, squeezing tight enough to send a pulse of blood through my ears, fog across my eyes, and as Eugene stuck his knee into my back and his fist into my jugular vein, I twisted round, tangling my chained feet against his knees, drew my head back and, biting down a hysterical laugh, slammed my forehead into the crack in his visor as hard as I could.

Plastic shattered, biting into my face, my skin, my eyes; a shriek came out of someone's lungs – mine? – and as a gun fired and a bullet shattered my shoulder blade in a primrose roar, my forehead brushed Eugene's cheek and

another gunshot. The body beneath me jerked, cried out in pain, and I held on, sweat running down my back, panting for breath, but I held on, my arm across the throat of the security guard beneath me, blood running down his back from where the bullet had broken his shoulder, popped one of his lungs like a can of Coke. He stared up at me, confused, trying to breathe and finding his lung expanding with blood not air.

A dead man in my arms.

His tongue flopped in his bloody mouth, his eyes bulged, and he didn't understand, and he died.

I scrambled back, bits of broken visor slipping down the inside of my suit.

Looked up.

Alice was staring at me. She held a gun with both hands, and it was pointed at me.

"Leontes!" she barked, and I stared back, empty-eyed, empty-brained. "Leontes! Your suit is breached, Leontes!"

I remembered that my feet were not chained, tried to get up, felt scar tissue tight across every muscle. Constriction in my chest, aching in my ribs, tasted blood on my mouth, heard a whining in my right ear and wondered if Eugene could remember a time when he had felt human, before this constancy of physical distress became all that he knew.

"Leontes! *Sir!*" Alice's voice was shaking, but the gun was not.

A picture of Coyle's phone – *Aeolus, Circe.*

Call and response.

Alice called Leontes, and Eugene responded . . .

. . . God knew what.

I took a step towards her, and as her finger pulled back the safety to fire, I stumbled, fell, landing breathless on my hands and knees, my palm slipping in the growing pool of blood spreading out from . . .

. . . whoever he'd been.

Whatever man it was who'd died, eyes cold at my side.

I looked up and met Alice's eye, and she knew I was not Eugene, and would not permit herself to believe it. I made no sound but launched myself from the floor towards her face, hands outstretched to tear at the mask that covered her head. I heard the gunshot, felt the shock of something below my lungs. She'd aimed low and wide, deliberately, and it wasn't enough to slow me down as I slammed into her, throwing her back through the open door of the cage and on to the floor beyond. I knelt on her chest, dragging at her suit as the blood ran down my trouser leg and someone jumped on my back and tried to pull me off, and I drove my elbow into their stomach as hard as I could and heard a *whomph* of air, managed to get my fingers under Alice's helmet, a bare inch, as she pushed her hands against my neck and chest, trying to drive me away. I could see a corner of her bare skin and, as the man I'd just thrown off tried again, hurling himself on to my back, I bent beneath him and pressed my lips into the side of her neck and jumped.

Alice Mair.

Good to be someone you know.

Above me, Eugene sagged under the weight of the man wrapped across his back. I drew my fist back and drove it as hard as I could into his face, felt his nose snap beneath my fingers. His body went limp. I kicked him off me, and as he rolled, so his attacker rolled with him, still clinging to Eugene with all his might. I pulled my hazmat helmet back down over my suit, and as the final man in the room untangled himself from Eugene, I crawled to my feet and gasped, "Help him! For God's sake help him!"

The man looked at me, looked at Eugene, fallen to the floor.

His eyes roamed over my suit, stained with Eugene's blood, but he saw no tear.

"It's in him!" I shrieked, overestimating how high my voice could climb. "Help him!"

If he looked close, too close, he'd see the tiny gap between suit and helmet where I'd wormed my fingers in to touch Alice's skin. Or perhaps he wouldn't. Perhaps there was too much blood to see.

Then he got to his feet, ran to the door, stuck his head outside and roared, "Help us! Somebody help us!"

This "us" included me.

Chapter 52

East Berlin.

There are many ways to tell when you've crossed that now unsung line from West to East Berlin. Trees shorter, roads straighter, new buildings that much newer. All these things are the external indicators; for internal, I find nothing gives the game away quite so much as discovering yourself in a windowless concrete industrial workshop on whose walls are written the immortal words: CONFIDENT IN OUR STRENGTH.

Capitalism's self-confidence is infinite, but never quite so vividly pronounced as that of its socialist rivals.

Running feet, running people, raised voices. Duck and cover.

A medical team, fully dressed in hazmat suits, kneeling over Eugene. The inside of my colleague's helmet was steaming up. I cowered against the wall, dreading the moment someone asked me my half of a call sign or something as simple as my true name.

I needed to get out of this suit. I needed skin.

Vomiting wouldn't hurt either.

I bent over double, hands around my belly, and gave the preliminary shudders of a woman about to puke. The sight of nausea is often enough to induce nausea in those who see it. People cleared out of my path as I staggered, head down, into the corridor.

They believed that I was Eugene.

Let them believe it. If I was lucky, Eugene wouldn't wake any time soon. If I was unlucky, some bright spark would watch CCTV footage of the last thirty seconds and spot the moment when my fingers brushed against Alice's neck, and that would be that. Either way, time was a factor.

I headed away from the cage, away from the commotion, into the bowels of the building.

It had perhaps once been a factory; heavy metal doors led off to concrete caverns where the empty pipes of extractor fans hung down like jungle vines. Most was still empty space, but some computers had been wheeled in, server racks and cooling fans in a maze of unadorned copper and silicon. Around these worked the men and women of this institution, whatever it may be, some in suits, some in ties, some in loafers. None carried guns, though one door guarded a collection of padlocked cases whose contents, I guessed, were rather more explosive than a set of disco lights. I avoided people, kept my head down, hands to my belly, a woman running for the toilet. I was having a bad day, speak to me at your peril. I'd counted seventeen strangers by the time I found the unlabelled grey door to the women's toilet, eighteen by the time the woman in the solitary stained cubicle emerged, saw me, smiled and said, "You all right, hun?"

I scampered into the cubicle.

Never speak when you can get away with saying nothing at all.

There was something important I'd left with Alice Mair.

I got down on my hands and knees in front of the orange-flecked toilet bowel and stuck two fingers down my throat.

Anyone who says that inducing vomiting can be therapeutic lies.

It took four attempts before my body got through hot spasms and down to the more important business of throwing up. When done, I sat, sweating and wretched, my arm draped over the edge of the seat, and tried to get my breathing under control. When I could muster the will to look, there, floating among the sticky orange stomach contents from my day, including the near-digested burger I'd had on Kaufurstendam, was Spunkmaster13's second USB stick.

Ghosts are lazy.

Not stupid.

I took off my helmet, my gloves.

Under my suit I was wearing a T-shirt and a pair of black leggings. As an outfit it wasn't ideal, but neither was it soaked in Eugene's blood.

I moved through the building. I smiled at strangers and nodded at those who nodded at me and kept my eyes low when I could, and when a man with a pencil tucked behind his ear stopped me with a hand on my arm to ask what was happening with Kepler, they'd heard something bad, I nearly jumped out of instinct, and said, it's OK. It'll all be OK. And walked on.

It took a while to find an unattended computer. I stepped into the bare grey office and wished the door had a lock. The facility felt temporary – dull flat desks in dull flat rooms, not a picture, nor a Post-it note out of place, none of the detritus of an ordinary working environment. The computers were new enough to feel clean in what they did, but old enough for the processor to whine like a puppy begging for RAM. I didn't bother to guess a login, but shoved Johannes' USB stick – minus the worst of the puke – into the nearest portal, waited just long enough to see lines of incomprehensible code begin to flow and started rifling the desk. The best thing to do with Spunkmaster's technology was let it get on by itself.

The desk was, like everything else in this place, unadorned. Not a snotty tissue or half-eaten sandwich to state that this was anything other than a low-budget film set. I wondered if the walls, when kicked, wouldn't reveal themselves to be cardboard, gleaming cameras and laughing watchers behind them

remembering the day they tried to burn me alive

Eugene kicking me because he wanted to, and where is Coyle?

Who cares where Coyle is.

The computer unlocked.

It did so without even a satisfying flashing icon or a note from Johannes stating his brilliance. A thing which had been locked now was not. Email loaded, revealing that the owner of this computer was one P. L. Trent, and of all the jobs in all the secret hidden organisations of the world, he'd managed to pick finance manager.

Even hidden organisations of specialist assassins, I supposed, needed accountants.

I copied the most recent twelve months of email straight on to Johannes' USB stick and started downloading hard-drive files. As they transferred, my eye wandered briefly over the in-box of P. L. Trent and I found myself irritated at how many words were dedicated to arguments over travel receipts and photocopier ink. Only one name cropped up with enough regularity for me to note it – Aquarius. Aquarius contracts stipulate X amount of medical insurance; Aquarius no longer pays for meals bought while on assignment whose value exceeds five euros. Aquarius likes to kill ghosts.

Accounts are boring; accounts are important.

I pulled my USB stick from the machine and stood up to the wailing of a general alarm.

Someone, somewhere, had pressed a button or pulled a cord, or whatever it was people in this business did when they realised they were in trouble. Perhaps someone had bothered to look at the CCTV. Perhaps Eugene had opened his eyes, and he'd known what to answer to "Leontes". And when the doctor asked him, who was the last person you saw, he'd said Alice.

Time to go.

Chapter 53

It is said that ghosts do not care for the bodies they wear. We gorge. We feast, we dine, we slouch. We spend money that is not our own, lie with man and woman, woman and man, and when we are done, and the bones are broken and the skin is torn, we move on, leaving nothing but flesh behind.

In the best of circumstances I believe myself to be better than this.

These were not the best of circumstances.

The alarm was a klaxon, blasting from little black speakers which might have, in a different time, encouraged the working masses to reflect upon the glory of their struggle. Now it was a cry of distress, loud enough to make bubbles pop in my ears as I moved – neither walking nor running – through the clamour. There had to be protocols for this situation, but not knowing any, I fell back on brute force.

Rounding the corridor, I saw a man in a white shirt locking shut a heavy door as he glanced up at me and opened his mouth for what could only be the beginning of another round of code words I couldn't respond to. I bunched my hand into a fist and drove it as hard as I could into his nose. Something cracked and he fell, blood bursting between his fingers as he cupped his face. I drove my knee between his legs, and as he crumpled forward, flecking the wall with little drops of crimson blood, I put one arm across his throat and the palm of my hand against his face and hissed, "Exit. Now. Or I'll wear you."

His shoulders were broader than mine, his chest rose and swelled like the panting of a beached whale, but I dug my fingers hard into his skin and snarled, "Exit!"

"Stairs at the end of the corridor," he stammered. "Down three floors."

"What's the security like?" When he didn't answer, I snarled, "Tell me or I'll walk you straight into the nearest fucking bullet!"

"We go into twos. One watches the other, full gear."

"Guns? Suits?"

He managed a nod.

"What's the answer to your call sign? What's the call and response?"

He didn't answer.

"Tell me!"

Still no answer; he wanted to live. The sweat seeped in dark patches beneath his armpits, his stomach deflated and his spine tensed, but he did not speak.

I scowled, drew my hand back and drove his skull as hard as I could into the wall. Blood streaked down the concrete as he fell, and I stepped by him and ran towards the end of the corridor, my USB stick in the palm of my hand. The door ahead opened, and as the two men came through, half-dressed in rubber suits, guns in hand, I didn't slow but raised my hand and shouted, "Circe! Circe!"

They hesitated, the moment when doubt and fear combined, and in that moment I closed the distance, grabbed the first one by the neck

switched

shook Alice off as she staggered back, USB stick falling from her hand, raised my gun to my colleague and fired, point-blank range into his side, and as he fell I stepped past him and kicked the gun from his hand, turned back to Alice as she tried to regain her balance, grabbed her fingers, wrapping them round the butt of the gun and

switched

my fingers round the butt of the gun

pulled the trigger.

The man half into his suit fell, clutching at his thigh. I picked my USB stick up, felt the weight of the pistol in my fingers, and as the door slid towards its lock, rammed my foot into the gap, let myself through.

In the stairwell the alarm was muffled but still howling. I heard voices above, footsteps below, and descended. Small square windows lined the stairwell, letting in boxes of yellow light; below, a door slammed. I raised my gun and as the first man rounded the corner, dressed now in full hazmat, I put a bullet through his belly, just below the ribcage. His body swung sideways and I twisted by, heard a gunshot, felt mortar explode behind my left ear and ducked, curling up behind the bulk of the wounded man. Another gunshot snapped at the wall above my head, sending the sound of concrete and metal singing up the stairwell. As another bullet smacked overhead I grabbed the back of the injured man's suit and yanked it free from his trousers. A small inch of bare skin, I pressed my hand to it, closed my eyes and jumped.

The pain burst like the first hot light from the morning sun. I bit my teeth, felt blood in places it should not have flowed, reminded myself that my arms could still move, that my head could turn, that I could reach behind me, grab the gun from Alice's hands, turn again, look down, aim at the man who stood below me and fire.

As the man below me fell, Alice kicked me from behind and I slammed up against the railing of the stairwell, blood bursting across my chest, my sight, my tongue and my mind. I tried to grab her, but my hands were in unwieldy rubber gloves. She drove her elbow into my chest and I howled, an injured dog as humanity collapsed behind the pain, then she reached by me and grabbed the gun still in my hands. I held on tight, tried to wrap one leg around her chest, pin her in place, felt her hands over mine, felt something give around the sleeve and even as she sensed the rubber come away beneath her hand, I reached up to press my wrist against her neck, fumbling for an inch of skin, and it was *there.*

I snatched the gun from the man's hands and staggered off him, climbing breathless to my feet, heart rushing from Alice's adrenaline. Beneath me the injured man wailed, a long, low sound that hummed off the metal railings. I grabbed my USB stick once again, and half-ran, half-fell down the stairs.

How much easier all this would be if I weren't carrying something physical with me.

The door at the bottom was locked, an electronic panel whose code I did not know. Above I could hear shouting, see the slow drip-drip of blood spilling down the side of the stairwell. My mouth tasted sharp and vile. The nearest window was barely wide enough for a child to worm through and high above the stair, but there was street light outside and nothing better in here, so I levelled my gun at it and emptied the magazine. Glass crumpled, cracked and on the final shot shattered, falling like sleet. As footsteps thundered towards me I hauled myself up by my skinny arms, slithered forward, tearing skin on glassy teeth, blood slicing from my bare hands, my belly, my chest, and as the first gunshot snapped behind me I wriggled through the ruined window and flopped, head first, into the world outside.

A concrete car park framed by a concrete wall. I landed on my palms, felt something crack, pain shoot up through my right arm, then tingling numbness in my elbow. Tried to get up, fell, tried again. I wiggled the fingers of my right arm, and every bone and muscle, every tiny connection shrieked, and I did not move them again. A muzzle flash behind my left shoulder and a smack of bullet into concrete propelled me up, and, cradling my arm, cradling any part where the pressure of finger against skin might outweigh the shock still reverberating through my body, I ran.

Chapter 54

Alice Mair.

Nice body, shame about the use I was making of it.

I ran through the night, a bleeding woman underdressed for the weather, out on to an alien street in a place I did not know.

Let no one tell you that fear is fun or exhilarating. Their fear is the fear of the funfair ride where reason tells you the seat belt will keep you safe.

True fear is the fear of doubt; it is the mind that will not sleep, the open space at your back where the murderer stands with the axe. It is the gasp of a shadow passed whose cause you cannot see, the laughter of a stranger whose laugh, you know, laughs at you. It is the jumping of the heart when a car backfires in the street; it is the shaking hands that shake and shake as your thoughts do, until you laugh at it because you cannot comprehend that it is a thing for which you should weep. It is the flash of the snake's head as it turns in the forest, the startled jump of a deer, the furious flapping of a sparrow's wings and yes, I am human

I run.

And I am afraid.

*

Once upon a time

a long time ago

Hecuba came to me in the body of a man with great sideburns and an ivory cane, and said, "I've found them."

I was Victoria Whitten. Her parents had named her for a queen, and left her the wealth of a princess, and her husband had beaten her until I'd lost patience and stepped into Victoria's skin and beaten my husband. He now lived in Norwich, I in London, and once a month he wrote to me to assure me that he was well, and I did not reply.

We sat in my drawing room sipping tea as Hecuba said,

"A whole nest, right under our noses. They call themselves a brotherhood."

"Would you like a macaroon?"

He leaned forward, the end of his pink nose quivering, and said, "I've *found* them. Will you come with me?"

"To do what?"

"To stop them."

"Are we talking explosives?"

"Whatever it takes."

"I don't like knives," I explained, rolling a tiny macaroon between my well-tended fingertips. "I try not to shoot people unless necessary."

He sat back, one leg folding over another in a way which suggested that not so long ago Hecuba had been wearing skirts and was, at this moment, forgetting the nature of his own sex. "They *kill* us," he snapped. "They are beyond the law. Does that not interest you?"

"Interest – yes. Is that interest sufficient to motivate me into infiltrating, if you'll excuse my framing it so, a *den*, a lair even, one might go so far, a lair of individuals dedicated to my destruction, in order to kill them one at a time? No. I fear it is not."

"You've lost hosts," he retorted sharply. "Everyone's lost someone. Maybe not to these ones, maybe not to this new 'brotherhood', but down the years, people we've worn, they've gone to the fire, or the gallows, or the wall . . . "

"Because we drew attention to ourselves," I replied, putting my cup down. "We switched a little too much, or perhaps not enough, and we left too many stories behind. The pre-emptive mass murder of individuals set upon our destruction is, if you don't mind me saying so, a sure way to be noticed."

Hecuba's scowl deepened. There is a face which I have rarely seen since the 1880s. It was the face of that age, when sideburns erupted from the side of the head like whiskers on a water rat; when the moustache was an explosion of curling wax and could scowl something extraordinary. I have sometimes looked for that face, and found it only glaring out from the crabbed old men who squat in the shade of overcooked equatorial countries, or corrupted technocrats glowering through their insufficient pensions.

Hecuba scowled; his soul scowled with him.

"I had expected more from you, Ms Whitten," he said. "I had understood that you were an estate agent."

"I have been known to work as the same," I replied cordially. "And go to some considerable lengths to ensure that the products I procure are neither traceable nor provoke much remark when their circumstances change. And you are correct: I have lost hosts to men such as those you describe. They wore different clothes, had a different name, and yet the motives have always been the same. Fear. Ignorance. The usual motives for the predictable cloud of nebulous prejudice that dogs human history. I cannot say my experiences have made me wiser, or kinder, or bequeathed me a moral plinth from which I may preach my message to the crowd, but I have learned this: that the massed letting of blood never, but never, solves the problem. Naturally, should you pursue those who would pursue me, I would be a hypocrite to offer anything but my grateful thanks. Yet my thanks would be, I think, premature. For there is a near-infinity of men and women who are fearful and wish me harm, but only ever one of me, standing in the dark with knife in hand."

Hecuba grunted, rose to his feet. "I'll thank you for the tea, if no more."

I rose too, politely nodding in reply, and followed him to the door. He put his hand on the latch, then hesitated, half-turned.

"I am not some fool," he said at last, "that I do not see the reason in what you say. But I have one question of you, which is this: those that would hurt us are many; we are few. You are unique, a sum of experience beyond any other. Why do you give so much credit to the survival of men who are, next to you, common as muck, mindful as stones?"

I considered his question for a long moment, standing in the cold hall with its high ceiling. "I heard a story once. It was the story of a man called al-Mu'allim. One day a jinn came from the desert and possessed al-Mu'allim, and banished his senior wives but stayed and loved the youngest, who was beautiful and clever, a woman out of her time. They had a child, but the wife died, and the jinn fled. This is the story I have heard, from a long time ago. And do you know what it is to me?"

A shrug from Hecuba, who neither knew nor sensed he would much care.

"A story. That is all that the lives of other men ever are – a tale told about another. Including mine. It is the only trace we leave behind, quickly reported with the details blurred, soon forgotten."

Hecuba thought about this, then tutted.

"If that's all you think you are, then perhaps you're not worth the effort of saving. Goodbye, Ms Whitten."

"Goodbye," I replied. "Good luck."

Four days later the *London Gazette* reported on the killing of eleven men and three women in a warehouse near Silver Wharf. Two witnesses had survived. One claimed that the occupants of the wharf turned on each other, butchering their neighbours one after another, as though they were possessed by a demon.

The other survivor, who was far slower to speak, having had both eyes carefully gouged from their sockets, said no, that wasn't it at all.

It wasn't one demon.

It was two.

And as the second demon had pulled his eyes from his face, he'd laughed, a child-like laughter, and whispered:

"Do you like what you see?"

Chapter 55

There's always something to break.

First I broke a thick branch from a low spiny tree sprouting from a concrete wall.

With my branch I broke the window of the white van parked around the corner, and as its siren wailed, I reached down and unlocked the door from the inside. Then I broke a seat while crawling into the back, where I broke into the van's emergency kit and stole a tyre iron, flashlight and waterproof cagoule.

Then I broke the side panel of the steering column and stole the van.

My intention was not to go far.

Even if Aquarius couldn't follow a shrieking van with a broken window, the police might rouse themselves enough to ask a few questions.

I drove until I was beyond the search radius of a running man, then ditched the van and went, tyre iron under one arm, cagoule pulled over my vest, in search of something better.

I was in a district of Berlin where one-storey industrial blocks squatted amid a grid of streets, overshadowed by glowering tower blocks and great advertising boards declaring the wonders of cheap petrol, good vacuum cleaners and locally traded plumbing parts. The buses were few and far between, and I hadn't a cent to pay for a ride. I wandered down the middle of an empty shopping street which provided the area's worldly goods: cheap laundry, fresh tomatoes and cans of fruit.

The laundrette was the place to begin.

I smashed at the padlock on the shutter until it gave, then smashed at the glass behind the shutter until I had carved myself an access route. An alarm began to wail, but at this hour locals would be slow to stir, and the police slower yet to answer, and even if anyone did, arrest was the very least of my problems.

I smashed open the till and was rewarded with not a cent for my troubles. In the back I rifled through plastic-sheathed clothes hanging on a rail, forgetting for a moment that I was smaller, more neatly built than Nathan Coyle, and that a cocktail dress was more my style than a tuxedo. A small red box on the highest corner of a shelf caught my eye; smashed open, it revealed thirty euros in one-euro coins and twenty-cent pieces, an emergency supply gratefully received.

I thought I heard a siren in the distance so made a quick exit, shattered glass crunching beneath my feet, Alice's fingerprints all over the crime scene, for what little that might matter in the long run.

A cold night to be lost in a strange city.

I wanted to sleep, and so did my body.

My mouth tasted of bile, arm throbbed, ribs ached. At some point I must have hit me harder than I realised.

I turned my face towards what I guessed to be the centre of the city, navigating by the towers, and began the long walk towards morning.

Chapter 56

The coming of dawn did not so much lighten the sky as shift it from blue to grey, scored by the hissing of falling rain.

I wanted out of this skin.

Another day, another internet café.

I love the internet.

Online banking! Facebook!

I struggle now to recall my existence before these two miracles of technology, to remember precisely how – dear God but I shudder to think of it – how hard I had to labour to gather information on my body's friends, acquaintances, past and wealth. The weeks spent shadowing a target, the long nights cataloguing people met, stories told, the eavesdropping and the subterfuges I had to engage in to crack the secrets of my skins – yet now, oh most precious now, most wonderful of wonders, *Facebook*! The entire life, the personality, every friend and family member catalogued and listed in perfect traceable glory, just one password away, assuming the skin even bothers to log out. Facebook! How did I ever live a life of reckless possession without you?

And glory above glories, online banking.

Miraculous, wonderful, a delight, for all I need to do is remember a name, a password, a code, and in any body, in any skin, I can sit down in front of a computer and move monies around from one place to another, send myself credit here or there without ever having to wear the same skin twice. Gone are the days when I would bury a rich man's money beneath a secluded tree, to return to it in a poor man's body when time came to move on; now the tree is the world, and the earth is automated.

Technology, I thank you.

The city woke, and I longed to sleep.

Beneath my stolen clothes my skin throbbed from a dozen untreated slices. I wanted to scratch, but when my fingers brushed beneath my arm I felt the lumpen protrusions of embedded glass and flinched away, repulsed by my own flesh.

I bought an hour on a computer in an all-night internet café, among the international callers trying to catch their mothers in Taiwan, the insomniac shoppers and the quiet downloaders of internet porn.

An hour on a computer netted me three hundred euros transferred to the nearest ATM.

Another euro bought a hot dog from a man with a steaming cart who gave me extra onion with a cry of, "You're up early, ma'am. Rough night?"

"Good God," I replied. "Is it morning?"

Two hundred and fifty euros netted me a small laptop to call my own.

I sat in the dullest corner of the darkest café I could find, fighting the urge, the need to jump bodies, forcing myself to stay still and in discomfort, and slipped in the only object that had made a switch unviable – my little stomach-stained USB stick.

What may be said of the organisation that dubs itself Aquarius?

If it was half as good at protecting its data as it was its people, I don't think I'd stand a chance.

Emails, folders, pictures, accounts, personnel files – more documents than the eye could read in a day, in a week, ransacked by Spunkmaster13's malicious toy.

Most of it banal.

Even secret bunkers of murderous men need to order toilet paper in bulk. Even murderers run out of rubber bands.

I tried searching for *Nathan Coyle* and located an email with a little red flag by it.

The message said: *Compromised.*

That was all.

I searched for *Kepler*.

It was the same file that Coyle had taken with him to Istanbul, with only one addendum. Now the first image in the document was not Josephine, but Coyle.

I tried other names.

Hecuba.

Nearly thirty pictures and names, stretching back over four and a half years. They ended in one last face, a woman in a headscarf, head turned to one side, a bullet hole in her skull and another in her throat, lying where she'd fallen on the steps of Senefelderplatz. Hecuba had jumped into her while running, and worn the body eleven seconds before the pursuit team took her down.

More names, more faces.

Kuanyin, who died wearing the body of a man who'd sacrificed his life so that the beaten rag of Eugene's ravaged flesh might endure a little longer.

Names led to more names: code names I didn't recognise, some I did. Marionette, poisoned in St Petersburg. Huang Li, shot in Tokyo. Charlemagne, who, realising he was pursued, fled into the body of a seven-year-old boy, proclaiming, you'll never do it. You'll never kill me, not a child. In a way he was right, for Aquarius took the child and strapped him down, experimented for weeks on their living subject, cutting out pieces of brain one cluster at a time in search of some miracle mechanism that might yet save the body from the ghost. He was already comatose when his heart stopped, but *which* mind slumbered, Aquarius did not know, and an unknown boy was buried in a field outside Seville.

Aquarius were not afraid of experimenting on ghosts.

Or their hosts.

Perhaps Hecuba had been right when he refused my macaroons all those years ago.

Janus.

The file was thick but patchy. It began in 1993, speculating on Janus' prior activities, largely incorrectly. It missed 2001–4 but caught up again with Janus as she moved into a long-term body in Barcelona. The skin had terminal lymphoma, and I was surprised at how long Janus stuck around in the dying flesh.

The newest picture showed a middle-aged Japanese woman in a Parisian café, her hat pulled low, her scarf high against the wind. The newspaper on the table before her was three weeks ago.

Galileo.

Fascination overwhelmed caution; I opened the file.

Pictures, snippets.

A face from 2002, another from 1984. A note suggesting Galileo boarded such a plane at such a time, but switched to another passenger during the flight. A face half-turned towards the photographer, a shadow on a window, a receipt from a meal, a copy of a bank statement as the account was drained. Edinburgh, 1983. Someone had tipped off the men who would become Aquarius and they'd nearly got him. Nearly was not good enough.

A picture of Coyle in hospital, tubes and bandages. Corpses laid on the dockside, at their back, the stern of a ship, *Santa Rosa* in black and a policeman trying hard not to vomit.

These were the fragments, the rare glimpses of Galileo's life that had been compiled, and as I flicked through them with increasing astonishment, the certainty grew upon me that almost every single piece of it, barring a few noble exceptions, was wrong.

Only one more task remained.

I searched for *Josephine Cebula.*

Chapter 57

Three euros bought me a ride to Zehlendorf.

School children slushed through the growing rain, kicking dark water in growing puddles. Pedestrians ran for cover as vans swished by, ducking the spray.

Back to a quiet house in a quiet street where no harm could possibly befall any man.

Back to Coyle.

The house was silent as I let myself in, lights off, rooms empty.

Nathan Coyle lay where I'd left him, handcuffed to a stone-cold radiator, his head on one side, asleep.

I walked towards him slowly, tiny laptop tucked under one arm. The floor creaked beneath my feet, and his body jerked, eyes flying open, hand tugging against the handcuff. The gag was still – miraculously – in place, and as he blinked himself to full awareness, his eyes fell on me and widened first in surprise then rage.

I, Alice Mair, partner of the man who called himself Nathan Coyle – folded myself on to the floor just out of the reach of his legs and opened the laptop.

He made a strangled sound against his gag; heels pounded on the floor.

I said, "There's something I want to show you."

Another noise, rage popping against his eyelids, skin flushing red as he tried to throw himself at me through sheer force of will.

I pushed the USB stick into the machine, let the files unfold.

"I stole these," I said, "from Aquarius. At a brief glance, it's clear that I've got account information, personnel information, emails, correspondence, documentation. Enough to destroy Aquarius by remote control, wearing bank managers and clerks, nothing more."

He tore again at the cuffs, a throat-deep animal snarl tangling mutely on the gag.

"However," I went on, "what I want to show to you is this."

I turned the laptop screen so he could see the images as I opened them. "This is the file of the entity you call Galileo. It's patchy – remarkably more so than any other file, including my own. Here we see, for example, a shot of a man in 1957 who may or may not have been Galileo. Here, the corpses of the *Milli Vra*, a ferry whose passengers went mad and killed each other one by one on a midnight voyage. Here's a photo –" I pushed the screen a little closer "– of an individual reported to be Galileo, taken in 2006. A New York gentleman. Observe the dapper dress, the smart black shoes, the professionally manicured nails. I can see why someone might want to be this man – he doubtless has dinner parties and attends all the best shows. But look a little closer –" my finger tapped the screen "– and observe where his neck meets his collar. Do you see?"

For a moment curiosity overwhelmed Coyle's pride, and there was a flicker in his eye as he saw the infiltration of broken capillaries and torn-up veins running through the surface of the stranger's skin in a reddish burst, just above the collar.

I ploughed on. "Most people are hypersensitive about their skin – it's what strangers see, what they judge – and any anomaly, anything which may not conform to the image they wish to project of social perfection, they disguise. No such effort is being made here. What may we conclude? Either that this gentleman doesn't care for appearances, which seems unlikely considering the neatness of his apparel, or that lesions are a common feature of his flesh and he no longer regards their appearance as anomalous. What do you think?"

Coyle, behind his gag and chains, thought nothing. His struggles had slowed. Now he lay still, staring at the photo which he must have stared at a hundred times before, of a man alleged to be Galileo.

I let him stare, then flicked over to the next. "How about this? Female, early twenties, stunning, absolutely. I would, wouldn't you? For a day in that skin, for an hour of that pride. But then look – really look. Observe her shoes where they meet the ankle. Observe the plasters. Blisters and blood – the price of being desirable, you might say, but I say no. There are few irritations as inescapable as badly fitting shoes. And your file says that this woman was Galileo for three months?" I flicked through more pictures, fast now, shaking my head. "Blisters, more blisters! And this!" Another photo, another face. "Do you really think *he* was Galileo?" I demanded, holding up the laptop incredulously for Coyle's inspection. "Gold watch, silk shirt, all very appealing. But look, I mean *look* at his face! *The man has a glass eye.*"

Coyle was frozen, shoulders slumped, legs straight. Quieter, I flicked through more photos, shaking my head, a tut, a sigh. "These are not Galileo. Three months with blisters, two with lesions on the skin? Look at her – she's *old*. Her face has been maintained with creams, but her fingers are withered, they show her age because so many people in tending their faces forget their hands. No ghost would wear her for more than a few minutes. Back problems, arthritis – any estate agent worth their skin could tell you no. Not for any ghost. Galileo wants to be loved. He wants to look in the mirror and love his face, and see his face loving him back. He wants to kiss his reflection, feel a shudder of delight when his hands touch his skin. He wants strangers to fall into his arms because he's beautiful, so beautiful, and when he fucks them he wants to flick, one to the other and back again, a breath, a second. He wants to love everyone and everything all at once, as long as everyone and everything loves him. And when he kills, it's because he looks in the mirror and sees only contempt staring back, and he needs to destroy that face, so he cuts it off, and then looks again and still can't find any beauty in it, so kills again, and again, and ... Well. I won't go on. You know this story better than most. You should also know, therefore, that these people are not Galileo. Even if they were ... Here ... "

I turned to the final photograph, dated 2001, of a woman lounging across a leather sofa, a cocktail in her hand. "November 2001 to January 2002. I grant you there are no physical deformities in this individual, nothing obvious disbarring her from being a suitable habitation, but I know where Galileo was in November 2001. I know who he was. And he was *not* her."

So saying, I closed my laptop.

Coyle was motionless.

My eyes felt sticky inside, full of weight.

"Aquarius experiments on ghosts." The words fell from my tongue. "The torture isn't about cooperation. It's limit testing. They want to know how we work. Look at Galileo's file. Look at Josephine's – at her real file, not the tissue of lies they gave you to read. Look again at Frankfurt, ask yourself if this was a vaccination programme or something else entirely. Consider the data they gathered, observe the direction of their enquiries, the resources available. Ask yourself why the researchers died, and why in so much pain. Look at my file, look at dates, times, places, see if I was in Frankfurt when they were killed. Look at Josephine's face in the CCTV camera and ask who is looking back at you. Understand that as I have a history with Galileo, so it has a history with me, and this is not the first time we have danced around each other in the course of our lives. Ask yourself: who in Aquarius has been losing time. But don't tell. Whatever happens, do not tell them what you find. You're compromised now."

I stood up.

"I'm going," I said, barely bothering to glance at him as I spoke. "I'll send someone to pick you up. You can keep the laptop, the money. I can't take it with me. But this —" my fist tightened around Schwarb's USB stick "– is mine. Tell your bosses that. And ask them why, of all the ghosts they've broken and all the skins they've killed, they lied about Galileo."

I nudged the laptop closer to him with the end of my foot so that it was just within his reach.

Walked away.

Chapter 58

You must travel light when you wear another's skin.

Everything you own belongs to someone else.

Everything you value you must leave behind.

It is not I who made a family.

It is not I who have a home.

It is someone else, whose face I borrowed for a little while, whose life I lived and who now may live the life I lived as I move on.

Time to go.

I went to the post office and sent my USB stick first class to a PO box in Edinburgh, where some time I had worn a skin whose name was

something-son

and had opened an account and been careful never to close it. Because even a ghost needs something to call their own.

I headed to the airport.

This is how I run.

I am Alice.

I stand in the departures lounge of Brandenburg airport, and as the crowds bustle around me on their way to the luggage check-in, I spread my fingers wide and brush

a child holding her mother's hand who walks towards the check-in desk for flights to Athens, and as I look up into my mother's face I decide that actually this body is a little too young and a little too puffy-eyed from an early-morning start, so I switch into

Mum, straight back and wearing a belt a little too tight across the belly, I support my child as she staggers, only to reach out and politely tap the guard who stands by the oversize luggage counter to say, "Excuse me?" and as he turns, brush my fingers against his neck to become

oversize luggage porter, my arms folded, my breath stinking of cigarette smoke, I smile at mum and resolve either to get out of this body or get some mint into it as soon as possible. I march towards the security gate, calling out to the bored guard who confiscates all liquids and bottles over a hundred millilitres (verily, though they be empty, they shall be confiscated), "You got a cigarette?"

She turns, rolling her eyes at my approach, and as she does I catch her hand and

pull my hand free from the sticky grasp of the confused oversize baggage porter, tut and say, "Cigarettes will kill you, you know?" and turn, pushing my way through the winding queues for the security gate. The crowds are thick and unwilling to part, even for a woman in uniform, so I am

teenager slouching with drum and bass roaring through my headphones. I pull the cord free in disgust and, eardrums still ringing, reach out for

businessman, standing crooked, hip down, shoulders twisted, impatient for the flight, who reaches for

father, no longer listening to his wife,

who touches the arm of

student carrying too much stuff and none of it what she needs who stands at the head of the queue, and her heart is racing even though mine is not and I wonder precisely what else she's carrying to induce such terror of the X-ray machine, but perhaps now is not the time to find out, so as the security guard passes me the tray for my personal belongings I brush his fingers and

straighten up, smiling my most reassuring smile at the shaking student and turn to my colleague, bored staring at the X-ray screen, and say, "Hey, you got the time?"

My colleague barely glances up from her monotonous study to grunt her reply, by which time I'm on the other side of the counter and into

baggage checker, who's just been through a woman's under-wear, and the woman is bright red, ashamed of all her pink lace, though I,

as I move into her and pack up my bag again, think it's really rather charming and not nearly so sexual as perhaps she intends it, and as I sweep through customs and towards duty free, I feel in my pocket for my ticket, and see it is to San Francisco and sigh, and go looking for someone who might be heading for Paris instead.

Chapter 59

My name is Salome.

This is what my passport says and I have nothing better to go on. I had been aiming for first class, but the queue was varied and my fingers were warm, so Salome I remained, knees pressed against the seat in front of me, window view, a vista of wing, engine and a scrap of sky.

Somewhere a USB stick containing the records of a company called Aquarius is heading towards Edinburgh.

In Zehlendorf police have received a tip-off that a man is hand-cuffed to a radiator, confused and afraid.

And I, who don't feel comfortable with a name like Salome and fancy myself more an Amelia, close my eyes as take-off pushes me into my seat and, with nothing in the world to call my own, think of Paris.

I heard a story once, in the basement of a Paris café where artists gathered to whisper of rebellion, and the music was soft, and the smell was strong coffee and cheap gin.

The story was told by a woman called Nour Sayegh, who studied not much at the Nouvelle Sorbonne and spoke French with an Algerian accent. There was a quality to her face that fascinated me, enthralled me, and as I sat among her fellow students – how I *love* freshers' week! – I wondered if I had not met her before, or worn the skin of her sister, and yet I could not place her features until at last she began to speak.

"My name is Nour Sayegh," she said, "and I carry the fire of the jinn."

A slow drumbeat, for this was a space for people who liked to perform, for students with dreams of the limelight and contempt for those who already had it, and as Nour told her tale – of her journeys in Africa, of her coming to France – she swayed to the music that ran beneath her words, plumping them up.

"My great-great-great-great-great-great-grandmother married a jinn," she said. "Her husband was a rich man in Cairo but he did not love my grandmother. She was an ornament in the house, not a woman at all. So my grandmother would weep, alone beneath the moonlight, and look towards the sacred waters of the Nile and pray to the ancient gods, to falcon Horus and gentle Isis, mother of all things, for some magic to change her husband's eye. She wept so softly, for she feared being seen to be sad, that only the little crickets clustered beneath her feet knew of her distress, and the breeze that blew from the sea. Until the jinn came. Fire of the desert, the knife-wind, he comes, he comes riding the sands, and his name is a thousand eyes without expression, *elf'ayyoun we'ain douna ta'beer, youharrik elqazb doun arreeh*, and his voice is stirs-the-reeds-without-wind, and his sword is starlight, and his eyes are the hot embers of a fallen sun.

"We do not know the true name of the jinn, nor why the crying of my grandmother lured him to her house, but when he saw her weeping in the garden he grew sad and took the form of a little boy, silver-skinned and ebon-haired, who asked, 'Why do you weep, mistress? Why do you weep?'

"'My husband does not love me,' she replied. 'I am his wife so must be with him, yet I cannot but lament this fate that has befallen me, for I see other wives, and see that they are in love, and feel the sting of my sorrow, crueller by compare.'

"Hearing these words, the jinn was greatly moved. 'Come away with me,' he said, 'and I shall love you as your husband.'

"'Allah forgive me that I should even consider the thought!' she replied. 'For I am wed to my husband and cannot permit another to violate my flesh! Get gone with you, jinn, for though I know you spoke in kindness, yet your words are still obscene!'

"The jinn, confused, departed. 'What strange ways these mortals have,' he mused, 'to be so trapped by prisons of their own creation. Why then, if I am to have her, I must be as her husband is!' So saying, the jinn made himself a vapour, and slithered into her husband's room, where he lay, great and panting from a night of loving some other wife. And the jinn wriggled up the husband's nose and wrapped himself around his heart, so that when dawn came it was the jinn, not the husband, who roused himself from sleep, turned to the hussy by his side and barked, 'Get gone, whore!'

"This woman fled, weeping, from the bed, while the jinn, now become the husband, went straight to the room of my grandmother and said, 'Forgive me my past cruelties; I am your husband and will honour you with all the duty and care that is within my power to give.'

"My grandmother, being a shrewd woman, at once marvelled at this change and expressed only cautious duty towards her husband, not believing his speech. Yet as the weeks went by, and the jinn showed his dedication to her, she softened and began to hope, to pray, that this sudden change in her husband might be true.

"'My lord,' she said to him one night, 'there is such alteration in your nature that, if you permit me to say it, you barely seem to be the man I married.'

"At this the jinn puffed up with pride. 'Indeed,' he said. 'It is you that has altered me, fulfilled me and made me the better man.'

"With these words, they were happy together, but my grandmother could not help but remember the jinn in the garden, promising forbidden adventures to her, and as she looked at her husband she wondered. Was this man her husband, or was she ensorcelled by a fiery creature of the desert, a jinn of the sands?

But if she was, what could be done? For the jinn are a great mixed race, who delight, it is true, in playing tricks on men, but are also gentle and kind to their favourites and beloved of Allah. For recall the jinn who carried the starving prince to Baghdad on a wind of fire, or helped the wounded merchant reach the gates of Damascus. Remember that there are jinn who have loved, and served faithfully those they have loved, and guarded the wombs of the mothers as they brought forth their children on stormy nights. We too eagerly blame the jinn, accuse them of all our woes, forgetting their good deeds, which we often claim for our own.

"'You are much changed,' she murmured again to her husband, as they lay, naked lovers, beneath the leaves of the trees. 'You are much changed.'

"At this the jinn made to speak, but at once she interrupted him. 'It is said that the innocents will find their path to paradise. I know of no crimes of which I am guilty, but if I am to stay shriven, surely my best safety lies in innocence. Were a spirit of the deep to abuse me, why then I am abused. But were I to revel in that debasement, why I am a harlot and a witch, and should be branded for the same. Is it not so?'

"Hearing this, the jinn wisely did not speak, for he knew my grandmother's meaning. Instead, silent a long time they lay beneath the breath of the river's breeze, until at last he said, 'To love whom one loves, to be whom one would be, this does not seem against the will of the Creator. For he made you to love, and made you to life, and to deny this is to deny the will of Allah.'

"My grandmother shot the jinn a look of ivory arrows, piercing straight through his soul to the truth of his heart, so much that he almost leaped from the skin he was inhabiting; then she smiled and said, 'And if Allah made others to mischief?'

"'Then clearly,' he replied, 'there is a purpose.'

"For ten years the jinn remained by my grandmother's side, loving her as she loved him, and never did they speak of the alteration in her husband or question how it had come to pass but, as innocents do, accepted everything of each other, and were truly the loveliest couple in creation.

"Then war came to the land, and the soldiers came for the husband, who had in his former time committed some deep indiscretion against the rulers of Cairo. And as the soldiers took hold of the husband's arms, the jinn, incensed with anger and confused with terror, fled the body he had worn for ten years and vanished spinning into the night. Seeing this, the soldiers cried out against all sorcery and at once beheaded the husband where he stood, throwing his corpse to the crocodiles. My grandmother fell weeping by the crimson waters, but the soldiers called her a witch and took her to the jail, where first a judge, then a sacred wise man called her blasphemer. They threw her into the deepest dungeon in Cairo, where foul men practised against her evil acts, and every night she cried out for her jinn, for her husband, for her lost lover and protector, but he did not come, for jinn are as changeable as the moon, as fearful as the sea, and her cries were lost far beneath the stones.

"Her torment only ceased when the men who were her tormentors saw that she was with child. At this, many wanted her cast to the bottom of a pit, but one took pity on her and smuggled her out into the foggy night. Desperate and bleeding, she staggered through the streets, collapsing at last at the doors of a madrasa, where the kind imam took pity and nurtured her back to health.

"Yet the dungeon had wounded my grandmother deeper than flesh, and when the childbirth came, it was tormented, foul and bloody, for the child she was giving birth to was that of the jinn, and a creature as much fire as it was mortal. As it was born it burned my mother from the inside, its magical essence too much for her womb to bear, and seeing this infant as it fell mewling into the world, the imam was taken with a great confusion as to what he was to do. He turned to give the babe to his mother, but his mother was dead.

"Alone with the screaming child and the woman's corpse, the imam prayed to Allah for guidance, and as he did, it came to him that he became as a jinn himself, for his mind seemed to slip into that of the child's own, and within that little body he felt the terror, the pain, the grief, but above all the love that the child's father had felt for my dead grandmother, brighter than the flames that had destroyed her. Returning to his senses, he knew then that he could not kill the child, created though it was in a union of obscenity, for it was also a child of the purest love. So he raised the child, and in time that child became a man, and the man lay with women, and the women became my grandmothers, each gifted with a little of the jinn's blood, the desert's fire and the love of an immortal soul."

Nour Sayegh finished speaking, and as the half-attentive café beneath the Paris streets applauded her tale, I sat dumb in my corner and stared into the eyes of this child, who had come from the flesh of Ayesha bint Kamal and Abdul al-Mu'allim al-Ninowy; but also from my soul.

Chapter 60

Paris.

What may I say of Paris?

That the French never take no for an answer.

Wars, riots and rebellions, governments formed and over-thrown, regular as winter flu; crushing poverty and great wealth. Through all of this Paris has stayed Paris, crown of France, city of boulevards, chic and red wine.

In romantic movies Paris is the Seine and sentimental under-standings beneath the burgundy awnings of the local café, where waiters in crisp white aprons serve tiny croissants on silver plates and whisper philosophical truths about love.

In American thrillers Paris is corruption, its grimy Metro hiding beady-eyed strangers chewing unknown herbs in the corners of their mouths, who spit on the track and snigger at young women and chase each other down the cobbles of Montmartre.

To children Paris is the double-decker train and the Eiffel Tower; to wealthy adults it's the sound of champagne popping on the top-floor restaurant beside Notre-Dame. To nationalists it's the tricolour flying by the Arc de Triomphe, and to historians it's the same, though perhaps the historians look upon the red, white and blue with a little more circumspection.

To me Paris is a beautiful place to spend May, June and September, hideous in August, drab in February and at its most magical when the drains are opened to wash away yesterday's dirt, turning the city streets into a roaring fountain.

To Aquarius Paris was the last known location of the entity known as Janus.

I ditched Salome at the arrivals lounge of Charles de Gaulle airport and walked to the taxi rank in the security guard who'd been about to search me. There I caught a taxi driver by the arm, but was so repulsed by the stench of booze on my breath and the migraine pounding against the side of my skull that I went instead to my neighbour driver and slipped into him, easing cautiously out of the taxi rank with my hire sign off.

Roadworks on the Autoroute du Nord left me fuming, fingers drumming while the radio played bad Europop. When the traffic report kicked in, overriding the singer's expression of the notion that his lover was his light, his breath, his joy, his food, his buttered toast, it declared that the tailback ran all the way to the Périphérique, and with a hiss of frustration I pulled off the autoroute and went looking for a station.

At Drancy I caught the RER and a young woman with dyed blonde hair and, alone in the scratched corner of my carriage, rifled through my purse in search of who I was. I was Monique Darriet, and I was carrying fifty euros in notes and coins, a door key to location unknown, a tube of lipstick, a mobile phone, two condoms and an insulin kit. Pulling up my sleeve, a bracelet revealed me to be diabetic and asked that you dial for emergency assistance immediately.

I shuffled into an old man with a pencil moustache at Stade de France. He wasn't as handsome nor indeed as comfortable as Monique, but I wasn't in the mood to manage my blood sugars.

Only fools and the desperate stay near Gare du Nord or Gare de l'Est. Like nearly all major stations in every major city on the planet, all they're good for are thin coffee, overpriced cigarettes and the fumes of taxis waiting in ranks. Noise, bustle and a sense that nobody cares define the drab station concourses where money cannot buy a decent sandwich, and I made sure to be at least fifteen minutes' walk from them before I looked for a hotel.

Down a street too narrow for the height of houses that fronted it I found a thick black door with a bell pull that weighed as much as my old thin arms. The proprietor seemed surprised to have a guest, but I shook his hairy hand nonetheless and slammed the gate in the bemused face of my former host.

Inside, a windowless hall was lit by bare tungsten bulbs, the filaments wound like strands of DNA. The air smelt of warm breath and wood varnish. I trotted round to the back of the reception desk and assigned myself a suite on the top floor, marked it as paid for, tucked the key in a plant pot on the landing of the stairs, grabbed my coat and went to find a hearty meal and a missing ghost.

My body didn't need the food, but routine dies hard, and the mental compulsion to eat outweighed physical desire. As stew steamed before me and coffee cooled by my side, I watched the street and thought about Janus.

Three weeks ago she'd been photographed by Aquarius: a Japanese woman sitting in this very same café, newspaper on the table in front of her. She'd looked distracted, her eyes wandering off somewhere to the left of the lens, but then Janus probably had plenty to think about.

"Excuse me," I said to the waiter, pushing a very generous tip on to the tray, "I'm looking for a friend of mine. Osako Kuyeshi. Comes to this café sometimes. Have you seen her at all?"

Paris isn't as diverse as London or New York. A lone Japanese lady sipping coffee by herself had been noticed. As, indeed, had her absence.

I found her in outpatients at Georges–Pompidou, waiting for a CT scan. Slipping into a woman in hospital robes and thick support socks, I sat down by her and said, "Are you waiting for the scanner?"

She was.

"What's it for, can I ask?"

"I get cysts," she explained. "And I lost my memory."

"That's terrible for you. I've been waiting months," I grumbled, rolling my tongue against the false teeth glued to my gums. "I have terrible problems with my memory. One day I'm standing talking to this stranger on the train, next thing it's two months later and I'm down to my knickers in someone else's bedroom."

No! exclaimed Osako Kuyeshi. Not you too?

Yes! Shocking, it was, just shocking, I mean, they weren't even *my* knickers . . .

. . . but enough about me. Tell me about you.

Forty minutes later I walked out of the hospital, a junior doctor with a stethoscope round my neck.

Three days ago Osako Kuyeshi had opened her eyes and not known where she was. Five months of her life had vanished. She barely even spoke French; the last thing she remembered she was in Tokyo, waiting to collect her benefits. The doctors were baffled, so were the nice men who came to ask her questions about it as she sat waiting for the psychiatrist.

"It's all right," I'd said. "I'm sure something good will come of this."

I don't think so, she'd replied. My husband died last month, and now I'm alone. I don't think anything good will come ever again.

Osako had woken in an apartment not her own.

That was interesting.

If Janus had left Osako as an emergency move, she would have done so in a crowded street, a place hot with bodies to jump to.

An apartment sounded more planned, less alarmed.

I went to Sèvres-Lecourbe, south of the monument to military ambition that was Invalides, searching out Janus' new host.

The place turned out to be a holiday apartment, rented in Osako's name, though she couldn't remember the purchase. The first face that Osako had seen – young, green eyes and a purple veil – was the house cleaner, a Moroccan woman with flawless French and shoes going through at the toe, who exclaimed that she'd been asked about Madame Osako's condition already, first by the doctors, then by the men who came knocking on her door, and she had told them what she told me – that she had helped Osako when Madame stumbled.

And after Madame stumbled?

The cleaner wasn't sure. She remembered a stumble, then she stood in the street and Madame Osako was screaming, just screaming. Poor woman, is she all right?

"You found yourself in the street but cannot say how you got there?"

"Of course I can say!" she exclaimed. "I walked there! I can't remember why I walked there, but I must have walked there, because there I was!"

And in the street did you see someone walk away?

Funny thing: that was precisely the question the other men asked her too.

Janus, you two-faced god, where are you?

Osako to the cleaning woman, the cleaning woman to a stranger in the street.

Only he wasn't a stranger, because this was planned, this was something Janus had arranged, and the stranger was . . .

Monsieur Petrain, who lives at number 49, and there's only one question I really want to ask here, one question that will crack this case wide open:

"Monsieur Petrain. His arse. Would you describe it as 'tight'?"

Chapter 61

I remember Will, my gofer from the days of Marilyn Monroe, Aurangzeb and champagne.

I did not wear his body long, for he and I had a deal, and at the termination of our contract I shook him by the hand, and he was unafraid of my touch, and I said, "Good luck to you, Will."

He grinned and squeezed my palm and replied, "Likewise. Likewise."

Thirty-two years later I was sitting in Melissa Belvin in a diner off Columbus when a man entered. He was chubby without being fat, portly without being uncomfortable, and he ordered strong black coffee, a Danish pastry and a copy of the *New York Post.*

I watched him flick through political scandals, corruption, reports on dictators and economics, straight to the back. There he started earnestly on the sports pages, scouring each line of every article like a holy text.

After a while I walked over to him, swinging myself on to the high stool by the bar at his side.

His eyes flickered up to me from the paper and, perceiving no threat, returned to his reading. Others might have stopped to stare, for in my yellow dress and fair hair I was beautiful even by the rules of the time.

"How are the Dodgers doing?" I asked.

He glanced up again, re-evaluating then dismissing. "OK. But they can sure do better."

"Tough season?"

"It's always a tough season for the Dodgers. It's how they make success feel sweet."

That should have been that, but I said, "And how are you, William?"

His eyes focused fast, now trying to read the face that moments before he'd disregarded. "I'm not William. You're thinking of someone else."

"Then who are you?"

"I think you have me mistaken—"

"How's your memory?"

Silence, and now his eyes moved though his body was still, sweeping me top to bottom. "Jesus," he breathed. "*Jesus!* Look at you! Who the fuck are you?"

"I am Melissa."

"And how the fuck have you been, Melissa?"

"Well, thank you. Moving around a bit. You?"

"Good. Good! Fucking good! You still agenting? Is this —" he leaned back abruptly " – is this work?"

"I'm not in that line of business any more."

"Seriously?"

"Yes."

"What happened?"

"It became . . . difficult. I'm just a stranger, for now."

He stared, his mouth making the slow circular movements of a mind that wants to speak and can find no words. Then, having no wittier exclamations, he threw his hands into the air and exclaimed, "Fuck! You wanna get a drink?"

He was older, a well-lived age, a life that had progressed more slowly than the speed of years which had passed it by. In a bar off

Broadway he regaled me with the life and times of Harold Peake – a new name for a new man.

"So then I got into sport, I mean, like, bought into it, you know, as an investor. And I've got this house now – you have to come see it – out in New Jersey, and my partner – you've gotta meet my partner, he's just great, he's such a great guy – and we've got a garden, and I mow the lawn on Sundays, can you believe it? I *mow the lawn*! It's like, Jesus, from where you first met me to where I am today, it's like unbelievable."

That sounds great, I said. That sounds really nice.

His silence was the sudden sharp closing-off of a man afraid he has talked too much. "So 'Melissa'," he mumbled, "you must have been up to stuff. You must have seen some things. Tell me, what've you been, *who've* you been?"

"Nothing much to tell. I've been living quietly."

"Come on, come on! You're . . . you know . . . why would you live anything other than . . . you know!"

"As I said. Things have been quiet."

"You gotta come see the house. You gotta meet Joe."

"That would be . . . nice."

"Where you living at the moment?"

"A hotel on Columbus, near 84th."

"That's swell, but bet you don't get to mow the lawn?"

You guess correctly. I do not mow the lawn.

"Then come have dinner! Sunday? You can do Sunday, right? I mean, you're not jetting out of town?"

Sunday would be lovely. Give me the address.

The house was a mansion in New Jersey, a testimony to revival colonial pride all in white. The partner, Joe, was a man of gleaming teeth and impossible tan. The food was rich and served with guacamole on the side. The lawn was very mown.

"And where did you two meet?" Joe asked, kissing me on both cheeks.

"LA," explained Will. "Melissa was a runner at Paramount."

"That's wonderful – just wonderful! And are you still in the movies, Melissa? Did you know my boy in his wilder days? You look so young – what is your secret?"

Creams, I replied. I make my own creams.

The house was full of photos. Even the toilet boasted a framed portrait of the happy hugging couple. Shelves were lined with memorabilia. A plaster model of the Eiffel Tower, which changed colour with the temperature. A memorial mug from Santa Monica, a teddy-bear shark won at a fair in Vermont, the hat Joe had given back to Will the first time they met, when a gust of wind blew it off his head and into the arms of him who would be his lover. The painting of Rhode Island they'd bought together, to hang on the bare wall of their first apartment. They showed me every object, told me every story.

This is lovely, I said.

How lucky you must feel.

God! Joe replied. It's been such a ride, you know, like, such a ride.

At 5.45 p.m. Joe pulled out of the drive in a fat 4x4 to go to church, and I stayed behind, drinking port and eating cheese with Will in the back garden.

"You've built yourself a wonderful life here," I said as the leaves swayed on the beech tree and a child screamed in a neighbour's garden. "You must be proud."

Silence from Will, and I glanced over at him to see his hand white around the circumference of his glass, eyes turned into the setting sun.

"Proud. I guess so. I've done the things you're meant to do. Get a job, get a house, get a husband. I go to the dentist, clean the floors, plant the garden, have dinner with friends. Yeah, I'm proud. I've lived the American dream. I owe you that. But . . . I'm not so sure, any more, that the American dream is a thing to take pride in. You see the kids come back from Vietnam; you live through Watergate, watch the Russians point missiles at you which you just point straight back, and you think . . . yeah, I've got the perfect life. But it's someone else's idea of perfection. Someone told me to be proud, and I did it, and I'm proud, but the pride I got . . . I'm not so sure it's mine."

"What would you rather do?"

"Fuck," he groaned. "Fuck, what kind of question is that? How the fuck do I know what I'd rather do, I haven't done it. I've begged. I've been down on the street on my fucking knees and begged, and I know I don't want to do that. I know that this life is better – so much better it doesn't even seem like the same me living it. I know what I have is great because everyone tells me so, but how do *I* know? How do I know that what I do is better than being a surgeon, hands covered in beating blood? Or a soldier, a politician, an actor, a teacher, a preacher. How the fuck do I know that my better is anything more than the great big fat lie we tell ourselves to justify the slow fat nothing of our days. There isn't enough time in a life to find out if the other guy's better is better than yours, cos you'd have to lose everything you have to find out for yourself. In the old days our fathers dreamed of bringing liberty and prosperity to the whole of the human race, of building a perfect society, and somehow that became a dream of a bigger car and a bigger front window and our neighbours making apple pie, apple fucking pie. And we bought into it, the whole fucking country, we bought into it, and we're proud because our lawns are neat and our houses are warm in winter and cool in summer and – fuck!" He slammed his glass down, port slopping in bloody streaks over the side. "We're happy because we're too fucking scared, too fucking lazy to think of anything better to be."

Silence.

The playing child next door had fallen silent. Will unclasped his fingers from the glass, one at a time, and turned to me, swinging the full force of his body to bear.

"Can I ask you something? Can I ask you ... What do you think of this?" A sweep of his hand, covering the garden, the house. "Do you like it? You've been anyone you fucking want; you must have an idea. Should we be proud?"

I didn't answer.

"Come on, whatever-the-hell-your-name-is. Come on."

I laid my glass to one side. "Yes," I said at last. "You have something beautiful here."

"Do we? You could be a billionaire like that! You could be president of the USA without having to bother with the elections. Is what we've got so much?"

"Yes. You have something . . . enviable. Not just things. Anyone can buy things. Your house is full of stories. Everything is a story. You get to keep them."

"And that's enough?"

"Yes." I flinched even as I spoke the word. "Joe – do you love him?"

"Fuck, of course I do." He spoke the words, and I believed him, from the pain in his eyes to the horror in his voice. "I love him. But how do I know I love him? How do I know that this is love? I've got nothing else to measure it by, no way of knowing. What's enough? How you live, *who* you live, what's enough?"

"Nothing. Nothing is ever quite enough. No matter who you are, there's always something more to be had, which could be yours if only you were someone else."

"Make me like you." The words came so fast I barely heard them. He spoke again, eyes bright, fingers tight between his knees. "Make me like you."

"No."

"Why?"

"I don't know how."

"Come on . . . "

"No. I don't know how."

"Come on!" he hissed. "Come on. I'm begging. This is me, begging. I'm getting old, getting slow, I'm settling down and I know, I just fucking know, I'm going to die in this place, living this life. Make me like you."

"No."

"Melissa . . . "

I rose sharply, and he rose too. "No. This life you have is beautiful. It is clean, warm, dull and beautiful. You've built something from nothing, and what you want now would destroy it. No, that's not the point – it would destroy *you*. You become like me, and not only will you lose the what, you'll lose the *who* you have. Every means you have of self-definition, from the mole under your arm to the friends who pick you up when you're too drunk to drive, the memories you own and the stories you tell, the clothes you wear and the people you love, none of it will exist any more. They will belong to someone else. Someone else's stories. And all you are will be . . . an audience . . . to a life you cannot live. I will not help you. I cannot, and I will not."

I made to move – where, I wasn't quite sure, the bathroom perhaps, the door maybe – and Will lunged forward and grabbed me by the arm, "Melissa—"

I jumped.

Instinctive panic, the jolt of skin. I jumped, and a woman stood before me, blinking, dazed and confused. With a curse I caught her arm and jumped back before she could begin to scream, and in that second of uncertainty Will's hand fell from my arm and I turned and walked away, my heels *snap-snapping* on the garden stones as I headed for the door.

I was in the street by the time he caught up with me. "Melissa!"

He stood, wretched, behind me, shoulders down and back bent.

"I can't help. I don't know how."

"Please," he whispered, tears stinging the rims of his eyes. "Please."

"All men want to be someone else. It's what makes them do greater things with their lives. With the lives they can live."

I began to walk away, and he shuffled limply after, a few steps, no more. "And what about you?" he asked. "What do you do?"

"Nothing," I replied. "Nothing."

I left him there, walking until my walk became a run.

I am very good at running.

Chapter 62

Paris.

Monsieur Petrain, lawyer by day, tight-arsed Adonis by night. The moment I saw him from across the street, I knew he was Janus' type. Beneath his cotton shirt was a body that gleamed with taut energy ready to go. His arms were almost too buffed to fit in his sleeves, his jaw was square, his eyes were weak, and he seemed every bit the manifestation of clichéd vanity that I recalled from my dealings with Janus.

Nor was he alone.

Ghosts like company, and when newly inhabiting a body find it easy to buy the companionship that others earn.

Today Janus was buying company with Côtes-du-Rhône, served by a tight-lipped waiter to a table of four. The party sat at the back of a bistro whose speciality was duck and lychee cassoulet served on a bed of chard soaked in hand-picked Sicilian plums. The price was so high they didn't have the decency to put it on the menu, and if you had to ask, you probably couldn't pay.

As the sun set over Paris I sat in a dignified woman with antique pince-nez on the end of my nose, a smartphone in my bag and small alp of diamond on my fingers, ate mussels served in lemon cream with garlic mushrooms, and watched Janus hold court, a beautiful wealthy man who wasn't shy about being the centre of attention.

I was not the only one who watched.

While Paris is a hub of modern fashion, a hazmat suit would stand out. The Aquarius agents therefore dressed more suitably for the environment: long-sleeved shirts, trousers, gloves, high polo collars, hats pulled tight and low and, just peeping out here or there, full-body Lycra suits. The overall result, besides giving the impression of Inuit prepped for a harsh winter, was to leave an area of exposed skin no greater than the distance from the bottom of their furrowed eyebrows to the top of their snuggled-up chins. In winter they could just about pull off the look. How they hunted in summer I could not speculate.

Two of their number, perhaps bolder than their colleagues, were sitting in the window of the restaurant. They ate a starter (hopefully on expenses) of warm goats' cheese, roast nuts and butter-soaked prawns, only a hint of Lycra suits and shoulder holsters showing beneath their long-sleeved shirts.

To all of which Janus was, naturally, oblivious.

Why look for that which you do not suspect?

A roar of laughter from Janus' table declared that a particularly witty anecdote had just been delivered, along with an especially droll bottle of red burgundy, whose sweet bite and extreme price tag served only to enhance wit, ease appreciation. I slipped twenty euros on to the table, gathered my walking stick and handbag, and waddled out of the restaurant. Some time in its recent past this body had undergone an operation on its right hip, and now the weight of my spine created a constant sine curve of irritation and discomfort.

Outside the restaurant I took note of the blue van parked – illegally – on the other side of the street, clocked the man with the long sleeves and tight-fitting hat having his third cigarette of the twilight as he leaned against a lamp post, and finally noted the two men nestled against the high stone balustrade of a rooftop, their arms wrapped up tight against the cold, their shapes visible as two patches of blackness against the settling evening light.

I hobbled a few hundred yards before stumbling and catching the arm of the passing businessman with the briefcase into whom I jumped, turning at once to catch the respectable lady by my side before she could fall and murmuring, "Are you all right, Madame?"

Chivalry isn't dead.

In a rather more comfortable frame I circled the block twice, passing by the restaurant both times to check on Janus' entrenched circumstance, before I found who I was looking for. The traffic warden was in her early thirties, looked like she might have come from Cambodia or Laos, and her scowl was embedded in the curled downward corners of her lips.

I am Doris Tu, traffic enforcement officer.

I have an an iffy right shoulder and am in urgent need of glasses, but the odds of finding another traffic warden any time soon seemed remote, even on Parisian streets, so I stuck with what I could get.

Squinting against my own questionable eyesight, I half-fumbled my way back to the restaurant where Janus was on to the crème brûlée, one hand up the skirt of his nearest companion.

I crossed to the blue van opposite, its windows tinted, its lights off, and rapped on the glass.

A moment in which I fancied I heard half-mumbled exclamations of obscenity. The window wound down. A face peered at me from the shadows, hair ruffled from having just pulled off the balaclava that otherwise would have completely covered his features. Long-fingered gloves, the sleeves tucked in, trousers tucked into socks, and the gun left, for lack of a better choice, in his jacket pocket, he was Aquarius through and through. Whatever his martial prowess, his parking skills left a lot to be desired.

"You can't park here," I snapped in my sharpest, fastest French. "No stopping Monday to Friday 6 a.m. to 10 p.m.!"

"We're on a delivery," he mumbled as the floor creaked in the cabin behind him and the assembled assassins tried not to breathe.

"No stopping!" I snapped. "I'm going to have to give you a ticket. Licence, please!"

His mouth dropped.

I am Doris Tu, a woman determined to do her job.

I tried not to laugh.

"Driving licence!" I repeated, snapping my fingers beneath his nose.

And at the end of the day what is a covert agent to do?

Shoot the traffic warden?

He handed over his driving licence.

I pulled out a biro from my pocket and wrote the entirely fraudulent details down in Doris Tu's notebook, angling the docket away from the van so he couldn't see the glaring difference between my handwriting and the writing already in the book. "Hundred and twenty euros," I barked, passing him the ticket through the open window. "Eighty if you pay within fourteen days."

"Can I just pay now?"

I am bureaucracy on the move, serving the good people of Paris.

"No! And you have to move!"

"But you've already given me the ticket."

"Move!" I nearly shrieked the word. "Or I'll call the police!"

I am traffic warden. Fear my wrath.

He moved.

As the van pulled away from the kerb I walked away at a stately leg-swinging swagger.

Around the corner I darted into the nearest open shop, caught the arm of the first person I passed,

was irritated to discover that I had acne, a particularly hot spot burning above my left eyebrow, but so be it, no time to fuss,

and headed back the way I'd come.

I walked straight into the restaurant where a few minutes ago a dignified lady with a penchant for diamonds had eaten mussels in cream, up to the table where Janus sat and exclaimed, "Monsieur Petrain! Morgan is dead!"

Janus, a woman's thigh pressed to his own, looked up, confusion battling with irritation, before the professionalism of a ghost kicked in. "Morgan? How terrible!"

Ghosts lie. It's how we keep our friends.

"They sent me to find you at once!"

"Well yes," he murmured, thumb flicking against the edge of a fifty-euro bill. "I can see that they would."

"Morgan?" asked the woman draped across his left leg. "Who is Morgan?"

"My good friend Morgan," he replied quickly, easily. "How did it happen?" he added, eyes flicking to me as his thumb snapped back and forth against the note.

"His lungs," I replied. "The doctors always said that Michael Morgan would never live past fifty. Can you come?"

And finally, in not his finest hour of deductive reasoning, Janus understood.

"Of course," he said. "Of course. Let me settle up and I'll be right with you."

Three minutes later we walked beneath the red awnings and flaking shutters of the tight Paris streets and Janus said, "Who are you?"

"How many ghosts did you introduce to Morgan?"

"What are you doing here?" he hissed.

"We need to get somewhere crowded. Need to jump away."

"Why? I've only just moved to—"

"You're being followed. An organisation called Aquarius is right behind you. They tracked you from Madame Osako through the cleaner to Petrain, and so did I. I bought us a few minutes, that's all."

A curl at the corner of his mouth. "Why would you do this?"

"They killed Hecuba, Kuanyin, others. They call me Kepler. Their file on you is thick; their file on me is a lie, and their file on Galileo is a fake."

"Who's Galileo?"

"Miami. Galileo killed us. Come on, we need a crowd."

Chapter 63

Remember Miami.

November 2001.

At this time the Galileo file had her down as a beautiful woman with auburn hair who didn't need to wear heels to strut, lipstick to pout. Who she was, where she was, I do not know, but she was entirely herself, some other where.

It was unseasonably cold for the time of year. I had gone so far as to start carrying a light linen jacket to wear outside, and on the beach the sunbathers were almost cool enough to talk to each other, instead of the usual silent all-consuming sweat that defined the Florida sands.

I was Carla Hermandez, district attorney, and I had become myself for the sake of my flat. On the fourteenth floor of a Miami tower block, I had panoramic views of the entire city, the green explosion of Oleta to my right, the beach not fifteen minutes' walk away, and in my black marble bathroom a jacuzzi. All paid for by the criminal cartels I was meant to prosecute.

My sudden donation of a large percentage of my life savings to victim-support charities had therefore earned me the incredulity of my (dubious and sacked) accountant, and simultaneously a range of dinner invitations from people hoping to profit by my new-found philanthropy. Money buys friendship in even the most well-intentioned circles.

I eased into my body and lifestyle a little piece at a time: a friend dropped here, a phone disconnected there, a drink with a stranger in a bar, a jog along the beach, a gift to the concierge downstairs.

I was beginning to settle in when a voice said:

"I just *love* who you're wearing."

It was a fund-raiser for an anti-corruption charity. I had attended for the nibbles, the jazz and the irony. But there, resplendent in a blue taffeta dress, was Janus.

She had to be Janus.

No one else would have polished their teeth to such whiteness.

No one else would dare wear such long lacquered nails, such a low-cut dress, such high heels for such dainty legs.

No one else could have recognised that I, Carla Hermandez, was not myself.

"Darling," she exclaimed, looping one arm through mine, "I've been in Miami for nine months, and Carla Hermandez is a double-crossing bitch. A queen among bitches, a bitch that laughs the laugh and barks the bark, but still a bitch. And you –" she tapped my shoulder with her glass "– are clearly *not* Carla Hermandez. How are you, darling? How are you keeping?"

"Well," I replied, "Miss . . . ?"

"I am Ambrosia Jane. And if I ever meet them, I shall chide my parents for the name."

"What happened to Michael? Michael Morgan?"

A flicker passed across Janus' face, and softer than I'd ever heard her speak before she murmured, "Time to move on." Then her face flashed a smile again, too bright to be real. "I hear you've quit the business?"

"You mean district attorney?"

"I mean estate agenting. Such a shame; you were so good at it."

"Time to move on."

She laughed, brittle and false as cut glass. "I hope you're keeping busy in your retirement."

"I'm ... Yes. Keeping busy. Trying a few different things."

A flicker of concern across her high plucked brow. "Are you all right, sweet thing?" she murmured. "Have you ... had a bad experience?"

"I'm fine. You?"

"I'm fine too."

"Well then. There you are."

Silence, her eyes fixed on mine. I looked away. Her arm tightened against the crook of my elbow. Two women pressed together in a room of strangers, and stranger than could be known. "You know," she murmured, "for the last thirty years I've been looking after my body. I exercised, ate carefully, played golf – *golf* of all things. Walking away from all that work I put in was ... frustrating. But at least now I don't have to care about my figure. More champagne?"

"Thank you."

"Don't go anywhere," she said.

Stand on a balcony overlooking Miami.

Cars back to back, pairs of white lights in one direction, red in the other, glowing like angry ants stuck in a queue to the nest.

Look down.

Pick a body.

Any body.

As an estate agent, I picked my bodies carefully. The beautiful, the wealthy, the popular, the beloved. I picked apart their lives and made their lives my own.

More care, less artifice.

Look through the walls, and I can see seven million lives acted out as though their stories, their memories, were the defining point of the universe.

Which, in a way, they are.

I stand on a terrace fifteen floors up, at a party hosted by a charity whose name I can't remember but which is terribly, terribly grateful to me for turning over most of my savings to its account, and Miami isn't cold, not even in November; the most chilly Miami gets is when you step inside the foyers of arctic air conditioning,

but I shiver.

Then Janus is by my side. She is very beautiful, and she is young, and ancient, and careless, and free.

"More champagne?" she says.

I do not say no.

Some hours later, as the rising sun pushed shadows across my bedroom ceiling, Janus rolled over beside me and said, "Cancer."

"What?"

"I – Morgan, I, myself – developed lung cancer."

"I'm . . . sorry to hear that."

"It's a slow tumour – large but slow. It hasn't spread – hadn't spread. Left lung. I had excellent medical insurance. I think he'll live."

"You had a family."

I could have made it a question, but there was no point. The answer was easy, obvious, known.

"A wife, two children. Elsa, Amber. They're both grown up now. I was in a hurry. We're always in such a hurry, you and I. The treatment was chemotherapy, radiotherapy, drugs, and eventually a lung transplant. I did the radiotherapy and it was . . . fine. My wife, Paula, came with me on every trip. She was very brave. She carried on as if nothing was happening, which is what you need when you have . . . this thing. But when the hospital called, she was there by my side. Then my hair began to fall out, I was sick, cramps in my stomach, legs. My gums bled, my eyes ached, I was hot and dizzy and it wouldn't go away. Pain I have experienced . . . Would you believe I used to go to the dentist when I was Morgan? But nausea. Trapped sweating in a dying corpse, knowing that there's nothing you can do to make it stop, your own body trying to poison you from the inside out. It was . . . And Paula held my

250

hand and . . . I didn't mean to, it happened so fast. I was Morgan, and then he was lying on the bed beside me, his eyebrows falling out, and he was shouting, screaming, who are you, who are you, what's happening, so loud that Elsa came running too. She'd come for dad. To help me get through this, and I was so . . . I didn't mean to jump. I blew it. When Elsa came through the door and saw me – saw Morgan – and he didn't recognise her, didn't know her face. It was over. Just one second, just a moment, a tiny moment and . . . " She stopped, turned her face away from me. I waited. "My wife. Paula. She lied to me. She had arthritis, her hands had seized up, painful. She'd said that they were fine, not to worry, here – have another pillow. But I went into her and my fingers were . . . to even bend them hurt up to my elbows, hurt into my jaw, relentless. She'd lied to me as she brought me food and held me in the dark. My wife lied."

Janus was crying, silently, her back shaking, head buried.

I held her, tight and without a word, having nothing better to give.

And then the sun was up, and I said, "I've quit estate agenting."

She sat in the window, eating toast and honey, and I said,

"There was an affair in Edinburgh. A deal that went bad. A ghost who . . . I thought I knew. You hear rumours but you never know for certain until it happens to you. I sold her out. Gave her account information to some people."

"What people?"

"The kind of people who kill ghosts."

"Why?"

I thought about it then shrugged. "I didn't think she deserved to live."

Janus laughed.

Twelve hours later Janus was gone, and Ambrosia Jane was in the emergency room. The doctors inspected her for concussion, substance abuse, psychotic breakdown; prodded for the four months of lost time she had experienced between getting on a bus in

Tampa and waking up in South Beach with silk on her shoulders.

A week later a letter addressed to Carla Hermandez arrived at my apartment. It smelt of lavender and was signed, "Your fellow traveller and friend".

It contained an invitation to the *Fairview Royale*, a barge specialising in loud music and cheap wine: Please come if you can. There'll be fireworks.

You hear rumours.

A frigate in 1899 off the coast of Hong Kong. A cruiser in 1924, ferry in 1957.

Milli Vra, Alexandra, Santa Rosa.

You never believe it'll happen to you.

In the same way that a beautiful man in a Parisian café perhaps does not look for the men in Lycra who have come to end him. They've been there all along. You simply did not think they could be there for you.

I went to the Port of Miami, to have drinks on the *Fairview Royale*.

As the ship pulled away from the harbour I looked for Janus, and she found me.

She was wearing a young black woman with warm round cheeks and a shaven head.

She said, "Carla?" and there was a note of surprise in her voice. "What are you doing here?"

"I received an invite. I thought it was from you."

"I didn't send anything."

This is that moment. It is the second of realisation when the terror bites. It is the instant when paranoia raises its head and whispers, *Fear me. I was right all along.* You go forward, you go back; the choosing is all.

"We need to get off this ship," I breathed.

"Carla . . ."

"We *need* to get off this ship."

Janus didn't argue.

*

I am

partygoer, packet of pills in my pocket, vodka on my breath, waiter, blisters on my feet, trousers too tight at the groin.

I am sailor in childish white uniform who knocks on the door of the cabin and says, sir? A message, sir?

I am the captain of the ship, and I am taking the boat towards land as fast as I possibly can.

Janus is my first mate, arms folded, eyes fixed on the partying throng below.

"It's not a bomb," she – *he*, a young man in white buttoned socks – says at last. "If it was a bomb we'd be dead now."

"Maybe they're limiting casualties."

"They?"

"They. Whoever they are this time."

His eyes flicker to me, then back to the dancing below. "You've done this before," he murmurs.

"A couple of times."

"It might not be a trap."

"You believe that?"

"No."

I take us towards a concrete wharf, flattened sheds of an industrial quay, the swollen sides of container ships riding high in the water, silent monoliths overhead.

"When we arrive," I breathe, "don't stop, just run."

"Don't need to tell me, sweetheart."

I flinch. A first mate doesn't say "sweetheart" to his captain. It's wrong, the wrong words from the wrong mouth, it is ugly. In another time, another place, I would say something.

Not tonight.

Slow as an ox, stately as a fattened cow, I ease us in.

Janus didn't bother with the rope, waited for the ship to slow to walking pace and jumped. I killed the engines and, as we bounced against the quay, I too hopped overboard, landing awkwardly on crooked ankles, steadying myself and pushing up, heading towards land.

Janus was already running for the metal fence that ringed the quay, while behind us, someone, a confused waiter, seeing his captain and first mate depart, shouted, "Hey!"

I kept running, unsure where I was, heading for the bright lights of the city, a silent causeway between us and it, cranes overhead, yellow beasts for hauling containers the size of houses, cars parked on the other side of the fence, low buildings with ominous messages such as CUSTOMS & IMMIGRATION – OBEY ALL COMMANDS nailed to the door. Janus was ahead, running between great walls of crates, through the sodium-stained night towards the metal gate and the bright road beyond, and it occurred to me that no one might have spotted us, safe in our skins, until the moment when we ran.

"Janus!" I called as his footsteps slapped in the night. "Janus!"

Janus, the gate a few metres away, half-turned to look back at me and fell.

There was the sound of an angry wasp biting a distracted bear, and Janus was on the ground, legs crooked beneath him. For a moment I couldn't see the blood, but as I pressed my back against the crate wall and stared at the body lying not ten feet from my knocking knees, it began to spread. Fast at first, then somehow slower as the area it covered grew wider, the blood came from his back, from the hole the bullet had torn through his lung, and it occurred to me, not for the first time, that ghosts are predictable. Mark your target, take them out. Whoever was shooting at us knew our natures.

I looked and saw only dark tunnels of towering crates, a chain fence and a padlocked gate. Janus lay just out in the open, head rolled towards me, mouth working, blood and foam on his lips, trying to speak. I eased closer, back still pressed against the containers, until I was a foot and a half from him.

"Ca . . . ca . . . ca . . ."

The beginning of a sound that might have been a name.

Janus' left hand was outstretched to me, right hand limp as his life ran away, the breath bubbling up through the shattered remnants of his ribcage. I could almost reach his hand without exposing myself, grab it from cover. The blood trickled against the toe of my shoe.

I reached out, caught Janus' arm by the wrist, pulling with all my might, dragging his body through the blood, little waves of it shifting beneath him as the body began to turn.

A gun fired and Janus' body jerked. I saw his eyes go wide, a sharp punching-out of breath, felt the blood splatter against my face as the bullet slammed into his chest and

Janus jumped.

Into the only body that was available.

I screamed and so did Janus, the two of us in one falling back against the crate, shrieking as I pressed my hands against my head and Janus pulled my knees to our chin and we screamed to drown out the shrieking in my ears and screamed to silence the bursting in our brain and screamed because all the little blood vessels behind our eyes were peeling away from the optic nerve and our tear ducts were filling with iron and our nose was flooding with hot blood and our body was kicking and tearing against itself and I tried to shriek,

"Janus!"

but the body by my side was dead and someone else was howling with my tongue, the breath ripping my chest in two.

"Can't . . . get the . . . / Help! / Can't stop / can't breathe!"

With all the strength I had, I pushed myself from the wall, flopping on to hands and knees, and Janus tried to pick me up, one knee buckling and another dragging up, and I screamed, "Gunman! Crane / gotta move / body! Get body!" as Janus hauled us to our feet. Blood was running down my face, spilling from my nose as vessels ruptured. Pain lanced through my side as some internal piece of machinery tried, and failed, to maintain its usual function, but the brain wasn't having any of it, every part, every neuron, fit to bursting as Janus took a step, took another and I shrieked,

"Can't . . . breathe! / then . . . breathe!"

We tumbled again as I tried to stop our legs, focus only on getting air into my lungs, on that single conscious act of inhalation, and I managed to drag down a lungful before Janus, giddy with terror, pushed us back on to our feet and, falling, running, staggering, pulled us away from his already chilling corpse.

255

Janus ran, and I breathed, and tried not to use my eyes, filled with blood, or my ears, singing where the drums were beginning to rupture. Away from the crane, we saw a strip of metal fence and Janus ran towards it, but I managed to gasp, "No!" and drop us to the ground.

"Got to run / sniper on the crane / got to get / need a body! / run / sniper!"

I rolled on to my side, clasping my knees to my chest in an effort to hold Janus down. "Speak / now! / listen! / now! / listen to me! Listen! There's . . . sniper . . . gotta be / dying / I know / body dying! / listen! / gotta get out / listen! We're not getting over fence, saw . . . sheds back / back? / way we came few hundred yards / dying! / few hundred, get to shed, call cops / cops? / flesh with guns! / run!"

Janus hauled me to my feet and I let him, dedicated every thought I had through the red haze of pain to breathing, just breathing, let him manage the rest, arms, feet, even the direction as we stumbled through the dark. The customs sheds lay, grey blots on a grey land, visible between the crates, and as we neared them I felt something hot and sharp down my side, and we screamed but kept running as another part, muscle, organ, nerve, didn't matter, gave up trying.

"Run," I whispered as we paused on the edge of the crates. Ten yards between us and the shed, ten open yards and a sniper at our back. "Run!"

Janus ran and so did I, our legs flying as we tore across the ground and something bit the concrete by my back, smacked into the wall ahead of us, but the first was wide to the left, the second wide to the right, and we ran and Janus slammed our shoulder into the door of the cabin, which cracked and collapsed beneath our weight, tipping us shoulder first into the musty gloom within.

For a moment I lay as the blood seeped into my mouth and Janus shrieked and buzzed around my mind and tongue. I managed to open my eyes long enough to see a beige phone hanging on the wall, and hand over hand crawled towards it, each limb dressed in lead, each movement a kick against a wall, until Janus too seemed to see my intention and with a sudden surge forward propelled us to the phone.

911.

The ringing in my shattered eardrums sent bubbles through my face, I could feel them burst and pop inside my cheeks, along the line of my jaw, and as the operator came on to the line another surge of pain kicked through us and I nearly dropped the phone from my bloody hand.

"Help me / dying! / port / help me! / gun / help!"

A bullet smashed through the window above our head and with a shriek Janus dropped the phone and I dropped us, landing curled up on the floor, head in my hands. I pressed against my skull in case it burst even without the help of lead, and as the phone hung swinging by its cable I screamed, "Get me a fucking body!"

Another bullet slammed into the table behind me, and it occurred to me suddenly that these shots weren't muffled, weren't the silent wasp of a sniper's rifle, but were a revolver, high calibre, and getting closer.

"Coming," I hissed. "He's coming / oh god / got to move / where? / away / coming? / on foot / jesus jesus jesus / listen / oh god oh jesus jesus / listen we have to . . ."

Too late. Janus uncurled and crawled up on to our feet. "No, wait," I gasped, but he was already staggering out through the broken door, and for a second I saw a shape move by the containers, dark beneath the dull street light, then a forklift truck, disguised as a nine-millimetre bullet, slammed into my left leg, spun me against the door frame and dropped me back down on to the cabin floor from whence I came.

Janus screamed, and screamed, and kept on screaming, even as I scrambled back into the shelter of the cabin, pressing my hand against the growing shock, the growing cold, the growing mess that had been my thigh, and breathed in

until Janus screamed again

and breathed out, which he seemed to find easier, and it occurred to me that this was it, dead in a cabin in the Port of Miami, gunned down by a stranger in a stranger's body, and that all things considered, give or take a variation of geography and time, this was probably how it was always going to have been. How it always had to end.

Then the door opened at the other end of the cabin.

A flashlight swung into my face. Janus' jolt as he tried to flee sent puke into my mouth. The flashlight came towards us, and behind the light was a security guard, from his peaked black hat to the revolver on his hip, his face open in an expression of shock and concern, and as he knelt down beside me he said, "What the hell . . ."

Janus moved

faster than me. He caught the guard by the wrist

and was gone.

The security guard fell back on to his buttocks, a toddler learning to walk. Then full control kicked in: his eyes went from me to the door directly in front of us, and at once he fumbled at his side for his revolver, drawing it and locking it in place with a two-handed grip, the barrel fixed on the rectangle of light through which our assailant should walk. I lay beneath him, gasping for breath, the shock of my shattered limb beginning now to assert itself in strong, clean waves of physical pain, even as the blood slowed in my brain and I blinked scarlet tears from my eyes.

We waited, eyes on the door, Janus on one knee, torch beam and barrel pointing towards the exit.

Silence, and the hot slow passage of blood between my clenched fingertips.

"Where is he?" Janus whispered, for himself, not me. "Where is he?"

"Two doors," I wheezed, and at once Janus snapped round to face the other door, through which the security guard had come. The bouncing of the phone on its cord had subsided, so had the voice on the other end of the line. "Cops are coming," I added. "Help me."

Janus turned again, gun swinging from one door to another. "Where is he?" he breathed. "Where *is* he?"

"Help me!"

His eyes flickered down to me, then away again.

"I'm sorry, Carla," got to his feet, "I'm sorry," gun held in front, "I'm so sorry," and elbows bent, Janus turned and ran.

I lay in a body
 whose I do not know
 in a shed God knew where
 and didn't want to die.

My uniform was white, all the better for showing up the blood. I imagined that at some stage I'd taken a great deal of pride in the uniform. I'd pressed it, steamed it, made sure the crease down the trousers was just so. Perhaps, as I drove the boat
 because I was a captain

I'd reflected on ancient seafaring days when I'd guided tankers into port, or sailed through the twenty-foot waves of the Atlantic, or dressed as the god Poseidon for the young novices as they crossed the equator or the dateline or, on those rare occasions when fortune was fair and navigation liberal, both at once, whooping my way across the centre of the world.

That would have been when I was young, but who knew? Maybe I'd been the captain of a tourist barge my whole life, chugging through the bay. Maybe I'd lied on my CV. Maybe no one would remember my name, whatever that turned out to be. Maybe I was the last person left alive who loved the body I was going to die in.

I tried getting up.

Getting up wasn't happening.

I tried crawling for the door.

Crawling was within my repertoire, rolled out, snake-like on to my side, kicking with one good leg and pulling with my hands.

I thought I heard sirens, then thought I had imagined it.

A policeman's body would be ideal.

A policeman's body would come with a policeman's gun.

I crawled to the door through which Janus had fled, and peered through it at a sodium-soaked car park adorned with no cover save for one disregarded black van and one overflowing grey dustbin.

Somewhere out on the water a ship blared its horn, proud and lonely in the night. I crawled back across the floor to the still-dangling telephone. The police operator had given up, and the line hung silent, whining like a hurt child. I braced my back against the wall and pushed myself up high enough to get a blood-smeared finger into the top drawer of a desk, yanking it out on to the floor beside me. The owner, damn him to a lingering demise, kept neat papers, business cards and a photograph of his smiling wife and daughter inside. Not a stapler, pair of scissors or sawn-off shotgun in sight.

The next drawer offered up a more promising arsenal of paper clips, sticky notes, pencils, pencil sharpener and a mug proclaiming WE ARE THE BEST in heavy black letters around the side. I smashed the mug against the floor, fumbled through the pieces for one large enough to sit in the palm of my hand, sharp enough to draw blood, wrapped my fingers around it, my hand beneath my body, and lay down on my side, knees tucked in, head down. The doctors call it the recovery position, though all that was recovered was that warm sense of comfort you possessed when, as a child, you curled up by your mother's side and had not a care in the world.

If I survived this, I told myself, I would be a child again, if only for a few hours, and feel the warmth of unconditional love that forgave all sins.

A siren shrilled in the distance. It sounded too slow, too low, no urgency to it, no audible Doppler effect, and so I gripped my ceramic shard tighter and told myself that I was alone, always had been, and that was nothing new.

A footstep on concrete, taking its time.

Climbing the steps, a slightly different tone of concrete, hollow, ringing with bass. A footstep on carpet, the sound of breath. The hand that held the gun had no need to pull the safety off, that had already happened, but I fancied I could smell the cordite, taste the metal.

The breath above me moved.

Closer.

Denim crunched, haunched, hunched. A man squatted down, his elbows swinging out above his knees, wrists loose, hair white, gun in hand, and smiled at me, and he was

Will.

He was old now, not merely older. His skin was layered on top of itself like folds of cotton, his hair gone to reveal the irregularities of his skull, dotted with yellow. His hands were moulting, his eyes were grey with gum, but he was still William who loved the Dodgers when he was young, and Joe when he was old, and had dreamed of living for ever and becoming someone else.

Which, in a sense, he was.

I looked, and must have lost a little breath for my chest felt tighter, and he smiled, and though it was Will's lips that parted, it wasn't Will's smile that settled there, but someone else's, a Will who as a child had pulled the wings off flies, a Will who as a young man had been banished from his home and who had not, perhaps, in a single moment of change, chosen to share his body with a stranger for three weeks in California but had taken some other path, to some other person.

Not-Will, smiling still, looked my body up and down, taking in my face, my clothes, my shattered and bleeding leg. He reached out with his left hand and brushed my cheek, a lover's touch, felt the half-growth of beard across my chin, loosely tugged at my hair, scrutinising its colour. His hand drifted down, my neck, my chest, my thigh, and came to rest just above the gunshot wound in my leg, suspended an inch in the air.

Then he said, but the accent was all wrong, someone else's accent in Will's throat, "I thought you'd want to say goodbye."

Hand hovering, ready to scramble for a bullet in my leg, to dig it out with bare fingers, I had to breathe and couldn't control the heaving of my lungs, felt the ceramic between my fingertips, saw the veins blue-black on the base of Will's throat.

His head turned, pigeon-like, examining me, watching my face, my eyes. He said, "Do you love me?"

The question seemed to require a reply, and when I didn't give one, his fingers brushed, so delicate, through the blood across my leg, streaking the uniform, pain running through the remnants of my thigh, up through my chest, throbbing from elbow to skull.

"Do you love me?" he asked again. "I wanted to find someone that you loved. When I found him, I wasn't sure if I'd got it right. His kidneys are broken, there's tumors in his bones and when I looked, see, here . . . " He pulled my right hand from beneath my body, rested it on his side, pressing it into his flesh where a bulge protruded beneath his jacket, a distortion in the flesh – hernia on a good day, something worse on a bad. "Isn't it repulsive?" he asked, holding my hand in place, his warmth in my fingers. "Isn't it strange? Why would anyone love something as disgusting as this? And look!" He moved my hand, higher now. I grunted in pain as the motion shifted my body, dragging me after his enthusiasm, pressing my palm into his armpit, against his skin. "There's a mole here," he exclaimed. "I find that fascinating. I play with it all the time; did you? I tried kissing a man, but he didn't understand; he said there was something wrong. He didn't love me, though he swore he loved . . . Will." Hesitation, struggling to remember the name, trying it out. "He swore he loved Will, but not myself. I wanted to see if you felt the same way."

He leaned in close, his breath mixing with mine, lips close enough to kiss, and for a moment I thought he'd do just that, lip to lip, but he was looking into my eyes, trying to find something that was not there. "Do you love me?" he asked. "I looked into the mirror and I couldn't see it, but I thought . . . You've been me before; you've looked into my eyes so many times and you must have loved – loved my skin, my lips, my throat, my tongue. Did you? Do you love me? Will? Do you love me?"

Need. A child needing, imploring on Will's face.

No, not on Will's.

On his face.

On its face.

I didn't answer, couldn't think of a single thing to say.

"Sometimes I look at myself, and all I see is contempt. My face

is full of hatred and I think, why would it hate me, I am beautiful, but then I move, and I move, and I move, and it's all hatred,
all ugly every single time I try to smile and then ..." A shudder,
breath drawing in, going out. "Do you love me? Come on!" A
laugh that was lacking patience, a humour that had only a passing
wit. "Come on, Will. Do you or do you not love me?"

I tried to speak, yes, no, maybe, perhaps. Nothing formed as my
mind searched for the right answer, the way out, and couldn't work
out what that might be.

Will's face darkened. Eyebrows closing in, eyes crunching up
tight, a childish sulk on an ageing face, not Will's face now, I
hadn't ever seen it with such a look, couldn't call it his; he lunged
forward now and rammed the barrel of the gun hard enough into
my broken leg to make me scream, digging it in, and I howled, an
animal sound from a stranger's throat, my voice not so high as it
had been a few bodies ago but so much more intense, a lungful of
agony across my teeth, and I doubted if it had ever made such a
sound before but not-Will pressed harder and roared, his left hand
around my face, pulling it into his.

"Do you love me?!"

As he pressed the gun deeper, his cheek next to mine, I reached
up with the shard of shattered mug in my hand and drove it, as
hard as I could, into the top of Will's neck.

My bloody hand slipped and missed his windpipe, pushing
instead into the soft flesh beneath his jaw. Fresh red blood spurted
out as ceramic edge penetrated skin, punching through the bottom
of his mouth beneath his tongue, and he fell back even as I rolled
on to him, putting both my knees on top of the arm that held the
gun and twisting it. A bullet fired, a twitch in the finger, and
another, great bone-jarring jumps of noise and light, but I held on,
held on, as beneath me the hot body writhed and choked, coughing blood, eyes goggled and face pale, and as I prised the gun from
his fingers and curled backwards, kicking my way free of him and
scrambling back.

Then he looked up into my face and, with a piece of coffee
mug sticking through his jaw, he smiled. "D-d-do." The sound

tangled with the blood in his mouth, a rivulet spouting at the corner of his lips. He coughed, sending droplets splattering in my face, and tried again. "D-do you l-like ... w-what you see?"

I raised the gun in my one good hand. His smile widened to a grin. His teeth were fake, dentures stuck in with gum, stained with blood. I turned my face away and pulled the trigger.

Chapter 64

Bodies.

No one can track a ghost during rush hour.

A crowded train. A busy station. Shoulder to shoulder, skin brushes skin, breath breathes breath, we inhale the sweat of the tall man's armpits, crush the old lady's feet beneath our boots.

I

whoever I am

rode the Paris Metro from here to there, surfing the arterial pulse of strangers' flesh.

Where Janus was, who Janus was, I didn't care, as long as someone who was Janus was where I needed him, her, whoever, when the journey was done.

I slipped from skin to skin, a bump, a shudder, a slowing-down and a speeding-up, a swaying of the carriage, a stepping on another's foot, I am

a child dressed in school uniform,

an old man bent double over his stick.

I bleed in the body of a woman on the first day of her period, ache down to the soles of my tired builder's feet.

I crave alcohol, my nose burst and swollen from too much of the same.

The doors open and I am young again, and beautiful, dressed for summer in a slinky dress and hoping that the goosebumps on my flesh will not detract from the glamour I seek to express.

I am hungry
and now I am full,
desperate to pee by the carriage window,
eating crisps in the seat by the door.
I wear silk.
I wear nylon.
I loosen my tie.
I hurt in leather shoes.
My motion is constant, my skins are stationary, but by the brush of a hand on the rush-hour train
I am everyone.
I am no one at all.
I ride the train to Gare de Lyon.
To Janus.
To somebody else.

An uninspiring station of minimal merit.

The nearest food is on the other side of a flagstone concourse where nothing grows and no one waits.

The trains are roaring TGVs heading to Montpellier, Nice, Marseille. The commuter trains are full of suburban dreamers, men and women who aspire to boulevards lined with fir trees and the sound of old men playing boules. I become one of these women for a minute, my suit sharp, briefcase heavy, a copy of the latest thing, by the latest recommended cultural wonder, tucked under my arm. My ticket is to Troyes, where the streets are clean and the mayor always says hello. I look for platform 10, and see a woman eating a baguette, devouring a baguette, standing by the barrier. Her hair is fair, her face is young, her dress is small and black, her coat is lined with fur, and she wears upon her wedding finger a band of silver studded with jade. The wedding finger taps out a rhythm, and the rhythm is one-two-three, one-two-three, one-two-three, while feet move, almost imperceptibly, to the motion of the waltz.

I stand by her side, start to hum a tune, the same style, the same beat. We do not look at each other until she finishes her baguette and says, "I hope I didn't just ditch a very beautiful body for nothing."

"You didn't."

"You have a plan?"

"Where's your ticket to?"

"I don't have a ticket. I saw her on the train and suddenly realised that I hadn't finished my dinner."

"You're married," I said.

Janus shrugged. "I've got two condoms in my bag and a spare pair of black lace pants. I think I'm having an affair."

"If you say so. Either way, you don't have a ticket, and unless you know the pin number to your host's credit card . . . ?"

Janus sighed, brushing crumbs off the white collar of her fluffy coat. "What do you suggest?"

"A train out of here."

"They can't have followed us. I changed dozens of times."

"Yet the fact remains that they found you," I replied, eyes still moving everywhere except over her. "They found me."

"Fine," she grunted. "Pick a train. I'll find someone boring to wear on it."

We caught the Montpellier TGV.

I caught a man whose wallet proclaimed him to be Sebastian Puis, owner of three credit cards, one library card, one gym membership, four supermarket loyalty cards and a voucher for a free haircut at a salon in Nice.

Janus rode Marillion Buclare, dark hair, deep puppy eyes and a pendant around her neck which proclaimed "Love" in Farsi. The train was not so crowded that Sebastian and Marillion could not have sat together. We did not.

Sebastian Puis owned an iPod. As the train began the long slow hum of acceleration out of the station, I flicked through its contents. I had heard almost none of the music he possessed, most of which appeared to be some sort of French rap. Twenty minutes

267

later I laid the iPod down. Sometimes even I struggle to get into character.

Across the aisle a boy of fifteen gestured furiously at his teenage companion. Stick with me, he said, stick with me and I'll see you all right. Them kids at school, they think they're something, but they're not, they're all talk talk talk, they don't know, I know, I've lived it, I've fucking lived it, I'll see you're good. Got a phone? Gimme. I'm gonna prank-call my brother again. He gets so mad. Just so mad. It's amazing. This one time I called him fifteen times in a day, then sent him a picture of my balls. It was the best. I'm the fucking best, I'll see you all right.

I tried to tune him out, staring out across the darkening flatlands of Northern France, and thought without words, remembered without feeling.

A stranger approaches in the street.

Says you are beautiful.

Their warmth, your skin.

There is no loneliness more lonely than to be alone in a crowd. No awkwardness more unsettling than the inside joke you do not comprehend.

We fall in love too easily, ghosts such as I.

Chapter 65

In my younger days I associated south with warmth. From the north to the south there was, I imagined, a softening of the winters, a brightening of the summers. To grasp that a place could be both south and blisteringly cold took more bitter experience in more blue-lipped bodies than I care to recount. I would come to the coast of the Mediterranean unprepared for the slicing rains and frost-stained ground, abandoning the high-cheeked, slim creature I wore in favour of meatier locals with flubber around their bellies in the hope that a change of circulatory system might dull the distress of climate.

Sebastian Puis was not warm. Scrambling off the TGV in Montpellier station – as average a mainline building as any in France – I was immediately struck by how cold my fingertips became in the biting wind and how thin my coat felt against the pouring rain. I huddled by the *tabac* with its paraphernalia of cigarettes, chocolate and packs of heretic-themed playing cards, and waited for Marillion Buclare. Marillion Buclare did not come, but rather a woman in a fur stole of russet fox, the nose hanging forlornly down by her shoulder, approached me with a cry of "Is that still you?"

Her chins were many and layered, painted the same brilliant white as her face. Her jowls hung beneath the line of her jaw; her hair was an ozone catastrophe; her fingers were blood red, her lips purple, and as she swept upon me I had a sensation of being a rowing boat before the prow of an oncoming battleship. "Good God," she blurted. "You look terrible."

Janus, resplendent in . . .

"I feel like a Greta – do I look like a Greta to you?"

. . . in a woman whose name was almost certainly not Greta, flicked through a handbag hanging by a gold chain and with a cry of "Can I pick them, or can I pick them?" waved a fat wad of euros around for all to see.

I smiled the long-suffering smile of the embarrassed son meeting his extravagant mother, took Janus gently by the arm and angled her away from the gaze of the station. "Marillion?"

"Let her go in the lady's loo. She has a bit of a rash, poor thing. Don't look at me like that," she added, slapping me on the arm. "I hopped half a dozen times before picking up marvellous Greta. What do you think?"

"I don't think she's your type."

"I think I'm hers," she retorted. "And if I am not now, then I will be. I will become so, yes? No one can follow a ghost through a subway; not even Galileo."

I scowled. "No more unnecessary jumping. They may not track us through rush hour but what will they do when the hospital report comes in for Marillion? That will give them a city, a place to start looking."

"Why, my dear precious thing," she breathed, "I do believe you're frightened."

"If you had been shot as many times as I have in the last few days, you too would hear the beating of the drum."

"Then we should have gone to the airport, flown to a place with no name, a hillside of tumbling shacks and shanties where the hospitals won't ask and the records won't tell."

"Perhaps," I replied. "But there's more here than just them and us."

"There's never more."

"Galileo is inside Aquarius."

"What makes you sure?"

"Why else would his file be a lie?"

"That's conjecture, not proof. Even if it were true, I don't see why you need me."

"Our kind never work together. We are competitors in a world of beautiful bodies and excessive tastes. In Miami we behaved exactly as ghosts would – we jumped and we ran, and we were gunned down for our mistakes. Just now we did precisely what you'd expect – we ran into rush hour, ditched our bodies for something rich and easy. Ghosts don't cooperate. Let's cooperate. No more unnecessary jumps."

Janus turned away, preening at her reflection in a window. "Such a shame. I could have changed into someone less fashionable."

We caught a taxi from the station.

The driver understood that his role was to be grizzled, gruff and terse. Strangers visiting his city for the first time might mistake all of the above for a symptom of deep wisdom as long as they didn't perceive it for the antipathy it clearly was. Beyond my own sallow reflection in the window, I watched a city which had moved too fast to ever truly understand what it wanted to be. Beneath the overhanging remains of a Roman aqueduct, car parks and silver-grey bollards lined the boulevards and little winding streets. Between the coffee shop and the supermarket selling wine in six-euro cartons with a tap on the end, the green flashing light of a pharmacy, two snakes coiled around a staff. Swaying cedars pushed against dark-needled pines; hedges of thorns hid the new apartments which crawled up the hills towards the northern edge of town.

The driver asked, "Holiday?"

No, I answered, and yes, Janus replied.

Stupid time to come for a holiday, he said. Should have come in summer or closer to Christmas. You'll have a horrible time now.

*

The hotel had purple ceilings, blue carpets and a motif of silver storks embossed into the walls. Janus paid with Greta's cash for two rooms for the night. Dinner was still being served; would we be dining?

No, I said, running my eye over a menu of twenty-euro steak and thirty-euro wine. All things considered, I doubted that we would.

Alone in a room that could have been anywhere in the world, I stripped off before a full-length mirror and assessed the body of Sebastian Puis. He wasn't my type, nor was I particularly comfortable with either his skin or his style. He hovered on the verge of being unhealthy grey, and from his chest and back tufts of hair sprouted in patchy clusters, unsure whether to give growth a try.

The urge to jump into someone darker, brighter, smoother, hairier – anything which could be firmly defined, seized upon as a starting ground for creating some sort of character – grew in my stomach. I rifled through Sebastian's bag but could see no evidence of his occupation. His phone, simple and sensible, I pulled the battery from, in expectation of the moment when a friend or loved one, perhaps waiting at Montpellier station still, began to agonise about his disappearance. Maybe a frightened mother was already on the phone to the police, who would reply that young men lead their own lives, and that if she was truly concerned she should call back, on the non-emergency line, at the end of two days. Gut instinct is never accepted as a measure for the disappearance of a loved one, and for that I thank police procedure heartily.

Study this face and guess its nature.

I might be a rakish wit, a piss-taking clown. Perhaps I'm soulful and lonely, sitting awake at night writing sonnets to an imagined love. My hands are soft, alien to manual labour; suck in my stomach and my ribcage protrudes with aching clarity, yet relax my belly and I look almost portly as it rounds out above my hips. My buttocks have suffered the repetitive light abrasion that comes from too long sitting in the same place; the inside of my left thigh was once scratched and now is healed. Am I a student, a designer, a software programmer, a young DJ with a lot of trend and not much taste? More important, am I gluten intolerant? Can I manage lactose, do I get shin splints, should I be careful when eating sugar, will the sting of a bee cause my lungs to collapse? How will I know until I make the mistakes that Sebastian Puis would not make, having already made them once before?

For a moment I miss the familiar weight of Nathan Coyle or the runner's confidence of Alice Mair.

We eat, Janus and I, in a small restaurant opposite a remnant of medieval wall. She orders cheese and wine and duck in simmering purple sauce. The owner/waiter/matron of the place asks me if I will be paying for my mother's meal. Janus forgets who she is and for a moment is indignant at the idea.

Conversation is hollow.

Do you know the city?

A little.

When were you last here?

A long time ago.

And who were you then?

I forget. But I wore yellow as I walked by the sea, and ate oysters from a nickel bucket. And you?

I was someone extraordinary.

I am always someone extraordinary, you see.

And then Janus said, "Why did you save *me*?" The question was so against the tenor of our conversation I was taken by surprise. "Our relationship has been ... temperamental, shall we say. You need help – you could have gone elsewhere."

"Galileo. You're the only one I know – besides myself and one other – who's met him."

"And Miami?" she murmured, prodding a piece of drooping vegetable with her fork. "What of that?"

I laid my cutlery down, folded my hands together beneath my chin. It feels like a gesture Sebastian Puis would not make, but then for this brief encounter, for this rare moment between old acquaintances, I am not he, but ...

... someone else.

"We ... understand flesh," I said at last. "We are connoisseurs of eyes and lips, hair and skin. The emotions which would otherwise drive the flesh, the ... complexity that arises from a life long lived, we perhaps lack. Like children, we flee from pain and deny our own responsibilities. This is the simple truth of our existence. Yet we have still lived as human. We still dread to die and feel all the things humans feel not merely as a chemical response, but as ... the only language we have left with which to speak. Had it been me who switched into a body without injury that night in Miami, I cannot guarantee that I would not have fled. I do not say this –" I added as she opened her mouth to speak "– to forgive you. You left me to die; that was the decision you made. As I understand fear and dread, and panic and pain, I also comprehend resentment, anger and betrayal. You saved your skin and left me to die in mine, and though I can comprehend the action I cannot forgive it."

"And if I repented?" she murmured. "If I ... apologised?"

"I don't know. I can't imagine how that might sound."

The end of a fingertip played with the hollow of her spoon. A moment came, a moment went, and that was all that there was to it. Our plates were removed, coffee presented, for you cannot have dinner and not have coffee, Monsieur, it simply is not a concept we are prepared to comprehend. And as she crumbled in a cube of brown sugar Janus said simply, "You were meant to have killed him."

"Who? I am caretaker to a whole cemetery of responsibilities."

"Galileo."

"I did kill him," I retorted, sharper than I'd meant. "I shot him, and when the police came I knelt over his body and there wasn't a pulse."

"And yet the rumours persist. *Milli Vra, Santa Rosa* ... "

"I didn't know you paid attention."

"I read newspapers. I'm particularly fond of the celebrity tattlers, but even the tabloid press will give a few inches to a ship found drifting in the dark, blood on the floor, survivors weeping in a barricaded room. And as we have discussed before, it is easy –

so very easy – for one of our nature to make a decision regarding the lives of others. You've tasted it. You know how it feels. Hecuba was inclined the same way. Families would slaughter each other, from the chambermaid to the master; only Hecuba killed those who threatened him, and you kill those who threaten the things you love, and you love everyone, don't you, Kepler?"

My teeth ground at the name, fingers rippled along the edge of the table.

"He wore . . . a host," I replied as Janus lifted her tiny coffee cup, little finger sticking out like an antenna. "His name was Will. He was my gofer, in the old days. Last time we met, we argued. He had this thing with his left leg, a muscle that cramped when twisted the wrong way. I don't know the cause, wasn't around long enough to get it checked out, but when it happened you could feel the tendons stand out beneath the bridge of your foot like they were going to pop right out from the skin. But he was a clean willing host in a city that wanted neither of us. He kept his nails trim and always carried mouthwash in a little bottle. He didn't ask questions. He was . . . good company. Not very often you can say that. Then he was Galileo. And he had to die, so I killed him, three shots to the chest. It would be safer to put a bullet in his brain, but I had this picture in my head, of Will's face, smashed up. Of his nose just exploding, of seeing his skull, of my – his – eyes staring, hanging out, and I should have put the bullets in his brain, but I didn't.

"Then I was the policeman and I took his pulse, and he didn't have one and I thought that's it, but the medics came and they started resuscitation and they failed. Of course they failed, but I imagine there must have been a moment. Perhaps a moment on the ambulance floor when a medic pushed down on his chest and what little blood there was left went through his arm and his skin touched the medic's skin and . . . and I don't know, because I wasn't there – I was . . . someone else by then – but I can almost guarantee you that the medic who called time of death on my Will, if questioned today, would have absolutely no memory of it. None at all."

"And so Galileo lives."

"It would appear to be so."

"Just because he is of us," she added sharply, "doesn't make him our responsibility." Even as she spoke the words, her shoulders uncurled, fingers relaxed over the end of her spoon. "Though he seems to have made us his."

"It's not just Galileo."

She waited.

"In Frankfurt Aquarius ran a medical trial. They were attempting to create a vaccine, to immunise people against us."

"Can that work?"

"I don't know. I doubt it. As it was, they didn't get very far. Four of their researchers were murdered. A woman called Josephine Cebula did it. She was worn. Aquarius blamed me."

"Why you?"

"I thought about that. Perhaps because I was convenient, because I showed up. But then I also thought about why they assumed that Josephine was somehow complicit in the act, instead of an unwilling host. I saw CCTV footage of her covered in blood, and to me it seemed obvious – blatant – that she was Galileo. That Galileo did the killing. But Aquarius blamed me, blamed her, and ordered us both killed. Host and ghost. That's not how these things usually work."

"How did they die?"

"Who?"

"The people your skin . . . that Galileo . . . killed."

"Badly. Drowned. Stabbed. Mutilated; it varied."

"Why?"

"Perhaps because they were developing a vaccine; perhaps that was a threat. But also . . . " I hesitated, drew in breath. Janus waited, a fork between two fingers, playing with it like a ball of string, watching. I ran my finger around the rim of my coffee cup, found I couldn't meet Janus' eye. "How did you become a ghost?"

"Badly," she replied.

"Violently? When I . . . died – I think it's fair to say that was the mechanism in my case – when I died, I held the ankle of the man

276

who'd killed me. That was my first jump. I watched myself bleed to death and shook my frozen corpse, trying to get back in, but of course the flesh was dead and I lived, and the watchmen arrested me for my murder, which seemed, in a way, fair. It was, as you say, a bad beginning. I take it your origins were no less glamorous?"

"Stabbed. In the stomach. Bled out. Jumped into the nurse who was trying to push my guts back in."

"Aurangzeb was hit by a car."

"Aurangzeb was an idiot."

"Kuanyin had ergot poisoning."

"She never told me that – *that* I can believe."

"The point is, our origins tend to be . . . traumatic."

"How is this relevant?"

"Consider an organisation like Aquarius, any organisation of that ilk – there are plenty to choose from. It kills ghosts for whatever reason. But no matter how many you destroy, we keep occurring, popping up like dandelions between the cracks. Perhaps you realise that there is a pattern in our origins; perhaps you conclude that violence, terror, pain, whatever – these are our creators. Aquarius can hardly eliminate violence, but not every murder in an alley creates one of our kind, not every ergot poisoning or death on a bedroom floor. There must be conditions above and beyond those presently observed. I've been a doctor now and then, and even I know that to vaccinate against a virus first you must understand the thing itself. You must know how it functions, how it replicates. In Frankfurt they may have been attempting to make a vaccine, certainly. But first they need to understand what it is they're vaccinating against, understand what *we* are."

"You propose that the vaccination programme could have been creating ghosts as well as destroying us?"

"I suggest that there is a mechanism in the human brain which can trigger a jump in a tiny minority of people at a time of trauma. Identify that, and perhaps you can prevent it manifesting. Perhaps you can kill us before we are born – genetic genocide. Perhaps you could do so much."

Silence.

Then, "Why Galileo? Why Frankfurt, four people dead?"

I pinched my fingertips together, bit my lip. "Permit me a different question. Why were the murders so brutal? You and I, we were created in a moment of violence, of brute force. *Milli Vra*, *Santa Rosa*, mass murders, fear, trauma, why? Perhaps because every few years Galileo looks in the mirror and realises that the face staring back doesn't love itself. Perhaps he tries to cut that look out of the mirror, and in doing so ... creates a situation. Or perhaps he looks in the mirror and sees something beautiful which will eventually die, and Galileo wants the perfect things to last for ever, and you and I, if we are careful, will last for ever. Perhaps Galileo wants to create ghosts. If that's the case, he too needs the same thing Aquarius does – to understand us. A trial to investigate vaccination can be permitted to go just far enough to discover the mechanism of our creation, but not too far. Not so far that it can actually inoculate against our existence. Just far enough."

"This is still supposition."

"Absolutely. But then we must add more evidence to this. If we suggest that Galileo, far from being ignorant of the Frankfurt trial, is in some manner aware of it, even manipulating it, then we can say that he is fairly well embedded in Aquarius. Embedded in the very organisation that is meant to destroy him. A series of murders in Frankfurt should have been blamed on him, and were instead put at my door. A host who any ghost would have worn – Josephine – was worn by me, and instead of ordering just my death, hers is ordered too. Clearing up loose ends, maybe. Or maybe more. Maybe we could call that jealousy. And who's sent to kill me? A man by the name of Nathan Coyle – a man with more cause to hate Galileo than he could ever find to despise me. Finally there's the Galileo file itself, which passes straight through incompetence and out the other side into lies. Plain and simple lies. Aquarius is protecting the single most violent member of our kind. Why?"

A half-laugh passed Janus' lips, humourless as a crocodile's wheeze. "Aquarius believed they were running a programme to destroy us, whereas Galileo was using the programme to create us. Absolutely marvellous."

"Mostly marvellous," I corrected. "But Josephine died."

Her smile was still there, frozen and distracted, smiling at a thing that had no humour. "You always were overattached to your skins. I'm surprised you don't have . . . a little sympathy for what Galileo has done."

"No. No sympathy. Some . . . inkling of comprehension for why. We move through skins. Today I am Sebastian. I have an iPod, a book, some clothes, these shoes, I am this face that I see in the mirror, and tomorrow I am . . . someone else, and I do not have any of the above. Today I have . . . you, in a sense. It may not be an association that either of us enjoys, but it is . . . a link. Something about which I can say, 'Yesterday this was so and tomorrow it shall be the same,' and that *is* something. Perhaps something good, in that it exists at all. Galileo . . . looks to make something – something that lasts, something that he did, regardless of who he was at its creation. So perhaps I can understand, but no, that is not the same as sympathy."

A bill was placed on the table.

I remembered that I was Janus' son and paid.

Sebastian didn't carry much cash. Here today, gone tomorrow.

Janus watched. "How did Galileo do it?" she asked. "How did he get so deep into Aquarius?"

I laughed.

Didn't know where the sound came from.

Sebastian Puis had a good laugh: it came right up through his belly, pushed his shoulders back. I liked it. It was the first thing about this body I admired.

"I think it was me," I said. "I think I made it happen."

Chapter 66

"Are you the estate agent?"

Do you like what you see?

"Are you the estate agent?" she'd said, and I'd looked up from my desk, and she was young, pampered and not at all herself.

Never mind the question on her lips; never mind her presence at my door.

This was Edinburgh in 1983, and no one dressed so well or spoke so fair. I leaned back and pictured her how she might truly be: a smaller meeker woman dressed in a shapeless old coat, her thick brogue tempered perhaps by a difficult upbringing that left her doubting her own mental and physical self-worth. Or maybe she was as her ghost had found her – heels a danger to tarmac, pointed and red, a skirt that barely covered her shapely behind, two hundred pounds of cotton and silk clinging to her breast, two thousand pounds of gold hanging about her neck. There were some – a few – who had the confidence to march around the city dressed in such a guise, but even the most vainglorious of self-admirers baulked at doing so casually.

"Are you the estate agent?" she said again, impatience rising in her tone, so I said yes.

"I need a man."

I resisted the obvious and gestured to the chair opposite my desk, won't you please, may I give ...

She was too busy for courtesy. "Young, strong – a complete medical history. That's the important part. I want cardiogram, blood tests, lung capacity test, allergies. Do you think you can do me someone ex-military?"

I could certainly look into it. Would madam be looking for a short-term or long-term habitation?

"Short. Doesn't matter about family history. And blond. I like blond. But not curly hair. And not too hairy on the back either. OK if he uses oils and shaves, but I don't want hairy when I collect."

Any particular needs more than an ex-military blond non-hairy physical hulk of a man with clean medical history and a penchant for razors?

She thought about it, then said, "It'd help if he has a boat."

"A boat?"

"Something nice. A yacht. Seagoing."

"I can certainly investigate, Miss ... "

She seemed to see me for the first time. "What?"

"What should I call you, Miss ... ?"

She stared down at herself as if surprised by both the question and her gender. Then her gaze returned to me, startled and clear. "Why the fuck should I know? Does it fucking matter?"

"I am an estate agent, the only one operating in this area. I have many clients, and considering how rapidly their appearances may change from meeting to meeting, I like to keep some sort of coherent client list for future reference."

"A name?"

"If you would."

She thought about it and smiled. "Call me Tasha. No – call me Tulia. I think I suit Tulia better." Then the smile was gone, and the memories which it stirred sank beneath the choppy waters of the present. "Now get me someone beautiful."

My commission for the job was fifty thousand pounds.

I found her Eddie Pearce, an ex-marine with a love of sailing. With the muscles beneath his neck he could have broken doors down; with the end of his finger he looked like he could lift my desk.

I said, do you like what you see?

Tasha — or perhaps Tulia — clapped her hands together with delight, exclaiming, "He's beautiful! He's so beautiful! Oh I *want* him!"

Can I ask what for?

What for? What kind of question is that? I want him because he's him! I want him because everything about him is enviable, everything about his body is handsome and toned, everything about his life is sensational. I want him because he sails with his face turned to the wind, because he has women who love him, men who adore him, strangers who look up when he walks by. I want him because I'm bored and he's something new. I want him because he's beautiful. Don't you understand? Don't you love him?

Yes, I said. I understand.

"But do you love him?" she demanded.

"Not yet. But perhaps I could."

She smiled at this, wrapping her arms about her chest as if to contain the jubilation welling up inside. "I love him already," she breathed. "I know he's going to love me too."

Two nights later she was on his yacht sailing out through the Firth of Forth towards grey seas and open horizons.

Four days after that the yacht was found drifting by a Dundee fisherman and his crew. When interviewed, he looked as if he had swallowed his own raw fish, which yet wriggled and writhed inside him. He spoke in the softest whisper of the things he had seen, and reported himself grateful, so very grateful, that at the moment his hand had brushed the skin of the one living thing inside he himself had passed out, to remember no more until waking on the shore.

Knowing I did not want to look, and knowing I had no choice, I read the autopsy report on Eddie Pearce. What acts, what violence, what violations that the mind could devise had perforated what little remained of his flesh, the deed prolonged over two days of suffering below the decks of his own vessel. Yet, the coroner concluded, somehow through all this there must have been at least an element of consent, for though his body was tortured with every constriction it could bear, still incredibly it had inflicted equal violation, equal pain upon the woman found barely conscious in the cabin besides his corpse, whose final words, as the fisherman pulled her up on to the deck, were a half-whispered

Do you like what you see?

Three days later my Edinburgh office was cleared, and I was someone else, standing on a railway platform.

Two days after that a document was sent anonymously to an organisation operating out of Geneva. It listed various accounts held across the globe. The most recent payment made had been to an estate agent in Edinburgh, for the sum of fifty thousand pounds, though if anyone bothered to look, they would find no record that the estate agent had existed at all.

Janus said you ratted out Galileo.

I said yes.

Good. Takes guts.

I said I sold him out to Aquarius. They weren't Aquarius then, just killers with a cause. Aquarius was who they became. I gave them everything they needed to track him, by his monies, by the accounts he used when he was some other skin.

I said that's why he tried to kill me in Miami

why so many skins died.

I thought I was helping Aquarius kill Galileo.

All I did was help him on his way.

Chapter 67

We walked back to the hotel in silence.

Alone, I lay down on the bed, flicked through my useless wallet, turned on the TV, swept through the channels one way, then back the other. Politics from Brussels, football from Marseille, beautiful cops from America, dangerous robbers from Russia, concerned journalists before the hulk of another burned-out-building-in-do-you-know-where?

I wondered if Sebastian Puis would have cared.

His face in the mirror looked like it was capable of guilt by remote control, but like most of the emotions his gently bristling chin expressed, he probably would have got over it quickly enough.

Hotel toothpaste is grainy and leaves a prickling aftertaste.

I turned the lights down and listened to stories of recession, development, light local tales of gap-toothed children excelling in a wildlife drawing competition and old women uniting against dog fouling, and as my mind began to drift, the newsreader cleared her throat and returned to the story of the moment, which, in among all the other moments, I'd somehow missed.

Two images, more fluent than the words.

A windswept reporter, shivering against the dead-night cold. She stood before the floodlights of the Brandenburg Gate, police behind and camera crews all around.

A shot – not from film itself, but of a film running on a computer screen, softly out of focus.

I listened to the story, and, hotel dressing gown pulled tight, padded down to the foyer. The girl behind the counter was sleepy, the computer by the lift was unattended. It took no time to find and a while to load. The YouTube video that was the centre of this breaking news was six hours old, had been pulled and re-released, pulled and re-released, and on its fifteenth reincarnation was at three hundred and forty-seven thousand one hundred and twelve hits and climbing.

The film itself is shot on a smartphone camera.

The filmmaker waves cheerfully to himself, his face giant, an angle that shoots up his nose as he proclaims in German, "This one's for you."

A series of floors and walls as he lays the phone down on an unseen stand, and then, resplendent beneath the lights of the Brandenburg Gate, he reaches into a large black bag and pulls from it a can of gasoline. Grinning, he throws it over himself, hair sticking to his face, suit dripping, and when the last drop has fallen he waves again at the camera, arms spread wide for the inspection of his audience.

A shout off screen and the filmmaker's face glows with delight. "Come over, you're just in time!" he calls, beckoning. From his pocket he removes a green cigarette lighter and as the security guard enters the frame, one hand on the pistol in his holster, another held out, calming, soothing, our filmmaker declares, "Smile! You're going to be famous!"

The words of the security guard are the inevitable half-stumbled placations of the moment, the please sir, calm sir, let me help you sir. He dare not approach, flinches back as our film-maker turns in the pool of spilt gasoline, revelling at the mess, until suddenly, sharp as the crack of a pane of glass, he stops, turns to the security guard, face vacant, hand outstretched and says, "Help me."

The guard hesitates, as who would not?

"Help me," he says again, fingers uncurled, imploring. "Help me. Please?"

The security guard is a good man.

His toe slipping on the edge of the pool of petrol, he reaches out, and his fingers brush the hand that implores.

The filmmaker staggers, and in that second the guard's outstretched hand becomes a bunched fist and he slams it into the filmmaker's jaw, pushing him up then dropping him down into the pool on the floor.

This moment occurs at 1.31 into the film.

Comments such as

OMG 1.31!!

or

Wow so thought that was gonna end different 1.31

fill the screen. One hundred and fifty-three viewers have even gone so far as to give what they're seeing a little thumbs-up. I wonder briefly if they looked beyond this moment before rendering their judgement.

Then the guard, all his previous fear and empty sounds turned to the dead silence of the competently self-aware, reaches down and plucks the cigarette lighter from the fallen man's hands. He steps back to the edge of the pool, and as the filmmaker shakes himself, blinks in bleary confusion, opens his eyes and looks up to see – as though for the very first time – his situation, the guard flicks back the cap from the lighter, looks direct to camera and breathes,

"Do you like what you see?"

Saturated in a pool of petrol, Johannes Schwarb, his face bewildered and mouth open, begins to get out a scream before the falling flame hits the ground.

The security guard waits for the body to stop burning before he reaches down, picks up the still-filming mobile phone and turns it off.

*

Janus watches in silence.

There is revulsion there, but not surprise.

When it is done, she says, "Who is it for?"

"What?"

"He said this one's for you. Who is it for?"

"Oh," I reply, briefly bewildered. "Me. Obviously. It's for me."

Chapter 68

The body of Sebastian Puis did not sleep that night.

I have surfed from host to host, night by night, never sleeping, and though my skin may be fresh as a spring flower, yet I remain tired. The only conclusion I can reach is that the mind – whatever loose concept of the same may be applied to myself – needs sleep as much as every muscle fibre, nerve and hormone-crunching cell.

Descending for breakfast out of the dumb sense that it was dawn and breakfast was what you did, I was only slightly surprised to find Janus not there. No one answered my knock on her bedroom door, and at the reception desk the clerk mumbled, "Yes, she went out this morning and left you this."

A yellow piece of hotel paper, a hand – child-like in its scrawled hugeness – proclaiming on it, *Popped out. Dinner, Saint-Guillaume, 53 rue de la Garde, 5 p.m.? xx*

Dinner and a kiss.

"Where is Saint-Guillaume?" I asked wearily.

The receptionist looked it up on a map. "Do you have a car?"

"No," I sighed. "But I'm sure I can find a lift."

*

Abandoning a body is dangerous.

If you cannot find the moment of the switch itself, then look for the next best thing. Find the patient who walked into the hospital, amnesiac and frightened, and ask them – what was the last thing *you* remember? And who was the last person you touched?

In those circumstances where a body must be abandoned without triggering the usual panoply of symptoms that may arouse attention, I recommend massive doses of mind-altering drugs.

Say what you will for the French; they know how to stock a pharmacy.

I took a gentle walk around the city, stopping on the way to pick up a drug here, a painkiller there, until my bag was sagging with the weight of questionable medication. I visited the cathedral, read a little more of my book and managed to restrain myself from editing the contents of Sebastian's iPod. I bought a map of the surrounding area and a bottle of water, tucked both into a brown paper bag and settled down on a bench opposite the emergency ward of the university hospital.

As it began to rain, sideways off the sea, I reached into my bag, pulled out a hefty handful of pills and downed them in a gulp of sugar-coated delirium. I waited ten minutes, stood up, leaving my map behind beneath the bench, and, surprised at how reluctant my own legs were to move and how tempting it was to laugh, swung my way towards the emergency room.

The receptionist at the entrance desk had a face designed to discourage sickness. Better a lingering disease, the furrows of her eye seemed to proclaim, than the customer care skills about to be revealed. I beamed, slouching across the desk, and let my packets of pills tumble from their bag. "Hi," I said. "I'm really, really high. Can I shake you by the hand?"

Jumping from a sober body to a drunk one is unpleasant.

Jumping from a stoned body to a sober one is, arguably, an even harsher return.

Needs must.

Fifteen minutes later – ten spent in the ladies' toilet reminding myself that my nausea was a psychological rather than physiological response – I was a male nurse with a straight back, short trousers and a set of car keys in my pocket. Five minutes walking round the car park with the electronic tag, looking for a flash of indicator lights, located my car. I paused long enough to turn my mobile phone off, and collect my map from beneath the bench, before settling into a car that smelt perfectly of me and heading north towards Saint-Guillaume.

Chapter 69

Once, in Milan, I was a woman with a handsome face and thick eyebrows that seemed always to rebuke the foolishness of what they beheld. I owned a little yellow Mini but, slipping into the driver's seat for the first time, I was shocked to discover how high the headrest, how close the brakes, my knees bumping up against the wheel. The back of the seat was pushed forward, crunching me down like a rally driver, and not two minutes into the drive I was forced to stop, readjust every part, tweak every mirror. Comfort and security thus restored, I spent four glorious days attending the most fashionable gatherings of the town, until at last a beautiful man in a suit approached me and said hello, and only after I'd started hitting on him did it become apparent that this unknown gentleman was my brother and he was perturbed by my behaviour.

Somewhat embarrassed, I moved swiftly on, and my host, it seemed, continued about her daily life as if oblivious to the time I had stolen from her. Until, that was, she tried to drive her car, which she crashed almost immediately into the side of a police truck, and was taken shrieking first to hospital, later to court.

Remarkable, the habits people will justify as normal.

I drive north as the rain thickens until it is a shimmering sheet sloshed across my windscreen, until the road is a grey fuzz of rebounding water, until the skies are black and the mountains vanish beneath the frozen skies, and I think of Galileo.

Chapter 70

Saint-Guillaume.

I had never been there before; doubt I'll go again.

The lights in their iron brackets along the steeply climbing streets were bubbles of pink hanging in the pouring air.

A single shop was open at the bottom of the hill, its back balcony overhanging a rocky river in full roar. The streets were empty save for the occasional outline of a smoker framed in an open door. Parking was difficult, finding my way through the downpour up the tight-spun stairways and byways near impossible. I cowered beneath the arch of a church and peered into the gloom for rue de la Garde. Eventually an old woman, her umbrella abandoned as useless against the slicing deluge, pointed me back down the hill and round the side of a bakery, its shutters barred and delivery van tucked up on the pavement for the night. I slipped and scrambled, my coat over my head, looking for number 53, warm lights behind the open shutters and closed window panes; hammered on the door, waited to be let in.

"It's open!"

A man's voice, calling from inside. Tried the handle and the door scraped open, heavy wood scratching along the granite floor.

A log fire burned within, the ceiling was low, the smell of onion heavy on the air. I looked for a restaurant sign and saw none; rather, a dining-room table neatly laid, lace tablecloth starched white, candle burning in an empty bottle in the middle. An open door, twisted trapezoid in its crooked frame, led to the smell of cooking and wine, and from within that hot glow came the man's voice again: "That you?"

"Greta?" I asked.

"I left her behind. Hope you don't mind."

I shook my dripping coat out by the fire and took in the neat plates displayed in a cabinet on one wall, the crucifix by the bookshelf, the picture of family children and family pets on the round table beneath the windows. "Janus," I called. "What's going on?"

"Dinner!" he replied. "I came here for a holiday a few months ago and suddenly remembered this little place – perfect, I thought, absolutely perfect! The perfect hideout!"

I pulled my shoes off, felt water seep from my socks as I wriggled my toes on the flagstones before the fire. From the kitchen came a sudden burst of sizzling, a gout of steam. I sidled towards it, ducking beneath the door frame, and beheld Janus.

He was tall, a habitual stoop having curved his shoulders and neck. A long-sleeved black shirt was buttoned tight around his wrists; long black trousers descended into a pair of mighty fur slippers. He tossed wine-soaked pork in a pan and as potatoes frothed beside him exclaimed, "Can you pass that?"

A hand flickered out towards an open bottle of wine. I passed it over without a word. The fingers which took it were red and yellow. Red beneath, yellow on top, where the scar tissue had healed in rivulets and pools. "Thanks." He poured wine into the hissing pan, then helped himself to a slurp. "Don't you love this place? I always thought I'd like to retire to a little village in the mountains."

"Retire from what?"

"I don't know. Anything. Actually I tried retiring a couple of times but I got bored. Politics politics politics. You know how hard it is to organise a village bake?"

"Not really."

"Nightmare!" he exclaimed. "Everyone's always got to be a leader."

I took the bottle of wine, smelt its fragrance, murmured, "Mind if . . . ?"

"Help yourself."

My hand shook as I poured, though I couldn't conceive of any satisfactory physiological reason why.

Glass in hand, I turned and looked him in the eye. There was only one eye to look in; the other had long since been removed or sealed over with the zigzag tissue that covered his face and neck, wriggling down beneath the collar of his shirt. It had possibly been a beautiful eye, sky-blue, now lost beneath the flesh-sunk savagery that was Janus' face. Feeling my stare, he glanced up briefly from the pan, smiled and kept on cooking.

I rolled the stem of the glass backwards and forwards between my fingertips.

"What's for dinner?"

"Pork, paprika, red wine, white beans, soft potatoes, black cabbage and a surprise dessert."

"I'm not sure if I can cope with many more surprises."

"You're strong, Kepler. You'll be just fine."

On the thin warped glass of the windows the rain tap-danced, noisy in the night.

"Where did you leave Greta?" I asked.

"On the train to Narbonne."

"Good call."

"I thought you'd approve. Took me a while to get back to where I wanted to be, but I came clean. Where'd you leave . . . whoever-he-was?"

"Hospital."

"What are you, some sort of . . . "

"Nurse. And you?"

"Marcel . . . something. Bit of a recluse."

"I see. Chemical or physical?"

"Gas fire," he replied with a shrug. "I'm having skin grafts; there are expanders, if you've heard of them, implanted in my back.

They're filled with saline and over the course of several months the skin stretches and grows around them until there's enough surplus to cut away and graft to somewhere more interesting. Fascinating stuff, really."

"You know this ... how?"

"Spent time in hospitals." The sharp double-strike of metal on metal as Janus tapped a spoon on the edge of a pan. "Stir this, will you?"

I stirred. "So," I said, "if we're still at the graft stage, I'm guessing the burns are fairly new?"

"Fairly."

"You in much pain?"

"There's morphine in the bedroom."

"You taken any?"

"No."

"Want me to get you some?"

"No."

"Want me to get you someone?"

"No."

Potatoes rose, potatoes fell, and I stirred the pot.

Janus' two scarred hands clapped together in command. The little finger on his right hand had been removed. So had the thumb. Now three fingers remained, over-long, over-stretched, against the stubbiness of their neighbours. "Dinner is served!"

I carried dishes into the dining room. Janus had over-catered. The pork was tender, the potatoes were soft, the cabbage tasted of pepper and the sauce was good enough to lick from the plate. I said, where'd you learn to cook like that?

He said, my wife.

Your wife?

Yes, he replied. My wife. Paula. The woman I married.

By the fireplace an old clock ticked away the seconds and Janus scraped sauce and potato fluff from the edge of his plate with the end of one half-dissolved fingertip.

Have you seen her since? I asked. Have you seen Paula Morgan, the woman you married?

Dead.

Dead?

Dead. Michael Morgan lived, Paula Morgan died. Perhaps she couldn't bear the loss of the man she loved and his replacement by a twenty-one-year-old child screaming in his old man's shell. Perhaps the arthritis was more than just arthritis. Perhaps she was tired. Perhaps she simply had enough. Who can say, in the lives of little people?

Janus' fingertip swept around the plate, scooping up another dribble of juice. His tongue, when it flicked out to collect the liquid, was shockingly whole, pink and unscathed. His bottom lip drooped, one side thicker than the other, as if a rat had gnawed it while Marcel slept.

You said you've spent time in hospitals.

Yes, I have.

I talked to Osako in Paris.

I loved Osako, Janus replied. Osako had lovely fingers.

She mentioned cysts.

Yes. That was a problem.

And Miami . . .

Are we going to talk about only the past, Kepler?

. . . in Miami your host on the *Fairview Royale*. She had no hair and I thought it was a style thing, but now I think back, she had no eyebrows too. And what about Greta? Interesting choice, older than your usual tight-arsed Adonis, all that make-up on such frail flesh . . .

Janus, licking sauce off the edge of his plate.

Sometimes, he said, it's good to experience something new.

"Janus –" I lay my fork to one side, press my hands into my lap "– is there something you want to tell me?"

"Why, certainly, sweetheart," he replied. "I'm dying."

"And how's that going for you?"

"Well. Really well. You know, I think it's probably the best thing I've done for a while."

"But never quite followed through on."

A slight intake of breath. "Not yet."

"Osako's cysts, they were more than just an inconvenience."

"Yes."

"But you ran away. Mr Petrain had such a lovely arse. You know, if you wanted to jump off a roof I'm sure you could have found someone with terminal ... whatever ... who'd be up for the plunge."

"Have you ever tried? Stood on the edge, looked at the fall, known it didn't have to be that way?"

"I'm not in a hurry to die."

"Yet."

"Seems to me you have the vision, not the commitment."

"Kepler ... "

"My name is Samir."

He twirled the stem of his wine glass back and forth between two fingers and thumb. Greta had done the same thing as we ate duck in Montpellier. It took a moment to remember not to be surprised.

"Done much research into Samir, have you?" he asked.

"Not really."

"Sloppy, for an estate agent. I always wondered why you did the work. Clearly it wasn't for the money or the flesh – you could have got both any other way. Was it the curiosity?"

"Something like that." Hard to look away from the glass, spinning, spinning between Janus' fingers. I spoke to pull my mind from it: "Easier to be in a body when you know its friends. Discernment is the first step to picking a skin, one we tragically tend to lack. Perhaps ... there is a kind of intimacy too. Say I decide to be a brain surgeon. Cutting heads open isn't what I'm interested in, that's not the point of 'brain surgeon' at all. I want to be someone admired by my peers, loved by my students and for new-found friends to look awed at my expertise. Do I love my mother? Is my smile real or forced? Do I wear purple spotted pants underneath my sensible brown trousers? I look at people in the same way an architect might look at a great house. This is a shack crumbling round the edges ... this a palace waiting to be filled ... here a tiny cottage of bitter resentments and half-lies; there a terraced house squashed between its friends. Watching their films, feeling their clothes, smelling their soap – there is something beautiful in the choice of soap a stranger makes. There is an intimacy that comes from that kind of knowing, and from our circumstances we can look with a sort of dispassion that need make no allowances for the sins of others, nor has no history that blinds it to the wonders before it. An estate agent looks at people, wonderful and whole, living their lives, and if you look long enough and hard enough, perhaps for a moment you can feel what that must be like. What it must be to be ... not just the skin, but the *person*. The whole thing, right down to the heart."

The glass was still between Janus' fingers, his eyes fixed on my face. At last:

"Were you never tempted to try and live a life? Ten years, twenty, a long-term host?"

"I could never follow through."

"Why not?"

"Because it was hard."

Silence, save for the ticking of the clock, the falling rain. Then, with a note of caution to his voice, "Kepler ... "

"Don't call me that."

"It's your name."

"It's a file."

"It's you."

"I'm Samir Chayet."

"No, you're not."

"It's what my driving licence says."

"No, you're not!" His fist hit the table, sending cutlery clattering. I caught my glass before it fell, looked up and saw his single brilliant eye burning at me across the tabletop. "Who is Samir Chayet?" he hissed. "Who is he? Is he funny? Is he dry, droll, witty, a magnificent lover, a ballroom dancer, a baker of dubious pies? What the fuck is Samir Chayet to you? How the fuck dare you dishonour him by taking his name, you useless fucking parasite!"

I held on to my glass by the bottom of its stem and waited for more. Janus exhaled, shuddering with more than merely effort, half-closed his eye, wrapped his fingers round the edge of the table, and then inhaled again, long and slow. "I *loathe* you," he breathed, teeth clenching round the words as they shivered out.

"That's OK. I'm not exactly enamoured of you either."

A laugh that dissolved into a choke of pain, as quickly as it had grown.

"Let me get you some morphine," I said. "I can—"

"No."

"You're in pain."

"That's fine. That's ... good."

"How can pain possibly be good?"

"Leave the fucking morphine!" he roared, and I flinched away. He breathed out, breathed in, slowing himself down, and, face turned towards nothing, murmured, "What do you know about Samir Chayet?"

"Why?"

"Tell me what you know."

"What is this?"

"Kepler – Samir – whatever. Tell me."

"I ... not much. I'm a nurse at the university hospital. I was finishing my shift, had car keys in my hand. I needed a car. I'm comfortable. It was an acquisition of opportunity, no more. Marcel—"

"My name is Janus."

"It's a ridiculous name."

"Is it?" he breathed. "I rather like it. I think it has ... weight. Time and power."

"Janus –" my fingers tight across the table edge "– what the hell is going on here?"

He opened his eye, but there was no anger in his broken face, no retribution, merely the cold resignation of an empty stare. "Galileo is coming." My flesh locked. No breath, no sound, no reply. "I called Osako – she was convenient too. I called her, said my name was Janus, said I was sorry, wished her well, that I had some money stashed she could take if she wanted it; I wouldn't be needing it any more. She cried and hung up. But I think she may have cried for just long enough."

"Long enough for what?" He didn't answer. I was on my feet, not sure how I'd got there. "Long enough for what?"

A sigh, a stretch, a flash of pain. "For Aquarius to trace the call," he replied. "Long enough, I think, for that."

"When?"

"I think . . ." he plucked a number from the air " . . . three hours ago."

"Did you . . . " The words stumbled on the tip of my tongue.

"Mention you? No. But by now it'll be too late to run; you'll only draw attention to yourself. I suppose the question therefore is, how well do you really know Samir Chayet?"

"Why? Why did you do this?"

"Kepler –" he spoke like a father, sad at a school report "– you are a slave trader. A murderer. A thief of time. But this isn't even about you. I'm far too self-important to enact petty revenge on a passing acquaintance such as yourself. What you must understand is, much as I loathe you, more than that – more a thousandfold than that – I find myself disgusting. Truly repugnant. The luxury of having armed killers prepared to do that which for so long I have longed to do to myself but lacked the courage to attempt is, it seems to me, such a rare privilege that I dare not pass it up."

The sound of rain.

I stood, hands locked on the back of a squat wooden chair, knuckles curling white. Janus swirled the last dregs of wine in the glass. Swallowed. His gaze wandered to look at nothing much, before drifting up to the ceiling, some other place.

Words surfaced and sank like potatoes in a pot, and I said nothing.

A bluff.

A practical joke.

A trick played by a tired old ghost too bitter and cynical to remember that within every pair of eyes that beholds him, a mind watches too.

I looked at Janus, and Janus, feeling my gaze, looked back at me, and he didn't care if I lived, and he didn't care if he died, and he was not lying.

I moved.

Across the room, to a low wooden door; duck through into a tiny toilet with a sloping roof, squint into the single mirror above the sink and stare into the face of Samir Chayet. Worn for four hours and counting, never regarded. I am in my early forties? Straight dark hair, cut close, beard trimmed – not brilliantly but with a serviceable pair of scissors – almost certainly by myself. My skin is sanded elm, my name could be French, could be Islamic; Algerian will do as a guess, but what then? A mother, a father, a birthplace, a language, a religion? I feel around my neck for a crucifix – none – check my fingers for rings, fumble in my pocket for wallet, phone. I switched my phone off on acquiring Samir, never be available to make a fool of yourself; now I thumb it back on and tear through my wallet. I carry fifty euros in cash, two debit cards with the same bank, an ID telling me what I already know – Samir Chayet, senior staff nurse. What does a senior staff nurse do? I knew this once, long ago, when I was a medical student in San Francisco, when I was young and painted my toenails. Times have changed. I left those toes behind when I grew bored with patients being diseased, and now Samir Chayet has new toys to play with, new rules to learn, and I know none of them.

The sound of Janus moving in the room next door. Three hours is a long time when you're armed men with access to a helicopter. Running water in the kitchen: Janus doing the dishes.

"You know, they're probably already here, yes?" he calls out.

Helpful.

Contents of the wallet. Credit cards are dangerous – easy to ask me for the pin number, easy to catch me when I get it wrong. A library card, a couple of loyalty cards, union membership, a receipt from a local golf course.

Who is this man, Samir Chayet?

I look in the mirror, run my fingers through my beard, my hair, down the edge of my sleeve. I stare into round brown eyes that as a child would have begged for more and never been denied. I feel my belly, a little saggy but not embarrassingly so. When I raise my eyebrows, it seems that my whole scalp rises; when I frown, it's as if my forehead is trying to touch my nose. I lift the lid of the toilet cistern, drop my wallet and phone inside and close it.

Right now the question of who Samir Chayet is is not as important as who he *seems* to be.

"Are you ready for pudding?" Janus' voice drifted through from the kitchen.

I stared at my reflection for a moment longer, and turned out the light.

"What is it?" I asked, slipping into the kitchen, but now my words were Maghrib Arabic, slow to pass and heavy to form.

Janus stood at the sink, a pair of yellow Marigolds pulled over his withered hands, suds of washing-up liquid hanging off the front of his shirt. His eyebrows rose at the sound of my voice, but in the same language with an eastern accent, he replied, "Crème caramel with a raspberry and vanilla sauce. Hand made by someone in a supermarket."

"It sounds lovely. Shall I dry?"

A flicker of surprise in the corner of his lips. "If you wouldn't mind."

I picked a tea towel off its hook, lined up at Janus' side, started methodically drying the dishes. "Ever tried making crème caramel? Yourself, I mean?" I asked, testing the words as they ran through me, remembering the shape of them, warming to my theme.

"Once. When I was a housewife in Buenos Aires. It collapsed in the pot, looked like banana puke."

"That often happens."

"You a chef?"

"I was, for a while."

"Were you any good?"

"Used too much chilli. Management were disappointed that I wasn't sticking to the style for which I had been acclaimed. I told them that it was bland and undersized. They told me to reform my ways or find a new job. I reformed my ways and found a new job."

"Sounds unfulfilling."

"I wanted to test a hypothesis."

"Which was?"

"That the tongue of a chef could taste more – biologically, I mean, that there was something chemical in its capacity to taste more fully – than any other man."

"And?" Curiosity lifted Janus' voice, the scourer ceased for a moment in its rounds across the dishes.

"Damned if I could see what the fuss was about. I have worn some of the greatest musicians of the day and still cannot hear the sublime in Mahler. I have dressed myself in the bodies of great dancers, and certainly my muscles were flexible enough for me to stand on one leg and suck my own big toe without strain, and yet . . . "

"Yet?"

"I was forced to conclude that, though the body was toned to perfection, without the confidence of experience the feat for which it was honed still evaded me. It was a deep disappointment the day I realised that the lungs of an opera singer and the legs of a ballerina were not enough to achieve perfection in the form itself."

"You didn't want the hard work."

"No one wants the hard work. I suppose you could say I lacked motivation."

We worked in silence; the fire burning in the room next door, until at last he said, "I imagine running looks bad."

"What?"

"If they're already here, I mean."

"Ah, yes. Running would raise a few questions."

"So," he went on, "you intend to bluff it out? Dress yourself as a civilian?"

"That's the plan."

"And you think drying the dishes will help?"

"I think that our kind never work together. I think that we are lonely. I think we want friends, that we need . . . companionship, more than company. I think that everyone's afraid, but more so when we are alone. We should have that pudding now."

"You're in for a treat."

I put the last dish on to the rack and drifted back into the living room as Janus emptied the fridge of its sugary confections. Two white plates of crème caramel adorned with magenta sauce were laid out for my consideration, a silver spoon beside each. I tried a sliver and was cautiously impressed. Janus sat opposite, his pudding untouched.

Then, "Did . . . "

I took another bite.

"Would you . . . " he tried again, his voice shaking round the edges. Stop. A slow breath in, a long breath out, and at last, "I think I will have that morphine now, please."

I laid my spoon down, leaned back in the chair. "No."

"No?"

"No. You want to die, be my guest. You want someone here to give you the strength to go through with it, an audience for your big moment – fine. You want to stop the pain, that's an entirely different matter."

His bones stuck up white beneath the ragged redness of his knuckles; his smile was wide, eyes narrow. "How long do you think you have left to live, Samir?"

"You took the answer out of my hands. We do that, you and I. You're a good cook."

"I worked hard for it. Are you not—"

His words were barely formed, the sound balanced on the edge of his tongue, when the lights went out.

There was no *thunk* of circuit breakers, no snap of electricity tearing itself apart. The lights were on and then they were off, and we sat together, shadows against the bright orange of the fire, the rain drumming on the window pane, the *drip-drip* of the kitchen tap as it emptied itself into a still-soapy sink smelling of chemical lime. I looked to where the shadow of Janus sat, back straight, neck locked, hands curled around the edge of the table.

We waited.

"Samir?"

"Yes?"

His voice shook, his hands knocked against the wood. "Thank you."

"For what?"

"Not running."

"As you said, it would have been predictable."

The *thump* of a boot outside the door, the flicker of a shadow across the window pane. I thought about all the rugs on the floor, how the water would destroy them. I pushed my plate away from the edge of the table lest its contents be spilt.

"Samir?" A stammering, a heat, that might have been acid tears on a ravaged face.

"Yes?"

"Good luck."

A metal object broke a pane of glass. I pulled my hands over my ears but still heard the flashbang roll on to the floor. I ducked beneath the table, and the light as it exploded knocked against the back of my brain. I curled up with my knees to my chin and my elbows covering my head as the front door slammed off its hinges, as heavy boots and heavy men charged in from the front, from the back, their trousers tucked into their socks, their sleeves taped around their gloves, and through the scream of my ears and the whining in my brain I half-heard Janus climb to his feet, hold his hands out wide and proclaim in cheerful bouncing English,

"I fucking *love* this body!"

He must have moved as he spoke, must have lunged, tried to grab, because the gunfire that ensued – a burst of silenced shots – kept going long after the body had fallen. I half-opened my eyes, and as my retinas strained to adjust to the restored gloom, I saw the pocked body of Marcel hit the floor on the other side of the table, each silenced shot a crater in his chest, one through his throat, another through his lower jaw, the final one to the head, and even as he lay there, the shooter fired and fired again, three more bursts, Marcel's shirt popping and splattering red blood as the bullets bit in, until silence descended save for the drumming of the rain.

Then, as was inevitable, someone put a knee in the small of my back, a gun against the base of my neck, and I begged for mercy in what I hoped was my very best Maghrib Arabic.

Chapter 71

Military hit squads never do things by half.

If you could throw some circuit breakers, why not cut a power cable.

If you could cut one power cable, why not cut all power to the town.

That'd be convenient.

I sat, knees tucked up in front of me, hands at my back growing numb from the cable ties, and watched heavily armed men lift the broken and bloody corpse of Marcel ... whoever he had been ... from the scarlet-soaked floor of his living room, deposit it in a black rubber bag and carry it outside. As they did this, more of their colleagues, all silenced pistols, balaclavas and a bare minimum of skin, stood over me, guns levelled at my head, their expressions unknown. Every now and then I begged. I begged for mercy, I begged for answers, I begged for them to leave me alone. I begged on behalf of my dear and beloved mother who would not live without me. I begged for my dreams not yet fulfilled. I begged for my life. And I did so in a language which they didn't speak.

Eleven men.

They could have killed Janus with fewer, but eleven there were, distinguishable only by height and movement. They swept the house by torchlight, examined the half-eaten remains of dinner on the table, the cutlery drying in the kitchen. They patted down my pockets and, finding no identification, barked in Parisian-accented French, Who are you? What is your name?

I made a guess at how French would sound if spoken with an Algerian accent and replied, I am Samir. I am Samir Chayet. Please don't kill me.

What are you doing here, Samir Chayet?

I was here to see Monsieur Marcel. Monsieur Marcel was going to help me.

Help you do what?

Help me get a job. He was friend with my cousin. Please. I don't speak your French well. Algerian, you see? I am Algerian. I have not been long in your country, please let me go; are you police?

They are not police. One of the skin-clad darknesses approaches another, murmurs in his ear. What is this, who is this man?

He claims to be Samir Chayet, Algerian. His French is poor. He has no identification papers on him. We can't be sure.

Eyes settle on me, study my face, and a voice breathes, Will he be missed?

Show no reaction. My French is not good enough to understand a conversation about my demise. Show no fear. Focus on the problem at hand. Focus on innocence.

Then a voice speaks, and its French is heavily accented, and even through the language barrier I recognise that sound, and against the fire I recognise that shape, that height, that build, and the voice says, "We can't stay here. Do we take him?"

And the voice is known, because it was once my own, a comforting heaviness as I twisted it round Turkish, Serbian and German, before shoving a sock in its mouth and leaving it handcuffed in silence to a radiator in Zehlendorf, all those faces ago, and the voice is that of Nathan Coyle, murderer, assassin, fanatic and, quite possibly, salvation.

His boss replies, "Take him,"
And this they proceed to do.

I sat, hands tied, head covered, in the back of a van in the middle
of nowhere, and I prayed.

It had been a long, long time since I'd prayed.

I rocked, and in breathless Arabic I gabbled my imprecations to
the All-Merciful, the All-Seeing, the Compassionate and Mighty,
and when I'd run out of clichés, I babbled a few more things
besides, until finally someone nearby shouted, "Will you please
shut him up?!"

A gloved hand pulled the bag from my head, caught me by the
chin, tugged my face round hard. I stared into eyes which had for
so long regarded me with contempt from the bathroom mirror
and heard a familiar voice proclaim in soft, poor French, "Quiet
now. Or we'll shut you up, understand?"

And for a moment I felt almost hurt that he didn't recognise me,
as if there might be something in my eyes, in a twitch of iris and
a contraction of pupil which whispered, *Hello, stranger.*

"Please," I whispered. "I didn't do anything wrong."

Coyle pulled the bag back over my head.

We slowed.

We stopped.

Hands pulled me from the vehicle. Through the cloth across my
face I saw nothing, not even the glow of the moon.

A voice called, Kestrel, help me!

Arms linked arms with mine, one on either side, led me along
tarmac, then gravel, then soil going steeply downhill. A rough path
which slipped beneath my feet as I stumbled in the darkness. The
sound of a stream rushing below, the cracking of twigs, stir of an
engine growing distant. In the darkness a bird shrieked, its midnight rest disrupted by the intruders, and mud became pebble,
became wet rounded stones, became a damp riverbed where I was
pushed to my knees.

"Please don't hurt me!" I wailed, in French, then Arabic, then

French again. "I am Samir Chayet. I have a mother, I have a sister; please, I never did anything!"

Two – three at the most – bodies moved around me. They have taken me here to die.

"Please," I sobbed, shaking in my bonds. "Please don't hurt me."

It's OK to piss yourself in these circumstances. It's only a physical thing.

The click of a gun near my head. This was not how I planned on things ending.

Janus.

Do you like what you see?

"Galileo."

The word slipped from my lips, a bare breath in the dark, and instantly hands were there, grabbing me by the throat, pulling my head back and up, and though I couldn't see him, I could feel Coyle's body against mine, his hands wrenching me up. "What did you say?" he hissed. "What did you say?"

"Step back," barked another, the man in charge, the man who, if I had to speculate, was going to do the killing.

"Galileo!" Coyle pulled the hood off my head and stared into my eyes, shook me and roared, "What do you know of Galileo?"

I stared up into his face and whispered, a bare breath in the cold night, "*He lives.*"

A shot in the dark, the single *snap* of a silenced pistol. I jerked, trying to work out where it had gone in. The hands that held me let go; I fell to my knees. So did Coyle. His face hovered an inch from mine, eyes wide, mouth shaping an O of surprise. I looked down at myself and saw no bullet wound. I looked up at him, and there was a shininess to his jacket, a growing patch of darkness that caught the torchlight and reflected it back crimson.

The crunch of the gunman's boots behind me, and there's only one him, it seems, just one man sent to kill two birds.

He looked past me into Coyle's eyes. "I'm sorry," he said, raising the gun. "I have to follow orders."

Overhead the clouds have cleared and the sky is sprawled with a thousand stars framing cliffs dug out by this busy little gorge. In daylight the place might have been beautiful: black stones washed with silver water. By torchlight strapped to the end of a silenced pistol it is a lonely place to die.

Coyle moved. In the dark I didn't see his hand close around the gun, but I felt the movement, saw torchlight twist and turn, heard the double *crack-crack* of pistols firing, the ground briefly illumin-ated chemical-yellow, heard the *smack* of lead against bone. I looked up and saw the gunman, weapon held to fire. He took a step, and his foot slipped on the rocks. Took another, and his legs went out beneath him. He fell, head cracking open on the stony ground, arm slapping into the flow of the river.

Coyle fell. First onto his belly, then his face; twisted to one side, bounced on the wet stones.

The headlights of the van were high above us, and no one shouted, no one cried foul murder, no one came.

"Coyle!" I hissed, and he tried to raise his head at the name. "Cut me loose!" His head sank back on to the stones. "I can help you, I can *help* you! Cut me loose!"

I shuffled like an infant on my knees towards him, saw the light glisten on the blood where it was beginning to seep through his shirt. "*Coyle!*" His eyes were open, and he made no answer. I bent down towards his face. Only a thin pale line showed around his eyes, all other parts of his skin protected by layers of fabric, plas-tic and tape. But it was enough, so I bent down and kissed him on the softness of his eyes

pain

I bit back on a scream, stuffed my arm into my mouth to hold it in, shaking, shuddering pain rocking through my body. It ran through the tight muscles of my neck, through my locked-up belly, down to my knees and exited through the throbbing soles of my feet. It originated from a bullet, low calibre and slowed by a silencer, but still a bullet, wedged in my right shoulder, in a bundle of nerves that shrieked their distress, shredding thought and blurring all other sense. In front of me Samir Chayet swayed, blinking in the dark. I pushed myself up on my left arm, heard blood roar behind my ears as Samir began to whisper the usual refrain of what, where, how, his voice rising as the panic began to bite. I slid on to my knees, fumbled at my chest, my trousers, my belt, until I found a small blade. "Wait," I whispered, and my voice was cracked, and as Samir spotted the rapidly cooling corpse to his left he began to shout, to cry out, to lament without much direction or sense.

"Wait," I hissed again, pulling the balaclava from my face. "Stay still."

He gasped in air as I rested the blade against his back, managed to pull down a sob. I turned the knife against the cable ties that bound his wrists and, with a jerk that nearly took me to the ground again, cut him free. He fell on to his hands and knees, shaking, and I rested the blade against his throat.

He froze, an animal locked in place. "Listen," I hissed, first in Arabic, then in French, remembering that the Samir I had played was not the Samir I had been. "I'm losing a lot of blood here. Touch my skin."

Terror, incomprehension in his eyes. I turned the knife a little with my wrist, letting him feel the scrape of it against his skin. "Touch my skin."

I let the blade track his throat as he leaned into me, hands shaking, and as his skin brushed against the side of my face I threw the knife into the darkness of the river and

switched.

My heart was racing, piss in my pants, sweat on my back, eyes burning with tears wanting to be shed, but blessed relief! With a cry Coyle fell back on the ground, clutching the hole in his shoulder, and I rubbed blood back into my hands and hissed, "Coyle!" I scrambled over to him, felt the blood hot on his shirt. "Do you carry medical supplies?"

"The van," he replied. "In the van."

"How far are we from a town?"

"Four miles, five – five!" His face twisted, legs kicked back against nothing as he writhed beneath me. Sometimes people writhe to get away from a thing that scares them, sometimes to

312

remind themselves that they have a body beyond the pain. This was both.

"I can help you! I can get you away from here. Your own people have betrayed you – are you listening to me?"

A half-nod, a wheeze of broken bloody breath.

"I can get you out of here, get you medical attention, but you need to trust me."

"Kepler?" Not much of a question, but he asked it anyway.

"I can help you, but you need to give me your call sign." A half-laugh that quickly dissolved into the pain. "Coyle!" I snarled. "Kestrel – whatever your name is – they are going to kill you. I can keep you alive. Tell me."

"Aurelius," he wheezed. "My . . . call sign is Aurelius."

I pressed my bare hand against his cheek. "If you're lying," I whispered, "we're both dead."

"You find out."

"I need your clothes," I said, reaching for his belt. His bloody hand pressed against my own, stopping it before I could undo the buckle. "I've seen it all before." His hand didn't move. "I need to hide my face."

His hand fell away, and I pulled his trousers free one leg at a time. His shirt crackled like Velcro as I peeled it away from him. Beneath it he wore blue Lycra, the blood glistening, moving like a living thing as it filled the fibres. His trousers were too short, his jacket too tight, and I felt almost surprised. I slipped his balaclava over my face, smelt his sweat within it. I picked up his gun, checked the magazine, pressed my own discarded shirt against his wound, felt him flinch.

"You'll be OK," I murmured, and was surprised at how level my own voice seemed. "You're going to make it."

"You don't know that," he replied.

I pulled the magazine from my gun, threw it aside, buried my hands in my pockets so that no man might see the bare skin. I began to climb back up the muddy path, the crooked riverside made more treacherous by the rain, towards the light of the truck on the road above.

Chapter 72

I had counted eleven men who went to Saint-Guillaume to kill a cripple by the name of Janus.

Only three were waiting by the truck, parked on the roadside above a stream, its headlights burning white. Two of them had even begun to relax, their balaclavas off to reveal one man, one woman, cigarettes glowing between their bare fingers. Hard to strike a light when your fingers are muffled by wool and silk; harder still to enjoy a gasp when your face is hidden from view.

Perhaps they didn't know the events by the river.

Perhaps they were to have been told that Coyle's death was accident, not execution.

Perhaps they were only following orders.

My hands were in my pockets, and my face was covered by wool, and I was a familiar shape on a darkened night, and I was alone.

The man by the van turned as I approached, called out, "Herodotus?"

"Aurelius," I replied, brisk and businesslike, then, "I think we're going to need a hammer."

Curiosity flickered on the face of the woman, but my words had been enough to carry me from the lip of the road to the back door of the van, an arm's reach from the nearest man, and so, without further ado, I pulled my hands from my pockets, and before he could even register my bare flesh, pressed them against his exposed face and jumped.

An aluminium coffee mug fell to the ground, bouncing along the road and into the overflowing gutter; Samir Chayet staggered and blinked, hands rising to the unfamiliar balaclava against his skin, and I drew the gun off my hip and put one bullet in the thigh of the woman and another into the belly of the man who stood beside her. As they fell, I stepped forward, pulled their guns from their respective holsters and, having nothing better to do with them, tossed them down the ravine, listening to them clatter away in the dark. My weapon still raised, I shuffled round to the driver's side of the van, and seeing no one inside, turned again to find Samir frozen in place, the balaclava limp in his hands.

"Hi," I said. "You're a nurse, yes? There's a man down by the stream in a Lycra suit. I'd like you to get him for me. He's been shot. These two have also been shot, though only time will tell if fatally. I'll kill you, them and anyone else who passes by if you don't do as I say, understand?"

He understood perfectly.

"Terrific," I exclaimed with forced brightness. "I think I saw a torch in the driver's compartment. I'll watch for your light."

Time moves more slowly in the dark.

A cheap plastic watch on my wrist glowed green, declaring the hour unsanitary for any reasonable thing. The sky's enthusiasm for the night's rain was fading to a thick sleepy mist that obscured the line where black cliff met starlight. I stood away from the head-lights of the van, gun in pocket, torch in hand, and watched the tiny bubble of Samir's light moving by the stream far below.

Of the two individuals I'd shot, the man with the belly wound had lost consciousness, a mercy, I felt, for all concerned. The woman was awake, her hands pressed over her thigh, her breath fast and ragged, eyes full of pain. The blood through her fingers

315

and the blood on the tarmac was bright and thin where torchlight touched it, black and endless when the light turned away. I'd missed her femoral artery, as her continued ability to breathe demonstrated, though she seemed unwilling to thank me for this.

I leaned against the side of the van and finished their coffee.

No one felt the urge to communicate.

Samir's light began to ascend. I waited, torch turned towards the top of the path, for the two muddy figures to emerge. Coyle had one arm across Samir's back, the other curled into his own shoulder where the blood still burned between his fingers. He looked, in the unforgiving beam of my torch, pale and grey, a blueish tinge to his lips. Samir's face was bursting red, teeth locked together with effort, lips peeled back like a horse ready to bolt.

"Put him inside," I said, gesturing to the back of the truck.

"What did you do?" Coyle breathed, his gaze skimming over the two fallen figures.

"Their boss shot you. I wasn't about to to ask for company policy."

Coyle didn't cry out as Samir eased him on to the vehicle floor, which I took for a bad sign. "You're a nurse – do something."

"Are you going to kill me?"

When I'd asked the same question, I'd done so in shaking Arabic, but now I heard Samir speak, his voice was clear confident French with a thick southern accent. In a way I felt the performance of Samir I'd given suited his features more than the reality he now presented. "I give you my word that if you patch this man up I will let you live. And if you run I'll kill you and everyone here. Do you understand?"

"I don't know you." I felt a flicker of admiration. Shaking, frozen Samir Chayet, who'd woken in the dark with his hands tied, was standing his ground in the middle of the night.

"Nor do you understand what happened, how you came to be here. Yet the simple fact is you can take a risk and run, or you can take a risk and stay, and with only the bare minimum of information available you must decide which is the greater."

He weighed up his options and chose the wiser.

*

Five minutes later, he said, "This man needs blood."

"Know your type?" I asked Coyle.

"Sure," he growled from the floor of the van. "You know yours?"

"My friend is such a wag," I confided to Samir. "He tries to cultivate this dry manly wit."

"Nonetheless," said the nurse, "he needs blood, or I can't promise what will happen."

"I'll get right on that. Keep the first-aid kit; the two folk bleeding outside the van are probably going to want it. One of them might have a mobile phone. I suggest you call the police – only the police – just as soon as we're gone."

Chapter 73

Samir Chayet was a black silhouette in the rear-view mirror as I drove away. For less than eight hours I'd worn him, and his life would never be the same.

Coyle lay on the floor of the van behind me, one hand pressed to the dressing against his shoulder, his breath ragged, his skin grey. I'd put his jacket back around his shoulders, a blanket round his legs, and still he shivered, teeth clattering as he said, "What now?"

"Ditch the van. Get you to a doctor."

"Am I your hostage?"

"That sounds like more trouble than it's worth."

"Why would you help me?"

"Help myself. Always. You going to stay awake?"

"You going to sedate me?"

"No."

"Then I'm staying awake."

I drove north, following the largest signs to the biggest roads. Judging from the water-carved crevices and black pines of the hills, I guessed I was heading deeper into the Massif Central, hunting out the lone motorway that had been forged across dry plateaux and sodden valleys of volcanic black. A phone rang on the passenger seat beside me; I ignored it. A few minutes later it rang again.

"You going to answer that?"

Coyle's voice, a bare shimmer from the back.

"Nope."

Sodium lighting announced the advent of the motorway. The signage promised turnings to ancient castles and towns of skilled artisans. The towns of skilled artisans offered medieval walls, Cathar monuments, Templar secrets, Hospitaller coats of arms, tourist shops in whose darkened windows hung swords, shields and ancient sigils, and perhaps drugs.

The phone rang again.

I ignored it.

Rang again.

Ignored it.

On the edge of a town I pulled into an empty supermarket car park.

The phone rang, a fifth time, bouncing insistent on the seat beside me.

I put it on speaker and answered.

A sharp intake of breath at the end of the line.

Then silence.

I sat back, eyes half-closed against the orange light of the car park, and waited.

Somewhere, someone else quite possibly did the same.

And silence.

The great roaring silence of the open line. If I strained I thought I could hear the gentle in and out of expectant breathing, steady and deliberate.

Behind me Coyle stirred, waiting for the conversation to begin.

I said not a word.

Breath on the line, and it seemed to me that, as our silence stretched — thirty seconds, forty, a minute — the breathing grew faster, brighter, and the word that came to mind was excited.

A child, gasping with delight, playing hide and seek somewhere in the dark.

I waited.

I was fine with waiting.

No code words were called, no response requested.

And there it was – the rising breath broke, burst out into a single bubble of sound.

A giggle.

"Hello," I said.

The sound stopped as suddenly as it had begun.

"I see you," I murmured. "I see *you*. You've come too late – step back, stretch out, try again. But I'll always see you, whoever you are."

Silence on the line.

"You shouldn't have ordered them to kill my host. I know why, I understand. But when the moment comes, that's the thing I want you to remember."

I hung up.

Pulled the battery out of the phone, tossed it under the seat.

Turned the engine back on, pulled out of the car park.

The wet *swoosh* of wheels over tarmac.

The *slap-slap-slap* of the windscreen wipers.

Then Coyle said, though perhaps he already knew, "Who was that?"

"I think you know."

"Why didn't he speak?" Coyle was levering himself up on his good arm, straining to see me in the driver's mirror.

"Nothing to say."

"Tell me who."

"Who do you think?"

"I want you to say."

I shrugged. "Galileo Galilei was a brilliant man. I find it offensive you'd use his name for that creature."

"All that we have ever done is try to stop it."

I tried to smile, though he couldn't see the expression; tried to shape my voice into something halfway reassuring. "Tell me – do you feel like you're losing time?"

320

He didn't answer.

"Sure you do," I sighed. "Everyone does. At two o'clock you sit down to read a book and then, what do you know, it's five in the afternoon and you're only two pages further in. Perhaps, as you walk home through familiar streets, you grow distracted, and when next you wrench your concentration back to where you're going you find you're already there but the hour is late – so much later than you think. A call logged on your phone you don't remember making; perhaps your pocket dialled it as you leaned against the table. A waiting room where the magazines are three years old and you can't be bothered but, oh my! The time has flown and you don't quite know why. All we need are a few seconds. To give my wallet to a woman I do not know. To kiss a stranger, make a telephone call, spit in the face of the man I love, punch a policeman, push a traveller in front of a train. To give an order in a voice known for its authority – Nathan Coyle must die. I can change your life in less than ten seconds. And when it's done, all you will be able to say as you stand before a jury of your peers is . . . you don't know what came over you. So tell me, Mr Nathan Coyle. Have you been losing time?"

Silence on the phone, silence in the van.

"Thought as much."

In the town of Cavaliere (LIVE THE PAST – tourist office open 10 a.m.–3 p.m. Monday–Thursday excluding siesta) a map pinned up by the beige-bricked church pointed to a small clinic, a door like any other tucked into a street of tight apartments whose only claim to fame was a tiny plastic sign stuck by the bell asking any would-be visitors to kindly refrain from smoking on the stairs.

I parked squarely in the middle of the street, left the engine running and crawled over the seat into the back. Coyle was still awake, still breathing, his eyes red and his fingers curled into claws. "Hanging on in there?" I asked.

"What do you think?"

"I wasn't really asking. Remember that it wasn't me who shot you. Remember that your own people ordered you dead."

"Why?"

"Why remember, or why did they give the order?"

"Both."

"I think you can guess," I replied, shifting my weight forward, hands folded comfortably between my knees. "Leaving aside the fact that you've been compromised by the entity known as Kepler, you're just a bit of a pain. You're obsessed with Galileo; you failed in your mission, and now you've read files that you probably shouldn't have. I imagine, despite my excellent advice, that you asked some questions. Questions like 'Why did Josephine have to die?' or 'Has Galileo ever been to Frankfurt?' or 'When you say vaccination programme, what precisely are your parameters?' or . . . whatever. Am I wrong?"

He didn't answer, and I was not wrong.

"As for why your friends decided to kill you – that's easier still. An order was given. A telephone rang or an email was sent, and whoever spoke knew the code words and had power and authority, and an order was given. And of course you have protocols, fail-safes against just this sort of situation, but then again a fail-safe is only as good as the person who created it. And who's to say who really gives the orders now?"

"You think . . . it's in Aquarius?"

"Yes."

"At the top?"

"Yes."

"How?"

"It's had time."

"Why?" Trying to fight more than pain now, trying to swallow more than morphine could numb. "Why?"

"Because you're useful. Because if I wanted to study ghosts – really study them – if I wanted to learn what makes us tick, I'd probably create an organisation like Aquarius too. Keep your enemies close, as the old words say."

He didn't answer, couldn't meet my eyes. His breathing was fast, struggling, skin shining with sweat.

"You're losing blood."

No answer.

"I can help you, but you'll need to do something for me."

"Do what?"

"I need you to tie me to the passenger seat and point a gun at me." His mouth widened first in question, then wider in comprehension. "You still want to kill me?"

Without hesitation, his mouth twisting in a smile that wasn't a smile: "Yes."

"You think it's a good idea?"

"Yes."

"You want to live?"

He didn't seem to have an answer to that one. I nodded at nothing in particular, held out my bare cold hands for his attention. He didn't move, one hand still cradling the bloody mess of his arm, head turned to one side. "Galileo ordered you dead," I murmured, "and Aquarius did it. Now I'm about as excited by this as you are, but unless you want to bleed out right here, right now, this is what it's going to have to be."

He levered himself up on one elbow. "Cable ties," he said, and "Give me your gun."

I hesitated.

Gave him my gun.

His finger tapped against the trigger, light as a conductor testing his baton, feeling the weight of it, considering his options. He sighted down it, then let it drop to his side. I strapped my hands to the hook that hung above the passenger's seat, tightening the cable ties with my teeth until they bit deep, and then a little bit more, for spite. The height of the van was awkward – I could neither stand straight nor sit down, but balanced, knees bent, arms raised, suspended like an old coat.

"OK," I said as Coyle watched me from the floor. "If you wouldn't mind?"

He crawled on to his knees, cradling the gun to his chest. Made it on to one foot, and for a moment I thought he'd fall, but then the other foot came in and with a half-step, half-stagger, he came towards me, eyes locked on mine.

A moment.

Just a moment, and I didn't know.

A mistake, perhaps?

His finger *tap-tap-tapped* against the trigger of the gun.

Too little time to plan, too little time to come up with anything better.

A mistake ever to let this man live?

Perhaps.

Perhaps this will be a very short learning curve.

Then he reached down and picked something black and grubby from the floor. A balaclava, long since discarded. A twist at the end of his lips that might have been a smile, he staggered towards me, waved it before my face, a command in gesture, not words. Open wide.

I licked my lips. "You in much pain, Nathan Coyle?" I asked.

"Find out," he replied. I tried not to gag as he pushed the damp black fabric into my mouth. It tickled the back of my throat, made me want to vomit. I swallowed and tasted wool, mud, cigarette smoke. *Tap-tap* went Coyle's trigger finger against the gun. The barrel brushed against my chest as he inspected his handiwork.

A moment.

He thought about it as the blood seeped through the whiteness of the bandage, dried brown on his fingers, around his throat.

He looked at me, and I looked at him.

His hand shook as he reached out for me, hovered an inch away from my hands, the whole arm rocking with more than just cold. I don't know if he intended the movement, or if the weight of his own fingertips became too much to bear. Skin brushed my skin,

and I jumped, giddy with the relief of it, and as the bleary-eyed would-be killer flopped against the ties that bound him to the roof of the van, I staggered back, clutching my arm, the pain now not so much a universal shrieking as a specific throbbing, the hot fire of it pulsing in time to the rhythm of my heart. I gasped, swayed against the side of the van, felt thin blood bubble through my skull, blinked tears from my eyes. My captive flopped against his bonds, then kicked out, tried to stagger upright and flopped again, shouting unheard words through the balaclava in his mouth. I waggled the gun at him and hissed, "Try me."

He fell silent, grew still.

I smiled my giddiest smile and slid, one shaking foot at a time, out of the van.

The night nurse took a long time to answer the door.

When she did, she saw first my face, grey and smeared with blood, and her features opened in shock and sympathy. Then she saw the bandages around my shoulder and chest, and I think understood what it was, what it might be, but by then I'd caught her by the index finger and,

as Coyle fell, I grabbed him round the middle and held him up. "OK," I whispered in my new, gentler voice. "You're OK."

I eased him down on to the steps, and as his eyes regained their focus he looked up into mine. "Kepler?"

"I'm going to get you blood," I replied. "And painkillers. What's your type?"

"You're really doing this?"

"Blood type. Now would be a good time to declare allergies too."

"A positive. I'm A positive."

"OK. Stay there. If your friend in the truck starts shouting, shoot him."

"Kepler?" he called as I skipped back up the stairs, light-limbed in my nurse's shoes. "He *is* my friend, you know that?"

"Sure. I guess how you handle that one is up to you."

The clinic was fluorescent white. I wore a uniform of unwashed blue, sensible shoes, too much lipstick, not enough coffee. I'd been watching the TV until the knock at my door. The screen showed poker, a camera pointing straight down at a green table, hands moving in and out as cards were flipped, chances lost. I let it play. A small reception area stood empty. The light of a vending machine glowed in a shadowed corner; the shutter was down across the desk.

Little rooms led off either side of a corridor, within them plastic beds draped with white. I checked doors until I found the most secure, patted down my pockets, found a bunch of keys. Lady Luck smiled on me that day – the door was all bolts and levers, not a combination to be found. Three of my eleven keys fitted the locks; the door opened.

The room beyond was a paradise of nasty drugs for nasty diseases. French pharmacies; nowhere in the world can you find as many potentially toxic formulas so readily available. The painkillers weren't hard to find – the most secure box in the room once again yielded to a heavy-duty key. The clinic's blood supplies were a bare minimum; the packs already had their intended destinations written on, for this old gentleman who can't make it to the hospital for his transfusion; for that young lady whose DNA turned against her before she was born. I stole a couple of pints, stuffed a plastic bag with saline, needles, sterile wipes, fresh bandages, sedatives and the long-hooked edge of a suture needle.

On the TV a player had folded, his last few chips taken by a rival. The crowd cheered, the presenter whooped as the broken contestant walked away to the swirl of golden lights. I let myself out, leaving all as I had found it.

Coyle sat where I had left him, and I was surprised.

The gun was in his lap, his head against the side of the staircase, his breathing long and ragged. He half-turned his head as I approached. "Find ... what you need?" Words came hard and slow. I helped him to his feet, supporting him gingerly, my hands either side of his chest.

"Yes. Put the gun away."

"Thought you wanted ... me to shoot someone."

"I've been this nurse for less than five minutes. People lose five minutes all the time. It's late, the dead of night. She can imagine that we came, imagine that we went, imagine that she imagined it. It's better that way."

"You do this a lot?" he asked, tucking the gun beneath the jacket draped loosely across his shoulders.

"Not habitually. Hold this."

He took the plastic bag I offered, out of instinct rather than choice. Offer a hand to shake, a bag to hold; do it fast enough, people don't think. As his fingers closed about the handle, my fingers closed about his and with a deep breath I

looked up into the nurse's eyes as she staggered and swayed.

Felt the pain pound through my body, nearly knocking me down.

Gripped the plastic bag tighter in my hand, turned and walked away.

In the clinic upstairs the TV played, the clock ticked, the lights burned, and nothing had changed between this minute and the last.

Back in the van.

I cut the man down who I'd suspended by his hands from a coat hook, and as his fingers came free, I jumped, faster than he could swing.

Coyle slumped to the floor as I spluttered dirty wool and pulled the balaclava from between my lips. My arms ached, my wrists were stung from a silent fight I'd had against my restraints. I eased Coyle on to his back, pulled the blanket over him once again, breathed, I have sedatives. I have painkillers.

Fuck your drugs, he replied, though I didn't think he felt the bravery in his words.

I drove a few miles, parked in an empty car park behind a shuttered warehouse where the CCTV cameras would not roam, settled down to work. I slung the first bag of blood from the same hook on the ceiling to which I had been tied. Peeled back the dressing from his wound, shone a torch into the bloody mess. Entry wound only, low calibre, I could still see the crunched-up end of the bullet gleaming near the surface of the skin. In the dark Coyle's hand grabbed my arm by the sleeve, then remembered its repulsion and slowly let go. "You . . . know anything about medicine?" he asked.

"Sure. Somewhere there's someone with most of a degree I earned."

"That doesn't comfort me."

I swapped the bandages, left the bullet there. "Morphine?"

"No."

"It's your body."

I felt his glare at the back of my neck as I climbed into the driver's seat.

Chapter 74

A service station on a winding motorway through the mountains.

Coyle didn't sleep, but neither did he speak, wrapped in blankets in the back of the van.

My body didn't carry money. Guns, knives – no cash.

I went into the service station anyway, ordered black coffee, two croque monsieurs. When I reached the bleary-eyed woman serving behind the counter, I put my coffee down, caught her by the hand. My former host swayed, dizzy and confused, and I opened the drawer of the till, grabbed a bundle of euros, pressed it into his fist.

His eyes had just about regained their focus, enough to look at me, to register my skin on his, before I jumped back.

I handed the cashier a twenty-euro note, and she seemed surprised to find her till already open, but looking into my smiling face she shook herself and asked no questions.

I perched on a cold metal bench beneath a red slate awning and let the coffee cool, untouched, by my side. A wet yellow sun was beginning to push up from the horizon, tiny and angry against a drained grey sky. It seemed a morning into which no colour could creep, try as it might. Low mist clung to the grass at the edge of the tarmac. Fat lorries grumbled away from the petrol pumps, engines roaring up to speed as they slipped on to the motorway.

I finished my sandwich and turned the mobile phone back on.

It took a while, settled down, showed a text message: *Do you like what you see?*

And then another, sent a few minutes later, its sender unable to resist: *This one's for you.* ☺

Smiley face.

A many-chinned driver, his padded red jacket flapping around his belly, passed me by. I asked him for the time, and as he made to answer caught his wrist, jumped, took the mobile phone from the proffered, unresisting hand, dropped it into my pocket, jumped back.

Less than five seconds.

Three, at a pinch.

I still felt my host's dizziness from my last departure.

Six thirty a.m., the driver told me when he stopped swaying. Better get moving before the traffic thickens.

In the gents' toilet I slipped into a cubicle, rolled up my sleeve, found a vein and pushed ten millilitres of sedative into my veins. This done, I stepped out, walked up to a man at the urinal and, speech already slurring, said, "Hit me."

He half-turned, so I grabbed him and

switched

trousers still around my knees, I hit him as hard as I could.

I was a big man, and what I lacked in regular exercise, I made up for with mass. Besides, the other guy was sedated.

He really didn't stand a chance.

Dawn in a French service station.

I look for a car.

Not a lorry – too many people have vested interests in lorries making it to their final destination. Night staff coming off shift are ideal, but it takes switches through

truck driver, breath stinking of mints, to

policeman, back heavy, an ache all down my left side, to cleaning lady

ah, the cleaning lady. Blue apron, dyed black hair, pale skin, thin arms, she's finished mopping the floor, and as I pause and check her pockets I find that I am the owner of a wallet with forty euros in, I have no pictures of family or loved ones, my mobile is off, ancient and unloved, and I am – blessed be – carrying a set of car keys.

I leave my mop against the wall, and collect my coffee and sandwiches from the bench on my way out.

Chapter 75

Coyle said, "Who the hell are you?"

"I am Irena Skarbek," I replied primly. "I am a cleaning lady."

"I can see you're a cleaning lady – the question is why you're a cleaning lady."

"Can't use this van, could be tracked. Dumped the phone in a lorry driver's pocket, hope he's going a long way at questionable speed."

"Aquarius will guess you ditched the phone."

I levered him up "A live signal is a live signal and should be followed no matter what. Even if it only buys us a few extra hours, I'm happy. Now, what kind of car do you think a woman like me drives?"

I drove a second-hand Renault that clunked and thumped its way on cracked suspension down the motorway. A plastic crucifix bounced irritatingly from the driver's mirror. A whole family of furry cats nodded their approval out of the back windscreen. The upholstery smelt of cigarette smoke, the gear stick was a little too stiff. On the tiny back seat my bags of medical equipment and bloody blankets lay, tumbled between collections of old CDs and battered maps.

Coyle sat in the passenger seat, head back, legs stretched, and watched my irritation grow. At last he said, "Shall I . . . ?" gesturing at the crucifix.

"If you wouldn't mind." He tucked it into the glove compartment, then hesitated, staring inside. "Anything interesting?" I asked.

"What? No. Not really. I . . . don't usually steal other people's cars."

"I do. All the time. Do I have a driving licence in there?"

"Does it matter if you don't?"

"I like to find all the paperwork. Makes it easier if you're going to stick around."

"Are you going to stick around?"

I shifted in my seat, testing the weight of my arms, heaviness of my back. "The body's tired," I admitted, "but so am I, so that's not really relevant. I haven't noticed any major muscular or skeletal problems; I'm not wearing a medical bracelet or carrying any sort of inhaler or EpiPen."

"EpiPen?"

"Bees, nuts, lactose, yeast, wheat, prawns – the list of things that can kill you is not to be underestimated. Check the glove compartment."

"I don't see anything like that."

"In that case, I imagine I'm sticking around. Sandwich?"

"I think," he said, slow and careful as I gestured at the still-steaming croque monsieur, "I might puke."

"No sandwich?"

"You haven't been shot much, have you?"

"I've been shot a lot. Far more than you, judging by your scars. I simply didn't hang around for the medical after effects."

"Piss to your sandwich," he explained.

We drove in silence.

Then, "Why Irena?"

"She had a car."

"Is that it?"

"She was coming off shift. After a night shift most people go

333

straight to bed. That's eight or nine hours in which no one should be expecting contact from her. I can do a lot in eight hours."

"That's it? That's the extent of your . . . discrimination?"

"If you're asking whether I would rather be a glamorous mid-twenty-something with perky breasts, a healthy bank account and pain-free teeth – yes. But they don't tend to hang around in service stations off the A75."

Coyle seemed too tired to manage his usual contempt.

I turned on the radio, flicked through a few stations, settled on unobtrusive jazz. The traffic coming from the north had headlights on, though the sun was getting high. Black clouds were striped with lines of rain. Roadside billboards advertised garden centres, fresh milk, the new season's clothes, crude political views and second-hand Fiats.

"Why are you helping me?"

Coyle's voice was heavy. His head rolled, eyes staring without seeing at the oncoming traffic. I turned the windscreen wipers up as the first of the rain began to thicken against the glass, slowed for the rising sheets of mist from the rear wheels of the cars ahead.

"Sentiment?" I suggested, and he hacked a coughing disdain. "You could help me."

"I could kill you."

"Not right now."

"I . . . have killed you. Killed your host. You talked about . . . retribution before."

"It's crossed my mind."

"What's changed?"

"I don't kill the foot soldiers. Not unless I have to. Also . . . "

"Also?"

"I spent a lot of time wearing your face. It would be disquieting to break it now."

"You told the man . . . the nurse, back by the stream."

"Samir?"

"Him. You told him that, given the circumstances in which he found himself, he had to weigh up the risks of his actions and decide whether to stay, whether to run. Why aren't you running?"

"Because I don't think you're as primed to shoot me as you once were."

"You stole my body."

"I gave it back."

"Left me handcuffed to a radiator."

"And told the police where to find you before you could starve to death. Really, if a pair of silver scales were to weigh up the justice of our causes, you'd find that my motivation to do you harm greatly exceeds any valid reason you could ever have to kill me. You murdered Josephine, would have killed more just to kill me. You gunned down Janus without a second thought, kidnapped me in the middle of dinner, and when I go to great lengths to keep you alive after your own side shoot you, all I get is rampant hostility and criticism. But if that doesn't satisfy you then here it is: Aquarius lied to you. They faked the Galileo file. They sent you across the world to gun down me and mine, but the one monster who really deserves his fate they left untouched. And when you get a little nervous on the subject, they try and kill you too. So to hell with the why and wherefore of our little arrangement. It's what you need. It's how you stay alive. And there's the end of it."

His teeth slid across his lower lip as he thought, eyes tight, fingers clawed. "I . . . shot Marigare."

"Mari . . ."

"The man who shot me. I wondered if . . . he might be . . . "

"No. He wasn't Galileo."

"No. I know. He was . . . one of us."

"He tried to kill you."

"Yes."

"Do you know why?"

"No."

"He said he was following orders."

"I know."

"I wouldn't take it personally. Galileo is Aquarius, and Aquarius doesn't even know it. Maybe the person who ordered you dead can't even remember doing it. Then again, someone has to take responsibility for following the orders, as well as giving the command. Either way, you fired in self-defence, so this one's probably not going to the top of the sin list."

His eyes flickered to me, fingers clenching. "You . . . want to find him? You want to kill Galileo?"

"Yes. I rather think I do."

"Why?"

"Deeds done. Friends remembered. But mostly, I think, because he wants me. We have both . . . taken action against the other, in our times, and now it appears that our relationship has a logic all of its own. It would be unwise of me not to respond accordingly. He gives us a bad name."

"Kepler—"

"Irena," I corrected automatically.

"—I think you did that yourself."

I said not a word.

On the radio a caller was shouting over the airwaves. He had a lot to shout about. Taxes – too high. Social security – too low. Hours of work – too long. Healthcare – too expensive.

What was his suggestion?

That people should try harder, of course! He'd tried his entire life and now he was living in a one-bedroom flat above a crêperie with not fifty euros to his name. He'd fought and he'd lost, but only others were to blame.

Thank you, caller, said the presenter as he cut him off. You sound like you've got some interesting stories to tell.

Then Coyle said, "You said you understood."

"What?"

"On the phone. You told . . . it that you knew why he ordered your host's . . . Josephine's death. You said you knew."

"Yes."

"Why. Tell me why."

"Because I loved her."

"Is that it?"

"Yes. I've known Galileo for nearly a hundred years. He – it –

336

loves to be loved. It is all that we ever want. We are beautiful and we are wealthy, and people love us for it, but it is not us that is loved, merely the life we are wearing. I loved Josephine. I was . . . happy when I was her. I was beautiful as Josephine. I was a person, when I was her, I *was* Josephine. Not some shadow playing a part, but her, whole and true, a truth that was more whole than anything she had been. It's that that makes beauty. Not leg or skin or breast or face, but wholeness, total and true. I was beautiful as Josephine, and Galileo . . . hasn't been beautiful for a very long time. He wanted to be in Edinburgh, needed to be in Miami, and forgot a very long time ago what beautiful really means. That is all."

Silence a while. Then, "I'm sorry. For Josephine. For your loss."

I didn't reply, and he said no more, but when I glanced up from the road there was a wetness in his eyes, and he turned his face away so I might not see any more.

Then he said, "Where are we now?" and his skin was yellow-grey, and his breathing was heavy, and his eyes were low.

And I said, "We're about to stop," and realised that this was now the case.

A hotel of little windows and iron walls, framing a car park.

I sat in the driver's seat for a few minutes and practised copying Irena's signature off the back of her debit card. It was no substitute for a pin code, but you make do.

The hotel was as close to a motel as the French could manage, though they would never admit to having sunk as low as the Americans in their hospitality. I asked for, and received, the cheapest room they had, and managed to pay for it in cash.

"Checkout is 10 a.m. tomorrow morning," explained the dull-eyed receptionist as he handed over a small key on a huge tag. "Breakfast is extra."

"That's OK. We'll be long gone."

The room was up a path of singing flagstones. A single cedar tree leaned over a curious ginger cat, which paused, one paw raised to its mouth like a child caught eating a sweet, to regard us as we staggered by, too much – far too much – of Coyle's weight draped across my back. Irena Skarbek had many pros, but upper-body strength was not one.

Coyle got blood on the sheets the moment he sank on to the bed. I piled blankets on top of him, fetched water to drink, and water in a jug to clean away the blood from his neck, his face, his hands. I fetched the remainder of my medical supplies from the car, and as I crossed the courtyard, a voice called out, hey you! Are you the cleaning lady? I've got a bone to pick with you.

No, I snapped in reply. Try someone else.

"Irena?" Coyle shivered beneath the sheets.

"Yes?"

"Where's Max?"

"Who's Max?"

"You were him until you were Irena. What did you do with him?"

"Left him sedated in the service station lavatory. I may have punched him too – only a little."

"He's a good man."

"Yeah," I sighed. "He was probably following orders too. Sorry about this." I slipped the needle under his skin, and though his lips curled and his eyes narrowed, he stayed still as the contents of the hypodermic entered his bloodstream. "Fingers," I said, and he obediently pressed three fingers over the cotton wool I laid over the vein. "Pressure for two minutes."

"What was it?"

"Sedative. You're going to have to sleep at some point."

"Why?"

"Because it's sleep or dead."

"I don't . . . understand why you need me," and already his voice was thickening. "You said you had what you needed to take down Aquarius. Why . . . do you need me?"

I shrugged, swinging my legs up to balance precariously on the corner of bed he wasn't already inhabiting, leaning back against the wall. "You shot my last ally. And it's always useful to have an obliging body."

"Is that what I am?" His eyes were drifting shut, his lips barely shaping the sounds.

"No. You're . . . something else."

He perhaps wanted to speak, but no words came.

I doubt I'd care for anything he had to say.

Chapter 76

I sleep.

It is a fitful process.

There is one bed in this tiny room, and though it's a double, Coyle is sprawled diagonally across it, and even if the smell of sweat weren't enough to set my delicate nose twitching, the blood seeps into the sheets.

I sleep on the floor, waking in awkward positions, one hand high, one hand squashed. Though the room is hot, I am cold, grateful that my muscles are already worn out, annoyed I haven't more flesh to keep in the heat.

I slip in and out of half-remembered dreams.

Dreams of

Janus. Two-faced god, who was beautiful as she lay down beside me in an apartment in Miami, sapphires in her hair. Who danced naked around the room, slapping his behind and exclaiming I love it. I love it I love it I love it. That had been when he was young, and handsome, and Michael Peter Morgan, who used to do tae kwon do, and would one day meet his perfect wife.

Janus-who-was-Marcel, melted lips and withered fingers, skin the colour of rotten tomato laced with maggoty worms, do you like what you see?

Dreams of Galileo.

He's mine.

He's beautiful.

He's mine.

Do you like what you see?

And I wake and for a moment cannot remember where I am, or who, and I feel sick, and sit on the edge of the toilet bowl, clutching it for a while, knowing I will not puke and wishing this body would.

The hotel is too cheap to provide toothpaste and my teeth are starting to ache.

Coyle sleeps soundly.

I have four euros left.

In the hotel lobby I wait on a low couch opposite the vending machine and flick through the newspapers.

When the chubby man with the blue shirt comes along, I put down my paper, get up and approach him, smiling.

"Excuse me," I say as he reaches for the wallet in his pocket. "Do you have the time?"

He looks up, bewildered, and as he does, my fingers brush his own.

I place my wallet on top of the vending machine, push it back just out of sight, before catching the wrist of Irena Skarbek again and,

still smiling, thanking the man for his assistance,

I sit back down and carry on reading the newspaper.

His dizziness passes. The man examines his hands, his pockets, the inside of his shirt, the floor around him and finally me. He looks me up and down, takes in my cleaner's uniform, wonders for a moment if I might be a thief but, seeing no evidence of the same, shakes himself and heads back upstairs.

Perhaps he left it in the bathroom, he thinks to himself. Or maybe beside the bed.

Funny, he could have sworn he had it when he came downstairs.

I wait until he is gone and retrieve his wallet from on top of the vending machine.

I have seventy-four euros, and my day is picking up.

I remember my first meeting with Galileo.

She was Tasha . . . or possibly Tulia.

I was Antonina Baryskina; I was young and beautiful, and for six months I played the cello and charmed the men of Moscow.

And when it was done, I was

(the names are hard to remember now)

Josef Brun, the grand duke's most trusted manservant. I wore a high-necked black tunic, tight black trousers, had a beard turning gently grey and was still recovering, I realised upon the instant of my arrival, from a stomach bug that I hadn't made known. Servants didn't get ill in 1912. It wasn't part of their job description.

I stood beside Antonina's chair as she swayed, dizzy and confused, then opened her eyes. It was the same chair, in the same room, at the same time of day when I had first met her, wearing this self-same body, so that it might appear to her that she had blinked, and nothing had changed. Her clothes were those she had worn that first time, her hair done in the same style, though six months had passed, and the sunlight had turned from autumn to spring.

Then her father said, "Antonina, we need to talk," and I bowed once and withdrew from the room.

The house echoed with her shrieking for three days.

I stayed, as a courtesy, in the gently aching body of Josef Brun. I did not do my servant's tasks, nor were they expected of me, but resided in the outhouse, away from the eyes of my peers, and now faked the stomach infection from which Josef had only just recovered. I read books, took a few discreet walks through the grounds, played chess against my shadow and lamented that I no longer had access to the music room of the house.

On the fourth night the grand old duke came to me and took the seat on the other side of the chess board.

Do you? he asked.

I did.

He played competently, but moved too fast, his impatience showing in reckless attacks and careless defences. I told myself I would play with mercy, but it is not a game where good intentions last, and soon his pieces were scattered across the board.

"You are leaving us tomorrow?" Casually, his fingers on a bishop, a thing that hardly mattered.

"Yes."

"Where will you go?"

"I'm not yet certain. South, perhaps. The western borders seem a little too . . . unsteady for my inclination."

"You fear war?"

"I consider it a possibility."

"Could you not spend such a conflict as . . . a general's wife? A minister's daughter? Some position away from the front lines?"

"I could. But in my experience war comes to us all, even – if not especially – the wives, sisters and mothers of those who fight. Womanhood is no protection from conflict. You wait for the news that comes. You dread, powerless and alone, forbidden to do what you would and fight for those you love."

"And who do you love, Josef?" he asked softly. "Who do you really love?"

I leaned back from the board, went to fold my arms, remembered my body, its station, and instead laid them on my lap. "If I am wife, then I love my husband. If I am sister, then I love my brother. If I am soldier, then I love my men. My privilege, if you will, is that I may choose to enter any life I please. Why would I be a man in a callous home? Why would I be a mother whose children I did not adore? I love my kin, otherwise I would not keep them. I love everyone that I am, otherwise I would not be them."

His eyes were fixed on the board, his eyebrows knotted together. "Are you not tempted to be me? Does my dukedom not attract you?"

"No, sir."

"Why not?"

I licked my lips, saw small eyes in his drooping face, noted the yellow spots on his hands, the stiff tendons about his neck, the curvature at the base of his spine where posture fought with age. He saw my speculation, blurted, "My age repulses you."

"No, sir. Not that, although age, if you do not have the opportunity to grow into it easily, can be a shock. You have power and the respect of your peers, and health, but I do not think you are ... beautiful. You lack that joy, or that love, which makes beauty more than the flesh that owns it." A muscle twitched in a cheek, a tiny movement, but enough. I pressed my hands together in apology. "I have spoken ... out of turn."

"No," he replied, more sharply than I think he meant, and then, softer, "No. You have spoken your mind. Very few do that around me. My daughter ... spits in my face, wishes me dead. Do you think I did the right thing in commissioning you? Do you think I acted with ... love?"

Silence.

"Come, sir, come." He tutted. "I have congratulated you on the liberty of your speech. Do not betray that compliment now."

"I believe you acted from love when you commissioned me to be your daughter. I believe you wish her well and through my intervention sought to give her that security in life which her own nature would not provide."

"But?" he grunted. "Get on with it."

"Sir ... this understanding has been of great benefit to both of us. But the question I must ask is this: if the security you wished for your daughter required another to achieve it, then do you not force that which is opposite to her nature upon her? Or perhaps I may put it like this: is the daughter you love the daughter you in fact have?"

His eyes upon the board, though he no longer saw the pieces.

"You did not say as much when you agreed to this contract."

"Nor was it in my interest to do so. But our arrangement is concluded, and you have asked for my thoughts, and there they are."

His finger settled on a pawn, moved it for the sake of moving, an irrelevant gesture in an already concluded game.

"My wife believes my daughter to be ill."

I waited, studied the board, leaning forward, enjoying the freedom of a man's clothes, which did not restrict me to polite straight backs and the little breaths of a corset.

"She believes the illness to be of the mind. She has said it for many years. Sometimes Antonina . . . has episodes. She will . . . cry out against people who are not there, name fancies which cannot be believed, tell tales. As a child I hoped it was merely a trick of her growing, some spark of her personality which might, one day, be almost charming. Now she is a young woman, and that hope diminishes. Before you came . . . she lay with a peasant boy. He was fourteen, she one year older, and when they were done she came running back to the house, still . . . unclean, and shrieked of the deed that she had done. I do not mean to say that she lamented it, but rather she danced around the room, laughed in our faces, hitched up her skirts to show us the dirt and nakedness of her act, spat in her mother's eye and told us she was free now. Free and blessed in the eyes of the Lord. I beat her that night. I beat her until even my wife, her child's spittle dry on her face, begged me to stop. I told no one. We waited for her wounds to heal before letting any living soul near the house – near her. I had hoped that your presence would heal our household, redeem my daughter's name, and do not think I have complaint. Your behaviour has been exemplary. Perhaps too much so. For these last few months I have almost at times forgotten that you are not my daughter. I watched her dance, laugh and smile. I heard her tell little jokes, bow to gentlemen of whom I approved, politely dismiss those whose spirits were too high. She has been appropriate with the servants, generous with her friends, welcoming to strangers, careful of her dignity. These last months my daughter has been everything I wanted her to be, and now . . . you are gone, and she returns, and I realise that it was not – nor was it ever – for my daughter's sake that I sought your services, but for mine. For a few months with the child I thought I had deserved. I do not know what to do."

He was weeping. The old duke was weeping, his hands pressed in little fists against his eyes, tears gleaming like icicles off the whiskers on his chin. I opened my mouth to speak, and no words came. I stared down at the board, noticed that checkmate was a few moves away, and I felt no triumph at the revelation. Tiny sobs, barely more than hiccups, swallowed before they could begin, broke from him and were gasped back down – the shame, said his clenched fists, the shame.

Then the duke raised his head, eyes raw, and whispered, "Would you be my daughter? Would you be her . . . a little longer?"

I shook my head.

"Please. Be my daughter. Be who she ought to be."

I reached out, laid my hands on his, pulled them gently down into his lap, spreading the fingers wide.

"No," I replied, and jumped.

My old servant Josef swayed before my eyes. "Stay there," I barked, and, tired bones creaking, face swollen and red from tears, I clambered to my feet. My legs ached more than I had imagined, a nerve twanged in my thigh, the duke too proud to carry the walking stick he clearly required.

The house was sleeping, the lamps turned down low as I climbed the stairs, limping, to Antonina's door. A chubby matron sat outside, the key around her waist. I removed it without a sound, and she, snoring through her flared nose, did not stir. I slipped into the darkness of the room.

All furniture was gone. Any object by which Antonina might do herself harm had been removed. The windows were barred, the curtains drawn, but the smell of urine and faeces rose from the smeared floors, overpowering the soap and brine.

A figure stirred in the shadows, dressed in a torn white gown which offered as little warmth as it did dignity. I had looked in the mirror so often and seen that face and found it lovely; now as it rose, hair wild and eyes set in vengeance, I saw only a tempest of growling youth and hatred.

"Antonina," I whispered. "Antonina," I breathed again, and, one leg hardly accepting the project at all, I sank down on to my knees before her. "Forgive me," I said. "Forgive me. I did you wrong. I have stolen time from you. I have taken your dignity, your name, your soul. I love you. Forgive me."

She stirred from the shadows of the room, shuffled towards me, one unsteady foot at a time. I stayed where I was, head bowed, hands clasped before me. She stopped, her feet and bare lower legs filling my vision. I looked up. Her hair was tangled across her face, around her neck, as if she had tried to hang herself with her own locks. She spat in my face. I flinched, and didn't move. She spat again. The liquid barely registered, already skin temperature, as it rolled down my forehead.

"I love you," I said, and she shook her head, covered her ears. "I love you." Reaching out, pressing my hands against her feet, rooting them in place. "I love you."

Her hands turned to claws, dragging them down across her own face, and with a sudden lurch she pulled her feet free from my fingers. There were no words, no shaping except her rage, only heat and wetness on my face as she lowered her mouth to the level of my eyes and screamed, screamed and screamed until at last she had no more breath, and I caught her by the shoulders and pulled her close. She bit and scratched, tore at my beard, my face, her nails digging into my wrinkled skin as if she would pull it from my skull, but I let her fight until at last even that strength seemed to leave her, and I held her tight.

The noise could not have been ignored. The servants came, along with my lady wife, who stood in the door and gaped at the sight she beheld. I shook my head at her, sending her away, and held my daughter closer still, her breath hot in the tangle of mine, until morning.

Then I was someone else, and I was gone.

Chapter 77

A shaking awake, a starting. The sun is setting, and I have dreamed of Galileo.

Coyle is still asleep on the bed. I wake him as the last vestiges of daylight fade.

"We have to keep moving."

"Where are we going?" he asks as I help him down to the car.

"Somewhere with trains."

We reached Lyon shortly after 8 p.m.

Like many old cities in France, Lyon was possessed of beautiful houses pressed against a sluggish river, of a high-towered cathedral and ancient buried walls, and of suburbs of grand *supermarchés*, sprawling car parks and low-rise clothing outlets in iron-ceilinged industrial sheds. I left Coyle slumbering in the car park of one which advertised itself with the immortal words EAT THE BEST, LIVE THE BEST, SHOP THE BEST! and went inside with my plundered euros. A child giggled on a tiny fireman's truck that rocked back and forth to the wailing of a siren. A small marquee, perfect, declared the billboard, for weddings and festive occasions, had been erected by the supermarket checkout counters for any casual shoppers looking for the ultimate spontaneous splurge. Cold steam drifted in grey wisps over fat vegetables, and the smell of yeast mixed with light jazz pumped from the bare pipes of the ceiling.

I bought bread, meat, water and an armful of men's clothes, all baggier than required. The woman behind the checkout counter wore a peaked green hat and a bewildered expression as my shopping drifted down the conveyer belt towards her.

"For my brother," I explained.

"He lets you buy trousers for him?"

"I'm good at dressing people."

Coyle was still asleep in the car.

"Coyle." I brushed his arm gingerly and, when he didn't stir, ran the back of my fingers, gentle as a feather, across his cheek. His eyes opened, flickering in the darkness of the car, registered where he was and who he was with, and recoiled. I swallowed and said, "We're in Lyon."

"What's in Lyon?"

"Public transport, mostly. Here."

"What's this?"

"Clean clothes. For you."

"Not for you?"

"If I wanted to change, it'd be more than the clothes I wear. Try them. I think I remembered your size."

He scowled but said, "Help me with the shirt?"

I turned the heater up, helped him fumble with buttons, peeled the ruined shirt away from his skin. Remarkably the dressing across his shoulder was neither saturated with blood nor falling away. By the faint light of the car park I felt around the edges of the wound and asked, "Does it burn?"

"No."

"How's the pain?"

"I'm coping. Your hands are cold."

"My circulation isn't fantastic. Here." I rolled a T-shirt down over his head, helped him manoeuvre one arm at a time into the sleeves, tucked it down around his trousers. He sat still and straight, breath steady, watching my every move. My fingers brushed the scar across his belly and he didn't flinch, but every fibre was tight, every muscle locked. "Fit OK?"

"Fine."

"I bought you a jumper too. It'll probably disintegrate in the first wash, but it's warm and clean."

"Thank you."

"You're welcome."

"Why are you bothering?"

I sighed and turned away. "You've got blood on the upholstery," I murmured. "Blood's hard to clean."

Roundabouts were the lock, patience the key, to any driver seeking to find their way into the middle of Lyon. I took us through one-way systems and down towards the river, where the hot young things of the city grew cold to the sound of 90s techno and noughties bass. I parked, illegally, in front of a grey stone church from whose porch the Virgin Mary gazed sorrowfully down at her straying flock and said, "We can't use the car any more."

"Why not?"

"Irena's been gone more than eight hours. If she had a shift tonight, it would have started a few hours ago. The last person I wore – Max – I left him at the service station . . . "

"You think Aquarius will have worked out who you are?"

"You know them better than I. Would you?"

"Yes. I think I might."

"Then we need to lose the car. It's public transport from now on. If we can get to Spain, or even Gibraltar, without setting off alarms, that'll make things easier. I need a drink."

"A drink?"

"Can you walk?"

"Is this the time for a drink?"

"Never better," I replied, pushing open the car door. "I'm a lady who likes tequila."

*

I had tequila, Coyle had orange juice.

In France orange juice means fizzy orange-coloured sugar from a spherical bottle.

We sat at the counter of a bar whose flat-screen TVs showed football and BMX. Only one game interested the crowd, and by their gripes it was both local and not going well. Coyle was sweating, one hand clenched around a paper napkin, his teeth drawn back across his lips.

The barman said, "You all right?"

And I replied, "He twisted his ankle."

"You should see a doctor. Sometimes these things are worse than you think."

"They usually are. More tequila?"

His eyes radiated scepticism, but economics guided his hand to another glass. Behind us someone scored, and the room groaned its universal dismay.

"You're knocking it back," grunted Coyle to the sound of sporting hearts breaking and the hissing of fresh beer.

"I'll let you into a secret. It's far easier to divert the world's attention away from a host if that host can be discovered intoxicated, bewildered, concussed or otherwise in an altered mental state upon her awakening."

"You're moving on?"

I took another slurp, felt salt crackle, alcohol burn, hissed in satisfaction at the effect. "There's a file – I stole records from Aquarius while in Berlin."

"You told me."

"And did you tell Aquarius?"

"I did. We ... *they* ... are afraid of you."

"I take it they didn't realise I was with Janus?"

"No."

"Why were you there?"

"It's my job," he replied. "It's what I do." Another drink; I put the empty glass to one side. "No. That's not it." His voice was for him, though I happened to hear it. "I asked about Galileo, and they reassigned me to Paris. At the time I thought it was ... At the time I didn't think. That's what I was doing there, as you ask."

My nails were hard and sharp as they rattled around the edge of the glass.

"I'm not going to help you hurt them," he breathed. "I won't help you against Aquarius, no matter what they did. If it was them who did it. You're not my friend. This is about Galileo – nothing more."

"I understand."

The busy roar of the football screen, the busy contempt of the disappointed fans lamenting the game. I ran my finger round the lip of the glass, which stoutly refused to hum.

Then, "New York," said Coyle. "There's a ... sponsor in New York. After Berlin, after you showed me the file, I tried to speak to him, but Aquarius said no. Told me you'd lied to me about Galileo, that it was what you did – spread the chaos. You put Alice in hospital, did you know that?"

"She was bruised but walking when I left her. The rest is psychological, nothing to do with me."

"Do you care?"

"Not right now."

He sipped his juice like it was whisky, salve to the wounds, old and new, still burning on his body. "I knew they were lying to me. You're a parasite, but you didn't lie. I guess I should thank you for that."

"Knock yourself out."

"A sponsor," he tried again. "There's a sponsor in New York."

"What does he sponsor?"

"Us. Aquarius. The units are kept largely separate. If one is infiltrated, the others should be safe, but there has to be some central authority, someone who watches it all. We aren't bad people. We don't hurt our own. If there were orders ... if Galileo is being protected ... the sponsor will know why."

"I wouldn't hold your breath on that count. Do you know who this sponsor is?"

"No."

"You know where to find him?"

Silence.

I squeezed the last dregs of lime into the bottom of my glass, watched the innards of the fruit pop between my fingers. "You're wondering if I'll kill him," I breathed. "If this is all just part of one big trick. It's a good instinct. It could keep you safe right up to that moment when your fear of being stabbed in the back means there's no one left to watch it. So don't ask yourself what I want or even who I am. Ask yourself only this: what could I do? Ten seconds are all I need to destroy a man. When you shot me on the steps in Taksim, I thought, Yes. Why not. I'll be him, I'll be her – I'll be someone – and I'll slit your throat. It'll only take a moment, and when the cops take me away, blood still warm on my skin, I'll be gone. All that your death would be to me, as I carried on with my life, was a few seconds. Consequences are for the flesh. Yet for some reason I couldn't fully fathom at the time, I let you live. I could have run. I'm very good at running. Now, having had a while to consider it, I think I spared you, whatever-your-name-is, because in trying to kill me you performed the single most personal act anyone has done for me in . . . I don't know how long. You tried to kill *me*. For all the things that I have done. I can barely describe the excitement of that feeling. So, here we are now, you and I, and I think you should know that my sentiments have perhaps evolved. Become a little more nuanced as, in the course of this merry round, I have come to know you, and, simply put, I love you. Curse me, hate me, spit on me, it's all the same – an act of revulsion against my very soul. Not who I seem to be, but who I actually am. You are beautiful. And I would no sooner hurt you than I would walk barefoot to Aleppo in a leper's skin."

Coyle drained the last of his juice, looked into the empty glass. "Well," he said at last, then stopped. "OK," he went on, after a moment's reflection. "Right."

I waggled my empty glass at the barman. "Tequila. More tequila."

"You haven't had enough, Madame?"

"I'll have had enough when I can't walk. And my lovely friend here is going to help me home."

The man shrugged as only a French barman can, all wisdom and apathy, and poured another glass. At my side Coyle had grown still. "And how am I helping you home, exactly?"

"What do you look for when you hunt my kind? Do you scour hospital records, looking for patients with sudden amnesia? Or is it financial blips, the poor man who suddenly starts buying, the rich man who gives it all away?"

"Both. We follow the carnage."

"But amnesia can be caused by all sorts of things. A hit on the head. A shock to the system. A chemical cocktail perhaps, that too."

"Kepler –" a note of warning, understanding seeped into his voice "– where is this going?"

"Every body I pick up, every body I leave behind, is someone else who can be traced. The car can be traced; Irena can be traced. Time to move on."

"To what? Another cleaning lady? Or more hookers and thieves – that's your style, isn't it?"

"Usually, yes. But circumstances are different. Irena isn't my only liability."

The penny, which had been balancing on the edge for a while, dropped. "No way."

"Coyle ... "

"Don't call me that. No fucking way!"

"Think about it ... "

"Is this why you let me sleep? Patched me up?"

"I didn't want you dead."

"Or too uncomfortable."

"A cooperative host, a willing body ... "

"Chemically corrected for your pleasure ... "

"Coyle!" I nearly shouted, pushed my hands into my lap, swallowed a lungful of cold dark air. "I can think of few bodies I would rather inhabit less than yours. I have rejected skins because they have itchy knees or their knuckles crack; do you really think I'd want to inhabit a body with a bullet wound if there was a better choice?"

"And if they find you?"

"I promise to do my very best to move into a more combat-ready skin at the earliest opportunity. What options do you have?"

"Plenty."

"You've still got a bullet in your shoulder."

"I can't imagine you'll be in a hurry to take it out."

"Your own people ..."

"I know!" He shouted now, hands slamming into the counter top, hard enough to make my glass jump, loud enough for heads to turn. He shrank down before the stares, seemed to curl in around his own core. "I know," he murmured. "I know."

"I can get you to New York."

"How?"

"I can get you to your sponsor. I won't hurt him. Have I lied to you? Have I killed?"

"You killed Eugene. In Berlin – you did that."

"Alice killed Eugene," I retorted. "She shot him because I was there, but he died and I lived. He'd have lived if you'd left me alone. I can get you to Galileo."

"I ... don't know. I need to think. You've ... drugged me. Talked. Jesus, you talk. I need to think."

I laid my hand gently on top of his.

"That's great," I said. "But I'm going to throw up, and we're all out of time."

His hand twitched, but he was far, far too late.

Chapter 78

I said, "Hi."

Coyle opened his eyes, licked his lips and said, "Where am I?"

"Dentist's."

His eyes wandered across the low ceiling, the white tiled floor, to me. "Who are you?"

"I am Nehra Beck, married, two kids, loyalty card for the local coffee shop, fastidious – some might say obsessive – collector of receipts."

"What time is it?"

"Midnight, give or take. I – or rather you – explained that it was an emergency and you'd pay, and when Nehra realised that I had a bullet in my shoulder he became a little distressed and I had to explain that my emergency wasn't so much about teeth, and then ... Well, here we are."

"Which day?"

"Same day," I replied. "Only a few hours gone. I'm sorry about just jumping in like that, but you were getting unreasonable and I was really very, very drunk. But once in I realised that this whole stoical thing you've been doing was actually secondary to the fact that the bullet has got to come out." I picked a pair of industrial-sized tweezers off the metal table at my side, clicked them together thoughtfully. "I figured a dentist might have enough happy drugs to ease the experience a little. I, for one, am looking forward to the after-effects."

Chapter 79

And then Coyle opened his eyes and I said: "I'm Babushka. Actually, I'm almost certainly not Babushka, but all I've got in my handbag is eighty euros cash, a set of front-door keys, a half-bottle of vodka, four condoms, a pack of paracetamol, pepper spray and these."

I tossed the business cards on to the bed where Coyle lay. He looked from them to me and back again, and said, "You look... surgical."

"Do I?" I ran my hands around the expansive shape of my body, my platinum-blonde hair draping down the side of my podgy white neck. "Well, yes, the breasts feel silicone and a bit undercooked, but I'd say that my face was all my own, wouldn't you?"

Coyle, lying on his back on the cheap hotel bed, scrutinised the copious quantities of bare flesh I sported, and said, "This is some sort of punishment, isn't it? Divine retribution?"

"Nonsense!" I exclaimed, flopping on to the bed beside him and sliding the cards back into my bag. "Babushka seemed a very pleasant woman. Cheap too. Fifty euros for two hours. You don't get rates like that in Paris, I can tell you. How are you feeling?"

Flinching with every press of his fingertips, he fumbled around the fresh bandages across his shoulder. "I don't remember much."

"That would be because you were stoned!" I sang out brightly, testing the rubbery ends of my bright white fingernails. "I knew you were stoned because I was the one who threw the drugs at you, but it took picking up Babushka here to realise just how high I – you – am. Are. You are. Enjoy it while it lasts. I was only checking in, so actually . . . " I reached out towards the soft skin of his cheek.

"Wait!"

I waited, eyebrows raised. Babushka had sensational plucked eyebrows, and I enjoyed raising them. Coyle sucked in a long slow breath. "You told me . . . you wanted a willing body. Someone who wouldn't scream, wouldn't run. And cheap though your . . . your Babushka is, if you take her anywhere outside this hotel room her pimp will come running, and you'll have more trouble than you want. So you need me, and you need me to cooperate. So just wait." I waited as Coyle pressed his fists against his forehead and drew in another shuddering breath. "Tell me how you get me to New York."

"I can walk you through customs," I replied simply. "I can ignore your boarding pass, stamp your passport, fail to search your bags. I could wear anyone I want to New York, fly first class, stretch my legs. But I'll get you there, if you let me."

"And what then? I wake up handcuffed to a radiator?"

"Or in a comfortable hotel room next to a lovely lady."

"Have you looked at yourself in the mirror?"

"No," I confessed. "But I took a good long stare at me when I came through the door. I was promising all sorts of wonderful delights – sexual thrills and erotic mysteries. I implied that I was very athletic." I stretched my legs, feeling the pull beneath my thighs and calves, and, curious, reached down and tried to touch my toes. My fingertips barely made it past my knees before tendons locked, muscles objected, and with a sigh I relaxed again. "Maybe I exaggerated. But I thought I had a tender smile. It laughed, but at itself. I think I am quite wonderful, in my way."

"Do you do this a lot? You hear about people who establish . . . relationships with people like you. I was never sure I could believe it."

"It's true. I've had a few in my time – gofers, if you will. Don't worry; I was always very well behaved. A cooperative body isn't something to be taken for granted. I'd never drive dangerously or have unprotected sex in a gofer; it wouldn't be professional. Never have sex at all, in fact, in a gofer – not without permission. A relationship like that is about someone who's willing to get you to the next appointment without all the fuss of jumping from waiter to chef to driver and back again. And a good gofer is . . . can be a friend. If they want to be."

"Did you love them too?"

"Yes. Of course I did. They knew what I was and trusted me. They trusted me with their naked skin. If that isn't an act of love, I don't know what is. I love all my hosts. I loved Josephine." His eyes glinted in the low tungsten light of the room, and he said not a word. "There was a time when I took everything I wanted by force. You – the actions of your kind – have somewhat resurrected that experience, those memories. But Josephine Cebula knew what she had agreed to. She and I made a bargain in the international departures lounge of Frankfurt airport, once I had proved to her all that I could do. I would wash her body, run my hands through her hair, over her naked flesh. I would dress her in brand-new clothes, stand before a mirror and turn myself this way and that, wonder if my bum looked big in red, small in blue. I would laugh her laugh, fill her belly with food, run her tongue along my teeth, kiss with her lips, caress with her fingertips, pull a stranger down on to her body in the quiet of the night and in her most secret voice whisper tales of romance in my lover's ears. All this I did, all this she permitted me to do, because I asked and did not take, and I . . . loved her. There is no giving greater than the gift she gave me, nor that I . . . meant to give her. A new life. A new her. A chance to be whoever she desired, and all this for a term of time no longer than the jail sentence given to a petty thief. But you killed her, Nathan Coyle. Whoever you are. You killed her."

I did not think I had heard a silence that ran so deep, burying itself in the very bones of the night.

He said, "I . . ."

And stopped.

Said, "It wasn't . . ."

Stopped again.

Some words on the tip of his tongue. Justifications perhaps, excuses. Following orders. Justice. Retribution. Poor decisions, too little time, too much pressure. Past history – poor Nathan Coyle, he's been hurt, he's been traumatised by events gone by, don't judge, not him, not for his actions freely taken.

The words rose to his lips and died before they could be expressed.

I watched them dissolve into him, burning as they burrowed deep into his flesh, until he looked away and said nothing at all.

I paced the room, turned on the TV.

Reports of . . .

. . . someone else's problems.

Turned the TV off again.

Waited.

Then he said, I want to brush my teeth.

Bathroom's right there. Knock yourself out.

He rose, painfully, testing the bandages across his arm and chest, feeling that they were good.

The bathroom door stood ajar, and from the bed I watched him move in and out of view against bright white light. When the tap had finished running, I eased back the bathroom door so that I might see him fully, and there he stood, hands pressed down on the edge of the sink, staring up into the mirror as if he too were only just seeing his face, he too was trying to solve the question of what shape it might become. I leaned against the door frame, a surgically skinned prostitute in a town where the rates were bad, the pimps difficult, the secrets of my trade hidden beneath new-washed cobbled streets. His eyes didn't move to me, didn't wander from the hypnotic weight of his own stare.

"If I say no?" he asked.

"Then I'll leave. I'll run to where my file on Aquarius will be. I'll tear them apart from the inside out and leave you alone."

"To die? Is that the threat?"

"I won't hurt you. Aquarius, Galileo ... your guess is as good as mine. But I won't hurt you."

He nodded once at his own reflection, then looked down into the depths of the sink, shoulders hunched, back bent, suddenly old before his time. "Do it," he said. "Do it."

I reached out, then hesitated, my fingers hovering above the bare skin of his back. "Do it!" he snarled, lips twisting, eyebrows knotted together and I pressed my fingers against his skin and, instinctive before his rage,

jumped.

I am Nathan Coyle. Here, the pounding of my heart. The heat in my eyes, the aching in my chest.

I am Nathan Coyle, standing hurt and breathless, a bewildered woman with an implausible name reeling in the doorway of the bathroom.

I am Nathan Coyle, looking up into the mirror at eyes that wanted to weep.

And for a moment, as I regard my reflection staring back at me, I wish to God that I were anyone else in the world.

Chapter 80

There are no planes from Lyon to New York.

Back on to the trains.

Passengers on a train are harder to track than cars.

The TGV, the push of acceleration, the roar of tunnels, the flat fields of northern France.

Back to Paris.

The passenger next to me, at a table of four, was an old man with an oversized newspaper.

I read the articles over his shoulder for a while, but his reading speed was slow, mine fast, and I was tired, and bored, and lonely, so I put one hand on his wrist and

jumped.

Coyle stirred by my side, saw the window, the countryside grey-green outside, heard the engine, smelt overpriced railway coffee and at last, his hand still on mine, saw me.

"We're not there yet?"

"Not yet."

"What is it?"

"I . . . wanted to say hello."

"Why?"

"I thought you might . . . want to know how we were doing?"
He stared at me, incredulous. "Sorry," I mumbled. "I . . . was just
trying to be nice."

I jumped back through the hot palm of his hand.

Back in Gare de Lyona, nd for a few seconds I left Coyle, who
staggered, catching his weight against the side of a ticket machine.

"What is it now?"

"We're low on money," I replied, fumbling in my pockets for
my wallet. "Here – take this." I pulled all the notes save one from
my wallet, held them out for Coyle.

He looked down with the contempt of a bishop for a fallen
angel, then folded the money into his fist. "Who are you?" he
asked as I put my far lighter wallet back into my pocket.

"Right now I'm a man who met a stranger and shook him by
the hand. So shake my hand, Nathan Coyle, and let's move on."

Slowly he uncurled his fingers and shook me gently by the
hand.

I rode the train to the airport, then the humming twin-carriaged
shuttle to the terminal. A woman stood opposite me, her hair fair,
her skin tanned, a green dress tied shut across her waist, her laugh
as she chatted with a friend on the phone dazzling and bright. She
was going to the car park, I decided, having returned from a sun-
soaked holiday in some southern clime, and for her tomorrow
held no dread of work or fear of jet lag, but rather a delight that
having departed, she was now returning to her waiting family and
friends, who would all cluster about to see her.

My fingers itched to brush her skin and have that laugh to call
my own, as my mother, father – perhaps even some adoring sib-
lings who as a child I squabbled with but are now all grown up and
fraternally in love – crushed me to their sides and called me their
little pumpkin, their dearest girl.

Then I looked round, and saw Nathan Coyle's reflection staring back at me from the window panes, and the doors opened,
and she was gone.

*

One ticket to New York, coming up.

And I was . . .

"Passport, please?"

Coyle blinked up at me, felt his hand upon my own, peeking through the little gap in the screen where weary travellers must place their passports upon attempting to leave this land. I smiled at him and said in cheerful, chatty French, "I'm going to look at your passport now, Mr Coyle," and prised my fingers free from his.

It was the first time I'd been inside a passport control booth, having never before felt the need. An uncomfortable high stool, foolproof equipment that I was too foolish to fully comprehend, a holstered gun tucked beneath the counter.

"Give it a few moments," I said, "then move on as if I've cleared you. I'll be a couple of bodies behind."

He nodded, and at my smile and cheery "Have a good flight!" shuffled like one half-asleep down through the line.

I scanned a few more passports, inspected a few more faces, just for the hell of it, wondering which might be criminal, which a smuggler. A bar code scanner beeped appreciatively when I waved a couple of passports at it, and up popped names and numbers on my screen which I made a show of studying while chubby tourists and harassed businessmen waited for me to clear them through. When one came along whose build seemed close enough to Coyle's, his hair of the same colour and a similar cut, I smiled especially brightly, reached out for his passport and, as his fingers brushed mine,

my fingers brushed back.

Nine bodies later, as Coyle stepped up to the metal detectors at border control, laying his bag down on the X-ray conveyor, I said, "You carrying anything dodgy, sir?" His eyes flashed to mine, for "dodgy" was not a word commonly expected of customs officers. I smiled and added, "Strip-search, sir?"

"Do we have the time?"

"Oh, sir," I chided, pushing his bag on to the conveyor belt, "don't you know how much more exciting it is to be touched by another's skin, instead of your own? But I can see you're not in the mood, and I've got an ingrown toenail; you go straight on through."

Then I was

businessman with horrific teeth, fillings that needed repair, heat in my gums, did he think this was normal?

sitting down beside Coyle in the international departures lounge, briefcase in one hand, paper cup in the other. "Tea?"

Coyle examined the cup, examined me, and without another word took the tea from my unresisting fingers. "Thank you."

"You're welcome. I brought some sugar too, in case you like it sweet."

"I don't."

"Never mind. Better for your teeth anyway."

He slurped tea; I leaned back, tucking my briefcase between my knees, rolling my tongue nervously around the ravaged inside of my mouth. Charles de Gaulle airport was like any airport in the world: there the duty free, here the chemist for those unsuspecting travellers whose hundred-millilitre bottles of shampoo were one millilitre too dangerous for airport security. There the smart-suited men trying to sell indulged strangers the latest sports car, here the bookshop of last month's greatest hits, tales of American lawyers with perfect teeth, American lovers with perfect lives, American killers who refuse to lie down and die.

Women in headscarves held their infant children by the hand and studied the departures board for the next plane to wherever. Tired travellers, stopping over on the way to something better, slumbered, heads back, tongues lolling, their boarding passes gripped tight against their slowly deflating chests. I fumbled in my pocket for my ticket, checked the flight, the time, the board overhead. "Can't even see where I'm supposed to go."

Coyle glanced down at the stub in my hand. "I think yours is delayed."

"Typical. Yours?"

"'Wait for announcements'."

"That could mean anything."

"I think it's a good thing."

"Are you sure?"

He glanced over at me, surprised. "You . . . don't like flying?"

"First time I crossed the Atlantic, it was in a Dutch race-built frigate called the *Nessy Reach*. Bloody dangerous business."

"But planes . . . ?"

"I dislike the universality of the threat with flying. First-class fat-cat or economy class with your knees pressed to your chin; if a plane falls, you're dead no matter who you are."

"My God," he exclaimed. "You're a coward."

"Am I? I suppose bravery must be defined relative to the deeds habitually available to he who faces it. I have been hired to do many of the things that brave man can't: leave a lover, attend a job interview, march to war. I grant you I had none of the emotional involvement in these acts that might have rendered them tricky, but still I have to ask . . . am I really a coward? I think the case could be argued both ways."

"All right – you're not a coward. You're merely operating by a different set of rules."

I smiled and said, "Want another cup of tea?"

"No. Thank you."

"I should let this body go. Flight delayed or not, the mind can only lose so much time."

"I know." He held out his hand, not looking, the fingers hanging loose like those of a queen waiting to be kissed.

"You're very brave," I said, resting my fingers in his skin.

Then there was the slow crawl to the runway.

Safety demonstrations. Chin to knees, oxygen from above, be sure to save yourself before you save a child or your friend.

A push of acceleration as we headed for the sky. I let my skull press back into the headrest of my seat, felt the chemically numbed throbbing in my shoulder and arm, resisted the urge to prod at the wound, watched the landscape turn from a thing of solid nature into a map of straight lines, roads and paths carved by a human hand, ordered the vegetarian meal and a bottle of water and, finding that the in-flight movies had even less merit than commonly supposed, played chess instead with an unknown passenger in seat D12, who lost quickly and didn't return for a rematch.

Then there was ocean beneath us and tiny clouds far below, and I was tired, and my shoulder ached, and my eyes hurt, and in a moment of temptation I became

round-faced man, too fat for my economy-class seat, belt chafing across my middle, my knees pressed up awkwardly, elbows jammed in, and as I shifted uncomfortably and the engines hummed and the drinks trolley clattered up and down the aisle, Coyle turned blearily to me and said:

"Brave?"

"What?"

"You called me brave."

"Did I?"

"A second ago."

"A few hours ago."

"Where are we now?"

"Somewhere over the Atlantic."

"What's the matter?"

"Matter?"

"Why are you . . . you?" he asked, gesturing at my more abundant flesh.

"I was . . . uncomfortable. Wanted to stretch my legs. This gentleman was in the way, so I thought I'd stretch his."

"I can believe that. You called me brave."

"Must have imagined it."

"A moment ago."

"I also called you a murderer, a blind fool and the killer of a woman I loved. All of which is true. Yet here we are, knuckling down and carrying on. I wouldn't be too worried about it."

"Are you going to be him long?"

I shifted awkwardly in my seat. "No," I said at last. "I'm too wide for the armrests – they're compressing my belly – and my knees hurt, and my feet feel splayed and flat, and I've got an after-taste of ginger ale in my mouth, and even if all this were not the case, I still think I'm a coronary risk. But if you want to watch a movie or something, I could take a wander round the plane? Upgrade to first class, perhaps."

"What are the movie choices like?"

"Appalling. Do you play chess?"

"What?"

"Do you play chess?"

"No. I mean yes, I play."

"Want a game?"

"With you?"

"Sure. Or challenge seat D12, but they won't give you much trouble."

"I'm not sure . . . "

"You let me wear your body, but you won't play me at chess?"

"One is grim necessity, the other feels like socialising."

"Suit yourself."

Silence a while. Then, "I'm not your friend. You understand that."

"Of course."

"In Berlin, in Istanbul, I meant everything I said. I believe everything that I believe. A few minutes here or there, a game of chess . . . it doesn't change what you are. What you represent. I let you . . . touch me . . . because I must, and it repulses me. I don't know why I'm explaining this to you."

"It's OK," I replied. "It'll be OK."

Silence.

As much as there is ever silence in the roar of a plane.

"So . . . do you want to sleep?" I asked, shifting awkwardly in my seat.

"Won't your body notice if you stay in too long?"

I shrugged. "Planes are boring. Most people are relieved to find that the hours have flown by, so to speak."

"I could do with some time."

"Fine."

"By myself."

I half-nodded at nothing in particular. "That's not a problem," I murmured, reaching out to touch my neighbour's hand. "I'll see you on the other side."

I am a first-class businesswoman.
    At home I probably do yoga.
    I eat prawns and drink champagne.
    Coyle sits alone, and so do I.

Chapter 81

Then there was ...

"Passport, please."

I beamed at the man behind the counter. Newark airport specialised in immigration officers whose every scowl seemed to say that, even if they couldn't stop you entering the United States, they sure as hell weren't going to make it easy.

I pushed the wallet that contained my tickets across the counter towards him, and as he reached down, lips already narrowing in the expectation of disappointment, I caught his wrist and said, "Welcome to New York."

Coyle caught his balance on the counter before him while I made a show of flicking through the little pouch of documents on the desk. "The Americans have a poker up their arse with security. Do you have a communicable disease?"

Coyle pressed his forehead against the palms of his hands, steadying himself in body and mind. "What?"

"I'm supposed to ask questions. Do you have a communicable disease?"

"Only you."

"Harsh. Have you ever been arrested for a crime of moral

turpitude? You know, I'm not sure I know what moral turpitude is, and I've been around."

"I've never been arrested," he replied carefully. "Is that your American accent?"

"I'm aiming for New Jersey."

"It's bad."

"I'm still warming up. It's as much about syntax as it is inflection. I'm on duty right now, so I probably won't be calling you dude or asking about the game because I'm the kind of man who takes pride in my uniform. Have you ever been or are you now involved in espionage or sabotage, or in terrorist activities, or in genocide? I think we can put a big yes down for all of the above."

"You planning on ratting me out to the US authorities?"

"I thought about it for a fanciful moment," I replied, pushing the travel documents back across the desk. "I also thought about walking you through the 'something to declare' aisle singing the North Korean national anthem, but I doubted anyone would find it funny. Here. You're nearly through."

For a few minutes a hot flush of panic overcame me as, prowling the conveyor belts, I sought but could not find Coyle.

Then I saw him, sitting with his back pressed against the wall, legs splayed across the floor, his hand pressed tightly against the place in his shoulder where the bandages were growing old, his face grey, his breathing steady. I squatted down beside him, wobbling in my high heels, and said, "You all right?"

He half-turned to look at me and saw, for a second, not me but my stewardess uniform, my little hat, my painted lips, and said, "I'm fine, I'm ... " then he hesitated, his eyes narrowing. "Are you you?" I held out a long-nailed hand to pull him to his feet. "I think you should know," he breathed, "that I've felt better."

"It's OK. I'll get you somewhere safe."

"Why can't you just get yourself there?"

"The fewer bodies I take off course, the fewer alarms I'll set ringing, the better I can protect you."

"You're doing this to protect me?"

"God knows," I replied, my fingers tightening around his cold arm, "I'm not doing it for your silky flesh."

Coyle had not lied.

I'd felt much, much better.

My fingers were icy cold as I shuffled into my seat on the train.

My stomach felt hot and empty, my shoulder throbbed with a dull heartbeat of its own. I staggered into the stainless-steel toilet on the stained steel train and as we bounced and rattled our way north pulled back my shirt to inspect the bandages. They seemed clean enough, but when I prodded around the area of the wound, pain shimmered down my spine, and I prodded no more.

Then I was

"Hi." As Coyle swayed before me I pushed the room key into his hand and said, "You're on the top floor. Take the lift. I've booked us in for one night."

He blinked up at me as I beamed from behind the reception desk, looked down at the room key pressed into his hand and, without a word, turned and began the shuffle towards the bank of brass-doored lifts. I waited until he was gone, called a porter over and followed.

The hotel was grand – more so than I'd grown accustomed to. The room came with a leather-clad bed, armchairs, en-suite bathroom of polished chrome, three layers of unwieldy curtain and a TV larger than a slumbering hippo. By the time I arrived, no luggage in hand, Coyle was already lying on the bed, feet hanging off the end, arms wrapped round his middle.

"Coyle?" He half-opened an eye to peer up at me. "You're going to be OK," I said. "I'll go out, find someone rich, get you more painkillers, more dressings."

"Who are you now?"

"I don't know. I'll get you what you need."

"I've never been shot before."

"I have. I know how you feel. You'll be fine."

"You don't know that. You never stick around long enough to find out."

"I'll be back in a bit."

"And who will you be when you come back?"

"Someone else. Someone new. Me."

I took the key to the room, stuffed it into the soil of a potted plant by the elevator, rode to the ground floor.

I shook the hand of the first man I saw emerge from the hotel restaurant, and as the porter blinked blearily before me slipped him a ten-dollar tip, thanked him politely and headed out into the New York streets.

The cold comes with bone-cracking intensity. Without pausing to let the skin register its distress, the Manhattan winter drives straight through to the heart, seeming to the unprotected wanderer that they are freezing from the inside out, though this cannot be the case. The wind off the water rushes up the streets, racing the yellow cab driver to his destination, swirls round the tower blocks, blasts you sideways at the crossroads, picks up newspaper and claws at your hair. Pharmacies in New York are as far removed from their French counterparts as frozen Alaska from Hawaiian beaches. Gone are the clinical whiteness, long counters and careful shelves; instead arise walls of advertisements and pledges, price slashes and guarantees that this cream can make your hair grow or this spray-on tan is the only path to sexual satisfaction. Squeeze through the laden shelves of shampoo and razors, emery boards and nail paint, and stand before a tiny desk where the clerk's eyes seem to say, if you cannot buy yourself a cure, then you are incurable.

I bought bandages, painkillers, the necessaries of first aid. I toyed with hopping into the clerk and grabbing an armful of antibiotics, just in case – but no. Unlike Coyle, my body would not stay put while I ransacked the shelves, so I would be patient until needs must.

I tried jogging through the streets of Manhattan, but my portly frame and aching knees were having none of it, so I waddled as fast as I could, face flushed and lungs heavy, back to the hotel.

The key to Coyle's room was still buried in the potted plant by the elevator door. I dug it out, shook the dirt off, let myself in.

Coyle lay where I had left him, blanket pulled up to his chin, shivering on the bed. I shook him gently by the leg, whispered, "Coyle."

His eyes opened slowly – dizziness giving way to startled fear at the sight of a stranger's face. "Kepler?" His voice was dry, tongue slow.

"I've got more meds. Do you need water?"

"Yes ... please."

I fetched a plastic cup from the bathroom, held his head as he levered up to drink, murmured, sip – small sips. Not too fast.

When he was done, I said, I need to look at your dressing now. Do what you have to, he replied.

A restless night.

Coyle slept, buried beneath the many sheets of the hotel bed.

I sat on the armchair opposite and didn't sleep a wink. Watching. Sometimes he woke, and I gave him water and painkillers, and pulled the blanket back about his chin and waited for him to sleep again. Sometimes he murmured half-heard whispers of deeds done and regrets remembered. I sat with my head in my hands and didn't watch the TV, didn't read a book, but listened and waited.

I found it hard to remember when I had last slept.

Struggled to recall where I was, how I had come to be there. The room was Bratislava or Belgrade or Berlin, and I was ...

a man who loved ...

a woman who said ...

something.

I looked in my wallet, found a name, found I didn't care. I had no interest in my face or my nature. I was someone, from somewhere, who happened to be myself. For whatever that was worth.

Dawn was a grey tinge around the edge of the curtains, a sucking out of colour from the room.

Coyle lay still, breathing steadily, heartbeat level. I washed my face in the polished sink, left the key to the room again in the pot by the elevator and went out to find New York's rush hour.

The Subway.

On the express you slide along the plastic seats with the deceleration of the train. The escalators *clack* irritatingly as you descend; the ticket barriers have a nasty bite as they open and close around you.

I rode the rush-hour train and, when the crowd was substantial enough, I
jumped
and jumped
and jumped again
moving without motion
leaving my body far behind.

Chapter 82

Coyle was awake when I returned to the hotel, watching the news.

The news was loud, opinionated and local. In the land of the free you are free to say whatever you want, regardless of whether you have anything to say.

I was the porter again, and as I shuffled in with a tray of fruit and croissants, I said, "I can't stay in this boy long – how are you feeling?"

Coyle's fingers unconsciously fumbled at the dressing over his shoulder. "Crap. But not too crap."

"Feel like food?"

"I'll give it a go."

He gave it a go and asked for more.

I said, "I really need to let this body get on with its work."

"I need to make a phone call."

"Who to?"

"A friend."

"What kind of friend?" His eyes slipped up sideways at me, a sharp stare. Back off. I pulled my flat cap off my head, scratched at the dark hair nestled beneath, a thin shower of dandruff from my fingertips. "OK. You trusted me, I guess I owe you that. But please don't do anything reckless."

"More reckless than stealing a porter's body for an hour?"

"Like I said, sometimes people are grateful to find the hours have passed. I'll go for a walk in someone discreet."

I went for a walk in someone discreet.

A woman, whose thick grey hair and overhanging eyelids proclaimed her to be old, but whose skin beneath my shirt was soft and pink, and whose arms, as I flexed them inside my sleeves, were sturdy and ready to work.

I walked the tourist's shuffle, for only tourists ever really walk in New York.

I walked to Washington Square and stood beneath the white arch raised by city forefathers who loathed imperialism but had a soft spot for its ego. In the grand central circle buskers competed with the pigeons and each other for the attention of passers-by. The last time I visited the square, I had turned the corner to find four hundred zombies, faces melting, skins grey, butcher's knives impaled through their skulls and sticking out of their spines, chatting about the weather. One zombie, his throat a bloody mess of latex and food colouring, had fallen behind the crowd, and stood beneath an oak tree on his mobile phone asking, where now? Which left do I take?

Now the sky was grey and the grass crackled underfoot, and only the bravest had ventured out from the university buildings that framed the square. One or two, in defiance of the threatening sky, hunched over the chess tables that marked the end of the would-be "chess district" of the city, complete with venerable shops and men who knew the difference between a Vienna and a king's gambit. One offered to play me for twenty-five dollars. I patted my pockets and was surprised to discover I had nearly three hundred stuffed into a soft leather wallet. I sat down to play – sure, why not?

I don't know how good you are, said my opponent. I won't gamble. It's money for the game, that's all.

That's fine, I replied. I'm only here to pass the time.

He said his name was Simon, and he lived at the Salvation Army shelter.

"I used to be an interior designer," he explained, tearing into my pieces like a lion with a lamb. "But the recession came, and now I do whatever jobs I can."

Like chess?

"I make maybe eighty bucks a day on the boards. Less now it's cold. Sometimes folk don't pay up, and the police don't do nothing about that, cos it's gambling and technically illegal, but they don't care so long as no drugs are being dealt under the table."

"Is there nothing you can do?"

"Against them who won't pay? Nah. Folk who think they're good don't always take well to losing."

"What happens when you lose?"

"I pay; wouldn't come back here if I didn't."

"How often do you lose?"

He sucked breath judiciously between his teeth, then let it out all at once, cheeks puffing. "Not so often that it ain't worth the risk."

I nodded and struggled to stay alive in the face of his attacks. He moved carefully, without raising his head from the board. The ends of the fingers on his left hand were lightly calloused; those on his right were not. His eyes were grey and heavy, his skin was deep coffee, his hair was turning white at the roots long before its time. I said, what's it like at the Salvation Army shelter?

It's a roof, he replied. They're strict, but it's a roof.

He beat me, but only just, and I shook his hand, felt the coldness in his fingertips, and though he was beautiful – so very beautiful – I had no desire to be him for even a day. I left fifty dollars on the table and went on my way.

I dropped my body where I had found it and went via

a woman with bum compressed achingly into her tight, bright skirt,

a policeman with the taste of nicotine gum in his mouth,

a courier with headphones turned up far too high beneath his helmet,

the cleaning woman who changed the sheets in every room, wedding ring too tight on her right hand

back to Coyle.

I knocked on the door of the room, called, "Service!"

To my surprise, Coyle answered, his face washed, his hair combed, some semblance of civility on his face. "Already?"

"Yes, already," I replied, tucking my trolley of white towels against the wall and pushing past him into the room. "I don't know what you've been up to, but this body is dying for a pee."

He was sitting on the end of the bed, legs swinging down to the floor, hands clasped, head bowed, when I returned.

"Did you have a good walk?" he asked.

"Sure. Saw some of the sights, took in a bit of atmosphere. Did you make your phone call?"

"Yes."

"And? Should I be expecting armed vengeance to come crashing out of the cupboard any moment now?"

"No. I told you. I called a friend."

"And who is this friend?"

"She'll help us meet the sponsor."

"And this sponsor will have answers for us? For you?"

"Yes. I think so."

I shrugged. "Fine then. Who now?"

Chapter 83

Too long since I slept.

My bodies are rested, and I am not.

We sat in a diner off Lafayette and East Houston Street, and waited.

Coyle waited with coffee.

I waited in an Asian student with bright orange hair, who carried in her purple rucksack books on . . .

"The medicinal applications of chitin."

"Really." An empty sound as Coyle prodded his cup of coffee.

"Good God." From the bottom of my bag I pulled out a small glass jar. Within it a creature as long as my index finger, fat as my thumb, rattled and bumped, its translucent wings flapping ineffectively against its prison walls. "No matter how old I get, I'm still always surprised by what I find in the bottom of my bag."

"Do you know anything about the medicinal applications of chitin?" asked Coyle as I returned my belongings to the gloom of the rucksack.

"Frankly, no."

"Then let's hope no one asks you too many questions. Ma'am?"

The waitress smiled, and just about restrained herself from doing a little bob as she topped up his coffee cup. "And for you, miss?"

"Do you do pancakes?"

"Sure we do!"

"With syrup?"

"Sweetie, all our pancakes come with syrup."

"Whatever you'd recommend, please."

"Sure thing!"

Coyle pressed his hands tighter against the coffee cup. "You're not diabetic, I take it?"

"I can't find any evidence that I am, and it feels like I haven't had breakfast yet."

"Do you eat constantly?"

"I eat when I'm hungry. It simply happens that sometimes I'm hungry several bodies in a row. And I will concede that knowing someone else will top up on salad and exercise when I'm done can induce a certain gluttony. You going to tell me anything about your friend?"

"She works for Aquarius."

"You'll forgive me if that doesn't fill me with confidence."

"I trust her."

"That's fine, but does she trust you? You and your bosses did part in a rather spectacular manner."

"She trusts me. We spoke. She trusts me. We ... have been close, sometimes."

"Did you tell her about me?"

"No."

"Do you want me to—"

"No," fast. Then, "No. I want ... this to be clean. Honest." He thought about it a moment longer. "And if something does happen, if she has ... If Aquarius do come, then I may ... need you." The words came out, slow and bitter. "What should I say your name is?"

"What? I suppose ... Susie. Call me Susie."

"OK then."

The pancakes came, a great pile of them, bacon in between,

syrup all over. I tucked in gleefully, running my finger round the edge of the plate to mop up the oozing sauce while Coyle tried not to look too sickened.

Then, as is always the way when meeting strangers, a woman who could have been anyone from anywhere sat down on the padded orange couch opposite us, and she wore long sleeves, long trousers, long gloves, a long silk scarf that was wound across her face and neck, long socks that vanished high up her trouser legs and probably tights underneath, and though it might have been a particularly in-depth sports section that weighed so heavily in the newspaper as she laid it down on the tabletop between us, it was more likely to be a .22 calibre revolver, loaded and ready to fire.

Coyle looked up into the thin strip of veil from which grey eyes stared, smiled and said, "Hi, Pam."

One of her gloved hands rested beneath the paper, the other pressed against the table's edge. Eyes flickered from Coyle to me, and back again. "Where did we meet?" she asked. Her accent was pure Manhattan, brisk and hard.

"Chicago, 2004," he replied. "You were wearing a blue dress."

"San Francisco, 2008. What did we eat on the night of the op?"

"Japanese. You had sushi, I had teriyaki, and in the morning you had the early flight and didn't want to wake me to say goodbye."

"Tell me what you said when I left."

"I said your husband was a lucky man, and I wouldn't tell a soul."

"And did you?" she asked, quick and sharp. "Did you tell a soul?"

"No, Pam. I didn't tell anyone. I am me."

For a moment her eyes lingered on his face, then slowly turned to me. "Who is this?"

"I'm Susie," I said. "I'm a friend."

"I don't know you."

"No. You don't."

"Pam," blurted Coyle, "I don't know what you've heard . . ."

"I heard that you were taken," she retorted. "An operation went wrong. There's an alert out on you. They say that you've been compromised by Janus."

"And what do you believe?"

"I believe that you're you. Don't think that makes this easy. Phil—"

"I'm Nathan now."

"OK, Nathan," she went on in the same breath. "You've been compromised twice in as many weeks. There are orders."

"And are you obeying them now? Are you going to do your job?"

"I ... don't know. I read the files you sent from Berlin."

"Did you tell anyone?" he asked, eyes rising fast, and this was news to me too.

"No."

"And?"

"And I can see different ways of looking at it."

"Marigare shot me; he had *orders* to shoot me."

Beneath the veil a flicker of her eyebrows. Surprise, perhaps disbelief. "Why?"

"We were bringing in a suspect, a possible ghost. Marigare decided the witness was compromised. We were supposed to ..." he rolled the words slowly around his mouth, like the taste of aniseed that won't wash away " ... eliminate the threat. We took the body down to the river, and it said Galileo."

"OK. Then?"

"Then Marigare shot me. 'Just following orders' and he shot me. In Berlin Kepler showed me the file and they lied to me, to *us*, Pam. They lied about what went down in Frankfurt, they lied about the hosts, they lied about Galileo, Kepler said—"

"Kepler lies."

"You've seen the Galileo file too. Do you believe it? You're the only one I trusted with it – what did you see?"

"You killed Marigare." Her voice was high, cutting through words she didn't want to hear.

"I ... Yes. He shot me. He looked right at me and knew my name and shot me, Pam."

Again her eyes flickered to me, quiet in my corner, then back to Coyle. "Say I believe you – how did you survive?"

The long breath Coyle exhaled was perhaps more expressive than any words. The gun beneath the newspaper turned my way. I wrapped my hands tight around my coffee mug. "Kepler," I said. "You call me Kepler."

An intake of breath. Her head rocked back, her arm jerked, the gun now turned firmly towards me, the muzzle sticking out a little from the newspaper. She didn't speak, too many words at once for any to be spoken out loud, so Coyle spoke instead, low and urgent: "She . . . *it's* no threat to us. It came here of its own accord."

"If you know my name," I added, "you'll know that I have Aquarius' computer records at my disposal, stolen from Berlin. I could have brought down Aquarius already, without 'Phil', without risking my neck. I'm here for Galileo – nothing more."

"You're working with *this*?" she hissed at Coyle.

"I would have died. She . . . it . . . " he spat the word, forcing the recollection of my being on to his lips " . . . it helped me survive. It hates Galileo and has done me no harm . . . "

"It tore Berlin to pieces."

"It saved my life."

"It's worn you," she hissed. "It's violated you. Christ, do you even know what it's done to you? Do you know what it's made you do?"

"I haven't—" I began, and she shrieked, shut up, shut up, loud enough for heads to turn, for Coyle to flinch, for her to shudder and force her voice down, her head down, a worm-like blue vein rising hot in the thin space between her eyes and her veil.

"Pam," Coyle's voice, soothing, "you disobeyed orders meeting me here. You read the Galileo file. I know you have. I know you understand. I know you know about . . . You understand what it is. What Galileo is. What he means to me. Now, perhaps you go through with your orders, perhaps you shoot me down, shoot this . . . girl in front of all these people. Or perhaps you have a team outside, ready to pick us up when we leave. I don't know. But whatever you decide, believe this: Galileo is inside *us*. Aquarius ran a trial in Frankfurt and he took it, corrupted it, used it. I . . . killed a woman. No. That's not even right. I murdered her. I murdered a woman on the steps of Taksim station because of Galileo's lies. He's been eating us up from the inside out, playing us. But . . . I did it. It was me. Kill me, don't kill me, but whatever you decide, I need you to stop Galileo."

She said nothing. Coyle reached out slowly across the table, rested his palm on top of her gloved hand and left it there. He left it there, and nothing changed, and she was crying without crying, refusing to let us see.

"Go," she whispered.

"If you want us to—"

"Go! Get out, go!"

"The sponsor—"

"Just go!" she snarled, and Coyle jerked his hand away, nodded once and, without another word, climbed to his feet. I followed, gathering up my rucksack in my skinny arms and scampering after him as he strode to the door.

"Coyle . . ." I murmured, but he shook his head, so I closed my mouth, and followed, and said nothing at all.

Chapter 84

We moved hotel.

I had borrowed a few too many bodies from our present abode to feel safe.

Coyle watched the news.

I paced up and down, and when noon came and noon went, I said, "I'm late for class."

"Then go to class," he replied, eyes not moving from the TV screen.

"I don't care about medical insects."

"Then find something you care about, Kepler, and do that."

I scowled and marched out of the hotel room, bag bouncing on my back.

I rode the Subway.

The insect in the jar in the bottom of my bag was growing feebler, rattling limply against the glass. I unscrewed the lid a little, let some air in, then did it up tight again. Laying the jar on the floor beside me, I reached out for the nearest passenger and, uncaring of who they were or how they seemed,

jumped.

I am beautiful, and I shop for beautiful things that will make me more so.

I am tourist, camera on my back, beige loafers on my feet, standing in the gallery of the Natural History Museum, staring up at the mighty monsters who died before me.

I am chubby businesswoman eating chocolate cake that she would probably shun and I adore.

I am schoolgirl, sitting with my legs folded beneath me in the library, reading of times gone by, tales told. And when my mother calls, I run to her side and hold her tight and she says, "Now then, what's this? What's the matter?" and she takes my head in her hands and presses her arms across my back and loves me, almost as much as I love her.

I am spotty student who sells T-shirts in the museum shop.

I am taxi driver who has stopped for a smoke.

I let myself get waved down by a stranger who asks to go to Union Station.

In the mirror I look at a puffy-faced man out of breath who doesn't want to talk and hasn't much to say, but hell, the sun is setting and this is New York City so I say, "Going home, sir?"

"No."

"Leaving town?"

"Yes."

"Business trip?"

"No."

"Personal?"

"Yes."

And there ends the conversation.

He doesn't tip me as I let him out.

I am . . .

someone, whoever, when the hooker picks me up.

I am quite drunk, hunched over my

another

whisky at the bar of an authentic Irish pub, made authentic, one can only assume, by the uncomfortable stools in the form of a three-leafed clover and the silent misery of the drunks.

She says, you want to go somewhere private?

I look into a face of blue veins and white lines, and say, sure. Why not.

Give me your hand.

Coyle doesn't seem to have moved when I return to the hotel. He glances up as I enter the room and doesn't bother to ask my name, so I don't bother to give it, walking straight into the bathroom.

I take off my shoes.

The high backs are biting against my ankles, and as I run my hands up and down the insides of my calves I feel the roughness of the skin and rifle through my bag until I find the medication that had to be there – a cocktail of prescription meds carefully cut in half to make them go that little bit further, a week's supply now become two because this body, with its twenty-two dollars and no credit card, can only afford one week more of meds.

I take two of the half-pills at once, stare into a painted face whose make-up cannot disguise the illness.

I am someone not long for this world.

I remember Janus-who-was-Marcel.

Osako Kuyeshi in a hospital gown.

I get cysts.

And I lost my memory.

Seems to me you have the vision, not the commitment.

Not long for this world suits me fine.

In the bedroom Coyle doesn't turn his face away from the TV as he says, "I called Pam."

"What'd she say?"

"She's arranged a meeting with the sponsor. Says he's very interested."

"Are you sure?"

"I heard the words."

"Are you sure it isn't a trap?"

"No."

"You two were lovers?"

"Yes."

"Was it sex, or was it her?"

"Both. It ended a long time ago."

I sat down on the bed, flexing out the ache in the soles of my feet. "Do you love her?"

"You say 'love' too easily, Kepler."

"No, not really – please don't call me that. The idea that love has to be a blazing romantic thing of monogamous stability is innately ludicrous. You loved your parents, perhaps, because they were the warmth you could flee to. You loved your first childhood crush with a passion that made your lips tingle, your flesh grow light in their presence. You loved your wife with the steadiness of an ocean against the shore; your lover with the blaze of a shooting star, your best friend with the confidence of a mountain. Love is a many-splendoured thing, as the old song says. So, Pam, do you love her?"

"No. Once. Yes. If bodies are ... in a specific time, a specific place. Yes. In my way."

"When's the meet?"

"Tomorrow morning."

"OK."

I tucked my knees up to my chin, let my head rest back against the wall. Coyle's eyes finally turned to me, looked me up and down. "Hooker?"

I hummed confirmation.

"You look ... pale."

"Dying." At this his head turned fully, eyebrows raised. "Not immediately," I added. "I've got medication in my bag for a dozen things, but I've cut the pills in half to make them go further. This is a good body."

"You're OK being in a dying body?"

"Isn't everyone?"

"Not you. Not your rules."

"I take my example from Janus. He ... Funny, I always thought of him as a she, always thought he was ... softer than the skin he

390

wore. He dressed himself in a body barely on the edge of life when he died. When he knew he was going to die. It was still murder in that he forced a man to hold his consciousness while you put a bullet into his head. It was still butchery. But we must die someone, somewhere. And yet we lack the courage to slip into the wrinkled hand of the old woman on the ventilator or kiss goodbye on the cheek of he whose heart is fluttering in death. Janus tried before, but never quite managed to go through with it. Unlike most, we have a choice in this regard."

"Are you planning on dying?"

"I plan on living until the moment I have no options left. But this is perhaps an unhealthy conversation before a day of entrapment and potential demise. How's your shoulder?"

"I'm not going to play tennis any time soon."

I ran my fingers through my straw-dyed hair, felt the crackle of broken ends and dying roots, licked my lips and nodded at nothing much in particular. "It is going to be a trap, you know."

"I don't know that. I don't know anything any more."

"The orders to kill you, to kill me, to kill Josephine – they all had to come from the top. If this sponsor is at the top, then either he's been worn by Galileo, is being worn by Galileo or is in contact with someone being worn by Galileo – whatever. Galileo knows we're coming. It'll be waiting. Maybe not in the sponsor, maybe not in anyone we know, but it'll be there."

"What do you suggest we do?"

I shrugged. "If we don't take this chance now, I doubt we'll get another. I just don't want it to be a big surprise."

"And if Galileo is the sponsor? Will you kill him?" he asked.

"Will you?"

"I don't know. I thought I would. I thought that, whoever Galileo was, whoever he wore, I'd kill him. If one man, or woman, died so that Galileo was dead, that seemed . . . an acceptable price. Now . . . I don't know what I'll do, if the moment comes."

I didn't answer. He pulled himself up higher, resting on his elbows, studying me. "When did you last sleep?"

"Sleep? This body sleeps during the day, I think."

"Not the body. You. When did you last sleep?"

"I . . . Not for a while."

"You should sleep."

"Will you . . . " The words stopped dead on my lips. I licked them again, cheap make-up beneath my tongue. "Will you be there when I wake?"

"Where else would I be?"

I sleep.

Attempt to sleep.

Coyle turns the lights down, the TV off, lies on his back on the top of the bed beside me.

I try to remember: when was the last time someone watched me, without my watching them?

I want to curl up against him.

If I were a child

or someone with a slighter frame

auburn-haired, perhaps, with delicate wrists

I'd curl up against his side and he'd hold me.

If I was somebody else.

I sleep with my clothes on, ready to run, ready to jump.

Listen to his breathing, as he is listening to mine.

A truck grumbling outside the window, a long way down.

Police siren distant in the night.

Rise and fall of another's chest.

There are words on the tip of my tongue.

I roll over, and he's awake by my side, eyes open, watching me.

I know at once that he doesn't find my body attractive, and indeed, in conventional terms, it isn't glamorous.

Nor am I at home in it.

I do not yet know how to be beautiful in this body.

I reach out instinctively for his hand, and hesitate.

He doesn't pull it away, watching me still.

My fingers are a centimetre from his.

I just want to touch.

Not jump, just touch.

Just feel another's pulse beneath my own.

He's waiting.

I've seen the look on his face before, but cannot now remember if it was his face that wore it, or mine.

I roll over, turning my back.

And I must sleep, for it is daytime, and the man whose name is not Nathan Coyle is still there.

Chapter 85

My name is . . .

Irena.

No. Irena was France; I don't feel like being an Irena again.

Marta. Marilyn. Greta. Sandra. Salome. Amelia. Lydia. Susie.

My handbag doesn't contain any evidence either way. This body has no name that isn't a descriptor. Whatever the story behind the pasty face that regards me from the mirror, the pills cut in half in my bag, I can't see it. I try to guess, but nothing convincing comes to mind and I seem unable to hold on to the basic tenets of even the simplest stories. Perhaps I ran away . . .

was taken from my home . . .

a father that beat . . .

a father who loved.

Perhaps, in this face, I see a woman wrongly convicted of stealing another woman's child, sent to prison, from which I emerged too scathed to live. Perhaps one time I tried drugs, and it went wrong, or I didn't try drugs but had within my heart no conviction of my own worth, and having so little faith in myself only served to prove, again and again, how accurate my self-assessment was.

Perhaps I have a daughter, crying alone at home for her mother.

Perhaps I have a husband, sitting in his underpants watching the hockey, a can of beer in one hand, a cap pulled down low over his puffy black eyes.

Perhaps I have none of these things at all, and my life is only the half-sliced pills and the next job to pay for the same.

Then Coyle is behind me, standing in the bathroom door, and he says, "Ready?"

"Nearly. There's somewhere I want to go first."

Nathan Coyle was not a man built for the women's department of any Sixth Avenue store. He sat on a small padded bench outside the changing cubicles, legs crossed and arms folded, and perhaps tried to imagine himself a doting husband waiting on his wife's selections. Skin flaking beneath my underwear, I tried on smart shirts, smart shoes, smart trousers, smart jewels, until at last, satisfied that I now looked like at worst a tired newsreader, I stepped out before him, twirled and said, "What do you think?"

He looked me over top to bottom. "You look . . . like someone else."

"It's all in the cut. Which do you prefer?" I held out my hand, in which two bracelets, one of silver, one of gold, lay for his inspection.

"If I were buying? Silver."

"I thought so too. But then the gold may fetch a few more dollars at the pawnbroker."

Revelation dawned, and he now took in the silk and linen, expensive shoes and designer bag. "You're giving her wealth in clothes?"

"I might also slip cash into her handbag."

"You think that'll make a difference?"

"You have a better idea?"

"No," he conceded, "I don't. Money . . . seems a crude compensation for the price you take."

"She sleeps a dreamless sleep and, a few hours later, she wakes and is some other place, dressed some other way. I may not know

395

much about my host, but I think I can guess that of the events in her life, this will not count as the worst."

"When first we met, I slept and woke, and the journey was from one bad place to somewhere worse."

"That was when I didn't love you," I replied, checking my reflection in the mirror. "Times change."

"You love yourself. Not your host."

I shrugged. "In relationships as intimate as mine I challenge you to find the difference." I turned back, happy with my ensemble; wealth not beauty adorned my back. "There. Do you like what you see?"

We rode the Subway. Too many people to find a seat, but as I bumped, shoulder to shoulder, arm to arm with the strangers on the train, I felt no urge to jump. My hands, buried in their new coat pockets, felt warm, fingers gently curled, tendons relaxed into their natural position. A beautiful man with long black hair and skin like melted chocolate smiled at me, and I smiled back and thought how nice it would be to experience the touch of his lips from the outside, a stranger kissing a stranger rather than myself. A child with a violin on its back stared up at me, studying my rich clothes, my expensive jewels. A pickpocket eyed my handbag and it occurred to me that the only reason I'd be him and stick his head through the nearest pane of glass was to protect my host. I looked him in the eye and smiled, and let him know in my smile that he was known to me. He fled at the next stop, searching for easier pickings, and I patted my bag of money and pills, felt the stretch of the leather in my new shoes, on my new feet, and it was good.

Then we were at 86th Street, the tide marks of Hurricane Sandy still visible on its walls where the water had risen over white tiles and red mosaic. The flow of well-jacketed, camera-slung strangers heading towards Fifth Avenue was thick enough to follow through the one-way streets towards Central Park. At Madison Avenue a small truck was attempting a delivery, causing a tailback of traffic which honked and roared its fury all the way down to East 72nd Street. Two blue-coated cops stood by, drinking their coffees beside a kiosk, ready to spring into action just as soon as the caffeine had hit.

Coyle walked a little ahead; I followed behind at an easy lollop, feeling warmer and more awake than I had felt for too many skins.

Then Coyle said, "Here."

I looked at what here was and laughed.

"Something funny?"

"Sure. You don't get the joke?"

"Humour was never my strong point. Come on."

I followed him up the steps, into the museum.

The New York Metropolitan Museum of Art.

Museum is too small a word. Museums are places you visit for a few hours – half a day at the most. A museum is somewhere to go on a Sunday afternoon when the weather is not so warm that you want to be in the park. A museum is a place to take that distant relative who you don't really know but promised a tour round the city. A museum is a repository of stories you were half-told as a child and then forgot when more pressing matters of sex and money overwhelmed your preoccupations.

The Metropolitan Museum of Art is not a museum, but rather a monument. It is a temple raised to peoples gone and stories lost, a haven of ancient beauties picked out by long-dead fingertips, an offering to the vanished craftsman and the mighty emperor. It is full of beautiful things that I want and cannot have for myself.

All of which said, the entrance fee, as I line up in the queue behind Coyle, would deflate anyone's good mood.

Coyle climbs the great stone stairs that lead up through great stone halls. At one end of the museum is an Egyptian temple, and between there and us are breastplates of gold, silver scimitars, statues of ancient emperors serene in death, and the axe that severed the necks of greedy princelings. Here are the chests of lacquer and pearl in which the opium smugglers carried their goods into China, pipes of the dreamers who withered while inhaling the scent. There the muskets that were fired at the rebellion of Cairo, the Koran that was rescued from the ashes of the mosque, blood still visible on the hand-inscribed pages. Here the ballgown of a Russian aristocrat who danced her way to the revolution; there fine blue porcelain from which Victorian wives once drank their Indian tea. All these things were once beautiful, and time has made them sacred.

Coyle wants to hurry through.

I say, stop, wait, I want to look at this.

We look.

A gallery of faces, portraits of kings and queens, presidents and their wives, revolutionaries and martyrs to their cause. They fascinate me, watching me as I watch them. Coyle says, we'll be late.

It'll wait a few more minutes, I reply. It'll wait.

"Kepler?"

I hum an answer, distracted, my eyes on the face of a woman who seems surprised that the painter has caught her there, face half-turned away from the canvas, eyes looking back over her shoulder as if a stranger had just that moment called her name when she had thought herself alone.

"Kepler."

"What?"

"I'm sorry. For Josephine."

The words are enough to make me look away. Coyle seems tiny beneath these faces, a little hunched-up thing of skin and flesh. Inhuman almost beneath the living canvas, his gaze turned down, words shrivelled in. "I'm sorry."

He's sorry for being wrong.

And again: I'm sorry.

Sorry for murder, which he called something else.

And one more time: I'm sorry.

Sorry for . . .

a list probably longer than the time we have available.

Then:

"If something goes wrong, if it's a trap. Be me."

"What?" My voice is a mumble. For a moment I cannot

remember what shoes I wear, what gender I am; my body is some other place.

"If Pam has ... If we're betrayed, if this isn't what it should be. The woman you are now, I think ... she is beautiful. Now that I look. Now that I can see ... her. As well as you. Both of you. I have done some things, and they were not ... Anyway ... "

He lets out a breath, draws in another. Where is that man who in a no-place in eastern Europe could calm his heart with a single thought, who looked up proud and knew himself to be right? I look for Nathan Coyle in his face and cannot see him. Someone else, the face of that man, vandalised, looks back.

"Anyway," he says again, drawing himself up a little straighter. "If you have to choose – if there comes a moment where you have to decide – then I want you to be me. I think ... it's better that way."

"All right," I reply, and find that it is. "All right then."

Then we reach a door, and a red rope has been drawn across it, barring us access, and a sign proclaims, CLOSED FOR SPECIAL OCCASION, and a single security guard, radio clipped to her belt, wears the look of one who long ago ceased to be impressed by anything.

"Kepler ... " Coyle wants to say something more, hesitates. "You never told me your name."

"No. You never told me yours. Does it matter?"

A hesitation, a half-shake of the head, and then, unexpected, beautiful, the smallest smile. "Good luck."

Then the woman called Pam appears from the circle-shaped doorway behind the guard and simply says, "They're with me."

The guard leaves.

We follow Pam inside.

Chapter 86

It was a Chinese tea garden.

Through a round door and then a square, a walkway covered with ceramic tiles ran around the edge of a courtyard, in which bamboo swayed, water dribbled into a pool of orange and white mottled carp, and twisted volcanic rocks like the trapped scream of a frozen monster writhed around the wall.

In the centre of it all a small wooden table had been laid, and on the table were a blue porcelain teapot, three porcelain cups and a silver stand of tiny cakes. A man sat, his back to the door, a grey scarf wound around his neck, black jacket and silver hair. He did not look up, did not cease his slow sipping as we approached, but rather Pam, her face still obscured by the grey veil she had worn when last we met, a gun tucked with no discretion at all in the pocket of her beige overcoat, stood between us and him, and even with her mouth and nose covered her eyes were grim.

"Stop," she barked at Coyle. "Tell me something I want to know."

"Elijah. My call sign is Elijah."

Her gaze turned to me. "Is this her?"

"This is Kepler," Coyle replied before I could speak.

She didn't answer, but with the little finger of one hand gestured me away from the table, towards the whitewashed wall. "You come within three metres of me, or anyone in this room, and I'll put you down," she breathed. "So I shall."

I raised my hands, let her guide me towards the nearest wall.

"Stop. Face the wall."

Hands still raised, I faced the whiteness of the wall.

Feet behind me, keeping their distance, keeping safe.

Coyle: She's not a threat.

Pam: That's a dumb thing to say.

"She came here knowing the risks."

"Then she's dumb as well as ugly." Pam's voice, high and out of tune.

Then a third voice, older than the rest, tired – the voice of the silver-haired man with the grey scarf – said, "You didn't ask me here to enjoy a lovers' spat, did you?"

There was

familiarity

in that voice.

Staring at a whitewashed wall, a gun at my back, fat carp swimming by my side, several thousand dollars' worth of jewels and clothes on my gently dying body.

I am Kepler, and I know who the sponsor is.

Then the voice spoke again. "Mr Coyle, may I offer you some tea?" The pouring of hot water into a white bone cup. "I understand you wanted to see me urgently. Normally I wouldn't be amenable to these encounters – particularly with one who appears to be as compromised as yourself – but Pamela raised some interesting points that I would like to discuss. Please. Sit."

A creaking of a chair, the tinkle of plate and cup.

"I am the sponsor," the voice went on after a suitable pause for the sipping of tea. "You should understand that I have very little day-to-day interest in the running of your organisation. Its activities are entirely of its own deciding. I merely . . . afford it some resources. As, indeed, I do for this museum. My interests are eclectic."

"Thank you, sir."

"For what?"

"For . . . the tea."

"You are most welcome."

"And for seeing me."

"There you are perhaps less welcome, especially considering the company you keep."

"Kepler has been . . . helpful."

"Mr Coyle, let me say right now that any statements you may make in support or sympathy towards the entity you have brought into this place will only serve to compromise you in my eyes. I would urge you to focus only on the single statement that aroused my and Pamela's interest in this affair."

"Galileo."

I flinched as Coyle said the word and imagined that perhaps he winced too, though at what recollection I could only guess.

"Indeed," murmured the sponsor. "Galileo. Pamela was kind enough to take me through the file last night. I had looked at it before, of course, though not with such a . . . critical eye. You allege that the entity Galileo has somehow entered your organisation?"

"Yes, sir, I do."

"Because Kepler says so?"

"Yes, sir, and for other reasons."

I stared at a white wall, my hands by my head, and wondered if this was how it felt to be a host. The world moves, and I am still, actions beyond my control turning, unseen, in the background. I am a woman who sells her body for medicines she cannot afford, and around me conspiracies were unravelled and tales told, and I stared at a wall and waited.

"Such as?"

"Frankfurt."

"Yes, the medical trials. What of them?"

"They were designed to create a vaccine against ghosts. I think Galileo subverted them instead, to gather data not on the destruction but the creation of creatures like him."

"Because?"

"I think Galileo murdered the researchers in Frankfurt."

402

"In itself not proof of anything."

"Kepler was blamed and her host too. I was ordered to kill them both. Why was I ordered to kill the host?"

"I don't know."

"You're the sponsor."

"And as I've said, my interests are varied, my tastes eclectic, and I do not make operational decisions. But now you work with the very entity that you sought to kill. Why?"

"Galileo."

A sigh, a shifting of weight. Perhaps now a cake was consumed; perhaps sugar was added to some gently cooling tea. I imagined delicate fingertips holding a French fancy by the edges, unwilling to damage the icing. The thought made me smile.

"Galileo." The sponsor's sigh, deep and old. "We always seem to come back to Galileo."

The fountain dribbled, the carp swam. Beyond the moon door a thousand people ebbed and flowed, their eyes turned to the wonders of the past.

Then the sponsor said, "Kepler."

I lifted my head at my name, didn't turn from the wall. Bodies moved in chairs behind me. "Kepler, look at me."

I turned, keeping my hands raised, looked into the eyes of the silver-haired man. His face was grey, stained with yellow spots beneath the sagging hollows of his eyes. His neck hung with skin like the soft fins of a seal; his eyes were deep dark and looked on me without hatred, without recognition, and I knew his name.

He cleared his throat and, one hand scratching irritably at the vest underneath his ironed white shirt, said, "Why are you here?"

"I share Coyle's interest in Galileo."

"Why?"

"It seems . . . right. Maybe that's not even it. We've . . . shared hosts. I wore her flesh; he wore mine. At first you could say we were competitors. Then it was retribution. I betrayed Galileo, and Galileo took revenge."

"What kind of revenge?"

403

"He wore someone I loved, and I killed him. He was . . . beautiful. I didn't have the heart to put a bullet in his brain. That was in Miami. And then in Berlin . . . I went to a friend for help, and Galileo burned him alive. He did it so that I might see. He said, 'Do you like what you see?' We always like what we see, people like us. We always see how something else could be better than what we have. Perhaps today, perhaps tomorrow, perhaps this face, perhaps these hands, perhaps . . . perhaps I will be better. Perhaps no one will care for the things I did when last I was someone else. Perhaps someone will love me. Perhaps they will love *me*. Perhaps if I love them enough, they'll have no choice but to love me in return. Do you like what you see? we ask, and the answer is yes, of course. I love it. I love it. If I am it, will you love me?

"That Galileo is a monstrosity is an evident truth. That he has penetrated your organisation, torn it to pieces, is again obvious. Galileo has ripped you apart. That Galileo is perhaps attempting, through research and violence, to create more of himself, to create children, if you will, a something, someone that will last – well, that is debatable. I doubt Galileo himself would be able to give you a fair assessment either way."

Again the sponsor scratched at his vest, rubbing across his chest, and I wondered what manner of surgical scars might lurk beneath, digging their way through the body of this stooped old man.

"You are the first—" He stopped and smiled at a joke only he could know. "You are nearly the first," he corrected, "creature of your kind I have spoken to. You do a better impression of human than I expected. I congratulate you. That Galileo may have . . . compromised us in ways we do not know, well, the matter is rather too repugnant to speak of, yet we must speak of it. You . . . suggest that orders have been given, and operatives have acted on them?"

"Yes."

"Orders given by Galileo?"

"By Galileo, through another's voice."

"We have protocols in place, of course, to prevent this."

"Your protocols are only as good as the people who created them. Galileo has been around for a long time. Perhaps when you agreed a code word with a friend, you agreed it with someone else entirely?"

"I find that difficult to believe."

"People always find difficult truths harder than easy lies."

His breath caught in his throat, as his hand scratched scratched scratched at his shirt. "And we should believe you: a murderer, a slaver, a—"

"Sir!" Coyle was on his feet.

"Whatever Coyle may say," his voice rose, cutting Coyle off, "do not think that your pretence of humanity begins to redeem the harm you have done!"

Pam was stepping clear of the table, out of Coyle's reach, and now the gun was in her hands.

"No, sir . . ."

"Michael Peter Morgan!" My voice, high and hot, sliced through the air, knocked the sponsor back on his seat, a shudder running through his cold withered hands. "How old are you now? Your body must be far advanced into its declining years, but you – twenties, thirties? At least thirty years younger than the flesh you are prisoner to. Tell me, when they killed Janus did you know that it was yourself you ordered dead? It was you they gunned down in that house in Saint-Guillaume; it was the hand that held your wife, the heart that loved your children, flesh of your flesh but soul of his soul. You lost so much time: you lost your youth; you blinked and it was gone, a brief nap, and when you wake you are this. A man of eclectic tastes, and who are you? I don't think you even know."

The old man, cramped and curled around his own pain, one hand hugging the edge of the table, the other pressed against his chest, raised gummy eyes to my face and hissed, "How do you know me?"

"I knew Janus. I knew the person you were in your real life." He opened his mouth to speak, but the corners curled in; no sound emerged. "Mr Morgan," I said, "have you been losing time?"

Silence.

Not-silence.

This is the silence of air moving through our lips.

This is the silence of muscles tight, blood running, hearts racing.

This is the silence of a whole world turning outside the door.

This is the roaring not-silence of minds that dare not think out loud.

"Mr Morgan," I breathed, "you studied economics at Harvard. You did tae kwon do, had terrible taste in clothes. Both parents dead by the time you were twenty-five, you were still a virgin when Janus took your flesh. You blinked, and when you opened your eyes your wife was crying by your side, and your daughters, Elsa and Amber, they didn't understand what had happened to their father. They thought he'd died. Death of the mind, not the body. I know this because I knew you, Mr Morgan. I shared a drink with you in the junior common room in Princeton in 1961, when I was ... someone else. Just doing my job. And since then you've hunted us for all you're worth with all the wealth that Janus left behind, but you're old now and all alone, and so I have to ask – have you been losing time?"

Silence.

The sponsor, breathing fast, ragged breath, head down, hands tight across his chest.

"Nathan," I murmured "step away from him."

Slowly he stepped back.

I advanced. Pam was moving now, watching me, her back to the wall, gun levelled at my chest, keeping her distance from everyone else in the room. I knelt down in front of him, seeing ancient liver-spotted hands that had been so young the last time they'd been his. I reached up slowly, palms open, fingers flexed, whispered, "I need to touch you, Mr Morgan. I need to know that you are who you say you are."

His head shaking, tears in his eyes, he couldn't speak, didn't stop me, could barely breathe. Coyle whispered, "Kepler ..." A question, a warning, but he wasn't going to stop me, not now, and before anyone could change their mind I grabbed Morgan's hands, held them tight, squeezed his fingers between my own and felt

nothing.

Only skin.

Just skin.

I let go, Morgan shaking now, the tears running through canyons on his face. He was young; he was so very young.

"Kepler?" Nathan's voice, high and urgent.

"He's not Galileo." I eased myself up, backing away from Morgan, giving myself a little space, room to breathe. My gaze swept the room: the ancient man not yet grown up, the injured killer, the woman in grey. "Nathan, when we came in here, you said 'Elijah'. What was Pamela's part of the recognition code?"

He opened his mouth to answer, then closed it again, turning to look into her eyes.

She giggled, pressing three fingers to her lower lip behind the veil. "Whoops," she said and fired.

Who she intended to fire at, clearly she couldn't decide, for there was a second in which her gun swung between Coyle and myself, before finally, almost with a shrug, she settled on me and pulled the trigger. By then I was already moving, which was why the bullet shattered my left arm, splitting bone in two with a *crack* I could feel in the hollows of my ears, but Coyle caught her by both wrists, and as she pulled the gun round he pushed her down, slamming his knee into her face, blood blooming across her scarf. I landed on the floor in a screaming haze of bewildered pain and blood, even as Pam

not-Pam

she-who-was-not-herself

she-who-was-Galileo

twisted round and drove her elbow into Coyle's throat. I heard two shots, the glass shattering in the ceiling overhead, a rainfall of shards, then three more shots that sang over my head and slammed into the wall, then the *click-click-click* of the pin on nothing at all, and Galileo, the scarf pulled back from her head to reveal golden hair and a soft blood-smeared face twisted with effort, slammed her open palm against Coyle's throat,

and it occurred to me

rather late in the day

that she wasn't wearing gloves.

Then the security guard, she with the face of stern rebuttal from the door, was inside the courtyard, radio in hand, shouting, stop, everyone, stop, and it was not Pamela who ran, but Coyle, blood pouring from his nose, bare hands outstretched for the woman's face.

From the floor I grabbed the guard's ankle, my fingers closing an instant before Galileo's, and I

jumped,

slamming my radio up into the flesh below Coyle's chin.

He staggered back, one arm sweeping a great smear of blood and nasal liquid across his face, over the side of his cheek and lips. I looked into my face

into Coyle's face

into the face that was Galileo

shook my head, thought about begging, thought about kneeling at his feet

but he drew his fist back to strike, and I dug my radio into the wound on his shoulder, twisting the butt as hard as I dared, and Coyle

not-Coyle

screamed, the animal scream of a beast caught in barbed wire, and slammed his fist into the side of my face hard enough to knock my teeth together inside my jaw. I tasted salt and blood and loose fillings as I fell. Coyle ran by me, heading for the door, staggered through the red rope that guarded the entrance and out into the crowds of the museum.

I crawled up on to my hands and knees and looked back.

Pamela, struggling to her feet, the gun useless in her hand.

My unnamed, abandoned host in beautiful new clothes, slowly going to ruin as blood seeped from her flesh. Morgan, still sitting on his chair, his eyes turned upwards at nothing at all, his hands loose by his side. Five shots Galileo had fired as she struggled for the gun; one of them had found their home in the sponsor's chest.

Pam's eyes turned slowly and settled on her master, the beginning of a choke that might become a sob rising from her throat, and there was no time, no time at all as I staggered on to my feet, picked up my radio and ran into the museum.

Chapter 87

At its busiest the Metropolitan Museum of Art can handle fifty thousand visitors a day.

This was not its busiest; there were probably only two or three thousand souls wandering through its halls.

I found Coyle gasping for breath at the top of the stairs, a small crowd of people tactfully trying not to stare. I slammed my knee into his chest, my elbow into his throat, pushing him back against the cold floor, and roared, "Who are you?!"

"Coyle!" he squeaked. "You know me as Coyle!"

"Who was I the night Marigare fired?" He didn't answer so I dug my elbow a little deeper, his eyes rolling, tongue flopping against his lips. "Who was I?!"

"Nurse! You were . . . Samir! Samir Chayet!"

"Who drove you to Lyon?"

"Irena. You. Irena!" The sound barely escaped past the weight of security guard pressing down on to him, the tips of his ears bright crimson.

I rolled off him as more onlookers gathered round our little scene. "Who did you touch?" I whispered. "Who did you touch?"

"A woman. She had red hair. My shoulder . . . "

"I hit it. Sorry."

Inspecting the crowd – woman with red hair, woman with red hair – I saw no such woman, but then that could mean nothing at all. "Get out," I hissed. "Get out of here."

"What?"

Pulled him to his feet. "Get out. Your injuries will protect you; she won't wear damaged skin. Shots have been fired; the police will be on their way. Get out!"

"I can't just—"

"Go!" My voice echoed down the staircase, bounced off hard, clean walls. I pushed him away from me, turned again to the crowd, snapped, "All of you, get out!"

His hand caught my sleeve as I turned. "Be me," he whispered. "No one else dies."

I jerked my arm away, shaking my head.

"Kepler!" He held on tighter, pulling me back. "I killed Josephine. It was me. I did it; I killed the woman you love. Be me! The woman you are now, she doesn't have to die; no one else has to die. Galileo knows me, knows my face. Be me!"

He was crying.

I hadn't ever seen Nathan Coyle cry.

I pulled my arm free of his grasp, pushed him away. "No," I said. "I love you."

And ran on through the crowd.

Galileo.

Who are you, Galileo?

I am security guard.

I am Japanese tourist admiring samurai swords.

I am schoolteacher taking notes on American sculpture.

I am student, sketching a statue of the goddess Kali as she dances on the skulls of her foes, slain in righteous retribution.

I am man who wants to sit down on a gallery bench.

Woman with flapjack stuck between my teeth.

I am catering staff pushing a tray of cakes.

Wanderer with audio guide pressed to my ear.

Usher with belt done up too tight around my underfed belly.

Every step there is someone new to be, every step a new shade of skin.

My flesh is silken soft, moisturised fresh this morning.

I have eczema beneath my elbow, red lumps up my arm.

I am old and stooped

fresh and beautiful

my skin is the colour of autumn sunset

pale as snow

dark as oil

so warm I feel every capillary tingle in my fresh wide lips

so cold that my toes are no more than slabs of defrosted meat blocking the ends of my shoes.

I move between the galleries, stand beneath the stones of Egyptian temples, before the gaze of medieval saints, looking for the one who looks for me.

Where are you, Galileo?

Won't be far.

Won't have run, not this time.

Do you like what you see?

We have come here for this, you and I.

Come to make an end of it.

Do you like what you see?

And then I am . . .

armed security, because shots were fired in the Chinese tea garden, and a man is dead in his chair, a wealthy man, a sponsor of a great many cultural events, and there are bullet holes in the wall, and bullet holes in the glass ceiling, whose panels have cracked to let in the angry sky, and a woman lies bleeding on the floor, a handbag full of money and no recollection of how she came to be in this place, and so armed security have sealed off the wing and the police are sealing off the gallery, but that's fine, Galileo, that's absolutely fine.

Because where there are policemen, there are weapons, there is armour, there is opportunity.

I slip into a man with a great flat nose, black hair cut close to my head. I am NYPD, New York's finest, shotgun held in both hands, body armour blue on chest, big black boots and knee pads, and I move with the team I've been assigned to because that is what I would do, and nod my answer to any questions, and do not speak, not knowing what it is I would say.

The NYPD seal off the Chinese tea room, set up cordons at the door, and where there were only half a dozen of us before, now there are twenty, thirty, trucks pulling up outside, and news crews too. A few hours and we'll have made headlines, GUNS FIRED AT THE METROPOLITAN MUSEUM OF ART, and just you wait because there's more to come; there'll be bullets flying.

Will you close the museum?

No, we will not close the museum.

You must close the museum, sir.

Do you know how long it will take, how much it will cost?

A man is dead, sir.

And that's a tragedy, but these things happen, and hell, you've already got the gun that did it, can you stop frightening our visitors?

I look around at the dozens of policemen and armed guards, and one of them is Galileo. We'll have both gone for a weapon, preferably carried by someone in full body armour, now look, just look, seek out the anomaly, the man who staggers, the man who is slow, the man who does not respond to his name, the man who falls behind. Look for him who does not belong, whose shoulders are not drawn back in pride, for him whose finger nervously taps the trigger guard of his weapon, for the one who too closely scrutinises his neighbours.

Who among you speaks French when he should not speak French?

Which of you loves the Mets but has "Yankees" on his underpants?

(Mr Whatever-your-name-is.)

Who cannot remember the number of their badge.

What they had for breakfast.

Their very name.

(I am Kepler.)

Who are you, Galileo?

Then a man comes up to me, revolver at his side, badge clipped to his leather belt, and says, "You got it, Jim?"

I turn and look into his eyes, and he must be my partner, and I must be Jim, and perhaps I do have it, whatever it is, but damned if I can tell him that.

Or perhaps my name isn't Jim at all.

He looks at me, and I look at him, and there is a moment which becomes a moment too long, and he smiles, trying to read the strangeness in my eyes, and I finger the trigger of my shotgun and wonder whether, at this very close range, he really stands a chance, even in the body armour. Or whether I do too.

"Jim?" he says again. "You got it?"

"No," I reply. "Not yet."

"Jim?" Irritation, worry in his voice. "Jim? Where is it?"

A moment, a doubt, a hesitation, and in the corner of my eye I see a movement that might be as innocent as the scratching of a nose, as circumspect as the tugging of an itchy earlobe, and I don't hesitate but reach out and press my fingers against my partner's neck and

blood splatters my face.

Point-blank range, blood and brain and little bits of skull, I stare into the face of the man who almost certainly was called Jim, and probably did have whatever it was I was asking for, stare into his eyes as he falls, crumpled like a paper cup before me, one hand slipping away from my neck, my shoulder as he drops, a dead weight to the floor, a bullet straight through the back of his head and out the forehead, slamming in a little bloody cloud into the pillar at my back.

Behind him, the shooter, a man of barely nineteen years old, gun held out in one hand, finger still resting on the trigger, policeman's cap pulled down over his eyes, giggles.

I grab my gun, and as the shooter's eyes widen in surprise put two in his chest and a third in his neck, firing as the arc of my weapon comes up from my hip, an empty sound of incoherent rage even as the body of the man I was rolls beneath my feet, his wet blood slipping under my shoes.

Arms grab me, pulling the gun from my hand, and I scream in fury as they take me down, three, four men knocking me off my feet, hands on my head, my face, my arms, but my fury is not for them, it's for the three other men pulling the shooter down, pulling Galileo down as the blood pops and bubbles around his throat, bursts upwards with every breath in great splatters, and then one of them steps away.

One of the men holding him down just steps away, and looks at me and smiles

and I scream again

and

a hand is against my face

I hold a hand against his face

pull it away from the writhing, bewildered body and myself free of the scrum and scream, "*Galileo!*"

He turns and runs.

I ran after him, leaving my bewildered colleagues behind, fumbled at my side, felt the gun, raised it to fire and he swerved round a corner, boundless giddy energy in his youthful, uniformed body, past statues of the serene Buddha, carved jade of fair Kuanyin, lute in hand, willow branches at her back. I fired and my shot went wide, impaling a screen of delicate wading birds brushed on to silk, which toppled as the people around screamed and parted before us, and then Galileo

staggered

and as he staggered his hand seemed to brush the arm of a woman dressed in purple and pigtails and I screamed again, "Galileo!"

And she looked back, and saw me coming, and saw that I saw *her*, and she ran on, beneath the dark wood of a Shinto arch, raised against all evil spirits, and swerved again, feet slipping on marble, into a room of violins and cellos, ivory-carved flutes and pearl-embossed guitars, a palace to the music of the ages, where she caught the arm of a man dressed all in white, who looked towards me and, seeing that I looked at him, for the first time showed a little fear, and he too ran, his feet faster than hers had been, his shoes more appropriate for the chase, throwing off his coat and bag as he fled through rustic scenes of haystacks and lambs, of dancing farmgirls and dying saints, and again a turn, and again he tried a switch, not running this time but sitting still and serene in the body of the guard by the door, but to hell with that, I raised my gun to fire, and seeing my face the guard threw himself, tooth and nail, towards me, and I pulled the trigger, knocking him back, and as he fell his hand caught the hand of the very same man he'd just been, who at once leaped back to his feet and turned and ran again, leaving the screaming guard behind him.

"*Galileo!*"

My voice, strange, a copper's throat, a smoker's lung, echoed through the corridors. Now he is a woman who throws her bag at me as I pursue, now she is a teenager with an incredible stride, a breathtaking burst of speed, and I am panting, gasping for breath, but I will not give up this chase or this body with its armour and gun, so as he rushes fresh-faced and full of air through the halls I sweat and pound after him, a clear shot – just give me a clear shot.

Crowds scream and part around us, like the ocean before an angry Moses as we move through halls of ancient totem poles pillaged from the Pacific, past cloaks of seashell taken from the backs of dead American priests. He jumps and is a she, she jumps and is a child, it jumps and is a man again as we pass monuments to the dead, ancient images of gods who faded when their worshippers forgot, carved tokens to speed departed souls on to the afterlife or sink their bodies into the embrace of those loving oceans whence they came.

There are policemen after us, security, but who knows who to pursue? A man who was Galileo is tackled to the ground; a woman who three bodies ago ran now stands and screams as guns are pointed in her face, who are you, who are you, why did you run? Run where? she gasps. Run why?

A figure in grey, Galileo is a child, straight black hair, pale beige

415

skin, grey uniform and knee-length socks. In one hand he holds a satchel, half-open to reveal the schoolbooks within; papers spilling from the bag as he runs down the hall.

A woman ahead. She's got a gun, the veil across her face is dishevelled. I can see bare skin about her wrists, eyes and throat, but she doesn't seem to care, raises the gun, levels it at

not the child

at me.

Pamela, back on her feet, I scream. "I'm Kepler, I'm Kepler!"

She doesn't seem to care, doesn't seem to perceive the child running towards her as she raises the gun and

fires.

I throw myself to the ground. I am policeman. I wear body armour, build up muscle tone, take long walks around my local beat ... or perhaps I don't. Perhaps I drive everywhere and live on doughnuts, and my heart is going to give out any moment. In all the fuss I didn't really have time to check. Either way, a bullet is a bullet, and we're all out of time.

I drop.

Zeus stares down at us, full of anger and sorrow at the deeds mortals do. Aphrodite combs her marble hair, Ares grapples with a raging warrior, Hercules strangles a snake, and two-faced Janus, god of gates, doorways, endings and times, laughs from one side of his face and weeps from the other, and I? I am cowering beneath a statue of Athena, goddess of wisdom and war, her face turned down in a serene smile, already knowing who will win.

Pam stands in the centre of the hall. She has followed the sound of gunfire, which makes her brave or foolish or otherwise emotionally involved. She doesn't fire again, but enough has already been done: people are running, fleeing from the gallery, pushing and shoving their way to the exit. Someone, somewhere has sounded an alarm, and an evacuation is under way, just like the NYPD wanted. On a stairway behind me someone falls, someone cries, someone sobs, and I remember Taksim station, where this all began, when I ran from a stranger's gun as Galileo runs from mine.

I am policeman.

I am meant to be obeyed.

I shout, "Everybody out!" but everybody has gone.

My hands are sweaty where they hold the gun, but my recovery time is impressive, heart already slipping down into steady double figures inside my chest.

"William ... "

A child's voice, sing-song. "Oh William!"

Who the hell is William?

(My Will, dead on a Miami dock.)

Ah yes.

I was a William once.

A long time ago.

I peep round the side of Athena, and there he is.

The schoolboy, Galileo, barely nine or ten years old. He's smiling, one hand in Pam's, the other still clasping his satchel. She stares at nothing, face greyer than her scarf, the gun still in her right hand, limp at her side. Of course. She came here without any gloves and now stands there, a picture of motherhood holding a child, and that child is Galileo.

I level my gun at the child, then turn it towards Pam.

The boy tuts. "But which one am I now?"

The boy staggers. Pam blinks, then smiles, her fingers tightening around the child's little fist. "Which one do you want me to be?" she asks, then she too sways as the child grins, pressing Pam's hand against his cheek like a cat brushing itself against its master's legs.

"Shoot me ... "

"or me?"

"Which one ... "

"first?"

He is she, she is he, clinging to each other, and in the moments when she is not he, she is terrified, tears rolling down her cheeks, and in the moments when he is not she, he is pissing his pants, a child lost and confused, clinging to a stranger's side and not knowing how he got there.

I stand.

The gun trained on some point between them both – best chance if I'm fast and they're slow.

I am New York's finest, called to the scene of the crime.

I am armed.

I am come to kill the child, Galileo.

Will, dying on a Miami dockside, the blood popping in his chest.

Johannes Schwarb, burned alive for all to see.

Do you like what you see?

I said, "I killed you before; I'll do it again."

Galileo grins, and as soon as the expression comes, it goes again, and, rubbing one eye with a fist, he stammers, "B-b-b-but please, sir, don't hurt the little boy."

I tighten my grip on the gun, level it at his skull. "I don't know you," I reply. "It will be a moment. That's all. Just another moment, and done."

My finger tightens against the trigger.

A shot.

Not mine.

Something slams into my back, into the bulletproof vest, knocking me down. I land on my hands and knees, gasping for breath, head ringing, Galileo before me. The shot frightened him and he must have jumped, because now she's standing there, breathless, gun raised ready to fire, a two-handed grip, and at her side the child is crying, standing bewildered, doesn't know where to go, doesn't understand.

Footsteps behind, approaching, by my side.

I half-turn my head, ribcage screaming at even that little movement, and Coyle is there, above me, a gun held tight, pointing at Pam, who tightens her grip and points straight back. "Remember me?" he asks. Galileo's head tilts on one side, curious. "Remember me?" Coyle's voice shook round the empty hall, off the sad smile of mother Hera, through the twisted limbs of raging Poseidon, into the cold white stones of the museum.

I tried to stagger up, and thought better of it, remained on my hands and knees, sucking in air. My jacket had stopped the shot, but not the shock, and now my ears rang and my tongue tasted of bitter adrenaline.

"Coyle ... " I wheezed.

"Shut up," he barked, eyes still fixed on Galileo. "Do you remember me?"

"No," she said. "Who are you?"

He draws in a breath. Is this hurt? Had he imagined his murder meant something to a creature like Galileo? "Boy. You!"

The child looked up.

"Get out of here."

The child didn't move.

"Run!" Coyle's voice echoed off stone walls, off statues of gods and monsters, and the child ran, leaving his satchel behind, slipping on the papers strewn across the floor.

Coyle kept the gun trained on Pam; she kept her gun trained on him. "Well," she said at last. "What now?"

Coyle's hand was shaking, but his voice shook more. "*Santa Rosa.* You wore me there. Do you remember?"

"No."

"I killed a woman – *you* killed her in *me*. Do you remember?"

Galileo shrugged.

Coyle's hands shook around the tight fist of the gun. "You stuck a knife in me. How can you not remember?!" A scream in the hall.

I think: you're getting hysterical, Nathan Coyle. Nothing.

Galileo remembered; she didn't remember.

Either way she didn't care.

"Nathan ... please ... " I tried to crawl to my feet, made it to my knees, made it to one knee, my hand shook as I reached for his gun. "Give me the gun. I'll do it. Give me the gun!"

"Oh! Do you love me?" Surprise, delight in Galileo's voice, she beamed at Coyle now, studying his face, her shoulders straightening, head coming up, delighted, a princess on display for her prince. "Do I love you too?"

Coyle's lower lip curled into his mouth, arms locked, fingers tight.

Then he lowered the gun.

Galileo smiled.

I lunged for my gun, throwing myself belly first across the floor, but even as my fingers reached the butt Coyle slammed his foot on to my hand, my fingers spasming, pain bouncing up through my elbow. He bent down, put an arm across my throat, dragged me up, pulled me so my body rested against his, his knees in my back, and levelled the gun to my head. "Sorry," he grunted. "Sorry."

"What are you doing?!"

"She's right. I love her. I love Pam. Not blazing love, not that. I love her . . . just enough. Just a tiny, tiny bit more than I hate Galileo."

"She dies or we die," I hissed. "That's how this ends!"

He hit me. It wasn't hard, but with the butt of a gun it didn't need to be. I slumped in his arms, felt blood running down behind my ear, his breath against my skin, his bare hand across my throat. "I killed Josephine," he whispered, so soft now, a voice only for me, a lover's sigh. "I killed her without a thought. I killed her even though you were gone. Do you remember?"

Galileo, watching.

Coyle licked his lips. "All right," he said. "OK then." His hands shook, his lips puckering in and out as if he wanted to swallow himself whole. Then he threw his gun away, let it clatter across the floor, pushed me to one side, straightened up, eyes on Galileo.

I fell, blood on my face, air in my lungs, rolling for breath, face burning, limbs cold.

Galileo tightened her grip on her gun, uncertain who to shoot first. I curled in close around my own aching body, squeezing my eyes shut, waiting for the shot, the pain, the end.

Then Coyle said, "Be me."

He wasn't speaking to me.

I looked up.

He was staring at Galileo, hands open by his sides.

"Be me," he said and took a step towards her.

Galileo put her head on one side. "Why?" she asked.

"Nathan." My voice was a scratching wheeze, my tongue barely moved. "Don't."

"Kepler loves me," he said. "He'll kill you regardless of who you are. I love you. I love you, I love . . . the one you wear. I won't let her die, not now, not after all . . . But Kepler won't kill me. I have killed . . . many people. I was following orders. You don't remember me, but I love you. Be me."

I crawled across the floor, grabbed Nathan's fallen gun, raised it. He stood between me and Galileo, blocking my shot. "Coyle! For God's sake get . . . "

His hand brushed Galileo's cheek, soft, lovers meeting after a long while. "Do you really want to be loved?" he asked. "Do you really want to know what it means?" Galileo's gun was pressed into his belly, but he didn't seem to care. "Kepler, when he was me, undressed me. Lay in a bath and felt heat go through my skin; crawled under blankets, stared into the mirror and saw my eyes. Do you want to know what love really means?"

"Nathan!" The word came as a sob from my throat, a heat running through my body, a terror in my hands. "Please!"

"He'll kill you," whispered Coyle, his lips caressing Galileo's ear. "He'll kill you without a thought because it will only take a second and he'll be gone. That's all this is to him. A moment that came, and a moment that passed. But I won't let that happen – not any more. He loves me. Kepler loves me, isn't that right?"

"No, please . . . "

His voice was soft now, so soft. "Listen to him. Have you ever heard anyone beg like that before?"

"No," said Galileo. "Not like that."

"That's love. It's not mercy, like we begged you for mercy on the *Santa Rosa*. It's not fear or pain or passing fancy. It's pure love, one creature for another. Kepler has been more intimate with me than any living creature. Kepler loves me. He would never hurt me. Do you understand?"

Galileo said, "Yes."

Coyle smiled, pressed his lips to Galileo's neck, held her tight. For a long while they stood there, the man and the woman. Her hands curled round to press against Coyle's back, to hold him closer still. It seemed that they were stone, a living statue, an embrace that could never end.

Then Coyle's hands dropped.

Pam staggered, confused, dizzy.

Coyle stayed where he was, head down, back straight. Pam's gaze swept the room, fell on me, her lips opening and closing, trying to find words to say.

Coyle raised his head and smiled at her. One hand caught her around the throat, holding her tight, the other grabbed the gun from her limp hands, turned it so the barrel was against her belly.

"No! Nathan! No!"

His head half-turned at the sound of my voice, but he didn't move, didn't take his fingers from Pam's skin. I threw the gun away, heard it clatter among Greek stones and Roman deities. "Let her go," I said. "I'll do whatever you want, go wherever, be whoever. Let her go."

His fingers brushed her neck, feeling its contours.

"Please."

Begging on my knees: please.

Coyle

not–Coyle

smiled.

Not his smile.

"Do you love me?" he asked.

I closed my eyes. "Yes."

"Do you love me?"

"Yes. I love you very much."

His fingers slipped from Pam's throat. He pushed her, very gently, away, saw her tear-streaked face, her running make-up, tutted. "Run along," he said. "Run along."

She ran.

I was alone with Galileo.

With Coyle.

With Galileo.

He came towards me, and I stayed. He stopped in front of me, smiled, looked into my eyes. The hand with the gun placed it against my skull. With his other he caught my chin, pulled me to my feet. I didn't resist. He held my face in his fingers, neither gentle nor hard, reached a conclusion, pulled me closer, pressed his lips against mine. Galileo kissed me, and I kissed Coyle back.

He let me go, looked again, his eyes filling with tears, his lips stretching back into an expression of excitement and delight. "You do love me!"

"Yes."

"You love *me*! You really love me, you love me!"

I stared into the face that had been my own, child-like now, distorted with joy, hope, wonder. The gun slipped down to his side, briefly forgotten as he reached round behind me to put his hand across my neck, pulling me in again to his embrace. He kissed like a man newly released from an island prison, and I held him tight to me and kissed him back, my right hand tangling in his hair, feeling the warmth of his skin, my left slipping around his side, beneath the loose weight of his arm.

My fingers brushed against his, found the weight of the gun still in his hand.

And it seemed to me, as he held me against his warm, familiar skin, that in that moment I was Nathan Coyle, and he was me. His flesh tangled with mine, his pulse beat against my skin, so I couldn't work out whose hand belonged to what body, whose leg pressed against whose thigh, whose lips tingled so. Rather, I knew then what Coyle would do, what he was doing even as Galileo pulled his lips away from mine and, the tears running freely down his face, stared into my eyes.

He loved me.

My fingers tightened around the gun in his hand, turning it gently towards his side.

He brushed my cheek with his finger, outlining the contours of my face. "Now," he said, "I know what love looks like."

I pulled the trigger.

Chapter 88

When the police find the body, it has already been found.

One of their number,

a man who is . . .

. . . someone . . .

a man with a gun,

is already there.

They call out, Aldama, show us your hands, Aldama, get away from the body, show us your hands.

He does not.

Instead he cradles the body of the man who lies dead, holding it like a child, and weeps.

They handcuff him anyway.

The medic asks him, what is your name?

What is your name?

He doesn't remember.

Shock, they say – it must be shock. Gets to us all eventually, even old Aldama.

A lieutenant brings him a cup of tea.

Their fingers brush as he passes him the cup.

Aldama says, what the fuck am I doing here? Why the fuck am I in handcuffs? What the fuck is going on?!

The lieutenant doesn't answer.

New York, in winter.

I walk, but walking is too slow, and I have lost my way. There is a bright winter sun somewhere overhead, but the buildings are higher than the sky and I cannot find my way through the shadows that fall into the streets.

I walk, and don't even notice the chill in my legs, the cold in my fingers. I must have had a coat, left it in the museum cloakroom; must have a bag, my name buried somewhere within it. A woman selling roast nuts and caramel sauce says,

"Hey! Lady! Are you OK?"

Am I lady?

Is that what I am today?

"Hey! Hey, you lost?"

"No. I'm not lost."

"You look a little lost."

"I'm not lost. I'm fine. Thank you."

Her mouth says, OK, but her eyes say, you lie, though about what precisely, she isn't so sure.

I walk away, aware now of all things, of my pin-thin legs and thick tights, my blue-tinged fingers and gently falling hair, and as awareness comes, so does the remembrance of blood in my veins and time in my eyes, but it was only a moment, and the moment passed.

I walk, and it is too slow; always, all things are too slow. Slow to travel and slow to learn, slow to study and slow to grow, slow to catch a husband, slow to get a wife, slow to age and slow to die. Too slow, this life, always too slow, and I

cannot stick around for very long. For someone has the thing I want, whatever that may be.

I walk

and then I run.

I race without moving, travel by touch.

My skin is wild in the wind
my breath is restless shock
and I am
woman, thick gloves woolly against the cold
man in yellow shoes who lost his way
I am the stranger who gave you the white flowers she carried
in her hand
the face you forget as it turned away
I am beautiful
until I see that she is more beautiful than me
and he more beautiful again
so beautiful, and never enough
I am the woman who stood on your foot on the train
jostled you in the queue
asked you for the time
I am the ancient man who has forgotten his name
the tired old woman who wished to be someone else.
I am no one.
I am Kepler.
I am love.
I am you.

MEET THE AUTHOR

Photo Credit: Siobhan Watts

Claire North is the pen name of Catherine Webb. She currently works as a theater lighting designer and is a fan of big cities, urban magic, Thai food and graffiti-spotting. She lives in London.

INTERVIEW

Where did the inspiration for Touch *come from?*

I wish I had a better answer than this, but here goes...

So I was walking through North London a few years ago on a freezing cold winter night, on my way to a dress rehearsal for a not-totally-brilliant show that I was lighting designer on. It was foggy, and there were commuters travelling home. I remember looking across the road where I was walking, to a park. There were lights above a path in the darkness, and I could see people moving in and out of the light. A figure appears in the light, then vanishes, then reappears a few metres later.

...and it was there. Looking at that, the idea of *Touch* popped into my head. Damned if I know why. I suspect there may be something to do with how you perceive others, how we perceive the lives that are around ours. For a moment as someone enters the light, you construct a story and an identity for them, then they vanish, carrying on with their lives, and reappear later, perhaps altered, perhaps not. But this is speculation. All I know for certain is watching that, as I walked to work, I stopped dead in the street and had a "hurrah" moment, and the rest is scribbling...

What were the main challenges you faced when writing this novel?

I think the hardest task is finding things that matter to Kepler. It's important for any narrative to pin down what matters to characters, and find how, by playing with these values, you can make the characters themselves change. Conventional fears—death, pain, injury, disease, romantic rejection, family worries, financial ruin, hunger, thirst—they don't apply. Kepler can hop away from them at the touch of a finger. The challenge therefore is to find what Kepler *does* invest in, and create a story that allows you to push against that.

Do you feel that it's a natural human desire to want to see life through another person's eyes?

I think it's both a desire and a fear. We live our lives in terror of how other people see us—a lot of the time we dress and speak in a terrified awareness not of who we are, but of who we wish to seem to be. Looking through someone else's eyes could reveal truths about ourselves we might not wish to perceive. That said, it also seems true to suggest that if humanity can envy a thing, we will. That may be a material object—we desire what *she* has or *he* has, but it may also be an idea. We envy the capacity of others to find the silver lining, or to always say the right thing, or to know the correct words for a difficult moment. In that sense, I suspect we all secretly desire to see the world through someone else's eyes in order to better ourselves in one way or another.

If you could live the life of any person in history, who would it be?

Oooohhh tricky. Women have had it pretty rubbish for the last few thousand years, which raises a dilemma for me. It'd be lovely to name a bastion of awesome such as Queen Zenobia or Ada Lovelace, but though Zenobia thrashed the Romans for a while, she did end up in chains, and Ada Lovelace died young, so perhaps we should resist the temptation to name someone famous or brilliant and instead aim more modestly to the unsung folk who managed to get through the last few thousand years without dying from plague, famine or war. That said, you could do a lot worse than to be a dowager empress of various courts—Ottoman and Chinese dowagers had it decent, if they made it through the assassinations.

If I was up for gender-swapping (which, given the question, seems valid) then perhaps someone like Michael Faraday? Decent innings, lived well most of his life and more importantly, both contributed to and experienced a fundamental change in science and through science how man perceives the universe. To see the world through the eyes of Michael Faraday—and to see the world *change*—would have been an incredible thing.

Did you deliberately set out to explore questions of gender and identity in this novel?

Um. Honestly. No. Characters and stories will naturally create their own questions, raise their own dilemmas. I didn't need to sit down and think about Kepler's gender or identity, or indeed what its lack of either might mean for the book—they were naturally arising consequences of the premise. It is the great beauty of fiction that, through telling a story, more than events may be unfolded; and in creating characters, more than dialogue may happen. Every story has its natural consequences, and I guess it was natural for Kepler's story to veer the way it did, regardless of any political gender I may have had!

Kepler travels a huge amount in this book—how do you research all of the locations?

Travel guides, photos, weather reports, film, Internet, chatting with friends who've been there...in some cases, my own personal experience! I've been to several places in the book as a tourist, and studied the history of a lot of cities where I send Kepler as part of my very rusty history degree. Also in fairness, a great deal of place-setting isn't about the big stuff, it's not "in this year the Eiffel Tower was built" but rather about little things—about how the food tastes, whether the buses run on time, the national drink, a local joke—all the stuff that characters would experience, rather than the big tourist-shaped facts that we might otherwise have to study and learn.

How would you imagine a film version of this novel to work?

With great difficulty. That's not a bad thing—awesomeness arises from such things; difficulty forces fantastic solutions. But there is the problem that your main character doesn't have a body to call its own; casting therefore has a tricky dilemma. Do you cast one actor who CGI/costume/physicality changes their way through the movie, or do you cast fifty actors who are all playing the same part? Either has merits and detractions, but thankfully people far more expert and savvy than me will be making these calls, and I'll be fascinated to see what they decide.

What can we expect from you next?

I've just delivered my third Claire North novel. Without wanting to reveal too much, it's the story of a woman who the world begins to forget. First her friends forget her, then her family, and she's forced to find her own way alone. It's somewhere between a thriller and a story of how she lives a life that no one else can remember, but which still can change the world.

INTRODUCING

If you enjoyed
TOUCH,
look out for

THE FIRST FIFTEEN LIVES
OF HARRY AUGUST

by Claire North

SOME STORIES CANNOT BE TOLD
IN JUST ONE LIFETIME.

Harry August is on his deathbed. Again.

*No matter what he does or the decisions he makes, when death
comes, Harry always returns to where he began, a child with
all the knowledge of a life he has already lived a dozen
times before. Nothing ever changes.*

Until now.

*As Harry nears the end of his eleventh life, a little girl appears
at his bedside. "I nearly missed you, Doctor August,"
she says. "I need to send a message."*

*This is the story of what Harry does next, and what he did
before, and how he tries to save a past he cannot change
and a future he cannot allow.*

Chapter 1

The second cataclysm began in my eleventh life, in 1996. I was dying my usual death, slipping away in a warm morphine haze, which she interrupted like an ice cube down my spine.

She was seven, I was seventy-eight. She had straight blonde hair worn in a long pigtail down her back, I had bright white hair, or at least the remnants of the same. I wore a hospital gown designed for sterile humility; she, bright-blue school uniform and a felt cap. She perched on the side of my bed, her feet dangling off it, and peered into my eyes. She examined the heart monitor plugged into my chest, observed where I'd disconnected the alarm, felt for my pulse, and said, "I nearly missed you, Dr August."

Her German was Berlin high, but she could have addressed me in any language of the world and still passed for respectable. She scratched at the back of her left leg, where her white knee-length socks had begun to itch from the rain outside. While scratching she said, "I need to send a message back through time. If time can be said to be important here. As you're conveniently dying, I ask you to relay it to the Clubs of your origin, as it has been passed down to me."

I tried to speak, but the words tumbled together on my tongue, and I said nothing.

"The world is ending," she said. "The message has come down from child to adult, child to adult, passed back down the generations from a thousand years forward in time. The world is ending and we cannot prevent it. So now it's up to you."

I found that Thai was the only language which wanted to pass my lips in any coherent form, and the only word which I seemed capable of forming was, why?

Not, I hasten to add, why was the world ending?

Why did it matter?

She smiled, and understood my meaning without needing it to be said. She leaned in close and murmured in my ear, "The world is ending, as it always must. But the end of the world is getting faster."

That was the beginning of the end.

Chapter 2

Let us begin at the beginning.

The Club, the cataclysm, my eleventh life and the deaths which followed – none peaceful – all are meaningless, a flash of violence that bursts and withers away, retribution without cause, until you understand where it all began.

My name is Harry August.

My father is Rory Edmond Hulne, my mother Elizabeth Leadmill, though I was not to know any of this until well until my third life.

I do not know whether to say that my father raped my mother or not. The law would have some difficulty in assessing the case; the jury could perhaps be swayed by a clever individual one way or the other. I am told that she did not scream, did not fight, didn't even say no when he came to her in the kitchen on the night of my conception, and in twenty-five inglorious minutes of passion – in that anger and jealousy and rage are passions of their kind – took revenge on his faithless wife by means of the kitchen girl. In this regard my mother was not forced, but then, as a girl of some twenty years old, living and working in my father's house, dependent for her future on his money and his family's goodwill, I would argue that she was given no chance to resist, coerced by her situation as much as by any blade held to the throat.

By the time my mother's pregnancy began to show, my father had returned to active duty in France, where he was to serve out the rest of the First World War as a largely undistinguished major in the Scots Guards. In a conflict where whole regiments could be wiped out in a single day, undistinguished was a rather enviable obtainment. It was therefore left to my paternal grandmother, Constance Hulne, to expel my mother from her home without a reference in the autumn of 1918. The man who was to become my adopted father – and yet a truer parent to me than any biological relation – took my mother to the local market on the back of his pony cart and left her there with some few shillings in her purse and a recommendation to seek the help of other distressed ladies of the county. A cousin, Alistair, who shared a mere one eighth of my mother's genetic material but whose surplus of wealth more than made up for a deficit of familial connections, gave my mother work on the floor of his Edinburgh paper mill; however, as she grew larger and increasingly unable to carry out her duties, she was quietly moved on by a junior official some three rungs away from the responsible party. In desperation, she wrote to my biological father, but the note was intercepted by my shrewd grandmother, who destroyed it before he could read my mother's plea, and so, on New Year's Eve 1918, my mother spent her last few pennies on the slow train from Edinburgh Waverley to Newcastle and, some ten miles north of Berwick-upon-Tweed, went into labour.

A trade unionist by the name of Douglas Crannich and his wife, Prudence, were the only two people present at my birth, in the ladies' washroom of the station. I am told that the stationmaster stood outside the door to prevent any innocent women coming inside, his hands clasped behind his back and his cap, crowned with snow, pulled down over his eyes in a manner I have always imagined as being rather hooded and malign. There were no doctors at the infirmary at this late hour and on this festive day, and the medic took over three hours to arrive. He came too late. The blood was already crystallising on the floor and Prudence Crannich was holding me in her arms at his arrival. My mother was dead. I have only the report of Douglas for the circumstances of her demise, but I believe she haemorrhaged out, and is buried in a grave marked "Lisa, d. 1 January 1919 – Angels Guide Her Into Light". Mrs Crannich, when the undertaker asked her what should be on the stone, realised that she had never known my mother's full name.

Some debate ensued about what to do with me, this suddenly orphaned child. I believe Mrs Crannich was sorely tempted to keep me for her own, but finances and practicality informed against this decision, as did Douglas Crannich's firm and literal interpretation of the law and rather more personal understanding of propriety. The child had a father, he exclaimed, and the father had a right to the child. This matter would have been rather moot, were it not that my mother was carrying about her person the address of my soon-to-be adopted father, Patrick August, presumably with the intention of enlisting his help in seeing my biological father, Rory Hulne. Enquiries were made as to whether this man, Patrick, could be my father, which caused quite a stir in the village as Patrick had been long married, childlessly, to my adopted mother, Harriet August, and a barren marriage in a border village, where the notion of the condom was regarded as taboo well into the 1970s, was always a topic of furious debate. The matter was so shocking that it very quickly made its way to the manor house itself, Hulne Hall, wherein resided my grandmother Constance, my two aunts Victoria and Alexandra, my cousin Clement, and Lydia, the unhappy wife of my father. I believe my grandmother immediately suspected whose child I was and the circumstances of my situation, but refused to take responsibility for me. It was Alexandra, my younger aunt, who showed a presence of mind and a compassion that the rest of her kin lacked, and seeing that suspicion would fairly quickly turn to her family once the truth of my dead mother's identity was revealed, approached Patrick and Harriet August with this offer – that if they were to adopt the child, and raise it as their own, the papers formally signed and witnessed by the Hulne family itself to quiet all rumours of an illegitimate affair, for no one carried authority like the inhabitants of Hulne Hall – then she would personally see to it that they received a monthly amount of money for their pains and to support the child, and that on his growing up she would ensure that his prospects were suitable – not excessive, mind, but neither the sorry situation of a bastard.

Patrick and Harriet debated a while, then accepted. I was raised as their child, as Harry August, and it wasn't until my second life that I began to understand where I was from, and what I was.